Paroxysm

Love, Murder and Justice in Post
Civil War Washington, DC

Gerald D. Otis

Cover Illustration: Sketch of Mary Harris by Edward Mason that appeared in Voorhees, Daniel. *Forty Years of Oratory*, Kansas City: Bowen-Merril, 1898.

For Connie

CHAPTER 1

Mary calmly made her way to the stairway on the west end of the Treasury building, mistakenly descending two floors rather than one and ending up in the basement. As she made her way back up the stairs and out the door to the east portico on 15th Street, a watchman apprehended her and brought her back into the hall. The body of the deceased had just been brought down and was lying about fifteen feet away. The watchman fumbled with the key while trying to open the watch room door, prompting Mary to exclaim, "For God's sake, get me into the room!" The watchman stayed with her in the room as another employee rushed to get his superior.

"I am Edwin Handy, justice of the peace," he said breathlessly, having just run up two flights of stairs.

"I am Mary Harris. I think you will want this," she said as she pulled the model 1859 Sharpe's Four Barrel pistol out of her pocket and handed it to him.

"Why did you shoot the man?"

Mary began to wave her arms wildly in the air, pulled on her hair, paced to and fro and dropped to her knees clutching the coat of Mr. Handy. "Why did I do it? Why did

I do it? I would give my life to save him." Handy lifted her to her feet and put her in a chair but she soon was up again, pacing about and fretting, dropping to the floor and grasping his coattails.

Hugh McCullough, Comptroller of the Currency, soon arrived and introduced himself to Miss Harris. Repeating her behavior with Mr. Handy, Mary again dropped to her knees, grasped his coattails and inquired beseechingly of the kind man "Is he dead?"

McCullough was under the impression that his employee, Adoniram Judson Burroughs, was still alive at that time but went out to check and when he returned he stated, "Yes, madam, he is dead."

Mary continued to pace as if in a frenzy and wailed, "Why did I do it? Oh, how I loved him! Why did I do it?"

"What was your relationship with Mr. Burroughs?" McCullough asked.

"I have known him for several years. We were to be married but he betrayed me and married another. I came here from Janesville, Wisconsin to prosecute him for breach of the promise of marriage"

"Did he injure you in any other way than breaking the engagement?"

"No, he did not. He was my best friend and always treated me respectfully."

McCullough gently posed the question, "Are you a virtuous girl?"

"Yes, as God is my witness," Mary replied.

George H. Walker of the metropolitan police arrived and took Mary into custody. They got into a hack to make the trip to jail. Nothing was said until Walker asked the prisoner if she had any friends in Washington.

"No, none at all. I have been to this city just once before, last summer, when I came to find Judson but he wasn't here so I returned to Chicago." As the hack turned from F Street onto 15th Street, Mary said, "I'll tell you all about it."

"I don't want to hear it. You may say something that can be held against you."

Notwithstanding his protests, Mary proceeded with her account, weeping continuously. "I don't wish sympathy for myself but for my family. Judson ruined my life. He talked me into leaving my home and friends in Burlington and my family disowned me. He seduced me and took me to a bad house in Chicago. I told him that if he did not live up to his promise of marriage, I would have my revenge, even if it meant my own life. I bought the pistol in Chicago and came here this morning to settle my scores." Arriving at the jail, Mary said, "If you will remain, I will explain it all to you."

"No madam. You may say something that will hurt your case. Select your counsel carefully and make your statement to him." At the prisoner's request, Mr. Walker sent a telegram to Louisa A. Devlin in Janesville, Wisconsin informing her that Mary had shot Burroughs and requesting that Miss Devlin come to Washington immediately.

***

Pacing in her cell, Mary's mind flitted from one thing to another. "Oh, God! I've really gotten myself into the soup this time. How am I going to get out of here? What will my family think of me? Will Louisa come? His wife must hate me. Why did I do it, for Christ's sake? Where am I going to get the money for a lawyer?"

Mary recalled when she had her first meeting with Judson. She was 12 years old and had just come to work in Mrs. Sue Alexander's millinery and fancy goods store. Her parents were just barely getting by on their farm outside of Burlington, Iowa and needed her to earn money for her clothes and school supplies. Mary felt marked as somehow inferior to her peers by this early challenge, but the childless Mrs. Alexander was a woman of refinement and culture and enjoyed the presence of the attractive, sprightly and good-natured little girl.

Mrs. Alexander would act as Mary's mentor and introduce her to other older and married women in the community who frequently visited her store and from whom Mary would receive advice and the benefit of their womanly experience. They all felt sorry for the lively young girl who was bright but had little formal education and they took great pleasure in trying to cultivate her manners and intellect to be acceptable in polite society. Mary was eager to learn and tried her best to please and impress these highly regarded women of the community.

Mrs. Alexander was in a back room when Judson entered the store and spotted Mary.

"Well, what have we here? Aren't you a little cutie. What's your name little girl?"

"Mary Harris. I just started working for Mrs. Alexander. She's in the back room. Is there something I can help you with?"

"Why yes, you can my little lovely," he said as he touched her on the arm. "My name is Judson. I just opened a mercantile store down the block and I was looking for some ties and pocket handkerchiefs that I could offer to men who come into my store."

"Those items are over there," said Mary pointing to a display counter. I'll get Mrs. Alexander."

"Oh, hello Mr. Burroughs," said Mrs. Alexander as she came out of the back room and recognized her customer. How is your new business going, then?"

"It's still pretty slow but I expect that it will pick up when people begin to know I'm here. I just came over to see if you had some items for men that I could put on consignment in my store. I can mark them up from what you charge and still make a little profit for myself."

Mrs. Alexander indicated that the items he was interested in were made for her by a local woman whose name she would not disclose but who would probably appreciate any additional business. They haggled some about the price and finally reached an agreement.

Before he left, Judson said, "I see you have a new helper. She certainly is a pretty little girl. She'll make someone a good wife in a few years."

When they were alone, Mrs. Alexander asked Mary what she thought of their new business neighbor.

"He certainly is handsome," said Mary, "but I was a little uncomfortable when he put his hand on my arm. He's not from around here is he?"

"Oh, you don't have to worry about Mr. Burroughs. He hails from a good religious family in Shelby, New York. He told me his father named him after Adoniram Judson, a Baptist missionary who was famous in the early part of the century for being imprisoned, starved and tortured for nearly two years during the Anglo – Burmese War. His brother is a minister in Chicago who has just started a school for preachers called Douglas College."

"How old is he? He looks kind of young to be running his own business."

"I think he told me he was about 21 years old. I think he's an ambitious young man and wants to get an early start on his career."

Over the next few years, Judson frequently dropped into the store and tried to provide Mary a man's perspective on the proper allure and social refinement of a woman. "A charming woman should wear just a hint of makeup to accentuate her attractive features," he told her. "She should dress in elegant but not ostentatious clothes and she should defer to the man she wishes to wed in all matters he considers important. Her mood should be cheerful and positive, she should show interest in whomever she talks to, and above all, she should not nag. Flirtation and displays of affection are quite desirable in private but not in public since they might tarnish one's reputation. Of course, the ideal woman should also know how to cook, sew, raise children and do other domestic tasks required of a housekeeper."

Mary presumed that Judson knew what he was talking about and appreciated his helpful suggestions about how to grow into the kind of woman that she admired. But Judson's business did not thrive and eventually he had to seek employment with Mrs. Alexander as her book keeper. Seeing each other for several hours a day, he and Mary grew to be close friends. Indeed, more than just friends as Mary would often sit on Judson's knee, tease him and play jokes on him, twirl her hands around his neck and, later, they would sneak kisses in the back room of the store.

By the time she was 16 years old, she acknowledged that what Judson considered important in a woman was reasonable enough, but she had a hunch there was more to attracting and holding a man than her social and homemaker skills. She asked Mrs. Winters, an older woman whom she visited frequently, what she thought of Judson's attractive qualities in a lady. She trusted Mrs. Winters to give her honest and useful information, not just the conventional teachings of the day.

"All of those things your friend has told you are either practical ones for running a household or they are important supports for a man's standing amongst his friends. But the tie that binds strongest of all is the intimate relationship that exists between a man and woman."

"Do you mean love?" Mary asked.

"Yes, honey, but don't underestimate the physical part of love. Men like to be able to brag about their wife and show her off in public, but they all will drop to their knees and beg for a good roll in the hay. It's almost like they lose all their reason when they get a hankering for what we've got and what we can do. It's the only real power we've got in this here so-called 'man's world.'"

"I know about the birds and the bees, Mrs. Winters. After all, I was raised on a farm. But with a man you can't be too forward or they'll just think you're a loose woman."

"No, you have to offer a little bit at a time, always holding something back and hinting that what is yet to come is even better than what they have already sampled. With Mr. Winters, God rest his soul, it was a year from the time he touched my breasts to the time we went to bed together. He would plead for me to go further but I would always hold out until he pledged himself to me a little bit more. It was only after he proposed marriage that I let him get into me. Once we did that a few times, he couldn't do without it and I knew I had him hooked. After that I could bring him around to my way of thinking on any matter by just cuddling up to him or, if need be, by withholding my favors. I made him feel that he was the ruler of the household but I was always the one who was really in control."

"Did you like the physical part, Mrs. Winters?"

"Sweetie, there were times when it was just out of this world. Of course, I had to teach him what to do, what I liked, but he was always eager to please me. The more I showed that I enjoyed it, the more amorous he became. And when I wasn't in the mood, I could always pretend I was and he wouldn't know the difference. Or I could have a sick headache. Or I could quickly oblige him in one of a number of ways and get on with what I wanted to do. Once you get the knack of it, men are really pretty easy to manage."

The clang of her cell door roused Mary from her reverie. "Here is your supper, Miss Harris, " said Mrs. Olson, the jail matron who attended to women prisoners. "Lights out in one hour. There are extra blankets on the shelf over there."

Mary picked at her meal, not feeling hungry even

though she had not eaten since morning before she left Baltimore. "I've got to keep my wits about me," she thought. "If I don't, I'll rot in this musty old building." Her sleep was fitful and filled with horrible nightmare images of being torn apart by an angry mob.

***

Mary awoke thinking about her first real sexual encounter with Judson. They were lying on a blanket in a secluded spot down by the river, having a picnic. Judson leaned over and gave Mary a peck on the cheek, to which Mary responded by drawing Jud closer for a prolonged and passionate kiss, surprising and delighting him. He soon became noticeably aroused and Mary moved her hand down to the protuberance in the front of his pants, gently outlining the bulge with her fingers. "Let me see it! I want to see it," she cried with glee as she unbuttoned his fly. Grinning from ear to ear because she was met with no censure or resistance, she proceeded to manually gratify Judson's desire. Afterwards, Jud heaped unending praise on Mary for her deft touch and inquired of her where she had learned such admirable skills. Mary, feeling pride in her accomplishment, responded, "What do you think I talk with all those older ladies about, my dear?"

Mrs. Olson called out, "Miss Harris, there's a reporter here from the *Chronicle* that wants to talk with you. Do you want to see him?"

"No, I don't want to see anyone."

"The warden said a sympathetic newspaper article might be helpful to you, that it might help flush out a lawyer that is willing to take your case for free."

Mary thought about it a few seconds and, intrigued by the possibility of getting a lawyer to defend her when she had no money, decided to not pass up an opportunity that could work in her favor. "Oh, alright, send him in."

In a few moments, Mr. Millburn, the warden, and the reporter entered her cell. Mary paced back and forth. "I don't know if I should answer any questions before I get a lawyer," said Mary.

"I don't want to intrude on your grief or cause you any discomfort," said the reporter "but if you don't get some public visibility, you may not get a very competent attorney to defend you. There are a lot of lawyers in this town and they all read the *Washington Chronicle,* so if we get your story out there, it is likely that one of them will come forward and offer his services pro bono. For my part, if your story is an interesting one, the public will want to read about it and my employer will sell a lot of newspapers."

"I can see the sense of that," said Mary. "What do you want to know?"

"Well, first off what is your name, how old are you, and where are you from?"

"My name is Mary Harris, I am nineteen years old and I am from Burlington, Iowa. My father is William Harris. Both my parents are poor Irish immigrants and work a farm."

"How did you become acquainted with Mr. Burroughs?"

Mary related how she had met Burroughs some seven years earlier and how their relationship had blossomed into an affectionate one even though her parents opposed it. "They continually told me that his family was too high for me, that he would never marry me and that I should not keep company with him. I disregarded them and continued to see him, and became more and more attached to him. Before he left Burlington, he asked me to marry him; I refused because I felt I was too young to disobey my parents in such a matter. He always protested his affection and his determination to make me his wife."

"What happened then?"

"We kept up a correspondence and occasionally met in Burlington or in towns nearby where he worked. At his request, I moved to Chicago to be near him. In August or September, a year ago, I received an anonymous note asking me to meet the writer at a house that I ascertained was one of the most notorious in Chicago. Miss Devlin said she thought the note was from Burroughs, and I wanted to determine the truth. I answered it, at her suggestion, promising to meet the writer at the place appointed. A friend of Miss Devlin in the post office watched for the person who came for the reply and his description of the person confirmed Miss Devlin's supposition that Mr. Burroughs was the person.

"I determined to go to the house appointed, and Miss Devlin went with me. The woman in charge of the house stated that the gentleman was not there at that time but that he had been before, and had instructed her not to answer the doorbell but permit him to do so, saying that unless the party he wished to see saw him, she would not come in. Her description further confirmed me in the belief that Mr. Burroughs was the person who had made the appointment."

"You said there was a second note?"

"Another note was received stating that the writer had unavoidably been absent from the city, and making another appointment, I resolved to go again, meantime taking measures to have the house watched. The person (whom I believe to have been Mr. Burroughs) did not go to the house, and when we went there again it was closed and we could not gain admittance. For sometime before this I had not seen Mr. Burroughs. The writer of the anonymous letter said he had seen me often and was much prepossessed in my favor and wanted to be a friend to me. Mr. Burroughs was a man of such marked appearance as not to be easily mistaken for another. I still felt most intense anxiety to be further satisfied, if possible, whether he whom I had so loved, and who has so protested his love for me, could be guilty of such baseness."

"What did you do to determine if this was so?"

"I went to see his brother, Professor Burroughs, and inquired of him whether Judson was in the city. He walked the floor, asked if I was from Iowa, and upon my answering in the affirmative, said that his brother had been there but had gone to Washington. Shortly after, I learned that he had been married by his brother, the professor, I think the day after I was there.

"I then determined to come to Washington and prosecute him but I continually deferred it until last August, when, Miss Devlin having repeatedly advised me to do so, and offered me all the aid in her power. I came here, only to learn that he had gone to Chicago with his wife. I immediately returned, and on reaching Chicago employed a lawyer and a detective."

"What did they find out?"

"I soon ascertained that he had again gone to Washington, but that his wife was believed to be in Chicago. I supposed that he would return for her, so I waited a long time with this expectation, but I subsequently learned that he had been there and gone without my knowledge. That renewed my resolve to come on here and secure redress, if possible, by prosecution, and at all hazards to see him. I had been disowned by my parents. I could not return to them.

"In Burlington, as well as Chicago, I had been reported to have had improper relations with him. This was never so and I was bent on vindicating my character. If the stories against me had been true, I would never have had the heart to come here to seek redress or to vindicate my repute. I believed I should wipe out the stain on my name by the prosecution or in some other way. I hardly knew how."

"When did you decide to shoot the man?"

"A few days before starting from Chicago (two weeks

ago), I was walking along the street and saw some pistols in a shop window. Having learned that many of the ladies in Chicago carried pistols, especially when traveling, I determined to buy one. The morning of the day I left Chicago, I examined the printed directions upon the wrapper accompanying the pistol and cartridges, and by following them, succeeded in loading it. I was then called to breakfast, and putting the revolver with my things, forgot to unload it; after I started I concluded to keep it loaded, but then had no intention of using it when I got here."

"What did you do once you got to Washington?"

"After my arrival here, I became almost frantic with a desire to see him, and put on a "nubia" (which I was not wont to wear) and a veil, and so disguised, went to the Treasury building, yesterday morning. I inquired to the room in which Mr. Burroughs was, and having learned that, walked up and down the hall for some time. Once I went to the door of the room, opened it a few inches, and saw him at his desk. The moment I looked at him, sitting there so comfortably, the thought of all I had suffered, and of his being the cause, enraged me and my hand involuntarily pulled back the trigger of the pistol in my pocket.

"I closed the door, and, stepping away, moved about again, I know not how or where, except that I kept my eye on his room until the men began to come out of their rooms. Then I placed myself where I knew he would have to come near me in going to the staircase. When he appeared, I felt suddenly lifted up. My arm was extended as stiff as iron, and I saw him fall. I knew nothing more until I was called back as I was leaving the building. Pray Sir, what will they do with me? If it was not for my poor father and mother I would not care."

***

"Are you ready for your newspapers, Mr. Bradley?"

"Yes, Doris, and a cup of coffee too, if you please."

The distinguished attorney was born in the newly formed District of Columbia two years after his father, the Assistant Postmaster General, came to the city when public offices were moved from Philadelphia. Joseph was one of the first schoolboys in the District and received a classical education at Yale College when he was but 18 years old. While he pursued his legal studies, he was employed as a clerk at the Supreme Court of the United States, which was then populated by such names as Clay, Webster, Calhoun, Crawford, Taney and Marshall. Joseph was admitted to the bar of the District of Columbia in 1824 and argued his first case before the Supreme Court when he was only 26 years old. From that day forward, he was involved in most of the great cases in the courts of the District.

Doris brought in the newspapers and a cup of coffee. "You may be interested in that article in the *Chronicle* about what happened at the Treasury Building yesterday."

Joseph took a sip of coffee and began to read the newspaper account: "The Washington Tragedy: An interview with Miss Harris – Her statement of her relations with the deceased." Joseph read down the page and then exclaimed to himself, "Harrumph! "What the hell is she doing talking to the newspapers before she has any legal counsel?"

Reading further, he thought to himself, "H'm. So he was robbing the cradle and her parents thought she, being of humble stock, was not good enough for him. But she wasn't totally naive either, being a little coquettish at times or just testing how strongly he was attracted to her. And she's trying to portray herself as a good girl who obeyed her parents."

Bradley pondered the significance of the mysterious admirer who wrote the anonymous letters and whether the accused was just trying to make herself appear quite desirable or if the victim would actually go to such lengths to discredit someone he did not yet know would make trouble for him if he were to jilt her.

Reading about her meeting with the brother of the deceased, Joseph observed, "So she claims she just wanted to defend her reputation with no thought of financial gain. I wonder what this Devlin woman hoped to get out of this. And did she really believe that she could win a breach of promise suit? The prosecution will claim she had no evidence of a contract to marry and was simply motivated by anger and the desire for vengeance."

Bradley's young colleague, William Fendall, came into the room. At 28 years of age, William was just beginning to practice law. He was from a well-known family that had its origin in the new world in 1656 when Josias Fendall was appointed the Proprietary Governor of the Maryland Colony.

William's father, Phillip Richard Fendall, had been the District Attorney for Washington City from 1841 to 1845 and again from 1849 to 1853. At present, his father was a prominent orator, attorney and investor in various properties and businesses in the Maryland, Washington and Virginia region as well as an expert on the philosophy and administration of James Madison. During the War of the Rebellion, he had two sons who served on the Union side and one son who served on the Confederate side, while William functioned as a courier carrying dispatches between various ships and the administration in Washington. At one point in 1861 William was detained in Richmond while traveling on a Spanish brigantine carrying messages from the Gulf Squadron to the Secretary of the Navy. Later, the elder Fendall had prevailed upon his old friend, Joseph H. Bradley, to help educate his son in the arts of legal practice.

"Good morning William. Sit down and have a cup of

coffee. Doris, please get a cup of coffee for our young friend. Have you seen today's *Chronicle* – the piece about the killing at the Treasury building yesterday?"

"Yes. I read it before I came over here. The whole town is talking about it, especially the women. The Supreme Court of the District is going to hear the case – sitting as a criminal court."

Glancing over at Fendall, Bradley said, "Now the prosecution is going to argue that it's first degree murder, and it sounds a lot like it to me. She donned a disguise and lay in wait for the victim – that's premeditation. And you can't claim insanity if you are motivated by common feelings like anger and revenge – that implies malicious intent. The defense will have to come up with something to change the meaning of that comment. On the other hand, she appears to have been directed by an irresistible impulse and acted as if in a trance, being 'lifted up' and her arm being 'stiff as iron,' like in demonstrations of mesmerism."

Doris brought in a cup of coffee for Fendall and left the room. "Maybe it could be argued that this article is hearsay and shouldn't be admitted," ventured the novice attorney.

Bradley finished reading the newspaper account describing how the reporter had contacted friends of the deceased to try to corroborate or refute the story of the prisoner. "It says here, 'They also state that Mr. Burroughs frequently told Miss Harris that he could not reciprocate her attachment, and could not marry her; notified her of his intended marriage to the lady (now left a widow by his sad decease) a short time before the wedding; called upon her with his bride soon after, and was well received. When the subject of his own marriage was mentioned to Miss Harris, she told him she was engaged to Mr. Devlin, the brother of the ladies with whom she had her home in Chicago.'"

Fendall said, "This is going to pose a problem for the defense, if the witnesses repeat this on the stand. These statements makes it doubtful that there was a current promise to marry and it makes it sound like the prisoner had moved on from the deceased and become engaged to another. I wonder how much of this is true and how much was just imagined by the reporter. He even got the victim's first name wrong - it was Judson, not Jackson. That makes me doubt that he got his facts straight."

"H'm," murmured Bradley. "It doesn't say who supplied this information. Maybe it was his brother."

Doris reentered the room. "Louisa Devlin and her sister are here. They are requesting that you represent Miss Harris in her trial, Mr. Bradley."

"Oh, shit! I don't want this case. It will be damn near impossible to get her off and I'm too busy the way it is." Show them in and I will make my excuses."

Doris brought in the Devlin sisters and introduced them to Bradley and Fendall. "Please be seated," said Bradley. "I understand you would like me to defend Miss Harris in her trial for killing Mr. Burroughs?"

"Yes, that is correct, responded Louisa Devlin," the older and taller of the two women. Unlike her younger sister, Jane, she would not be described as attractive.

"We have known Mary for some time now. She worked in our millinery shop and made her residence with us in Chicago and then in Janesville, Wisconsin. We have witnessed the contemptible treatment she has received from Burroughs and her deterioration in spirits since she learned of his marriage. We also know that she has not been in her right mind since he tried to lure her into a house of ill repute. We don't have much money but perhaps some schedule of payment could be worked out that would allow us to pay your fee."

Not wanting to get into a long discussion about the case, Bradley said, "I have just recently become aware of the nature of the case from a newspaper account and it looks to me like your friend is in a great deal of trouble. It is likely a case where it would prove difficult to successfully defend the accused. You don't have to worry about legal fees since the District will pay for a defense if your friend cannot afford to pay a lawyer."

"Perhaps if you saw her you would see how sweet and innocent a girl she is and how much she is suffering," Louisa remarked.

"Yes, maybe," Bradley replied doubtfully. "But in any event, I have a number of cases that I am working on already and it would be difficult for me to fit another one into my schedule right now."

Looking disheartened, Miss Devlin asked, "Then, would it be possible for you to help us find someone to defend her? We are not from this town and have no knowledge of where to go."

"It might be possible for me or my associate to do that. Give the address where you are staying to Doris and we will get back to you if we are able to find someone willing to take the case."

The women left the room and Bradley and Fendall looked at each other silently for a moment.

"Do you think anyone would want to take this case?" asked William.

"I certainly hope we can find some intrepid soul to take it on," replied Bradley.

***

Early in her imprisonment, the warden of the jail, thinking himself unobserved by his quarry, watched Mary pacing in her cell and heard her exclaim "I would not have killed him for the world. I loved him better than I do my life. Oh! I would have died for him, but he would have ruined me." Later, he observed that the pupil of her right eye was so occluded as to not look like an eye at all. Because of her frenzied behavior and this physical abnormality, he became concerned that she might suffer from some serious disease or do something to harm herself, so he had the prison doctor come in to see her.

"Hello, Miss Harris. I am Dr. Young. How do you feel today?"

"I am very sad and upset, doctor. I don't know what to do. I am from Burlington, Iowa and I am not well educated in the ways of big cities or of places like this. My parents are poor Irish farmers and they had to put me out to work at a young age. These four walls feel like they are closing in on me. Maybe I'm going crazy."

Ignoring any mental symptoms, the doctor gave credibility only to the prisoner's physical complaints. "Do you have any pains, any chills or unusual physical sensations?"

"I have very painful monthly periods that drive me to distraction sometimes, but that is about all. I really can't stand being cooped up like this. I fear I will lose my mind. Can't you do something to get me out of this room, at least for a while?"

"That would be very unusual, Miss Harris." Perturbed that a prisoner would be so presumptuous as to ask him a favor, the physician sought to induce a sense of shame in his client. "After all, you are being held here because you killed someone."

The doctor did not notice the brief flash of loathing that appeared on Mary's face before she began to wail as if being tortured, pull on her hair so strenuously as to eradicate it by the roots, pace rapidly back and forth and finally drop to her knees, sobbing profusely. Startled by the young woman's reaction, not wanting to appear to those who could hear the ruckus as a heartless person with no compassion, and wanting to quell the disturbance as quickly as possible, the doctor conceded that he would write a letter that the warden could present to the court requesting less restrictive confinement.

"Thank you. You are so very kind," said Mary disingenuously, as her sobs became less frequent and more muffled. "You must have a very difficult job here with all the different kinds of illnesses that are presented to you. I'm sure it must take a great deal of intelligence and learning to work in such a setting as this."

The physician looked at her for a long moment, having a vague feeling that he had been outfoxed, but not wanting to push his luck. "I do my best," he said.

The warden brought the letter to the court and it was granted that Mary would be allowed the privilege of being able to walk the passage near the warden's office when he was present. This made it possible, in the days to come, for her to receive her many visitors in more comfortable surroundings.

CHAPTER 2

Pacing back and forth in her cell, Mary's memory floated back to the time she had introduced Jud to the special spot on her body that she had discovered when she was just six years old and showed him how to massage it for her sensual enjoyment. Just as Mrs. Winters had predicted, Jud became more romantic as Mary expressed or simulated delight in his ministrations to her and each time she relieved his sexual tensions, he talked more of their future married life together. They imagined the big house they would have and how they would furnish it. He talked of dressing her in the finest garments, squiring her to dances, plays and dinners with the people important to advancement of his career. She imagined herself socializing with the prominent women in town, having various domestic pursuits and raising a crop of the most attractive children ever conceived.

The relationship continued on thus until Mary began to feel that she was, in Mrs. Winters metaphor, nearly ready to set the hook in her catch. But she also knew that Judson did not yet have a very solid record of success in running a business or working for someone else. She wanted to maintain her option to abandon him if he turned out not to have any potential for economic advancement. Although they both wanted to proceed to further sexual exploration, they also feared a pregnancy for which neither was ready.

Jud walked Mary home nearly every day but eventually her parents discouraged the relationship and visits at her family home, not because they thought it was inappropriate but because they thought that, due to the disparity in social status between the two families, he would never marry her. After that, Mary frequently met Jud in the home of one of Mary's older friends, using the excuse of "visiting Mrs. Winters" as a ready cover for her continuing relationship. Often they would stay quite late with the two of them acting every bit like lovers.

In 1858 Judson got into a quarrel with some of the members of his church and decided to leave town, believing that he had enemies there who would do their best to subvert anything he tried to do. He traveled to various towns in Iowa and Illinois, finding work as a clerk or bookkeeper wherever he could. When the war broke out, he made use of his talents in spoken communication and his flexible conscience to become a bounty broker and recruiter for the three-month service commitment initially asked for by President Lincoln. His territory was mainly in Iowa although he worked for the State of Illinois. This meant that he was functioning as a "poacher" in Iowa for recruits that would count for the quota required of the State of Illinois. He maintained a correspondence with Mary and would, on occasion, meet with her in hotels in towns distant from the prying eyes and disjointed noses of Burlington.

In late 1859 Mary sent Judson a letter containing a picture of her that showed how much she had matured physically and it so affected him that he proposed a meeting in Ottumwa the first of the month, emphasizing that she should come by herself so that there would be no one present who could prevent them from being alone together. This was to be a meeting where Mary would not only show Jud her new curves in person but also show him her newly acquired sensual knowledge.

Mary boarded the train to make the 90-mile ride to Ottumwa from Burlington. As the train approached Ottumwa from the south, she could see the towers of the recently completed Court House and the First Methodist Church peeking through the tree-covered bluff that arose on the north side of the Des Moines River valley. The city was about Mary's age and had quickly grown to a population of over 2000 thanks to good farm land, a railroad and the availability of coal in the area. The heart of the city was the Court Street Park, bounded by Third and Fourth Streets on the south and north sides and Market and Washington Streets on the east and west sides. The county court house was on Fourth and Court Street and St. Mary's Catholic Church, constructed of stone, was across the street. Court Street ran directly through the park and on up to the Fifth Street bluff where magnificent homes were being built by the most prosperous citizens of the town.

Judson was at the train station about noon when Mary arrived. He had a small handcart for her luggage and the two of them made their way up the boardwalk on Market Street just south of the park, where Judson had secured a room. Once inside, he dropped her bags on the floor and took her into his arms and kissed her fervently. "Would you like to go down stairs for lunch?" he asked.

"I had lunch on the train. Besides, I have something else in mind for right now," she said as she shed her clothes. Standing before him completely naked, she asked, "How did you like my picture I sent to you?"

"As I said in my letter back to you, it is a 'visible testimony of your loveliness' but it does not compare in the least to the vision I have before me right now," he said as he drew her near and caressed her right and then her left breast. Her nipples stood at attention and she kissed his neck, murmuring soft sounds of joy as she worked his finger against that spot where it felt so good.

Pushing Jud back, she helped him get out of his clothes and they kissed deeply as they fondled each other. Then Mary dropped to her knees and effected some further magic where upon Jud exclaimed, "Oh my God! Oh my God! How exquisite!"

The couple moved to the bed so Jud could recover his breath and the strength in his legs. "Did you learn that trick from your older lady friends too?" Jud teased.

"Well, from one of them," said Mary, smiling.

"She is a teacher who should be rewarded with the greatest treasures in the world. I would do so if I had any treasures to award."

"Don't you go getting any ideas about having an affair with my teacher," said Mary, in mock reproach.

Once his breathing returned to normal, Jud turned to Mary, who was lying on her back beside him, and said, "And now for you..."

It was not long before Mary exclaimed "Oh, such ecstasy, such bliss! I'm am most certainly in paradise!" As he moved back up beside her, Jud noted how her cheeks had acquired a blush of crimson.

It was a scene that would be repeated many times, sometimes without stopping to rest between climaxes, on that weekend in Ottumwa. Exhausted but exhilarated from engaging their passions, Mary and Jud would go down to one of the restaurants on Market Street and eat with gusto, the food seeming more brilliant and appealing than it had before this weekend. Then they would go for a walk in the park, commenting on how everything – the trees, the flowers and the birds - seemed so beautiful and beguiling. They would tell each other how much they adored one another.

Neither of them wanted that weekend to end but Mary had to get back to her job in Burlington and Jud had to organize recruitment rallies and find some more substitutes for the men who had already advanced him money to find replacements. They continued to write and made arrangements for a couple of meetings that were not to take place for one reason or another. It was not until October of 1860 that they were again able to meet alone together, this time in Mt. Pleasant, about 40 miles by train from Burlington. The thriving town on a high plain was known for its fertile loam and abundant natural resources. A source of pride for the community of about 4000 residents was that it was the first town west of the Mississippi to have a co-educational college, Iowa Wesleyan.

Being closer than Ottumwa, both Mary and Judson were concerned that they might meet someone on the streets who knew them from Burlington. They were quite watchful for familiar faces as they made their way from the train depot to the hotel. Mary knew that more than one of her older lady friends knew about their relationship and she felt that they at least tacitly endorsed it. However, Jud announced that he would rather it be the devil than one particular woman that he thought was critical of him. He believed that either the postmaster or the priest may have intercepted and read their letters. Once ensconced behind closed doors, however, they gave vent to their cravings as they had done in Ottumwa, those desires having become quite intense in the year since they were last together.

During a lull in their lustful preoccupations, Jud complained that he was impoverished and needed to find some way to make more money so that they might get married. He believed that he needed to make at least $10,000 per year in order to care for a wife and family in the manner he wished. "Will you wait for me?" Judson asked.

Mary thought the amount of money he wished for was quite extraordinary, since it was several times that of the average worker, but she also had visions of living in grand style at some point in the future. "Of course I will, dearest. You must know that it is only you that I love and care about. I know that fortune will smile on you one of these days. But I don't want to have to be limited to our special kisses and end up being an old lady before we get married and raise a family," she said jokingly.

A short time later, Judson wrote Mary and asked her to come to Chicago to be near him as he awaited formation of his company of three-month recruits. If it didn't work out, he said, they would get married and run away to California. Mary subsequently moved to Chicago and obtained work as a clerk at the city's premier bookstore, Sheldon & Company.

Judson took her to meet his brother and other members of his family at social events at the University of Chicago two or three times after she moved to Chicago in June of 1861. His brother privately expressed his disapproval of the young lady, primarily because of her lack of formal education.

"I'm sure she is a nice girl but she would be out of place in more refined circles," John told Judson. "I really think you should find someone who has at least finished high school."

Judson considered how the disparity in educational levels between the two of them might affect his social mobility, but at that point was not about to give up a bird in the hand – especially one that was more than willing to gratify his physical needs. But discretion was not one of Judson's virtues. He visited Mary so often at work and was so conspicuous in his affections that her boss complained to Judson's well-known brother to do something about it. Harassed and more than a little bit intimidated by his brother's social stature and economic success, Judson finally agreed to take Mary back to Burlington, explaining to her friends in that city that they were to be married in three weeks and that he did not want the woman he was to marry to any longer be a mere clerk in Chicago.

As the New Year holiday passed in 1862, Judson was dismayed by a letter he had received from Mary in which she threatened to burn all his letters and demanded the return of all her personal articles that she had sent to him. She had been angered by a letter he had written in which he off-handedly mentioned that he had gone out with "one or two respectable girls to pass the dreary hours" while distant from her.

Responding, he agreed to her demands but lamented "And must this be the finale of our enjoyment? Oh! My God, how bitter!"

He wrote that there must have been some kind of misunderstanding and begged her for a chance to explain himself to her in person. This was accomplished in Burlington a couple of months later. Mary seemed to be mollified by his explanation that the two girls meant nothing to him and that his involvement with them did not include any intimate contact. Although they sealed the rift with some of their special kisses in their favorite spot down by the river, the seeds of doubt had been planted, if not yet watered.

Judson managed to sign up enough recruits for the three-month stint in the army, but he declined to accept the position as captain of the unit. Thinking he might be able to strengthen his bargaining position, shortly after his meeting with Mary in Mount Pleasant, he began to work as an army recruiter for the State of Illinois for the newly instituted three-year enlistments. He had hoped to go to Washington to get a commission as a major but he had no military experience and it turned out that his expectations were again out of line with reality. He was for the second time offered a captain's rank if he brought in enough new recruits to fill out a company.

On September 5, 1862 Captain Burroughs' company, Company B, was formed as part of the 127th Illinois Volunteers with 103 soldiers other than himself. From the ranks, he promoted John R. Morgan to be his First Lieutenant and Frank J. Woodward to be his Second Lieutenant. Training was begun at Camp Douglas on the edge of Chicago along Lake Michigan and not far from the school started by Judson's brother, the University of Chicago. The camp's 60 acres was laid out in "squares" for the prison, hospitals, and the garrison. The latter included a parade ground and was surrounded by the quarters for the officers and men. Prisoners had constructed all the buildings for headquarters offices, officer's quarters, company barracks with kitchens, warehouses, prison barracks, a wash house, and a church. There were three 300-bed hospitals, one of them a small pox hospital. The single story barracks buildings were each 90 feet by 24 feet and could house up to 150 men in three-deck bunk beds arranged on each side.

Being an officer, Judson was able to avoid many of the indignities and drudgeries experienced by enlisted men. He didn't have to live in the barracks filled with a hundred obscene, noisy and sometimes drunken soldiers all hee-hawing, spitting or bragging all night long. He didn't have to wear the ill-fitting, itchy wool government-issue clothing or eat the "desecrated" vegetables. He didn't have to tote the 40 to 60 pound knapsack filled with clothes, bedding and half a tent. He didn't even have to learn how to master the Model 1853 Enfield rifled musket that was issued to each new recruit.

What he did have to do was learn how to swing a sword and bark out orders with authority. He had to learn the 101 *Articles of War*, which specified the responsibilities of officers and enlisted men and the consequences for certain kinds of offenses. And he had to stay one step ahead of the new recruits by attending classes teaching military tactics from Hardee's manual, *Rifle and Light Infantry Tactics For The Exercise and Maneuvers of Troops When Acting As Light Infantry Or Riflemen,* in order to teach them the movements the next day.

Within a month and a half, the men were beginning to look like real soldiers and the newly minted officers were able to give convincing presentations that they knew what they were doing, even though they had been trained under assumptions about maneuvers made obsolete by the increased accuracy and longer range of firearms with rifled barrels.

The regiment was given the disagreeable duty of guarding Union Army detainees who had been sent to Camp Douglas as part of the prisoner exchange at Harper's Ferry, where Stonewall Jackson had captured the garrison. Then they prepared to be sent by train and steamer to Memphis, Tennessee to join the Right Wing of the XVII Corps of the Army of the Tennessee under Major General William Tecumseh Sherman on November 9th. Sherman's army was intended to be a major force in the assault on the Confederate fort at Vicksburg, Mississippi.

Judson read *Harper's Weekly* and kept abreast of the various battles taking place on the western front. Most recently, he had read about the engagement at Antietum in mid-September, the most horrific one-day battle in American history. The 87,000 Union troops had losses amounting to 2,108 killed, 9,549 wounded, and 753 captured or missing. The numbers were staggering and Jud was more than a little apprehensive about becoming cannon fodder.

He knew that some of the men he recruited were planning on deserting even before they got to camp and 20 of them had already deserted en mass on one day,

September 6th, the day after mustering in. He heard rumblings about there being another mass exodus planned but didn't know when it would take place and he did not want to be an obvious part of a group of bounty jumpers.

Thinking it would be too difficult to come up with a plausible excuse once they boarded the train for Cairo, Illinois, he began to mull over what he might do before then. He thought about the record keeping in the army and judged it to be slipshod or non-existent. If he told his superiors that he was leaving for a promotion, they would probably never bother to verify his claim and just take him at his word.

"These guys are so gullible," he thought. "Besides, they don't have enough manpower to go chasing after all the men who have deserted already. That's my plan – simple and sweet."

So, on October 31, 1862, Adoniram Judson Burroughs told his superiors he had been offered a position as a major in another unit and walked off the base, his record showing that he "discharged for promotion." He was never to return to that camp and never again to appear in the roster of any Union regiment.

Of course he kept his uniform and wore it when it would serve his needs, such as to look official when he negotiated for an army substitute, or when he was trying to talk himself into a job, or simply to impress (and possibly seduce) the young socialites introduced to him by his brother. He told Mary, falsely, that he had fallen from his horse, broken his leg, and was unable to carry out the duties of an officer because of his injury. And, of course, their marriage would have to be postponed. He would be staying at his brother's place and seeking a different kind of work, probably in Chicago and possibly in Washington. He prevailed upon Mary to again move to Chicago, find a job, and make it possible for them to more readily carry on their relationship.

In March of 1863 Mary made the move to Chicago and found accommodations in a boarding house where two sisters from Baltimore had similarly found lodging. Louisa and Jane Devlin were planning on opening a millinery store and asked Mary if she would work for them as a clerk, bookkeeper and general manager since she had years of prior experience in that type of store. Mary, thinking she had a stroke of good luck at finding a job so quickly, agreed and began working in the store, just a block away, on the first of May. Judson visited Mary at the boarding house a couple of times and he saw her at the store on two occasions while wearing his uniform.

Because he was staying with his brother and she was living with the Devlins, it was not possible for them to simply meet at one of their residences and adjourn to a bedroom. Consequently, Judson began to urge Mary to meet him for a tryst at a house of assignation, a rooming house that provided for discrete short-term accommodations. Mary did some quick calculations of the time since she last ovulated and, after some misgivings and hesitation that were easily overcome by desire, she agreed.

The address on Quincy Street was only a few blocks from where Mary worked. She told her employer that she was going over to the University of Chicago to hear a lecture by Judson's brother and would be back in late afternoon. She wore a dark green veil so as not to be easily identified and carried a large bag that might pass as luggage. She met Judson at a café just down the street. Together they walked to the house, rang the bell, and when a woman answered, Judson said that they had reservations. Without them seeing any other inhabitants of the house, the woman in charge led them to their room. It was a pleasant enough room on the second floor, with nice views of the city from the windows and agreeable paintings hung on the walls, but perhaps a bit overdone with the red-flocked wallpaper.

Mary put her bag on the counter of the cabinet holding the water basin. Removing her hat and veil, she walked over and gazed out the window. Judson came up from behind and wrapped his arms around her, saying "I love you sweet Mollie," as he grasped a breast in each hand and kissed the back of her neck. Mary relaxed in his arms and sighed. He unlatched the catch on the back of her dress and helped her step out of it, hanging the garment on a convenient hook on the door. He removed his coat, shirt and trousers, throwing them on one of the chairs next to the bed. Both clad only in undergarments, they embraced for a long and passionate kiss.

Quickly dispensing with the last vestiges of clothing, they moved for the bed, lying down facing each other with hands exploring each other's sensitized skin and tongues probing each other. Lying still for a while, each of them contemplated what they desired next. Without actually deciding, they soon found themselves entwined as one. Mary began to lose her sense of her surroundings, being transported to a delirious kind of reality composed entirely of luxurious sensations. Later, when she lifted her head off Jud's chest to look him in the face, both of them broke into a smile that told them they had been somewhere exceptional, and they laughed.

Mary went over to the water basin and cleansed herself, brushed her hair and reapplied makeup that had been rubbed away or dissolved. Looking in the mirror, she asked coyly, "Do I look like I had a good time at the lecture?"

Jud laughed, "Judging from your rosy cheeks, I would say you had a most enjoyable afternoon on the college campus listening to Dr. Burroughs give one of his stuffy lectures."

When she got back home Louisa and Jane Devlin were

busy preparing dinner. "How was the lecture?" Louisa inquired.

"I had a wonderful time," Mary replied. "The lecture was kind of boring though."

"What was it about?" asked Jane

"Whether the extension of knowledge increases moral evil," Mary said, anticipating the question and reciting the conversation-stopping answer she had rehearsed with Judson.

"Sounds pretty profound," Jane commented.

"I didn't understand all of it but I enjoyed being with Judson," said Mary, shifting the focus of the conversation.

"Are you two going to get married?" asked Louisa.

"We had planned to get married in June but Judson has learned about the possibility of a job in Washington, DC and he thinks we should postpone the wedding until he knows for sure if he is going to get the appointment. He is going to go for an interview in April at the Treasury Department."

"Will you be moving to Washington if he gets the job then?" asked Jane.

"Yes, I presume so," said Mary. "When are we going to eat? I'm starved!"

***

Shortly after the murder, Mr. McCullough, Judson's boss at the Treasury, brought his wife with him to the jail to see Mary and inquire if there was anything they could do to mitigate her suffering or help her in a practical way. Mrs. McCullough became very interested in Mary and was greatly affected by her apparent mental agony. The girl seemed to be despairing and in a frenzy at the same time. She looked pale, paced the room, and loudly exclaimed, "Why did I do it?" over and over again. She would appear clear-minded and able to answer questions at one moment but then drift off into daydreams in the next. She seemed to be completely overwhelmed by her situation. Mr. McCullough later said that after seeing her for the first time, he finally knew what real mental suffering was, as opposed to the kind of suffering depicted in stage plays.

One of Mary's early and frequent visitors in February was a distinguished attorney from Burlington, Charles H. Phelps and his wife, Eunice, both of whom had known Mary for many years. Mr. Phelps was in Washington to attend a case being heard before the Supreme Court. They were concerned by what they saw – a Mary that was transformed from the happy, active, naturally intelligent girl they knew to one who was wild and haggard looking, restless, incoherent, and frequently contradicted herself within a few minutes of speaking on a subject. Mrs. Phelps, feeling sympathetic toward the young woman she had known since she was a child, spent many days with Mary in jail instead of enjoying the festivities taking place outside in the city.

When the Devlin sisters visited Mary after seeing Bradley, they told her of his rejection of their request to have him defend her. "We were informed that he is the best defense attorney in the District of Columbia," said Louisa. "What could we do to get him to reconsider and represent you?" Mary immediately thought of Mr. Phelps and presented the problem to the gentleman's wife the next time she visited. Mrs. Phelps pleaded with her husband who, in turn, sought out Bradley to see if he might convince him to come visit Miss Harris and assess the case directly himself. Impressed by the professional status of Mr. Phelps, the compassion his wife was showing for Miss Harris, and taking note of all the press coverage the case was getting already, Bradley decided go with Mr. Phelps to visit Mary in jail.

Mr. Phelps introduced Mary to Mr. Bradley. Joseph noted how petite she was and how childlike she appeared with her dark hair done in ringlets surrounding her face.

"I'm pleased to meet you, Mr. Bradley. I've heard so many good things about you, that you are the best attorney in Washington. I do wish you would take my case. I am feeling so alone and scared," she said with a quaver in her voice. "Mrs. Phelps has been very kind to visit me, encourages me and helps me as much as she can. I have known Mr. and Mrs. Phelps since I was just eight years old."

Eunice Phelps added, "She was such a sweet, happy, good tempered child but she always was a little restless. Her friends were strongly attached to her. We saw her with Burroughs frequently – he would come to the house often when he was in Burlington and she would read the letters she received from him when he was away. She always tried to please him and he seemed to pretty much control her in all respects."

"I see," said Bradley, turning to Mary. "I'm sure you must be a good person and you do need legal counsel but, as I explained to your friends, the Devlin sisters, I am very busy right now and would be unable to conduct the case in court.

Mary became quite animated, exclaiming, "What will I do? What will I do? This is all too much for me."

In a reassuring voice, Bradley said, "I also told your friends that I would see to it that a competent lawyer is found to defend you and I promise I will do that."

During the next few weeks, with increasing newspaper coverage in most areas of the country and strong opinions being expressed on both sides, the "Treasury Building Murder" became very salient in the public awareness. Mary had even more visitors who wanted to see the poor little girl who had her heart broken by the cad from a prominent Chicago family.

One visitor was Charles Mason, a prominent army officer (graduating first in Robert E. Lee's class of 1829 at West Point), lawyer and radical Democratic politician. He was not a follower of tradition and refused to be bound by legal precedent or technicalities. He wrote 166 of the 191 opinions for the Iowa Territorial Supreme Court and ruled that slavery in the Iowa Territory was "forever prohibited." As U. S. Commissioner of Patents, he reformed the patent application process and was the first person to hire a woman for a permanent position in a federal office. He tried to oust Lincoln from office in the 1864 election and currently was contemplating a second run for governor of Iowa in 1867.

Mary greeted him graciously. "What an honor it is to be visited by such a distinguished gentleman. How on earth did you choose to come visit such an insignificant little girl as me?"

"We have something in common, Mary. We have both lived on farms outside of Burlington, Iowa. I still have my farm there although right now I am involved in a patent law firm here in Washington called Mason, Fenwick and Lawrence. I knew your father from when I worked my own farm and have been reading in the papers about your recent troubles. There are a lot of people back home who feel very sympathetic toward you, especially the women." Mason knew that, while women could not vote, they nevertheless could have a great influence on their voting husbands and sons. "I thought I would stop by for a visit and see if there was anything I could do to help you."

"How generous of you, Mr. Mason. It gives me some hope that not everyone back home has abandoned me. My friends and I tried to get Mr. Joseph H. Bradley to represent me but he declined. Is it possible that you could be my lawyer?"

"No, Mary I don't practice that kind of law. I am a patent attorney. We represent the interests of people who invent things. Did Mr. Bradley say why he wouldn't take your case?"

"He said something about being too busy, but I think

maybe he just didn't want to do it. He probably just thinks I'm a silly dumb clod-buster who deserves what she gets."

"Don't put yourself down like that, Mary." Trying to boost her spirits, Mason said, "I think you are a tender-hearted and intelligent young girl who just got caught up in something too provocative of the sentiments for you to handle. Mr. Bradley is a very sought after lawyer and he is in court nearly all the time right now. I think he was telling you the truth. But I know him very well through our political party affairs, and maybe I can talk with him and help him figure out a way for him to represent you."

"You are so kind, Mr. Mason. Is there a Mrs. Mason?"

"Yes. Her name is Angelica, from the Gear family. We have been married 28 years and we have three lovely daughters who are all grown up."

"How lucky your wife is to have such a considerate and dependable husband. Oh, how I wish that it would have turned out like that for Judson and me!"

Katherine Abbey, middle-aged wife of a wealthy jeweler, traveled from New York City several times to visit Mary and promised to stay in Washington throughout the upcoming trial. She was a prominent socialite with interests in women's rights and was known for giving grand Christmas parties for poor children in New York City. She saw in Mary a reflection of her own past in that her first husband had abandoned her for another woman, an actress, within a year of their marriage. She was so heartbroken and dispirited that she was unable to even get out of bed for months afterwards. Fortunately, she was from a caring and well-to-do family that could sustain her in her time of need. Her mother and sisters took turns providing nourishment, washing clothes and bed linen and encouraging her to take steps to re-enter society.

Eventually, Katy pulled herself together and met a wonderful man who loved her dearly and respected her need to be a person in her own right rather than just a dutiful wife. But she never forgot the shock of having her understanding of the world be so totally shattered, the sense of aloneness, the feelings of failure and inadequacy, and the helplessness she experienced when her first husband told her, "I'm getting a divorce and there's nothing you can do to stop me."

And as she recovered her strength and began to get involved in life again, there was the anger – the pure fury at his betrayal of her, to say nothing of their wedding vows. She felt like a fool for having so blithely committed herself to someone she only thought she knew - perhaps she just saw in him what she wished to see. Yet she resented that he would think so little of her feelings that he could heartlessly cast her aside – only a monster could do such a thing.

Mary and Katy became very close as they shared their life stories over the course of several months. "We are two of a kind," said Katy. "And I have learned, over the years, that there are a lot of other women who have had similar experiences. We need to stick together and help each other."

"Yes," said Mary. "I would like that. Do you know Joseph Bradley? I was trying to get him to be my lawyer but he has refused."

"No, I don't. But I will see if my husband knows of him or knows someone who knows him. Maybe we can somehow persuade him to reconsider."

Another visitor who was to become one of Mary's supporters was Cornelius Wendell, the man who was at the time Printer to the Senate but was soon to be appointed Superintendent of Public Printing. He was a very powerful member of the Democratic Party, although he himself never held elective office. Mr. Wendell designed and directed the construction of the building used as the Government Printing Office and was widely known around the country, since his name appeared on most of the publications coming out of Washington. He was industrious, honest and dependable. But he was also known to be kind and generous, almost to a fault. He had a host of warm personal friends and worked behind the scenes, rather than in the forefront, to wield his kind of political power.

Wendell felt that those who were without power and resources needed someone with clout to speak up for them and Mary's story of heartbreak and of coming from a poor family and struggling to get ahead with little education tugged at his heart. He himself was a self-made man. Like Mary, he did not have the benefit of an early and formal education but he was earnest, naturally shrewd and worked hard to achieve his goals. He could understand her frustration and disappointment as well as her resentment at being used.

Mary had never heard of Wendell and was initially disinclined to see him when he first came to visit her in her cell. But the warden explained that he was a person of immense status in Washington and insisted that she see him.

"The warden tells me you are a printer. Why would you want to visit me? I have nothing to print."

"Mary, I am here to help in a more general way. I know you don't know me and must be surprised by my unannounced call, but I think I understand your troubles and I may be able to use some of my connections to assist in your defense. I myself have had to fight to make my way in this world without benefit of a formal education and I have met with a good deal of success. It helps to have good friends that will stand by you in difficult times. You are a pretty and intelligent girl and I know you can make it through this. You are still young and have a long life to look forward to."

Mary began to weep softly at this display of kindness and then caught herself. "Do you know Joseph H.

Bradley?" she inquired.

"Yes, as a matter of fact I do. How do you know Mr. Bradley?"

"I – my friends and I have tried to get him to represent me but he says he is too busy. Maybe he doesn't like me or he may just think I don't have a chance. I have heard that he is the best defense lawyer in town and I sure would like to have him for my attorney."

Reflecting on all the years that he had worked with Bradley in the Democratic Party, Wendell said confidently, "I think that might be arranged. You are right that he is the best defense attorney in town. He has been at it for over 35 years in this court and he has won the majority of his cases. I think I can coax him to be your lawyer. He owes me a favor or two."

Another person touched by some of the newspaper accounts of Mary's plight resided in the White House. Mrs. Abraham Lincoln sent Mary a bouquet of flowers that was to adorn her prison cell until after they wilted.

***

By the end of February, several important people that he respected had called on Joseph H. Bradley urging him to represent the defense in the trial of Mary Harris, and he suspected it was not a coincidence . They all seemed to be very passionate in the belief that this slender young farm girl from Iowa should receive a vigorous defense. Joseph wanted to comply with their wishes because they were old friends and he knew that doing favors for friends would subsequently put them in his debt. But he had also noticed the strong passions expressed on both sides in the press and thought that whoever represented her would be in the national limelight.

"The reporters don't seem to get enough of this Burroughs murder case, do they?" said Bradley, putting down his copy of the *Washington Chronicle*.

"No. It's the best thing since the war ended, as far as

they are concerned," said Fendall. "Some commentators think the public is just looking for some kind of diversion. One cynical reporter said it 'furnishes a lively subject of gossip amid the grave public questions now before the country.'"

"I think I will reconsider my stance on this case. Some known and responsible man has to take charge and, in the absence of any volunteers, it might as well be me." He went into his secretary's office. "Doris, see if my schedule can be rearranged so that I could be in court for the first two weeks in July and try to squeeze some time in where I can visit Miss Harris at the jail in late March. Set another appointment as soon as possible so I can tell her I can represent her, if it turns out to be possible."

Returning to his office, he addressed his young colleague. "You know who I think might be a good person to help us on this case?" he asked, rhetorically. "Dan Voorhees. Have you heard him give a speech?"

"No, I haven't," replied Fendall. "What is he like?"

"He's fantastic, especially on the stump! He gives a speech you can't turn away from – passionate, earthy, filled with eloquence that stirs the crowd. He's a tall drink of water, an imposing figure – that's why they call him the 'Tall Sycamore of the Wabash.' He can make the kind of appeal to the jury that we will need to win this case."

Thirty-eight year old Daniel Wolsey Voorhees had practiced law and was the federal district attorney for Indiana before being elected a Democratic representative in Congress. He was serving his third term and was an anti-war Copperhead with strong racial prejudice. He was suspicious of easterners, devoted to personal liberty, states rights and the Constitution and idealized the agrarian way of life that he felt was being destroyed by those currently in power.

"He sounds like a good pick. Maybe he could wax poetic during the summing up," said Fendall.

"I have an idea for the way we should approach this, said Bradley. "Since justice in the courtroom is largely a matter of theatrical presentation, what we should have is a phalanx of powerful lawyers marching in representing the defense. Besides Voorhees, we could get Mason. He has already contacted me to pressure me to take the case. His specialty is patents but he still qualifies as a lawyer and his appearance would be just for show anyway."

"Judge James Hughes from Indiana might also be available," said Fendall. "He is kind of between jobs right now and could probably use another source of income."

Hughes, another one of Bradley's Democratic Party pals and a Mexican-American War veteran, had practiced law in Indiana and then was appointed judge of the sixth judicial district in Indiana. He served one term in Congress and then was appointed judge of the United States Court of Claims from 1860 to 1864. After he resigned, he was elected to the Indiana House of Representative but apparently had contracted "Potomac Fever" and wanted to return to live in Washington.

"I can see it all now," said Bradley, smiling at his own dramatization and waving his hands before his eyes as if viewing the scene itself. "We all march in with the defendant, five Democrats – Bradley, Voorhees, Mason, Hughes, Fendall – the cream of the crop. Maybe we can get Wendell and Katharine Abbey to tag along – all staunch defenders of this poor little girl whose affections were toyed with and ultimately betrayed by a scoundrel, the deceitful suitor. That should be enough to intimidate the prosecution as well as the jury, for God's sake."

CHAPTER 3

When Bradley had seen Mary in jail in February with Mr. and Mrs. Phelps, he noticed that, while the four of them were talking about some subject, Mary broke into the conversation with an irrelevant matter that she had related to Mrs. Phelps just a few minutes earlier. After they left the cell Bradley asked Mr. Phelps if he had seen that and he responded, "Yes. I have observed that sort of thing several times since seeing her here in Washington. She is quite odd at times and at others she seems as if nothing is wrong. When we knew her in Burlington, she was a happy, carefree spirit. Of course, that was before she shot Burroughs. I think it would be helpful if you spent some time getting to know her and make observations of your own about her peculiarities and keep a record of them." Because he was busy in court, Bradley did not have much time to visit with Mary until the end of March.

In the last week of February, Bradley saw Mary accompanied by Dr. Nichols. He had intended to see if she could talk rationally about her history. He found Mary in a state of heightened excitement. Bradley inquired, "What has made you so upset, Miss Harris?"

"Someone sent me this newspaper article about Judson," she said, handing it to Bradley.

He quickly read the article, which told of a séance in which the spirit of Burroughs was evoked and made an appearance. The article related the conversation that occurred between the medium and Burroughs. It suggested that the deceased Burroughs felt he was unjustly put to death at a young age, before he could see the birth of his son. It quoted the spirit as saying, "There was no reason for her to kill me. I had done nothing to deserve such violence."

"Do you have faith in this science or do you have doubts about it, Mr. Bradley"

"I am inclined to be skeptical about anyone who claims to have super natural powers," said Bradley. "I don't think you should worry your pretty little head about such nonsense. This reporter is just trying to make a name for himself at your expense. Such is the nature of reporters – they have to write something to make them stand out from the pack. Put it out of your mind." He reached over and took Mary's pulse – over 110 beats per minute. He felt the top of her head and it was hot to the touch, while her hands were cold. The pupil of one eye was so dilated as to nearly cover the iris.

Mary continued on, impervious to Bradley's touch and glances at his watch to time her pulse. "Judson betrayed me and ruined my life. His brother, the holy man, contradicted his vows to God and lied to me. The only person I may have wronged is Judson's poor wife, who is with child and will not have a man around to help raise it. I do hope she can find it in her heart to forgive me."

When Bradley got back to his office, he made note of what had transpired in his interview with Mary, a practice he conscientiously continued throughout the time he saw her.

Many events in April of 1865 caused the citizens of Washington to be preoccupied with the news. On April 9th Lee surrendered at Appomattox, effectively ending the

Civil War. On the 14th John Wilkes Booth assassinated President Lincoln and everyone in Washington was obsessed with the hunt for the conspirators. Five of them were caught on the 17th and on the 26th Booth was shot and another conspirator was apprehended at a farmhouse in Virginia. The trial of the surviving conspirators began on May 10th and continued for many weeks.

It was not until April 25th that Bradley had his next visit with Mary. She was suffering from a very violent attack of erysipelas of the head, an infection of the skin that Bradley had himself contracted at one time. When he arrived he found Mary sitting with her back to an open window through which flowed a stream of cold air. She was bathing her head with a handkerchief and cold water and Bradley, dressed in heavy winter clothes, could not tolerate sitting in the draft. He exclaimed, "Good God girl, you'll catch your death sitting in that cold wind with a wet cloth on your head!"

Mary paid neither Bradley nor the cold breeze any mind. He reached over and felt her pulse – 120 beats per minute. He felt the top of her head, which was hot even with cold air blowing on it. She appeared listless and inert. Her facial features were fixed and she stared off into space, the pupil of her eye dilated as in the past. She did not blink.

"Has anything happened to frighten you?" Bradley asked.

"No....no," was the soft reply.

"Did anyone treat you with rudeness?"

"No."

"Have you been thinking about the last two years of your life?"

Mary nodded her head. "Mr. Bradley, do you think me a very bad girl? They say I have killed Burroughs, and have me locked up, and it must be so, but I can't believe it is real. I like Burroughs. I can see him now. I have seen him here in this very chamber since I have been here. It can't be so." She twisted her handkerchief and looked up at Bradley with beseeching eyes. "Tell me the truth. I know you will tell me the truth."

Bradley said, "Miss Mary, I know it must seem like a dream to you. I know is hard for you to apprehend the reality of it. But, yes, you did kill Burroughs. He is dead and you could not have seen him since you have been here. It would have to be the workings of your imagination that brought you these images. I am sorry but these are the facts."

Bradley tried to be as reassuring as he could under the circumstances. Mary cried and eventually calmed down. But shortly she again became distraught.

"I have suffered all my life. I have no friends. I have been whipped and beaten without any good reason."

"Who was it that punished you so?" inquired Bradley.

"My father and sometimes my mother. And the school kids sometimes ganged up on me.

"I have never intentionally harmed any human being. I stay awake at night trying to remember if I have given anyone cause to hate me." She stole a quick glance at Bradley to find a sad and sympathetic expression on his face.

"Surely there must have been some people who cared about you. What about Mrs. Alexander, who took you in and gave you employment at her shop?"

"Yes there were a few and I dearly love those who love me and treat me kindly and I would do anything in the world for them, but none of them have ever really loved me," she said, unmindful of the contradiction in her own utterance. "Even members of my church persecuted me because I was going to marry someone not a member, but I don't believe that is a good reason to persecute a person. I can't help it that I fell in love with someone who belonged to a different church. I have prayed long and earnestly and know that God will forgive me, even if all the people in the world should turn against me."

Bradley noted that Mary's face continued to be expressionless and her right eye had its peculiar character. She gave only glancing looks at her attorney, who again checked her pulse and found it to be 120. Her head was so hot that it gave off steam and the bath water soon evaporated. She again broke into tears but, after about two hours, she calmed down and was in full possession of her faculties when Bradley took his leave.

He continued to see the prisoner two or three times per week and in May began to obtain a complete history from his client. She told of her first meeting with Adoniram Judson Burroughs.

"He used to make suggestions about books for me to read. He had a good education and had read a lot of books. He encouraged me to study and thought I was bright and should go further in school. He got me to try out different things to see what I liked best and he introduced me to kinds of entertainment I had never experienced before. He showed me how some things were more pleasing to the eye and ear than others and he helped me to learn how to think about problems and issues, what sort of things to consider when making decisions. He pointed out to me the kinds of things to talk about when trying to make conversation in polite society."

Reinterpreting her comments in anticipation of presenting them in the forthcoming trial, Bradley remarked, "He directed your reading and had a great deal of influence over you. He stimulated your ambition and molded your tastes, habits and manners to those of his own. He shaped your character, thought and feelings into what he wanted to see in a woman."

"Yes, I suppose you could say that. I looked up to him and thought him a good man and wanted to please him."

"I see," said Bradley. "You were falling under his

spell."

"He wasn't always like a stuffy teacher or a father," said Mary. "I remember when he lost his business and came to keep books for Mrs. Alexander. We used to sneak off into the back room and he would put me on his knee and I would put my arms around his neck and kiss him on the mouth. He would try to hide this from Mrs. Alexander and I would play tricks on him – tease him or be provocative in front of her just to get his goat. It was great fun," she laughed in recalling the scene. "Once Mrs. Alexander caught us and Judson became bright red with embarrassment," she squealed with girlish glee. "I didn't think there was any harm in it and afterward we would kiss in front of Mrs. Alexander without trying to hide it. She didn't seem to think there was any great harm in it either."

"Were you always attracted to Burroughs?" asked Bradley.

"No. At first I didn't much care for him. But after he lost his business and was persecuted and reviled by so many people in town, and he would tell Mrs. Alexander how sad and disappointed he was, I began to feel sympathy toward him. I respected him as a good man who had been wronged and slowly I began to like and love him. He always treated me with respect and positive regard. I don't remember an instance where he was inappropriate in word or sentiment."

"He was preparing you to be a fitting, true, faithful and loving wife," said Bradley, as if in summation.

"He always seemed to be cheered when in the presence of his 'little Mollie' and would summon up strength and courage not to be beaten by his enemies. His interest and regard for me grew the more we knew each other."

The next time Bradley saw Mary, he asked her about the letters she had received with the signature J. P.

Greenwood. He brought the letters with him and showed them to Mary to refresh her memory in case she could not remember the details. The first letter read as follows:

Chicago, September 8ᵗʰ, 1863

Miss Molly Harris, Chicago – Dear Molly: I am aware that it is stepping somewhat beyond the bounds of true propriety for a comparative stranger to address a note to a young lady requesting her to meet him, but my hope is that you will excuse the presumption and accede to my request. I have had the pleasure of seeing you several times, but have never had the honor of an introduction. Now, my dear Molly, I have some things to say to you that I know you will be glad to hear, and I know of no better way to say them than for you to meet me, say on Friday, September 11ᵗʰ at 94 Quincy street at one and a half o'clock in the afternoon. I am perfectly well acquainted with the lady who keeps the house, and I know that we can talk there without interruption. You will, perhaps, have some hesitancy in coming, but you need not have, as I can assure you my sole motive in requesting the interview is that we may become acquainted, and that mutual friendship may result from it. I am confident that I can convince you with a few words of conversation, that my sole desire is to be your friend, and I think a meeting would do us both good. Will you come? Do.

If you would rather I see you at some other place, please write where and I will come. If you think it improper to meet me, I hope you will at least answer this note and state your objections.

Your friend,

J. P. Greenwood

Bradley asked, "What did you do when you received this note?"

"I took it right away to Louisa Devlin after I left the post office and showed it to her. I thought the handwriting looked like that of Burroughs and when I asked her, she thought it did too. She thought we should try to find out for sure who sent the letter and she devised a response indicating the time of a meeting and delivered it to the post office right away. We went to the house at the time requested but could not gain admittance and left."

The second letter was received on September 12, 1863 and read:

Chicago, September 12, 1863

Dear Miss Molly: Your favor of Thursday was duly received, and I was sorry to read that you could not come at the hour I appointed. Unfortunately, I had previous business engagement at half-past three o'clock, which is my excuse for not coming. My engagement was of such a nature that it was almost impossible for me to neglect it. I should have been most happy to see you. I have been absent of the city since Friday night; have just returned this evening, and I now embrace the first leisure moment to say to you that I will see you on Tuesday, at half-past two o'clock, at the place formerly designated (94 Quincy street) provided it is perfectly satisfactory to you. I am very anxious to cultivate your acquaintance, which I think will result to our mutual good, and I hope you will grant me the privilege of proving to you that I only desire to be your friend.

I will here say that I have had the pleasure of seeing you several times, but never have had an introduction.

If you cannot come at the time I have appointed, please say by note when you can come; or, if you prefer seeing me at some other place than 94 Quincy, if you will be kind enough to state the time and place, I will, if possible, see you.

Your friend,

J. P. Greenwood

"And how did you respond to this letter," Bradley inquired.

"Louisa composed another response and took it to the

post office that same day. It was a Saturday. She showed the envelope and address to the clerk and told him to take special note of the person who called for the letter, especially his hand, and describe him when she returned. On Monday, she returned for the answer and the clerk described the man to her. She came back and got me and we both went over and the clerk told us the man was of medium height and about 170 pounds with black hair, a heavy black beard and a set ring on his finger. He described the ring and I said 'That's it. That's the ring I gave Burroughs.' I showed him a picture of Burroughs in uniform and he said it might be the same person except for the dress and his beard was about an inch higher. The next day Louisa and I went out to Dr. Burroughs house and learned that Judson had been in town and I was more confident that it was him who had written the letters."

Later in the day, Bradley sent for Louisa Devlin and asked her to verify Mary's story, if she could. Miss Devlin did so and stated that she thought the handwriting was the same as that of Burroughs. She could not remember the name of the post office clerk and said she did not think he was still in the employ of the post office.

"Do you think there is any possibility that Mary wrote the letters herself?"

"Oh, I'm sure not. She is such a sweet young thing. She doesn't have a devious mind like you lawyers and she is not skeptical of people like us older women who have been deceived too many times."

"What was the effect on Mary when she figured out it was Burroughs who wrote the letters?"

"She became very excited and said she never thought he would turn out to be such a rascal. I think that is when the changes started in her. She started acting odd and not getting enough sleep. She attacked my sister with a carving knife and beat her with a brush at one time. She destroyed a quilt another one of my sisters had brought out to show us."

"Please help me and make some notes of all the strange things you observed Mary do. When the time comes, I'll have you testify as to what they were. It is very important because we have to build a case for her not being in her right mind when she shot Burroughs. Don't tell Mary that is our strategy just yet as she may not approve. I will tell her just before the trial begins."

On May 22, Maggie, the girl who attended Mary while she was incarcerated, came to Bradley's office and said something was wrong with her charge and that she had asked to see her lawyer. When he arrived at the jail, he found Mary standing next to the washbasin bathing her head with water and bay rum. Bradley had given her a preparation to help keep her hair from falling out, along with the bay rum for cleansing afterward, but she had still lost much of her hair from the erysipelas. Mary rushed toward him, twisting her handkerchief as she approached.

Bradley asked, "Did the things Mrs. S brought you meet with your approval?"

Mary was not distracted. Unsmiling, she had a rigid expression that was as colorless as white marble, Bradley thought to himself, and he observed that her cornea appeared clouded as if by injection. When her gaze met his, her facial expression seemed to be an unsettled combination of both anger and alarm.

"I am not going to stay here any longer, Mr. Bradley. I am going out – I am. I won't stay. I want you to take me out, Mr. Bradley."

He replied "Yes, Miss Mary. That's all right. I don't wonder at it. You have had a long and hard time of it and I would like to get you out."

"Then take me out – take me out now. I wont stay another minute."

"Well wait a minute, till we pack your things."

Moving rapidly and stopping only briefly, Mary twisted

her handkerchief continuously. "I don't care about the things. I am going now!"

"But look at those bars and...," Bradley cautioned.

"Bars – bars, what do I care about bars? Do you think they could keep me. Haven't I a will, and what are bars then?"

Speaking as if to a child, Bradley said, "I could not squeeze you through them and the only way will be to put you in my pocket, and so get by the guards. We must wait and make no noise to arouse their suspicion. Sit down quietly for a little while and tell me all about it."

When Mary sat down next to him, Bradley took her pulse – 120 again. Her pupils were dilated and her hair was disheveled. He stood and said, "Let me apply that bay rum and water," as he applied the solution to her temples. He felt her forehead and it was as cold as marble while a few inches away the top of her head was so hot as to be uncomfortable to the hand. He dipped the cloth into the solution again and applied it to the top of her head, repeating the procedure a few times.

Sitting down next to her he said, "Now tell us all about it. What has happened?"

"Mr. Bradley, I can't stay here. I can't sleep. I have not slept for two weeks. As soon as I begin to close my eyes, I am roused up, the cry of murder is ringing in my ears. It comes from the passage, it is in the room, with most horrid shrieks of pain, cursing and dreadful language; and overhead a crowd of men are stamping and shouting and yelling; and all around me are the most dreadful noises. I can't stay here. I won't stay here another night. Let them take me out and hang me! That is all they can do. Let them do it now!"

She started to rise but Bradley restrained her. "Sit still. Wait a moment; you haven't told me all yet; I must know all, Mary, before I take you out."

Mary gazed at him so long as to make him

53

uncomfortable and then, in a mournful voice said, "Mr. Bradley, do you think me a very bad girl? I have prayed to God to forgive me; but indeed I never meant to do any human being any harm. Do you think Mrs. Burroughs hates me?"

"There, there, Miss Mary," Bradley said as he wiped away a large tear that had hung on her eyelash.

"No, no. Not so! Let me get another handkerchief." She let out a choking sob, tears flowing without restraint until she again became calm. Bradley tried to make small talk to distract her from the disturbing feelings she was experiencing. Mary stared off into the indefinite distance, body and face fixed in position.

"Yes, I loved him. Oh! How I loved him! And how she must hate me. I don't like to be hated. I never harmed anybody. Its me that was hurt and they told lies about me." She shuddered and sighed again.

"I don't think she hates you," said Bradley.

"How do you know? You do not know her; you did not know him. I knew him for seven years and he loved me; I know he did; and he loves me now. He doesn't love her as he did me. He has loved me ever since I was a little child. He used to scold me so and tell me of my faults."

"Well, Miss Mary, you will not listen to the advice of a friend who has some experience in the world but you *must* do as I say while you are here."

"Must? must?"

"Yes, must" Bradley said, "for I am here as your counsel and friend."

"Friend, have I any friends?"

Bradley replied, "Yes, many. You can have no better friend than Miss Devlin; and I have seen Mrs. Phelps here, who, instead of enjoying the festivities taking place outside in the city what with the inauguration of Andrew Johnson, the new president, locked herself up here with you and her husband – warm friends, who have known you from childhood; and Mrs. Fales who has looked after you as a mother."

"Yes," she said, "yes, Mrs. Fales; she is a good soul ain't she? And she does come to see me and she brings me such comfort." She smiled and added "when she can get time from the soldiers."

***

The storm being over for the time being, Bradley retired to his office. Young Fendall was there and they began to discuss the case of Mary Harris. "I think I might call myself as a witness," Bradley said. "I have had a number of years handling clients such as Mary Harris and I am capable of making unbiased observations – certainly just as objective observations as any doctor."

"It's very unusual for a lawyer to call himself as a witness and it may raise some eyebrows in the legal community," Fendall volunteered. "On the other hand, you can paint the picture of the client and her circumstance that you want the jurors to see. You can cast the jurors' problem – whether to convict or excuse - into a framework that works for the defense."

"Exactly," said Bradley. "I think the trick in this case is going to be how to persuade the jury to accept our view of things rather than the prosecutions view. And it's not just their reasoning that we must convince but also their hearts. In fact, their hearts may be the most important part."

Fendall, having seen Bradley in action in the court room several times before, said, "I agree that if anyone can pull it off, it will be you."

"By the way," said Bradley, "I'd like you to make a trip to Chicago, Burlington and Janesville to collect some depositions that we can introduce in court from people who knew Mary in those places. Of course, we are looking for people who held Mary in high regard but also nose around to see if there are any people who might favor the prosecution and present a problem for us. We don't want to be blindsided by any sleeper witnesses that the district attorney, Carrington, might collar."

"I'll arrange to take the train to Burlington tomorrow and then I will cover Janesville and Chicago on the way back," said Fendall.

When Bradley saw Mary, about 11:00 am the next day, a Saturday, she was pale, restless, and not disposed to talk, but greeted him with a smile. Although Bradley had, in fact, read the newspaper article containing the interview Mary granted to a reporter the first day she was in jail, he told her he had not read it because he had heard from someone that it contained a falsehood about her, namely that Burroughs had seduced her. He maintained this fiction because he wanted to be able to claim ignorance of the information if there was no other way of avoiding it in court. But he wanted to figure out additional ways of blunting the effect of that interview on the jury in the event that it was brought up.

He introduced the subject to Mary and her facial expression turned to that of fury. She half arose, clenched her hand into a fist and leaned toward Bradley with a furrowed brow. "Mr. Bradley, what do you mean? Did that man say that of me and Burroughs, and that I told him so?" She stared off into space and became rigid.

Bradley took her hands in his and rubbed them to warm them up and said in a soothing voice, "There, there Miss Mary." Her pulse was again up to 120 beats per minute. Hoping to avoid a revival of the scene of the day before, Bradley shifted the conversation. "Why, Miss Mary, you could not have slept well for you have actually been dreaming while I was talking to you; wake up!"

"Did I dream aloud?" Soon she said, "There was something I wanted to tell you as it might be of some use, but I can't think what it was. Oh! It was about that article that man who came to me wrote in the *Chronicle*. I have it in my trunk and will show it to you."

Bradley was again evasive and Mary commented, "If I knew Mrs. Burroughs did not hate me, it would take a terrible load off my mind. I should have just quietly submitted to my fate when Burroughs deserted me. People point at me and say such dreadful things about me. When I learned of his marriage, I just wished that I could die."

About that time Mrs. Fales arrived loaded down with flowers and parcels for the prisoner. Mary's demeanor shifted from gloom and doom to brightness and cheer. Mrs. Fales had brought Mary a fine bouquet of flowers from her own garden as well as a container of fresh strawberries. There were other parcels from well-wishers whom Mary did not know.

"How very kind of them to think of me even though they don't know me. Maybe..." she said, leaving the sentence unfinished and looking up with a smile on her face.

Bradley noticed her whole being become animated and exude fun and gaiety. He wondered whether that was her natural temperament and thought to himself, "At least that is what I will put in my notes: Mary is naturally joyous and bird-like." Relieved that she had been distracted and he didn't have to cope with another one of her spells, he took his leave.

Mary had not forgotten Bradley's concern, however, and the following Tuesday Maggie again came and told him of her condition. When he arrived at the jail, an unsmiling Mary immediately confronted him.

"Did you say the trial was fixed for the first Monday in July? Will it certainly be then?"

"Yes."

"Well will that man be a witness?"

"What man?"

"The one that came with Milburn and wrote that

article in the *Chronicle*."

"I do not know, why?"

"What did you say was in that paper?"

Bradley told her what he understood was in the paper and said that the reason he had never read it was that he knew it was false.

"Would you like to see it?"

"Yes"

Mary went to her trunk and retrieved the newspaper article and said "There it is; there are falsehoods in it but not of that kind."

Bradley could see that she was becoming agitated. He took the paper and said, "Well, I'll read it some other time. What's the matter with you today? You do not seem well; you are pale, and your eyes are heavy and I do not like those red spots on your cheeks."

"Oh," she replied, "nothing but I can't sleep. I do not know that I have closed my eyes since you were here two weeks ago."

"Why, I was here only on Saturday last; don't you remember Mrs. Fales coming in and giving you those flowers and other things, and about her bonnet?" He hoped that Mary would become gleeful and laugh as she had done on Saturday, so that he would have more evidence of her natural temperament.

Mary complied with her attorney's implicit wishes and told of how joyful she had been in the early years of her relationship with Burroughs. She told of pranks she had played on Burroughs and how she would pester Mrs. Alexander with questions about love and such.

"You ought to have seen me then, Mr. Bradley; I weighed 116 pounds. I was a fat dowdy. I loved to laugh and dance and play, and I was as full of mischief as I could be. Oh, how happy, how happy I was!"

Suddenly she stopped, looked Bradley straight in the eyes and said, "Mr. Bradley, do you think me a very bad girl? Do you not believe God will forgive me? I know I have done wrong but I have prayed to be forgiven. I pray daily for it."

Noting the expression of remorse, the lawyer saw a chance to also obtain testimony as to his client's motivation. "Did you mean to harm Burroughs? Bradley asked."

"I have been wicked," Mary replied, "but indeed I did not mean it. I did not mean to hurt anybody. I would not have hurt Burroughs for the world. I liked Burroughs. I did love him, and I was so happy, so happy."

Uh, huh, Bradley thought to himself, there's lack of malicious intent. Now for state of mind. He asked out loud, "How then did you manage to commit the crime?"

"How did I do it? I know it must have been me, and they are right to shut me up."

"You know it must have been you? It sounds like you have a hard time believing it was really you."

"Yes, it is all like it was a dream now. As I told you before, I have a hard time realizing it but I know it must have been me."

"Don't say anymore," Mary. "I think I know that you must have been in a different – a peculiar - kind of mental state when you shot Burroughs."

Bradley jotted down notes of his encounter with Mary, recording her naturally joyful temperament and summarizing that she was now remorseful and that she had no malicious intent to harm Burroughs and was in a deranged mental state when she shot him. The next day he tried to get Dr. Nichols to see her but the physician was not available so he went himself.

He found Mary pale and exhausted and pacing back and forth in her room. He asked her to read the *Chronicle* article to him. She read it through and commented on it in a clear and accurate manner. She made the kinds of observations any intelligent reader would have made and he was struck by the quickness of her apprehension and her astuteness in seeing how the content related to her case. No latent mental disturbance was in evidence: consciousness was clear and full of energy; perceptions were keen; memory was very acute. He found it hard to believe that she had not been to sleep for a week.

He was starting to leave when she said, "Don't go yet. There is something else I want to tell you. It has flitted across my mind several times while we were talking but I couldn't think of it now. Sit down, please, and wait a minute."

After a while she said, "Mrs. Abbey has been here and she says Mrs. Burroughs is in Chicago, and she thinks she does not hate me. She says she has a little child – Burroughs' child. I want you to go with me and see it. Oh! how I would love it" she said with a radiant expression on her face. "That would not be wrong would it, Mr. Bradley? His child! Oh! if the mother would only not hate me, and would let me see that little child and give it one kiss I would be so happy. I would not hurt it. It would not be wrong, would it, Mr. Bradley?"

Bradley thought for a moment about how he would enter this encounter in his notes. "Delicate, a soft tenderness mingled with a deep and hopeless sorrow," he projected his own feelings onto the object of his scrutiny.

Just at that time there came floating in from outside music from the bands of the grand review that was in progress. Mary stopped, realizing her request was unrealistic given the circumstances and wanting to avoid the embarrassment of being denied. She listened, and looked at Bradley.

"I forgot," she said calmly. "Everybody is out today but me. I'm sure you want to go and to see the review. I am sorry I detained you."

"No, I saw one yesterday."

"Yes," she said, "but our western men are to pass

today, and I'll tell you at another time what I wanted to say. I wish you would see our western men. By the way, I wanted to tell you that those things your wife got for me are just right. How good she is, and your daughter too, to take so much trouble for me, and I can do nothing in return."

"We have all taken you into our family, Mary. My wife and daughter are happy to do whatever they can to make your life a little more bearable while you have to stay in this place."

***

When Bradley got back to his office, Fendall was there, having returned from arranging for the collection of depositions in Burlington, Chicago and Janesville. "What did you find out?" asked Bradley.

"Mr. and Mrs. Phelps both knew Mary in Burlington from a young age, thought her to be happy and intelligent and saw her frequently with Burroughs. Mrs. Phelps testimony will support the idea that Mary tried to please Burroughs in all respects."

"That's about what I expected from my conversations with them at the jail. Their depositions will help us establish that Burroughs had an undue amount of influence on this sprightly young girl. What we will go for is the controlling relationship over this innocent and trusting young thing."

Fendall continued his report. "Mrs. Mary Jane Winters agreed that Mary had no other motive than to please Burroughs and fulfill her engagement with him. When Burroughs brought Mary back from Chicago, he told Mrs. Winters that they were to be married in three weeks. She also confirmed that he had a ring on his finger that Mary had given him."

"Good, good," said Bradley. "That's more evidence that there was, in fact, an engagement and that Burroughs had Mary wrapped around his finger, both figuratively and literally."

"Mrs. Louisa Hall," Fendall went on, "will swear that, although she knew nothing of their relationship other than that told to her by Mary, she felt Burroughs had complete control of her affections."

"There you have our case," said Bradley. "She was totally dominated by this Mesmer of the heart, and depositions cannot be cross-examined. When he jilted her, she went crazy. To be more precise, she began to have 'periods of paroxysmal insanity.'"

"Then there's Mrs. Eliza J. Harris of Chicago," Fendall continued. "Burroughs spent nearly every evening with Mary at her house and often stayed very late. She was never told of an engagement, but she agreed when I offered the proposition that she always presumed they were engaged because they acted like lovers. When I asked if there was a change in Mary's behavior after Burroughs married Amelia Louise Boggs, she said that Mary believed Burroughs had been false to her all along and claimed that he wanted to take her to an assignation house. She brooded over this day and night and would become very excited, pacing from one end of the room to the other."

"Good job, William. You got the witnesses to put the right slant on their testimony. There is definitely a knack to asking questions so as to get the kinds of answers you want and I think you have acquired the skill."

Fendall was gratified that he had pleased his mentor and replied, "Thanks, boss! We also will be getting the deposition of the lawyer she hired in Chicago to bring suit against Burroughs for breach of the promise of marriage. When I asked if he thought it would be safe for Mary to meet with Burroughs alone, he said 'No'. I can tell you more about that later. Right now, I want to mention something else I discovered."

"What is that?" asked Bradley.

"Dr. John Curtis Burroughs, the deceased's brother, has been spreading money around in the places I've been, trying to get people to testify to support his brother's good name and/or discredit some witnesses. He has supplied funds for a Mr. Goode and a Mr. Hartwell to travel to Washington to tell of seeing Mary at parties in Chicago. They supposedly will say that she appeared cheerful and without mental derangement. It appears that Judge Freer was acting as intermediary for the payments. In Janesville he had contact with a Mr. Danes and two possible suitors – a Mr. Strong and a Mr. Mosely – all through contact with a policeman by the name of Barbee. In Chicago, he had someone contact an Ellen Mills of 94 Quincy Street and he may have arranged for her to disappear for a while."

"H'm. Very interesting, " said Bradley. "We can easily discredit any testimony regarding Mary's mental state from anyone who is not a doctor specializing in such cases. It would not be surprising that an attractive girl like Mary would have other suitors but the prosecution would have to present evidence that there was something there beside mere casual contact for it to have any significance. I would like to find out more about this Ellen Mills, however. If she doesn't appear, maybe we can turn the good reverend's contact with her to our advantage."

On June 20th, less than 2 weeks before the trial was to begin, Mary told Bradley she could not sleep, but actually meant that her sleep did not refresh her. Dr. Young had prescribed port for her and that quieted her down but when she slept, she had such frightful dreams her sleep was disturbed and fitful. In spite of her fatigue, she was self-possessed, and showed a clear, quick, comprehending mind. She corrected some erroneous assumptions Bradley had made and she spoke of how grateful she was for the unwavering regard of some of her friends.

Bradley had brought with him the letters from Burroughs that she had earlier given to him to peruse. He handed them to her and she scattered them out on the bed.

"Some of these I would not like to hear read in court," said Mary. "They might give the wrong impression or reveal things that would be embarrassing to me."

"If the court knows your relationship to Burroughs, I don't think there is a one of them that couldn't be seen. But I will defer to your sensitivities, if you like. We just want to introduce the letters to establish the fact that there was a long intimate relationship between you and Burroughs and that there was an implied promise to marry if not an actual written contract. We don't need to titillate the desires of the jury."

They were both looking over the letters trying to select those to present and those to withhold, when Mary, clutching a letter in her hand, exclaimed "Yes, that's the way you led me to believe that you were perfect, and trained my mind so as to make me think and feel as I thought you did!"

"Good, that's the kind of influence we want to show that he had over you" said Bradley, handing her a portion of a letter in which Judson speaks of the hostility of the Catholics toward him because they had discovered she was about to marry outside of the church.

"Yes," she said, "and I believed him, and I believed he would marry me; and I would have married him at all risks, persecuted as he was on all hands. But it is too late now; he has married another woman."

Fendall entered the room bringing a box for her and she became quite relaxed and laughed and talked as though nothing had occurred to disturb her. Bradley jotted down in his notes that prior to Fendall's appearance, she was abstracted, gloomy, excited or nervous, and that her moods changed rapidly.

***

Over in the District Attorney's office Edward C. Carrington was discussing the prosecution's case with his assistant, Nathaniel Wilson. Carrington was 40 years old, the son of General Edward C. Carrington, an officer of distinction in the Revolution as well as the War of 1812 and foreman of the jury that acquitted Aaron Burr of treason. His mother, Eliza Henry Preston was the daughter of General Francis Preston and his maternal grandmother was related to the great orator Patrick Henry. The District Attorney himself was a graduate of Virginia Military Academy, saw service in the Mexican War and was promoted to Brigadier General of the District of Columbia Militia during the Civil War. He was appointed U. S. District Attorney for the District of Columbia on April 17, 1861.

"This looks like an open and shut case, to me, Nate. Mary Harris got mad when Burroughs jilted her, thought about getting her revenge for a year and a half, and finally got up the courage to go shoot the poor bastard. Can't say as I blame her, but it's still premeditated murder and she's got to pay for it."

"What strategy do you think the defense will use?" asked Wilson.

"Oh, they'll pull out the old insanity defense. Bradley has used temporary or 'paroxysmal' insanity before and I suppose he will try it again. But there's no way it will work. There's no evidence she is insane now and he has to show there was a provocation that occurred with insufficient time for a return to a normal mental state. The last thing that might be considered a provocation in this case happened nearly a year and a half ago and to any reasonable person, that is sufficient time to cool off from the passion of the moment. I don't think we have anything to worry about. All we have to do is show that she had a motive – revenge – that she bought the weapon well in advance of the crime and laid in wait for the victim – showing premeditation - and that she was the one who pulled the trigger."

"I hope you're right," said Nate. "Bradley is a pretty cagey old coot. He's gotten people off before with his slick oratory."

"Bah! No way this time," responded Carrington.

CHAPTER 4

On the same day that four of the Lincoln conspirators were to be hanged and buried in the courtyard of the Old Arsenal Prison at First and A Street, the paddy wagon carrying Mary Harris from jail wended its way the five miles down Massachusetts Avenue and onto D Street where it meets Indiana Avenue. A large group of lawyers, reporters and curious citizens milled around in the Acropolis-styled Old City Hall. In 1863 the District's newly formed Supreme Court began sharing occupancy of the stuccoed brick building, located half way between the White House and the Capitol, with some municipal government offices. Waiting to enter the courtroom, a tall lanky man wearing a press badge leaned against one of the two marble columns in the beautiful south portico. Spotting what he thought was a familiar face moving toward him in the crowd, he righted his posture and waved his hand, at the same time trying to associate a name with the face.

"Bill Douglas?"

The younger man came closer and responded, "Well, I'll be! If it isn't Francis Richardson," he said extending his hand. "I haven't seen you since Cold Harbor. You were with Adelbert Ames' brigade under William F. Smith and I was next door with the brigade of William S. Truex. God, that was a horrible waste of life – 7000 casualties - and there wasn't any military justification for it. Grant really screwed up on that one. After the fighting in the Wilderness and then all these stinking, bloated bodies left on the battlefield at Cold Harbor while Lee and Grant sit around passing notes – it was disgusting. That's what caused me to get out of the war correspondent business. I couldn't take it. All the smoke, noise and gore made me sick. I got a job covering the police blotter with the New York *Times.* At least those killings make a certain amount of sense."

"I know what you mean," said Francis. "Most of us didn't stay in the field more than a year. I lasted two years in the Bohemian Brigade and then got a position with the *Baltimore Sun*," said the older man. "A lot of our boys didn't just remain detached, objective reporters. Some really stuck their necks out and managed to survive by the skin of their teeth. George Alfred Townsend – he wrote under the moniker of 'Gath' – he's trying to get a memorial built for us war correspondents over by Antietam."

"That would be real fitting," said Douglas. "My newspaper sent me down here to cover this 'jilted lover kills boyfriend' story. The editors all seem to think this is going to be a big human interest series."

"I'm here for the same reason. This story is different from the usual ones we cover around here and its been given a lot of press already, even before the trial. Bradley has assembled quite an impressive group to represent the defense. He's a crafty old fart so I think you can expect a bit of drama in the courtroom. The show should sell a lot of newspapers," he said, chuckling.

Francis was one of 26 reporters based in the District

of Columbia. Most of the local newspapers – the *National Intelligencer*, the *Washington Chronicle*, the *Telegraph*, the *Globe* – were considered mere party organs. Newsmen for the District newspapers enjoyed a cozy relationship with senators, representatives, cabinet members, foreign ministers, even vice presidents. It was common for public officials to visit offices down on Newspaper Row and discuss the news or matters that were about to become news. They considered reporters to be sources of influence and befriending them allowed the politician to present an issue as he wished it to be presented. Reporters considered all confidences provided by public men to be sacrosanct and they never betrayed their trust.

During a big event, like an inauguration, there was a great demand for reportorial services and editors would map out a military style plan well in advance of the event, assigning reporters to the White House, the president elect, the parade, the reviewing stand, the senate chamber and to incidents that would occur on the streets. Usually, a woman reporter would cover the inaugural ball. If he could get three or four different newspapers to carry his stories, a good reporter in Washington could expect to make $10,000 to $20,000 a year, placing him in the upper one percent of the population in terms of income. A side benefit, for those who liked to take risks, was the possibility of speculation, since reporters often obtained advance notice on legislation affecting taxes and other financial interests.

Richardson's newspaper, the *Baltimore Sun*, was the newspaper that most everyone in Washington depended upon for news and was not considered just another party organ. The editor subscribed to Samuel Bowles view that the newspaper is to be "the high priest of history, the vitalizer of society, the world's great informer, the earth's high censor, the medium of public thought and opinion,

and the circulating life blood of the whole human mind."
More down to earth, Francis believed in honest and
objective reporting and that newspapers should have a
policy of strictest truth and honor as a matter of
conscience.

"How long do you think the trial will last, Francis?"

"Probably several days," said Richardson.

About 9:30 the clerk of the court indicated to the
crowd that they would be allowed to file into the
courtroom. Seats closest to the bar were reserved for the
recognizable elite of the legal fraternity in Washington
while reporters were seated next closest to the action,
followed by the merely curious citizens, many of whom
were women. The two old war correspondent friends took
seats next to each other.

Escorted by Joseph Bradley, Cornelius Wendell and
Mrs. Abbey of New York, the prisoner entered the
courtroom at 10 o'clock on Friday, July 7[th.] She was
dressed in a black silk dress and a tight-fitting coat of the
same material, trimmed with braid and beads. A black
bonnet trimmed in straw framed her black hair, worn in
ringlets, and her facial features were hidden behind a
black veil.

Mary took a seat between Mr. Bradley and Judge
Mason of Iowa. Judge James Hughes and Daniel Voorhees,
both of Indiana and William Y. Fendell were also present
for the defense. Seated behind them were Louisa and Jane
Devlin and Mrs. Abbey. District Attorney Edward C.
Carrington and Assistant District Attorney Nathaniel
Wilson represented the prosecution. The jury was called
and answered to their names. Then Judge Andrew Wylie
asked Mr. Carrington to read the indictment.

"Gentlemen: You have been subjected to a very
searching examination by the Court and in reply to the
questions of his honor, you have stated that you have no
prejudice against the prisoner at the bar. (Turning toward

the prisoner) I am sure of this. How could you have any prejudice against her for she is a woman, and a woman in distress? That, in itself, is enough to commend her to the sympathy of every generous and noble-hearted man.

"On the other hand, you have sworn, with equal emphasis and solemnity, that you have no prejudice in her favor, and no conscientious scruples in regard to the subject of capital punishment. You have sworn that your minds are ready to discharge the high and awful duty which falls upon you in a spirit of perfect impartiality and to execute the law as it is, without reference to your peculiar views as to what it should be."

"I stand here today to plead the cause of woman – gentle, lovely, virtuous woman – associated in our minds, from earliest infancy, with all that is good, amiable, and attractive. Woman, more than man, is interested in the preservation of peace and order, and in the enforcement of law. To consign an innocent woman to a false doom would be horrible indeed! To allow a great crime to go unpunished, however, because the guilty agent happened to be a woman, would be an act of cowardice, a criminal imbecility.

"The prosecuting officer, who, from a feeling of sympathy, fails to state the law with perfect candor, is unfaithful to his trust. The witness, who, from sympathy, testifies untruly, stains his soul with perjury. And the juror, who, from sympathy, renders a verdict inconsistent with the law and the evidence, commits the same awful crime, in the sight of God and his country.

"Obedience to the law is the safeguard of us all. We must be cruel, only in order to be kind. We must punish the guilty in order to protect the innocent. Loyalty to law and government is obedience to Heaven. Crime must be punished, because God commands it."

Richardson thought that the DA had correctly perceived sympathetic feelings toward the defendant.

Masculine notions of chivalry were the most likely threats to his case and he needed to make a preemptory attempt to defuse their effects on the jury. His strategy was to cast such feelings as irrational emotional reactions that should be avoided because they degrade the judgment process. Giving into them, he implies, is stupid, cowardly and a moral crime. He reminds the jury that their divine oath requires them to be objective in making their judgments and that they must set aside any such feelings toward the accused because of her sex or because she might be subject to the death penalty. Obedience to the law is more important than sympathy in bringing about justice. Moreover, God is watching.

Proceeding to define the way he wanted the jury to consider their problem - arriving at a judgment regarding the guilt or innocence of Mary Harris – the District Attorney laid out a series of questions they had to resolve by examination of the evidence presented in the case and by pointing out legal definitions of terms and points of law.

"Four questions are submitted to you for your consideration. First, was the homicide charged in this indictment committed within the jurisdiction of this court? Secondly, if so, was it by the prisoner at the bar. Thirdly, is it felonious, justifiable, or excusable? And fourthly, if felonious, what is the quality of the homicide? Is it murder, or is it manslaughter? – there being no grades of murder in the District of Columbia, as there are in many of the States of the Union.

"Every homicide is presumed to be felonious murder until the contrary appears from the evidence. Therefore, if I show this homicide was committed by the prisoner, the burden of proof will be upon her to show that it was either excusable, or, if felonious, was committed under such circumstances as would mitigate the offense from murder to manslaughter.

"It is a vulgar error to say that where a party takes life in passion, it is manslaughter. *There must be provocation, and a sufficient and recent provocation, to justify that passion.* Both passion and provocation must concur. A man may take the life of another in the tempest and whirlwind of passion but it is still murder, unless it results from provocation. And that provocation must not only be sufficient, but recent, for if there is sufficient time for passion to subside and reason to resume its sway, it is still murder. What is sufficient cooling-time is a question of law for the Court. Whether the facts show sufficient cooling-time, is a question for the jury.

"Where the party's mind is so affected by disease as to render him an irresponsible being, this is called excusable homicide by reason of insanity. It is a vulgar error that insanity renders a party irresponsible for his conduct. Gentlemen of the jury, this is not so. Every man who commits a crime is at the time more or less insane.

"Passion is temporary insanity. Reason is for the time dethroned, and passion holds sway. But in order to acquit a party upon the ground of insanity you must be satisfied from the evidence that the mind was so affected as to render the party incapable of distinguishing between right and wrong as to the act committed; or that the will was so affected as to be entirely beyond his control, rendering him a mere automaton, and his acts involuntary.

"Motive, you will observe, is utterly incompatible with the idea of insanity. Therefore, if it appears from the evidence that this homicide was committed in the spirit of revenge – to avenge some wrong – it is a deathblow to the plea of insanity.

"It is my duty to remind you that if you acquit the party upon the ground of insanity, you should find that verdict special: not guilty by reason of insanity; in order that the Judge may certify the fact to the Secretary of the Interior, and have the unfortunate accused confined within the walls of the insane asylum.

"Of course it is not for me to anticipate the defense," Carrington continued, doing so nonetheless. "I am merely stating general principles. If this appears from the evidence to be a case neither of justifiable nor excusable homicide, the next question to be considered by the jury will be whether this be murder or manslaughter. You will observe from the definition of these two grades of offense, that malice is the distinguishing characteristic.

"Felonious homicide with malice is murder. Felonious homicide without malice is manslaughter. Now, malice is of two kinds: malice in law is where a party takes life wantonly, that is to say, without sufficient excuse in law; and it does not imply either hatred, envy, or revenge. Malice in law is that quality or feeling of the human heart that permits a man to injure another whom he neither hates nor envies, and against whom he has no grudge, and whom, perhaps, he has never seen.

"Malice in fact is malice in the ordinary acceptation of the term, and frequently implies hatred, envy, and revenge, and is manifested by lying in wait for the party injured, or by antecedent threats and menaces. Hatred is a feeling of hostility against some particular person. Envy is a feeling of chagrin and mortification at the real or supposed superiority of another. Revenge is that red and bloody demon lurking in every depraved and malignant heart, prompting to those crimes that shock and outrage human nature."

Douglas scribbled in his notebook, "DA distinguishes between murder, justifiable homicide and excusable homicide. Knows defense will argue that the accused suffered from diminished capacity due to some form of insanity - trying to undermine that strategy by arguing that if the accused had any kind of motive in killing Burroughs – hatred, envy, revenge - she could not use the insanity defense. Presence of 'malice' makes the killing murder and not manslaughter, in the legal eyes of Carrington."

The prosecution continued with a vivid and dramatic depiction of the events leading up to the killing of Burroughs, including interjections of shock and outrage, presumptions about what was in Mary's heart and mind, and shaming reminders that a woman - Burroughs's wife - was left a widow and his child was left an orphan by the acts of the accused.

"Having briefly stated these general principles, I shall proceed to briefly recapitulate the facts in the case which you are sworn to try. I think I am warranted in saying you have never tried a similar case before. It is unprecedented in the annals of crime. We expect to show that the prisoner at the bar armed herself with a deadly weapon in the city of Chicago. That she came to Washington, repaired to the Treasury building, and inquired of the doorkeeper for Mr. Burroughs. That she was received with that kindness and courtesy characteristic of the American people in any position of life, whenever approached by a lady, or one bearing the appearance of a lady.

"The doorkeeper told her that there were two persons of that name employed in the Treasury Department. She looked at the book where the names of the employees were recorded, and turning to the name of Adoniram J. Burroughs, said *he* was the gentleman whom she desired to see. She went to the room, turned the bolt, when she saw the object of her search, standing at his desk in the discharge of official duty. An old lady sitting near by attracted by the bright luster of her black eyes, rose from her seat, and was about to ask her in.

"Her envy was excited. Good heavens! What was there to excite this unchristian and pitiable spirit? She measured him, she marked him, she resolved upon his death. She retraced her steps down the hall then, turning to the left, she took her stand behind a high clock, which reaches from the floor almost to the ceiling. Here she sat awaiting the approach of her unsuspecting victim.

"Great God! What a position for a woman! Armed with a deadly weapon, and with malice in her heart, in a public building in the metropolis of a Christian nation, stands an American woman contemplating the crime of murder.

"She could hear the ticking of the clock; she could observe the movements of the hands. There was time for passion to subside and for reason to resume its sway. One would suppose that she could have seen with the eye of fancy the wife pointing to her child, and hear her voice:

'Oh! thinkest thou not how wretched we should be,
A widow I, and helpless orphan he?'

"The clock strikes; the labors of the day are ended. The clerks are returning to their respective places of abode. Young Burroughs, full of life, and joy, and hope, is going to his home, where his faithful wife, an honest, true-hearted woman, is anxiously expecting her husband's return, unconscious of the slightest design upon his life or personal safety.

"Alas! Alas! How ignorant of the terrible fate that awaits him, for almost at that very moment the instrument of death is pointed at his back by the assassin's hand. He is walking down the hall in company with a friend, engaged in conversation. As he passes the clock the prisoner draws her pistol, and without a word of warning or of notice, aims and fires, inflicting a mortal wound. He reels, exclaims 'Oh,' turns again, and endeavors to make his escape.

"Was not that enough to satisfy the assassin's revenge? No, gentlemen of the jury. She steps into the center of the hall, deliberately cocks her pistol, and aims directly at his head, as will appear from the impression made upon the wall, which will remain a lasting memorial of this cruel and bloody tragedy. But this was a useless expenditure of ammunition. Her object was accomplished, her revenge was satisfied; the body of her victim lies bleeding, at her feet.

"You see the flash, you hear the report, and in a moment the poor trembling spirit of Adoniram J. Burroughs stands frightened and appalled before the bar of eternal justice. Horrible, horrible, most horrible! Cut off in the very blossom of his sins, no reckoning made, unconsecrated, and untempered, he goes to his long account with all his imperfections on his head.

"She is arrested but still she is calm, cool, and collected, showing no emotion, until the mangled and bleeding corpse of her victim is brought into her presence. Then she begins to cry and tear her hair. In the strong and expressive language of this indictment, 'moved and seduced by the devil,' she commits the murder; but, when the deed is done, the devil leaves her, and she hears the voice of her God, 'Thou shalt do no murder.' She sounds the alarm, and then she suffers, in anticipation of the awful retribution of an outraged and violated law.

'Revenge, sweet at first, bitter ere long,
Back on itself recoils.'

"Is this some terrible dream?

"I have stated to you that I know nothing of my own personal knowledge. I never saw the prisoner until she was brought into the presence of the Court. But, if these facts appear in evidence, shall I insult your intelligence by arguing that this is a case of murder – willful, deliberate, cold-blooded murder – aggravated by cruelty, barbarity, and a savage disregard of human life, unrelieved by a single circumstance? To call it by any other name would be a libel upon the religion and the laws of that God we adore, and the country we love."

In his final comments, Carrington tries to tap into the juror's community pride by offering a challenge to them to repair the sullied reputation of the nation's capital by getting tough on crime, crime that is brought to them by outsiders.

"Why did the prisoner at the bar not kill him in Chicago, if she had suffered any wrong, either real or imaginary, at his hands? Ah, gentlemen, did she suppose, as many others do, that here in the nation's capitol, crime could be committed with impunity? As a citizen of Washington, as an American lawyer, proud of my country and her institutions, I hope this error will be corrected; for this is the metropolis of the nation, the great radiating point, and strangers from abroad judge of the habits, customs, and manners of our people from the citizens of the federal metropolis.

"Unfortunately for us, the city of Washington has acquired the reputation abroad of being the city of licentiousness, violence, and crime. But the citizens of Washington themselves are a law-loving, law-abiding, religious people. We are indebted to eminent criminals who come from a distance, for this unenviable reputation. It is the rendezvous for thieves, garrotters, murders, and adventurers. The city swarms with wicked men and women, and public safety depends upon the firmness and integrity of the judiciary.

"I charge you, gentlemen of the jury, maintain your dignity and your self-respect. Let it no longer be considered that crime may be committed with impunity in the national metropolis, and that jurors will refuse to discharge their duty with firmness and fidelity."

Douglas whispered to Richardson, "The crime rate isn't any worse here than in other parts of the country, is it?"

"Not that I'm aware of," Francis whispered back.

Assuming that by now there was a large proportion of those present that needed to use the bathroom, and it being a logical place for a break in the proceedings, Judge Wiley called a recess. Richardson and Douglas made it to the lavatory before most of the crowd could find it and afterwards went out on the south steps for a smoke.

Richardson asked, "Where are you staying, Bill?"

"At the Willard. It's close, the food is good and the service is fast. And it's a good place to hear the local gossip."

"That's for sure," said Francis. "William Howard Russel, the British war correspondent who came over here at the beginning of the war, used to say that at any given moment it contained more 'scheming, plotting, planning heads' than any same-sized building in the world."

"That's the Willard, alright. Where do you live, Francis?"

"I have a place over on North Capitol. It was built over the ruins of a pair of townhouses designed by George Washington back in 1798. The British burned the originals down in 1814 but it was rebuilt and is now owned by Rear Admiral Charles Wilkes. It sits on a little hill because they've lowered the street twice since it was built so they could drag slabs of marble down to the capitol building. But it is comfortable and close to places I need to go, as a reporter."

"Is there a Mrs. Richardson?"

"Not yet, but I'm working on it. How about yourself?"

"No. I've got to get established as a newspaper man before I dare take that step. Besides, I haven't been quite right since the war and I wouldn't want to subject a woman to a life of grief."

Francis took a long studious look at his old friend and said, "I understand. It's something that's hard to get over." Flashes of his own experiences on the battlefield crept into his awareness but he quickly pushed them out of mind. Tapping the dead ashes from his pipe on the bottom of his boot, he said, "We better get inside before the trial resumes."

CHAPTER 5

Judge Wiley directed the focus of the proceedings to the counsel for the defense. Joseph H. Bradley was dressed in an immaculate beige three-piece suit, his long white hair, mustache and beard impeccably groomed for the occasion. He arose, shifted his gaze to the table occupied by the prosecution, and, with the hint of a sneer, launched an attack on the prosecution's implied claim of sympathetic bias toward the defendant, asserting that it was irrelevant, and declaring the indictment against his client to be a gross overstatement.

"I have nothing to say to you, gentlemen of the jury, on behalf of the prisoner as a young lady, or even as a woman, nor have I any appeal to make to you on the ground of chivalry or of manhood. Those are questions outside of the present inquiry. I shall call upon you to decide this case upon the facts as they shall be presented to you from the written and oral proof, and if the accused, in your judgment, shall be possessed of one tenth of the guilt just now attributed to her by the District Attorney, I shall join him and ask for her condemnation, and that she shall suffer the severest penalty."

He then began to paint the picture of Mary Harris that he wished the jury to see - that of a naive and innocent young girl whose sympathies were played upon by a much older man who encouraged her to defy her parents, sculpted her sentiments, and falsely led her to believe he would marry her.

"The prisoner is of Irish descent. She has had few advantages of early education and moral culture. When about nine years of age, she was a little girl employed in a store kept by a lady in Burlington, Iowa – a millinery and fancy store, where some gentleman's belongings were kept, such as pocket-handkerchiefs, neckties, etc. While there she first attracted the attention of the deceased. She was then a bright and beautiful child, he fondled her as such, and she returned his caresses.

"The lady with whom she was thus employed is represented as one of refinement and culture, mingling in the society of the place, and in every respect admirably fitted for the training of such a child. Burroughs was at that time engaged in business, keeping a store not far from the one in which the accused was thus employed, and passed by the store every day. He was frequently in the store obtaining articles of gentleman's wear and use, and was treated as a friend. He failed in business after two or three years and then was employed by this lady to keep and post her books, and thus was thrown more closely into the society and association of the accused.

"Time passed on. He left the city of Burlington and on the first of November, 1858, wrote to the accused the first letter which ever passed between them. That letter will be offered in evidence. At this time she was about thirteen years of age, not more. He was a man of education and knowledge of the world, her senior at that time of more than double her years. During their acquaintance, he had cultivated her intellect, and assisted in refining her manners, and thus she became fitted for, and was admitted into, the best society of Burlington. From that time forth, so long as she continued to reside in Burlington, she was received as the friend of ladies of the highest character and repute, well known in that town. Her associations were with the children of these ladies, principally among married ladies, and of persons older than herself. She went very little into general society.

"The correspondence thus begun was continued for five years. So much of that will be laid before you as will enable you to see the character of the relations existing between the parties. I have here ninety-two letters, taken from the correspondence, extending from the year 1858, and including the year 1863. They will show how by degrees he formed, shaped, and molded her mind, feelings, habits, tastes, and her intellectual and moral character. They will show how completely she was identified with all his life that he took no grave step in life without first communicating to her. All his hopes, fears, and disappointments were found out in this correspondence, and in the interviews that from time to time were referred to in it.

"His expectations and prospects were disappointed. He had a quarrel in Burlington, and was dismissed from his church. He poured out into her ear all his grief and suffering, and although at first she did not even like him, yet by degrees, as time passed, she began to believe that he was persecuted and trodden down. She believed him a good man in adversity. He was always good to her. Her liking increased until at last she began to love and when she gave her heart she gave her whole soul with it. She thought and acted as and for him. She trusted with the whole trust of a woman's confidence when once given.

"Her father disapproved of this correspondence, disapproved of the man. He interfered, prohibited, and attempted to prevent. He did prevent his visits at his house, and treated her with some severity.

"They then poured the tale of their love and their difficulties into the ear of one of the most intelligent, refined, and estimable ladies of that town, and she permitted them to visit at her house. Her deposition will be read to you.

"He persuaded the accused to leave her father's house and go to Chicago in search of employment, in which city he was residing, and where he was looking forward to the formation of a military company to go into the service of the United States. She did so. His attentions to her there were such that one of her employers, a gentleman keeping the principal bookstore in that city, took the brother of the deceased to task. Shortly afterwards, or about that time, she left Chicago and returned to her father's house.

"She remained in Burlington for some time afterwards, retaining all her former associations, becoming more and more endeared to the ladies with whom she was thus associated, until again, in the spring of 1863, he prevailed on her once more to go to Chicago, where he was then residing, to seek employment there.

"Previous to that time he had in the most distinct terms informed a lady, whose testimony will be presented to you, the fact of a marriage engagement existing between himself and the accused. The day was fixed for the celebration of the marriage. His plan was, if he succeeded in forming this company, and was mustered into the service, to marry then. But as her parents were so much opposed to her marrying him, they being Catholics and he a Baptist, he determined if he did not succeed in the formation of this company, thus obtaining a subsistence for himself and wife, to go to California, or some other place remote from the town of Burlington.

"An accident, a broken leg, prevented him from going

into the military service, and the marriage was postponed. Subsequently the day was fixed, and when she returned from Chicago the first time she was accompanied by him and he then told this lady, as his excuse for his return to Burlington, that he did not wish his wife to be employed any longer as a clerk.

"They were then to be married within three weeks. At a subsequent period, as is shown in one of his letters, her priest discovered the fact of her intended marriage out of the church, and in that letter he inveighs in strong terms against the espionage upon the correspondence, which was then carried on between him and her.

"Subsequently to this, and after her return to Chicago in the spring of 1863, the period of her marriage was fixed in the month of June of that year. He came to Washington in search of employment, and obtained it in one of the public offices, and then, instead of writing to her to make arrangements for marriage, he wrote to her, proposing, if she would come to Washington, he would find employment for her in one of the public departments.

"Not a word was said of marriage. This was the first incident in the course of their long correspondence and intercourse that startled her, and led her to entertain the first doubt of the character of the professions he had made her. The contents of that letter were communicated to her friend in Burlington.

"The last time they were seen before that visit to Washington they were in such a position to each other as could only indicate an actual engagement of marriage within a short time. She sitting at his knee, he playing with her curls. She was a young girl of 17 years of age, pure and spotless; he a man well known in society, with long experience in the ways of the world – a man of education and refinement.

"Shortly after her arrival in Chicago, in the spring of 1863, she formed the acquaintance of the two Misses

Devlin, who had left Baltimore with means to establish themselves in the millinery and fancy goods business in the city of Chicago. The accused at that time wrote rapidly and had an excellent hand, and had had some experience under her former instructor in bookkeeping. She was taken into the employment of the Misses Devlin as clerk and bookkeeper, and occasionally assistant saleswoman. She was with them when the deceased parted from her to come to Washington, and with them she has lived until the 30th day of January last. She has occupied the same chamber with both, and the same bed with Miss Louisa Devlin from that time during the whole time she was with them.

"During that summer she received few attentions and went out but little. In fact, her life was spent in her correspondence and looking forward to the fruits of that correspondence – a union with the deceased. Her spirits were cheerful and happy – bird-like. Her manner was full of life and animation. The livelong day was a day of happiness to her. Not a cloud darkened her prospects, and she expected in June of that year to be married and come to Washington to live.

"The summer passed in the fond hope of their being married. She was at that time in high health, fleshy beyond the ordinary degree of girls of her age, of high, pure, healthy color, attractive, yet as I have said, not seeking society, but living within herself, and with the two friends whom she had thus made.

"On the receipt of a letter dated the 7th of August, she answered him, and told him where she was residing with the Misses Devlin, and that he could meet her at their store on the Sunday following. She and the Misses Devlin were at the store. He did not come; but a day or two afterwards he did come in the evening, and spent more than an hour in company with the accused, during the greater part of which time he held her hand. They were within the view of the two Misses Devlins all the time, and they spoke of the interview as an interview between lovers. They parted as friends, with his promise to see her the next day or the day after, and she with the expectation of seeing him, and having an opportunity to hear from him more fully the history of his prospects and his conditions, and to have the period of that marriage finally fixed.

"She heard no more of him until she received a letter dated the 24th of August, written in terms of warm friendship, and speaking of the long correspondence which had passed between them, and of his failure to fulfill their engagements by reason of his want of means; speaking of the strength of his friendship for her, and declaring that, but for the adverse fortunes which had pursued him, she should have shared in all his prosperity long before that.

"Still she was not alarmed. But on the 8th of September she received from the post office in Chicago a letter in a feigned handwriting, with a feigned signature, but still exhibiting such marked traces of the genuine handwriting of the deceased as to leave little doubt, upon investigation, that he was the author of it, inviting her to meet him at a house, No. 94 Quincy street, Chicago, at the same time declaring that he was an entire stranger to her, and professing the warmest friendship for her.

"She exhibited that letter to her friends, the Misses Devlin, and they were of the opinion that it was written by the deceased. Up to that time, if the suspicion had crossed the mind of the accused, she would have rejected it, and did then reject it with indignation, because no passage in the life of the deceased and herself had ever led her to suppose that he could be guilty of such an offense as that letter implied.

"They made inquires immediately as to the character of the house, and found it was an assignation house of the worst character in town. Miss Louisa Devlin of her own accord said she would reply to the letter, and did write the answer, signed the name of Miss Harris, and deposited it in the post office herself.

"On the 14th of September a reply was received. In the meantime Miss Devlin had gone to the post office and requested the delivery clerk to note particularly who should call for the letter with that address, J. B. Greenwood, telling him it was a matter of some interest, and she asked him particularly to observe his hand, to see if there was anything remarkable as to that.

"On the 14th of September, as I have stated, they received a reply dated the 12th of September. Both of these letters will be given in evidence to you. Miss Devlin went to the post office and inquired whether the letter she had written had been taken out, and on his replying that it had, asked the clerk to describe the man to her. Having received a description she returned to the store, took the accused to the post office with her, and there let her hear the clerk's description.

"The clerk gave the description minutely and accurately; and being asked if he observed any peculiarity about the hand, said "Yes; he wore a set ring, dark, but part light colored, on the little finger of his left hand." Miss Harris immediately exclaimed, "That is the very ring I gave him." In the testimony of one of the ladies from Burlington, you will find a minute description of that ring, and the fact sworn to that it was given by the accused to the deceased long before as a pledge of her love.

"Still, not satisfied with the description of the person and of the ring, they exhibited to him a full-length photograph of the deceased in the military uniform of a captain, which will also be exhibited to you. The clerk immediately, exclaimed 'That is the same person, except that the man who called for the letter was dressed in citizen's clothes, and his whiskers and beard were not quite so large as they appear to be in the picture.'

"Still, not satisfied with all this accumulative proof, Miss Jane Devlin and the accused went in open day to the house 94 Quincy Street, and there called for the woman who kept it. She met them there, and entered into conversation with them. They asked her to describe the man who had made that appointment. She said, 'He was here on such a day,' (naming it) and told me when the bell was pulled not to answer it, for he would sit at the window by the side of the door, where he could see the lady come up the steps, and he himself would answer the bell, and when she saw him, she would answer without hesitation; but, if she saw any third person there, she might be repelled without entering. She knew him so long a time and well, that she would enter without hesitation.

"She stated he was there when they were coming, but seeing two of them coming together, he had made his escape by a back way. They asked her to describe him, and she did so with such minute accuracy as to overcome the accused, and put her in such a state of excitement that Miss Devlin dared not take her back through the open street through which they came, but by a back way got her to the store.

"The next day the keeper of that house called at the store, and they exhibited to her the photograph of the deceased, in military dress. She immediately exclaimed, 'That is the very man, except that he did not have on military clothes.'

"Thus convinced, and overwhelmed with the discovery, Miss Louisa Devlin went out to see the brother of the deceased, to know whether his brother was in town or not. She saw him, and he assured her that he was not in town at that time, but had been a few days before. The next day the accused, taking with her all the mementos of the affection which had so long existed between herself and the deceased – the letters, photograph, etc. – went with them to this brother, a reverend clergyman, presiding over a college close to Chicago, and carrying with her these two letters, containing these infamous propositions, inquired if his brother was in town.

"He told her he was not; yet she says she saw him as she was going out to that reverend gentleman's, coming into town in one of the horse-cars, passing her on the road. That denial shocked and startled her. She was sure it was not true; for she had seen him, as she believed, rise up in the car, as they met and passed each other, and looked out of the window to see her. She could not be mistaken.

"She showed him these last two letters, and he denied that they were in his brother's handwriting. He had denied that the brother was there and he treated her with harshness and with severity. Fortunately for the truth and the cause of justice, she retained possession of all the articles she thus carried with her to surrender; and we have them here in court, and will exhibit them to you.

"On the day that she had this interview with this reverend brother, and within an hour or two afterwards, he performed the marriage ceremony for the deceased with the lady who now survives him, and who has been overwhelmed in the distress caused, not by us, but by those who produced the causes which have led to this unhappy result.

"A few days after this, she saw the notice of the marriage of the deceased in one of the public papers of Chicago, and immediately afterwards was seized with an attack of physical disease with which she had never before been disturbed, and which, at regular periodical intervals, has continued to visit her to this day.

"From that time forth her character and her physical condition were all changed. The light of her existence had gone out. She became moody, melancholy, depressed, and exceedingly quiet; and yet, during the intervals of these attacks, she went about her business mechanically, and to all external appearance, except to those who saw her intimately, and except so far as the loss of flesh was concerned, she continued the same.

"She was then visited by one of the most skillful physicians of Chicago, who treated her solely for the physical disease, he having had no intimation of the moral causes that aggravated and produced it. On a recurrence of one of these attacks in midwinter, in intensely cold weather, she got up in the night, with nothing on but her nightclothes, went into an adjoining chamber, and lay upon the floor. She resisted all arguments, and persisted in lying there; and this she repeated at different times during that winter, in the inclement climate of Chicago."

Bradley proceeded to cite numerous instances of odd behavior on the part of Miss Harris that he believed justified or implied a diagnosis of insanity. On one occasion she awoke early on a winter's day and indicated an intention to go for a walk on the lakeshore, only with great difficulty being restrained by Louisa Devlin. On another occasion she attacked Jane Devlin with a carving knife when the latter indicated with disgust that she did not want to hear the defendant read any more letters written by Burroughs. After Louisa Devlin again restrained her, she tried to jump out of the window but was persuaded to leave by the door. Jane followed her as she walked to the Tremont Hotel and the two Devlin sisters subsequently enlisted the aid of a friend from Burlington to try to convince her to return home, which she did later in the evening "clothed in her right mind."

Another time, at their store and without provocation, Mary was said to have attacked a customer with a large pincushion with a brick in it. She also was alleged to have attacked Jane Devlin several times even though they seemed to have subsequently become close friends. In 1864, when a third Devlin sister came to visit and was showing them an elegant and costly piece of silk patchwork, Mary, without any apparent cause for it, attempted to cut, hack, and destroy it and had to be locked up in a different room. She then attempted to force the door and to deface the Devlin's carpet.

"Thus, some months would pass without any extraordinary excitement. In July of 1864, before they left Chicago, the accused had employed counsel to bring suit against the deceased for breach of promise of marriage. The testimony of that counsel will be read in the cause, and you will see the condition of her mind at that time, the object of her instituting that suit, and the skill with which the deceased evaded an arrest to respond to that suit, while in Chicago on a visit of three weeks or more. The writ was placed in the hands of an astute detective officer, and yet he failed to serve it.

"After that she endeavored to persuade her lawyer to accompany her to Washington for the purpose of having the suit brought here. He dissuaded her from this course, and refused to come; yet, when she found it was impossible to serve the writ in Chicago, she, alone, unbefriended, the little, quiet, frail being you see before you, prevailed upon Miss Devlin to furnish her with money to come to Washington, that she might sue him here.

"The Misses Devlin believing that that would bring more quiet to her mind than anything else, as it would lead to a thorough exposition of his conduct, and purify her character from every shadow of doubt or suspicion which might be cast upon it by the circumstances of his desertion, these being the things which were preying upon her mind, furnished her with the means to come. She visited Washington, and on her arrival here found that he had gone, as she understood it, back to Chicago on that same day. She took the return train without stopping, and went back to Chicago."

"Long before that, and almost a year ago, she had

purchased a toy pistol – a Sharpe's four-barreled revolver – which lay in her open trunk, and which Miss Devlin saw; and when she remonstrated with her to know why she spent her money so foolishly, she answered that many ladies went armed, and she was afraid every day that Dr. Burroughs and his brother would snatch her up on the street and carry her off to some place where she would never be heard of again, and she had bought it for her defense.

"On the first occasion of her leaving Janesville to come to Washington, which was about the 1st of January, she put into her trunk a pile of the letters she had received from the deceased, and, with them, threw into the trunk that pistol, which will be exhibited to you, and which, you will see, has never been used. When and under what circumstances she loaded it, or it was loaded, does not appear in the progress of the case.

"She reached Baltimore, consigned to the parents of the Misses Devlin in that city. She was there taken sick, and remained three weeks, when she was visited with this periodical attack of physical disease. Recovering from that, she made an arrangement with the lady at whose house she was staying, to purchase for her a return ticket to Washington, for the 30th of January.

"A lady who occupied the chamber with her will state to you the facts and circumstances, exhibiting the condition of the accused at that time. You will find that on Saturday she communicated to this lady the whole history of her life, read to her the letters which she had received from the deceased, and commented upon them; and she read until past two o'clock on Saturday night, when this lady fell asleep, leaving her still awake reading and commenting upon those letters.

"The next day, (Sunday), she told her story to the lady of the house where she lived; told her that she was coming here; told her of her love for the deceased, and of the agony she had suffered, without uttering one word of reproach against him. She believed her character had been stained, and she was coming here to vindicate in our courts that character. She said he was poor and she did not seek compensation in damages. All she desired was to have her character vindicated.

"Sunday night was passed as was Saturday night, in reading and arranging these letters to be submitted to counsel in Washington. She had a card with the name on it of some professional gentleman she was to visit here. Her companion again went to sleep, leaving her sitting up engaged in thus arranging the letters. They had agreed to pass that Monday evening in attending a lecture of Henry Ward Beecher in Baltimore, and her companion cautioned her not to take a train on her return later than four o'clock, or she would not be on in time. When she awoke she found the accused was still at work, preparing to come to Washington with a pile of letters tied up, and the pistol lying on the bureau. She left her thus engaged. Shortly afterwards, for it was then late, the lady at whose house she was stopping, called to her from the foot of the stairs, and told her to make haste, or she would be too late; and in her hurry she threw her bundle of letters into the trunk, put the pistol in her pocket, and thus started for Washington.

"Arriving here she went to the Treasury Department, and opening the door of the room, saw the deceased sitting at his table. She did not stealthily open the door and peep in, but opened it wide enough to present her whole form to view to any one in the room who might be looking in that direction; and stood there long enough to have a lady who was employed in the room see her, and be able to recognize her as the same lady she had seen there last fall, and who was about to invite her in when she closed the door and walked away. Her appearance struck the lady at the time – especially the character and expression of the eye.

"An hour subsequent to this, while standing in the hall, the deceased passed by her, and under an impulse which she could not resist, she drew her pistol and fired. He turned, looked at her, and exclaimed, 'Oh, my God,' and fled. Just before he fell, as he turned the angle of the hall, to pass down stairs, she fired a second time. She then calmly walked down the steps without anybody molesting her, and walked, as she supposed, out of the door of the building she had entered. She was then arrested and carried back.

"She was calm, moving, as it were, mechanically, without shedding a tear. She was taken into a room, and immediately afterwards Mr. Handy, a justice of the peace, came in. On his telling her he was a justice of the peace, she immediately surrendered the pistol. She then for the first time began to yield to the paroxysm of despair, which continued for days afterwards. She tore her hair, threw herself upon the floor, and on her knees, and was raised repeatedly by Mr. Handy, or Mr. McCullough, or both. To both she exclaimed, when they asked why she did it, 'Why did I do it? Oh God, how I loved him. I loved him better than life itself.'

"A policeman was present during all this time, and in the course of that interview Mr. McCullough asked her – 'If he had wronged her in any other way than by desertion.' She said 'No,' and immediately relapsed into this terrible state of excitement. Upon Mr. McCullough again fixing her attention and asking her if she was a virtuous woman, she exclaimed, 'As God is my judge, I am pure,' and instantly again relapsed into a frenzied state of excitement. It is said that on the way to the jail, she communicated to the officer having her in charge, a story diametrically opposed to the one she had told Mr. McCullough; and upon that, we understand, the prosecution will rely.

"I have no hesitation in saying from my own

observation and experience, that during that period of time, from the 25th of April to the 20th of June, which was the last day of my observations, there have been three occasions in which she was undoubtedly insane. She was insane from moral causes, aggravated by disease of the body. This is our defense. A pure, virtuous, chaste, delicate little girl, not more than twenty years of age at this time, whose frame is wasting and whose spirits are gone, whose heart is broken, in a paroxysm of insanity has slain the man who has brought upon her all this suffering.

"That is our defense, and we will expect to show this by the facts in the case, and the opinion of medical witnesses of the highest character. During her confinement, Dr. Nichols has visited her. He will be present in court, and hear all the testimony in the case. The physician who attended her in Chicago will be here and examined as a witness, and from the testimony of these gentlemen, and the facts of this case, I have no doubt you will have the satisfaction of leaving that box with the conviction in your minds that the prisoner at the bar is not guilty of any crime toward God or man, although she has been the instrument of taking the life of another."

It being near the end of the day, Judge Wiley adjourned the court until the following morning. Francis Richardson and Bill Douglas filed out of the courtroom with the other observers.

Douglas asked Richardson, "Want to come down to the Willard and have a drink at the Round Robin? We can shoot the breeze, get caught up, and the *Times* will buy us dinner."

"Sounds good to me," said Francis. "The bar is renowned in the District for its mint juleps and one of those would really hit the spot on a hot day like today. Let's hike over to Pennsylvania Avenue and catch one of the cars going down to 14th Street." They walked the two blocks over to the main thoroughfare and jumped on one of the horse-drawn streetcars operated by the Washington and Georgetown Railroad which came by every ten minutes or so.

A short time later they got off at the entrance to the elegant six-story Willard Hotel. Passing through the ornate lobby, they made their way directly to the bar. It was still relatively early for the dinner crowd so there weren't many patrons for the three bartenders standing in front of the huge glass mirrors. Both men took positions at the carved mahogany bar, putting a foot on the brass rail while leaning against the brass guard that ran around the top of the counter. They ordered mint juleps and watched as one of the bartenders pressed fresh mint leaves against the walls of two silver goblets with a silver spoon, gently bruising the leaves before removing them from the containers. The goblets were filled half way with cracked ice before a mellow oak-aged bourbon was poured slowly over it. In a separate container, granulated sugar was slowly mixed with ice-cold limestone water and then poured over the ice and bourbon. Garnished with a sprig of fresh mint, the concoctions were placed before each of the reporters as beads of moisture formed on the silver goblets. Douglas put the tab for the drinks on his hotel room account and the two retired to a table where they could talk without concern for being overheard.

"I think this trial is shaping up to be an interesting contest," said Douglas. "The opposing counsels paint quite different pictures of the defendant. The prosecution portrays her as a jealous, hate filled strumpet out for revenge. The defense describes her as a sincere, hard-working, kind-hearted little thing that was taken advantage by the overbearing older man of the world. Bradley makes much of Miss Harris's acceptance by the upstanding ladies of the community yet these ladies did not warn her about Burroughs even though he failed at his business, was kicked out of his church, showed inappropriate behavior in public toward her when she worked in the bookstore and, on the face of it, appeared to be robbing the cradle."

"Right," said Richardson. "And the prosecution sees it as a clear case of murder and thinks the jury should focus on just a few critical legal questions to make their decision while the defense claims that she was crazy when she shot him and sporadically at other times and therefore the jury should find her blameless. At the same time, they are claiming that her actions were justified by the dastardliness of the victim's betrayal of such a dewy-eyed, pure-hearted young girl."

"Maybe I've been working the police beat too long, but there are some things about the girl's story that just don't seem to add up in my mind," said Douglas. "Like, why did Louisa Devlin write the letter in response to the Greenwood letter rather than Mary herself? There was not much content to it, according to what Bradley said, and Mary certainly would have been capable of writing it. I wonder if they will introduce that letter into the court record or if it will be simply accepted without questioning it?

"And the question of the length of Burroughs's beard at the time of the Greenwood letters was not addressed. You remember, the clerk said it was different from the picture. And the reported conversation with the lady from 94 Quincy Street is all hearsay. All the information about the conversation was from Mary or the Devlins. And, of course, all the information about the defendant's periodical disease and its origin on the day she saw the marriage notice in the paper is from Mary. If she made the connection of her painful periods with learning about Burroughs's marriage, why didn't she tell her doctor about it?

"Good points," said Richardson. "The counsel for the defense certainly tried to minimize the implications for premeditation in his treatment of the matter of the pistol. I mean she bought it seven months before the murder, not on her way to the Treasury building. I don't know about you, but the first time I used a pistol I couldn't hit the broad side of a barn, so to claim she never practiced with it, yet hit him with her first shot, is hard to believe. And he just used some rhetorical slight of hand to explain how and why she ended up taking the pistol and not the letters when she went into the District from Baltimore. Did you catch the part where he said the pistol hadn't even been used? Maybe he got carried away with his own grandiloquence. After all, it was the murder weapon and she did give it to the justice of the peace."

"No, I didn't catch that one," said Douglas. "But I did catch that he called it a 'toy' gun, seeming to imply that it was not the kind to be used by any sensible person intent on murder. I also caught his re-characterization of her calmness at the scene of the crime as being like an automaton, as if in a trance or insane. And her period of excitement became a 'paroxysm of despair.'"

"Yes, we'll probably see a lot of that as the trial proceeds. I think the most significant question is raised by the defendant's newspaper interview that appeared in the *Chronicle* shortly after she was arrested. Her statements in that interview made it sound like a revenge crime but here Bradley treats it, not like a confession, but as if her statements were insignificant or misconstrued. I suspect the DA will nail him on that someplace along the line."

"Do you think there will be any influence on the jury because of the hanging of Mary Surratt? There seems to be some guilt floating around the country about having hung a woman. There were quite a few people outraged that President Johnson didn't commute her sentence."

"Hmm," mused Richardson. "I hadn't thought of that

but there might be some sympathy that accrues to Miss Harris as a result of it. I guess we will see."

Having finished their drinks, the gentlemen moved into one of the smaller dinning rooms, one with a round domed ceiling with molding above that was similar to the decorative treatment at the top of the capitol building. Four huge palm trees towered over the tables, which were arranged for more intimate conversation than in the large dinning halls.

Richardson ordered the special – mock-turtle soup, corned beef and cabbage and parsley potatoes. Douglas had the fish of the day with green beans and rice. Blackberry pie and coffee would follow the meal. Conversation shifted to their days as war correspondents.

CHAPTER 6

District Attorney Carrington was still confident that his logic would prevail, that Bradley and his crew would not be able to get certain information and opinions entered into evidence and thereby try to justify a "paroxysmal insanity" defense. All he needed to prove, he thought, was that Mary Harris committed the homicide and that she did so with premeditation and malice.

He called Dr. John C. Riley who testified that Burroughs had died from loss of blood due to a gunshot wound that entered the body two inches to the left of the spine and between the fourth and fifth rib. Alfred Everett, a clerk who worked next to Burroughs and was trying to catch up to the victim in the hallway when he was shot, testified that Mary fired her revolver a second time and then went downstairs into the basement. He said that he had Dr. Herbert follow her, ran to his supervisor's office to report what had happened and to get help to carry Burroughs. He described Mary as being cool and self-possessed at the time.

Charles Sengstack, the watchman who arrested Mary as she was going toward the south steps, testified that

Mary showed no evidence of emotion or excitement until the body was brought to rest about 15 to 20 feet from her, at which time she became very excited and threw her hands up in the air in a dramatic manner.

William Schelley, the doorkeeper at the main entrance, testified that he allowed Mary to enter even though it was after hours because she said she was waiting for a man and a woman friend. He said she subsequently disappeared from the chair where he asked her to wait. Samuel Stearns, another doorkeeper, testified that Mary asked the whereabouts of Burroughs and he directed her upstairs to the Office of the Comptroller of the Currency.

Edwin G. Handy, who was in charge of the watchmen, reported that Mary surrendered her revolver to him as soon as he introduced himself as a justice of the peace. He described her as "very much excited" at the time as evidenced by walking back and forth and throwing her hands in the air. When he asked her why she had killed Burroughs, she did not answer but instead repeated the question and added, "I would give my life to save him."

A critical witness was George H. Walker, an officer with the metropolitan police who escorted Mary to jail. He testified that Mary told him that she had warned Burroughs that if he didn't comply with his promises of marriage, that she would have revenge on him, even at the risk of her own life. He said that Mary confessed to him that she had bought her pistol in Chicago and come to Washington with that purpose in mind and had accomplished her objective.

Hugh McCullough, who had been appointed Secretary of the Treasury since the time of the shooting, testified that Mary replied in the negative when he asked her if Burroughs had harmed her in any other way besides the abandonment. She swore to God that she was a "virtuous girl" when he posed that question to her. Although he described Mary as being in a frenzy just after the shooting and believing her to be in agony "too great for tears," he said that she was able to answer questions clearly and coherently.

The final witness called for the prosecution, Mrs. Woodbridge, was a woman who worked at a desk next to Burroughs and spotted Mary when she opened the door to the office. She testified that the prisoner was the same person she saw that day. On cross-examination by Mr. Bradley, she said that Mary "had the appearance of being much excited."

"Objection, your honor!" shouted out Assistant District Attorney Wilson. "The question asks for an opinion of the witness. It is a well-settled principle that the opinions of witnesses are not admissible. Where facts are at issue, it is incompetent for the witness to express an opinion. This question is a mixture of fact and law, and it is for the jury to determine the condition of the prisoner's mind. Only expert witnesses are able to state opinions and since this question goes to the prisoner's state of mind, the appropriate expert would be a physician or one who is qualified by study and experience to make such judgments." Mr. Wilson went on to cite a number of authorities that appeared to support his argument.

Judge Hughes, for the defense, countered that they were not asking of the witness a judgment about the prisoner's sanity or lack thereof, but simply what her impression was of her state of mind, since the witness could not send a photograph to the jury of how the prisoner looked at the time. He also said there are exceptions to the general rule, as stated by the prosecution, whereupon he cited his own authorities.

Bradley rose and stated, "For the past forty years, most of the States have made a distinction between an expert's opinion as to a person's mental condition and that of an ordinary person who bases his judgment on facts that he has observed but to exclude the rational conclusions of such a person is contrary to all rule."

Judge Wiley, for the Court, ruled that non-experts are competent to give an opinion as a general rule, but in the present case the evidence is that she had never seen the prisoner before in her life and therefore had no basis for forming a general opinion as to her sanity or insanity. The defense reserved an exception to this ruling.

Mr. Carrington abruptly announced, "The Government rests its case, your honor."

Judge Wiley declared a short recess before the defense began to call its witnesses. Bill Douglas looked at Francis Richardson, sitting next to him, and asked, "Is that it? Is that the total of the prosecution's case?"

"It appears to be," said Richardson. "The District Attorney seems to be satisfied that he has shown that the prisoner was indeed the person who had committed the homicide, that it was neither justifiable nor excusable, that the defendant was not insane at the time of the murder, that she acted with premeditation, and that the crime was motivated by malice in fact in the form of hatred and revenge. He thinks that is all that it is necessary to show in order to get a conviction."

"So the defense has to get the jury to disregard the testimony of Mr. Walker and buy the claim that the defendant was insane?" asked Douglas rhetorically.

The first defense witness after the recess was William W. Danenhower, who supervised Burroughs in his job in the Fourth Auditor's Office. He acknowledged that, when shown the letters written by Burroughs to Miss Harris, all except one appeared to be in the handwriting of Burroughs. Bradley tried to offer one of the letters into evidence and the Court asked why he was doing so.

Bradley responded, "We are trying to show the relationship between Burroughs and Miss Harris and the effect it had on the prisoner, causing her insanity."

"Objection," asserted Mr. Carrington. "The date of the letter is too remote and it is simply signed 'Incog.' It cannot be established that it was from Burroughs. I know what the esteemed counsel for the defense is trying to do but the letter is not admissible as evidence to show insanity," said Carrington.

Judge Hughes for the defense said, "We want to enter this entire bundle of letters into evidence in order to show an unbroken chain of correspondence, establishing the most intimate relations, the relations of betrothal between the deceased and the defendant. He was a man of 32 years while she was just a little girl," he said. "He trained her up to make her his wife and she knew no different until his marriage to another was announced," he said, only to interject another disparagement of the deceased, "except for his proposal to meet her at a house of assignation. We expect to establish the connecting evidence to show that the shock, disappointment, shame, and mortification of this news unsettled her reason and this was her state of mind at the time of the homicide."

Judge Wiley, for the Court, ruled that while insanity in itself is an appropriate defense, it would be inappropriate to go back into past history in order to establish it. Bradley argued that the letters should be admitted if it were necessary to show that the insanity was not feigned. Judge Wiley responded that, if there were a change in this aspect of the case, the Court would reconsider.

Carrington said, "I am ready to prove that Burroughs never wronged Miss Harris in any way."

Bradley sarcastically countered, "I wouldn't take any man's word for that when I have evidence of the victim's guilt in his own handwriting." The latter assertion was based on the unproven claim that Burroughs had written the Greenwood letters.

Over the objections of Mr. Carrington, Bradley had read into evidence the depositions received from witnesses in Burlington, Iowa. Charles H. Phelps, a lawyer who knew Mary from the age of eight or ten and estimated her current age to be 21 years, said she was good tempered, happy, naturally intelligent but tended to be nervous. When he saw her in jail in Washington he said she had a wild look, appeared haggard and was incoherent and contradictory. His wife, Eunice, testified that Mary's sole motive and desire in life was to please Burroughs and stated that, "He controlled her in all respects."

Mary Jane Winters testified that she knew Mary for 10 years and that the girl came to her for advice on all matters. Echoing the testimony of Mrs. Phelps, perhaps too closely to believe that it was not coached, she stated that Mary had no motive or aim in life except to please Burroughs and fulfill her engagement to him, that Burroughs was the master of Mary's heart and affections. She related that in May of 1861 Burroughs told her that he and Mary were engaged to be married and that he did not dare go to Mary's parents home because they were opposed to him.

When Burroughs brought Mary back home from Chicago after her first move there, Mrs. Winters said he told her that he was trying to raise a company of men for the war and if he succeeded they would be married in three weeks and, if not, they would marry and go off to California. She subsequently learned from Mary that Burroughs had broken his leg and would not be able to enter the military service. She testified that Burroughs had a ring on his finger and refused to remove it because he said it had been placed there with a wish.

Mrs. Louisa Hall deposed that, although her knowledge of the relationship between Mary and Burroughs was all received through Mary, she felt that Burroughs had complete control of her affections and swayed her as he wished.

"I object to these depositions, your honor!" said Carrington. "The facts are not admissible and the mode of proof is objectionable. The evidence showing an engagement in 1863 is not admissible when the crime was committed in 1865. The question is not how the deceased treated the prisoner, but how she was affected when the homicide was committed. If insanity is established, the cause is immaterial."

Judge Wiley, ruling for the Court, agreed with Bradley's argument. "If insanity is shown at some time anterior to the homicide, the evidence might be important as tending to show whether the insanity is real or feigned at the time the homicide was committed."

"Before that there should be some evidence to show insanity and the last two witnesses show her sanity," said Carrington.

Wiley remained on the fence when he responded, "There is something here that the jury can consider but whether or not it can be relied upon is another question."

"Your honor, it seems to me that if a young lady engages herself to a gentleman in 1858 and, in 1865, seven years after, creeps up behind him and shoots him in the back for fancied wrongs, it does not show that degree of insanity which makes the party an irresponsible agent. If she had done the act in a month, or even a year, there might be some excuse. Will it be allowed to give in evidence an injury inflicted five or six years before the homicide, in justification of the crime?

"Statements by the deceased to the defendant are not offered to show insanity but rather the cause thereof. The question of whether or not a marriage agreement existed in 1861 is a collateral issue. This is not a suit brought by the prisoner for a breach of marriage promise; this is a criminal prosecution, wherein the United States is one party, and the prisoner at the bar the other.

"The deceased is a third party in a suit for violation of

law and his evidence is mere hearsay! Moreover, declarations of a deceased party, with but few exceptions, are generally never admitted in evidence. If these depositions are admitted, we will produce rebutting testimony to show that, in point of fact, no marriage agreement existed!"

Judge Wiley ruled that the defense was trying to show that a well known, recognized cause of insanity existed in this case, and that the depositions could be entered into evidence. Mr. Bradley then offered into evidence the letter referred to in Mrs. Winter's testimony.

"Objection!" yelled Mr. Wilson. "The paper he holds is a mere mutilated part of a letter and shows no connection with the prisoner. It is but a half sheet with no signature and simply headed, 'Dear Little Mollie'."

Bradley responded, "It has been shown that the letter is in Burroughs' handwriting and was in the possession of the accused."

The letter was admitted into evidence and supported the testimony of Mrs. Winters. The deposition of Mrs. Eliza J. Harris, who knew Mary in both Burlington and Chicago, was then read to the jury. She testified that Mary and Burroughs spent nearly every evening at her house and stayed very late. Mary never told her of an actual engagement but she always assumed it because they acted "in all respects like lovers."

The witness said she noted a change in Mary after Burroughs married Amelia Louise Boggs. Mary came to the witness's room two or three times a day and related all her troubles, which she said were wearing her out and affecting her health. She brooded day and night because Burroughs had all along been false to her and wanted to take her to an assignation house.

Lewis H. Davis, the Chicago lawyer who took Mary's suit against Burroughs deposed that he thought Mary's motive in filing the suit was to vindicate her character and honor because her friends felt she had been disgraced. According to him, Mary spoke in terms of righteous indignation at mention of the invitation to the house of ill repute and he believed that, after she was satisfied that Burroughs had written the Greenwood letters, her love turned to hate. However, when he offered to try to settle the matter by talking with Burroughs' friends, Mary would not allow it.

"I must again object to these depositions," said the District Attorney. "These events occurred a year and a half before the homicide. The fact that she tried to file suit shows her sanity rather than insanity. She understood her remedy. She knew, like a discreet and intelligent person, that her proper course, if she had been wronged, was to institute a suit for breach of marriage contract. Mr. Davis also gave his opinion as to her motive and went on to state her mental condition when that is actually a matter of law. This would make the witness a member of the jury rather than a witness. It is the *jury's* job to form an opinion as to her mental state!"

Judge Wylie ruled that the law gives the prisoner the privilege of obtaining from a previously acquainted witness his or her opinion as to the sanity or insanity of the party at the time or previous to the commission of the offense. "Since this question seems to be constantly coming up, I want to make another point. This question of insanity is one of the most difficult to comprehend and to manage. There are so many degrees of it, so many species of it, the human mind is so easily affected, so subject to being influenced and becoming diseased, that the ablest writers of the law have acknowledged their inability to draw satisfactory lines by which to test whether a party under given circumstances acted under an insane impulse, insanity of mind, or otherwise. The most sure and legal term to use is *non compos mentis* – not mentally capable - and the witness can testify whether the prisoner was a reasonable being, capable of deciding properly upon any subject brought before him. Therefore, I admit the evidence and it can go to the jury."

Stunned by this ruling, Carrington fell into his chair, staring at the ceiling as Mr. Fendall proceeded to read extracts from the letters Mary had allowed to be presented in court, about one third of the total of 92 letters.

Douglas nudged Richardson and whispered, "What's going on with the prosecution? Why don't they raise the issue of this selection of letters from the total being biased? Why don't they ask that Mary's letters back to Burroughs be also read into evidence?"

Richardson, using his note pad to mask his mouth from the bench, whispered back, "They are in shock. They were blindsided by Wiley's ruling. Apparently the judge felt satisfied that he had maintained fairness by bending over backward to allow questionable testimony into the evidence to be considered by the jury."

Most of the excerpts of letters were rather innocuous, simply showing that Burroughs and Mary Harris had a long-term affectionate relationship, much of it composed of correspondence. Mr. Fendall read one letter in complete detail since Bradley believed it would illustrate Burroughs silver tongued persuasiveness and win the sympathy of the jury.

Writing as if speaking in an Irish brogue, Burroughs began, *"O! My Dear Little Rosebud: Is it after making me crazy that you are, or is for making me heart jump clear up into the throat of me till I'm kilt entirely, that you're saking after, that you send all the way from Burlington such a picture as would make the holy Virgin Mary blush again? O, holy St. Peter! What am I to do? My head grows giddy, and divil a bit can I sa. My hands fly up above the head of me; me fingers stick right out sidewise; me hair stands on end; me eyes steck out so far ahead of me, I* can only touch them with me hand, and I go runnin up the strate an' back again like mad! O, holy Virgin Mary, intercede for me! For divil a bit of rason have I got left, an' I'm mad intirely. You know, darling, when a person is bitten by a venomous snake, his skin assumes the color of the snake. If an abominable snake has such an effect on man, is it strange that when bewitched by the sweetest-looking Irish girl that ever lived, he should become an Irishman? Who wouldn't be anything to be the recipient of such favor as was I on Saturday evening? How am I to thank you for such a favor? O, joyous surprise! Glad source of delirious joy!"

Shifting back into his normal discourse, Burroughs wrote, *"Many times I had longed for your picture, and let my imagination dwell upon the receipt of it, but durst not ask you for it, for reasons I will give you if we ever meet – not now; but it is the more grateful, coming as a surprise of inexpressible delight. Really, Mollie, as I returned from the post office after receiving it, I felt so light I could with difficulty walk the ground; I could scarcely avoid flying. I wanted to button everybody I met, and show them what I had got; and it required all the sense of propriety I could command to keep myself from doing so.*

"O! that beautiful picture! Beautiful! Beautiful! Beautiful! And my beautiful! Beautiful Mollie! What can I now say for her? I cannot say – words fail me. Could I see her, I might, perhaps, express faintly what are my feelings, as reawakened by such visible testimony of her loveliness.

"O, Mollie, Mollie! You have turned my dry, sterile, old bachelor's heart into a gushing fountain of glad emotion, and warm genial affection; and Mollie – dear, darling Mollie – is the source and end of all. Would I had a hundred Pike's Peak's fortunes to lay at her feet, and the affection of a hundred hearts to lavish upon her. If 'another Mollie' were to contest the claim to my love, she

would stand but a poor chance now, if not before. When you were remarking concerning the change (improvement) that had taken place in your personal appearance, were you trying to make me understand that you had added to your already redundant stock of beauty? I did not fully take the hint then; I understand now. Nature has surpassed herself in bestowing new charms when the measure was already full, running over, and Mollie herself is taken by surprise at her own new excellencies. I understand it all now, and in a most effective way have you adopted to bring the fact to my comprehension, and as modest and winning as effective. Your beautiful picture! I have to look at it the last thing before I put out the light at bed-time and the first thing in the morning, before even I put myself in a condition to have any one (unless it were some one to whom I sustained a different relation than I ever yet sustained) to look at me, unless by accident, as occurred once in B., at my boarding house, when, from my long white robe, I was mistaken for a Catholic priest. Had my back been turned, they (the women who saw me) would have taken me for one of their own number, unless they had carried their scenting-box far in, in which case I presume they would have discovered their mistake.

"And many times during the day do I look again and again at this beautiful shadow of a more beautiful substance, and each time draws forth some fresh exclamation of swelling admiration.

"Do not, my dear Mollie, let that accursed blotch on your neck be left to mar such a beautiful person as yours. You have neglected it already too long. Do so no more.

"Perhaps, dear girl, you will think me extravagant and excessive at my expressions of delight at the receipt of your picture; perhaps I am fulsome, nauseating even. But remember the circumstances. A man would justly be thought a fool, who, going to the town pump, would clasp

his hands and dance with wild exclamations of delight at the sight of the water; but on the desert where water had not been seen for many long, weary days, he would be thought perfectly sound, and all would rejoice with him. Were I with you, enjoying the richer favor of your presence, though I would receive your picture as a precious treasure, yet I would not go quite crazy over it, but would seek to exhibit good common sense. As it is, away off in the wilderness, among Arabs, hideous to behold, and worse to mingle with, I am like the man in the desert at the sight of water. So, under the circumstances, I hope you will excuse me, dearest, if I do plaster it on rather thick. I would not resort to gross flattery of your personal appearance, though your charms were those of Venus, (and I do not think them short of it) for I possess too much of sincere regard for your best interests to turn flatterer, and injure you with extravagant praise. I would rather tell you of your faults, and show forth my regard and appreciation of you by the unmistakable evidence of duty faithfully performed.

"'Faithful are the wounds of a friend, but kisses of an enemy are deceitful.' If I speak warmly in your praise, it is but for the free gushing forth of uncontrolled feelings, and you know by experience may ring the din of hated chiding in your ears, and make you wish – O! so much! – it might but cease. But when I chide you, Mollie, I would rather take you in my arms, and soften the harsh accents by the soothing caresses of true, kind, and warm affection; for I am not a tyrant nor a bear in disposition; neither would I be the fitful cat, that utters her fondness in tones of winning tenderness at one moment, and plants her claws to the quick in her darling pets the next. But I would be as I have professed, your true friend; in advance asking pardon for his many failings. Will you believe me, Mollie? And will you understand me, as I make my imperfect efforts to express my sentiments; while I protest I could *tell you a dam sight better if I could see you! And, my dear, dear Mollie, shall I not see you at Ottumwa the first of the month? Dear girl, I want to urge you to come, if at all practicable, and don't let small considerations prevent you, and come in such a way as not to be tied up to somebody else, so to prevent our being together most of the time, mind you.*

"*I broke my promise, and did not write Sunday, but it was not because I had not intended to; but because I could not get a minute to myself. Today has been rather dull, and I have snatched the odd moments to write you this broken letter. Will you accept it, darling, as the honest though poor expression of the warm sentiments of my heart, while I thank you again and again for your beautiful picture.*"

Mr. Fendall indicated that across the top of the letter was written the following: "*Miss H was up here to visit H about four weeks since, and H will go to B in about two weeks. If you see her, she will tell you all about me. I call at their house quite frequently. You know she married __ who used to live in B. Perhaps she will make you believe I have found another 'Mollie' up here. There are one or two respectable girls here that I go with to pass away the dreary hours; but compared with my dear little Rosebud, they are – I'll not say what.*"

A few more letters were read before the court adjourned. The next day, the sixth day of the trial, the crowd was greater than usual. There were many ladies present, many of them seated within the bar. Miss Harris was brought in accompanied by her entourage of attorneys and lady friends shortly after 10 o'clock and was escorted to her usual seat.

Mr. Bradley continued to read excerpts from letters written by Burroughs to Miss Harris. In one of them, the writer expresses regret that someone has found out about the engagement between them and in a couple of other letters he relates fears that their correspondence has been intercepted by the postmaster or the priest. In yet another, he indicates that he tires of the life of a bachelor and "...could live very happily with a pretty little black-eyed, curly headed lady, whose name I will not mention." He suggests meetings at hotels in towns away from Burlington and says he has "...evidence of the fullness of your affection."

One letter refers to a tiff between them, in which it appears that Mary has asked for the return of things she has given him while he says that she can burn all his letters if she wants. He laments the end of their relationship in this postscript: "And must this be the finale of our enjoyment? Oh! my God, how bitter!" The estrangement was short-lived, however, and within two months their correspondence was back on affectionate terms.

Bradley called Miss Louisa Devlin to the stand. After some preliminary questions to establish her relationship with the defendant, he asked her about Mary's health when she first came to live with and work for her.

"State what was her temper and disposition during that time."

"Her temper was good and her disposition also," said Miss Devlin.

"How as to her spirits? State whether she was lively or melancholy?"

"She was very lively in disposition."

"What did you observe in regard to her going into society?"

"She went into no society whatever, except that that I was in. There were very few that we associated with."

"Did you at any time, during the period that Miss Harris was living with you, see the deceased, Mr. Burroughs?"

"I did. I saw the deceased twice at our boarding

house, in March, 1863, where she boarded."

"Was she boarding at the same house with you?"

"Yes, sir. I saw him, also, twice at my store during that summer."

"Did you learn from him or her, when both were together at that time, whether he was paying his attentions to her or not?"

"I never had any conversation with them."

"Did you have an opportunity to read the letters Mary received from Burroughs so as to become acquainted with his handwriting?"

"Yes, sir."

"State whether, after she had resided with you some time, you observed any change in Miss Harris; and state about the time when you observed such change."

"Well, the change was after the marriage of Burroughs, in September, 1863. Previous to that time the cheerfulness of character which I have described, and kindly disposition continued."

"State as accurately as you can how that change established itself?"

"After the receipt of these anonymous letters, and feeling satisfied that it was Burroughs who wrote them, she became almost frantic, and at such times she would not know what she was doing or saying. During that night she commenced to cry, and continued crying almost incessantly for two or three days and then at intervals for two or three weeks, sometimes every night, sometimes two or three nights in a week."

Bradley proceeded to question Louisa Devlin about several incidents she observed in which Mary displayed odd or violent behavior: the incident where she tried to go on a walk along the lake shore while it was still dark; the time Mary chased Jane Devlin with a carving knife; the occasion when Mary struck Jane with a window brush; and the incident where she tried to destroy a silk quilt belonging to another sister and threatened to spread preserves on all the carpets in the house unless she was released from her room; and instances where she commenced to tear up books, clothing, and anything she could lay her hands on.

The counsel for the defense then showed the witness Burroughs's letter of August 7, 1863 and she testified that it was in his handwriting and the same handwriting as all the other letters.

"State whether you saw that letter at or about the time it was received by Miss Harris, and where you saw it?"

"I do not recollect where I saw that letter, but she read me the letter, though at the time I did not see the handwriting."

"Now look at this envelope and the letter therein enclosed." Bradley presented Miss Devlin with the letter of September 8, 1863 and signed J. P. Greenwood. "State whether you saw it at or about the time of its date?"

"I saw this on the date she received it."

"In whose handwriting, in your judgment, is that letter?"

"In my judgment it is in the same handwriting as the others – Burroughs's."

"In the meanwhile, or immediately or shortly after the date of that first letter, of the 7th of August, had you seen Mr. Burroughs, and where did you see him?"

"I saw him about five or six weeks before he was married, the date I do not know. He called at my store to see Miss Harris."

"State whether or not he had any interview with Miss Harris at that time?"

"Yes, sir. He remained in my store then with her for about an hour or an hour and a half."

"Did you see him at the store at any other time?"

"Yes, sir. I had seen him at the store once before."

"Are you able to say Miss Harris never saw him after this interview of which I speak?"

"Never that I know of."

"State whether or not she was constantly in the store for months before the receipt of this letter?"

"She was."

"Could she have left, so as to have had an interview with him anywhere?"

"No, sir. She could not have been gone an hour without my knowing where she was. She and I went and returned from the store, and also remained and slept together."

"Where did you see this last letter and what were all the circumstances connected with it?"

"This letter I saw in the house when Miss Harris brought it from the post office. She read it and then remarked, 'Who in the world could have written the likes of this to me?' She read it first to me and then I looked over it. I went and inquired what kind of house it was and when I found out what sort of place it was, I proposed to answer the letter, and find out who had written it. I wrote the answer and signed her name to it."

"State whether or not the letter is in the handwriting of Mr. Burroughs."

"Yes, sir. I think it is."

The two Greenwood letters then being read and offered into evidence, Mr. Bradley continued questioning Louisa Devlin. "Can you recollect whether or not you gave any instructions to the postmaster in regard to that letter of September 12, 1863?"

"I showed the envelope and the address to the clerk in the post office, and told him to look particularly at the person who called for that letter, and describe him to me when I called. He said that he would do so. I told him to look particularly at his hand."

"What happened then?"

"I deposited the second response on the 12th and called for the answer on Monday, the 14th by myself. Then I got Miss Harris and returned to the post office where the clerk described the person who got the letter. He said he was a man who weighed about 170 pounds, that he had black hair, a heavy black beard, a rather pretty hand for a man of his size, was of medium height, and on his finger wore a set ring. Miss Harris turned round and said, 'That is the ring I gave Mr. Burroughs.' She then handed the clerk a photograph."

"Is this the photograph (handing the witness a *carte-de-visite* of Burroughs in military uniform)?"

"That is it. After looking at it, he said, 'Well, yes' and then hesitated but afterwards added, 'I do not know, as the beard on this is higher than he wore it.' I asked him how much higher and he said, 'Well, I guess something about an inch.' He said it might be the same person; that he could tell more accurately if this person was in the clothes he appeared in when he came to the post office. He said the person who called for the letter was in citizen's dress, with a heavy outside coat on."

"What effect did this information have on Miss Harris?"

"She got very excited and said she never thought he would turn out to be such a rascal."

"Do you know whether or not that same day she started to go out to the place where she supposed Mr. Burroughs to be?"

"I went out on that same day (Monday, the 14th) to call upon the Rev. Dr. Burroughs to know from him if his brother was in town. He was and this made Mary more confident it was him that had written the two letters. She said she would go the next day and return his likeness, and all the letters she had of his, to Dr. Burroughs, and would let him know what a great rascal his brother was."

"How long was she gone?"

"I can't say exactly. She might have been gone over two hours. She said she showed the anonymous letters to Dr. Burroughs and he tried to persuade her that it was not his brother who had written them. He told her his brother had been in Chicago but had returned to Washington on the sixth of September, before the first Greenwood letter had been delivered. She then said that he acted in such a strange manner towards her, his hand trembled, and she thought there was some plot between him and his brother about the affair. She did not tell him she had these other letters, but concluded to bring them back again. It was the 15th of September. She also told me that she saw A. J. Burroughs coming in the cars as she was going out; that he poked his head out of the cars and looked at her."

Bradley inquired of the witness if she had seen a pistol in the possession of Miss Harris. Miss Devlin responded that she had, that the accused had told her she bought it because she believed Dr. Burroughs and his brother were plotting to abduct her and take her where she would never be seen again. She said the prisoner told her she didn't know how to use it. She did not think Mary had practiced with it because she didn't know how to charge it.

CHAPTER 7

Mr. Wilson handled the cross-examination of Miss Devlin. He began by posing questions the answers to which had been covered in previous testimony. Then he asked her whether or not Miss Harris had "any attendants – any beaux, any admirers?"

"No, sir," was the reply from Miss Devlin.

"Did you ever know of her going out into society – to parties?"

"She has been to the theater a few times, that is all."

"Whom did she go with?"

"Some of her friends from Burlington."

"Young gentlemen?"

"Yes, sir," she replied, betraying no awareness of the contradiction with her testimony given just a few seconds prior.

"Who were they?"

"I have heard their names – been introduced to them, but really I have forgotten."

"How many times do you suppose she went to the theater?"

"Only five or six times a year. Sometimes I went with

her."

Wilson continued, "Did you ever, during that time, see any exhibitions of ill-temper, hear any impatient or hasty remarks, know of her being particularly unwell, see any change in her spirits?"

"No, sir."

Shifting the focus to Burroughs, Wilson inquired when she had seen the first letter signed J. P. Greenwood.

"You are positive it is in Burroughs's handwriting?"

"I am."

"What resemblance do you see between this letter and the other letters that were shown to you?"

"I see a general resemblance, and particularly the 'Chicago' – that looks precisely the same."

"Here is one dated February 11. Observe the 'Chicago' there. Will you state any points of resemblance in these two letters?"

"Objection! Calls for a conclusion from the witness!"

"Objection sustained," said Judge Wiley.

"Do you remember the day of the week when the second letter was received?"

"Yes, sir. Saturday the 12th of September. I know it was Saturday because I marked it down in a small pocket book. I do not know where the book is now. I made a memorandum of the fact that Miss Harris received a certain anonymous letter on the 12th."

"Why did you make that entry in the book?"

"Because I wanted to find out who had written that letter and when."

"You did not make an entry of the receipt of the first letter?"

"No, sir. Miss Harris showed it to me and went and got other letters and compared them with this, and then said, 'Look here, these are in the same handwriting!'"

"Was your sister present at the time?"

"Yes, sir. She thought it was Burroughs's writing too."

"Did Miss Harris say anything else at the time this letter was first read?"

"She said he was a great rascal for – after having corresponded with her for so long, been engaged to be married to her, thinking as much of him as she did, and he thinking as much of her as he had led her to believe he did – trying to bring her to an assignation house. This she said quite often."

"What time on Monday was it that you called on this clerk at the post office?"

"About noon."

"Do you know who that clerk was?"

"I do not."

"Had you ever seen him before?"

"No, sir."

"Do you know his name?"

"I have heard it, but I have since forgotten it."

"What kind of a looking man was he?"

"I could not exactly say. He wore whiskers."

"Do you see him in this courtroom?"

"I do not know as I would be able to recognize the man now, it has been so long ago. I think he was a middle-age man. He stood at the gentleman's general delivery."

"Was any thing said about there being a number of persons in Chicago who looked like that picture?"

"No, sir."

"How many times did Miss Harris strike your sister with the window brush?"

"Some three or four times before I succeeded in taking the brush from her."

"Were the blows violent?"

"Yes, sir."

"How long did your struggle for the brush continue?"

"Some ten or fifteen minutes. She did not speak but looked very excited and wild."

"She was the only one you had employed at that time as clerk?"

"That is my business," Miss Devlin responded with finality.

Mr. Wilson was rather nonplussed and didn't know what to make of her response, thinking it rather odd. Then he continued, "After you observed these little irregularities of which you have spoken, did you continue her in your employment?"

"Yes, sir."

"Put as much confidence in her as before, allowed her the same privileges?"

"Yes, sir."

"Did you mention these peculiarities to any of her friends?"

"Yes, one. Mrs. Harris in Chicago because she was an intimate acquaintance, having known her in Burlington."

"Did you mention these facts to her father?"

"I did not know her father."

"Did you ever consult the superintendent of the Insane Asylum or express any desire to have her confined? Did you ever have occasion to restrain her liberty in any way?"

"No, sir."

"Did you observe at that time that she had an appreciation of her duties, and the moral qualities of any act that she committed – was capable of deciding what was right and wrong, as well as at other times?"

"Yes, sir. I observed that."

"At this time, after you had observed these irregularities to which you have testified, did you observe any change in the state of her mind or morals?"

"Yes, sir. When she would be in these excited fits she would try to get out on the street. She acted entirely different from what she did at other times."

"Was she at such times incapable of judging between

right and wrong?"

"Yes, sir."

"How long would these attacks last?"

"Sometimes they would last five or six hours. Then they would pass off."

"Then it was only during this temporary illness that you observed these exhibitions to which you have testified?"

"Sometimes she would not be ill at all when she would take them."

"Did you ever see her attempt to make an attack upon any person who came into the store, or upon any one except members of the family?"

"Upon one lady in Chicago. She took up a very heavy pincushion, that had a brick in it to make it lay flat, that was lying on the table and threw it at her. I don't remember what we were talking about."

"Was the lady seriously injured?"

"No sir. She never did any serious injury to anyone. She was a quick-tempered girl when she became nervous."

"She never did any serious injury to anyone," repeated Mr. Wilson as he looked at the jury. Allowing a pregnant pause for emphasis, he continued, "Why didn't you advise Miss Harris to write to Burroughs when the suspicions came into your minds that he had written the Greenwood letters?"

"I thought she wouldn't get a direct answer from him if she did. He was not going to tell her he had written those letters."

"Hadn't you known Mr. Burroughs to be a man of high character previous to that?"

"I did not know what his character was."

"Did you not suggest to your friend and employee the impropriety of carrying a pistol?"

"I did not."

"Did you threaten to discharge her from your employment if she did not abandon the habit of carrying this pistol?"

"I did not."

"Did you inform her father about it, by letter or otherwise?"

"I did not."

"Did she ever tell you that the reason of her engagement being broken off with Burroughs was owing to her being engaged to someone else?"

"No, sir. She never told me she was engaged to any person but him."

On redirect, Bradley asked, "Did she ever tell you that the engagement between herself and Burroughs was broken off?"

"No, sir."

Bradley continued, "You were asked why you did not communicate these peculiarities to her father. Were her relations with her father friendly at that time?"

"She told me they were not because she corresponded with Burroughs. Her father did not consider his reputation to be a very good one. She left her father's house to come to Chicago to seek employment because she could not live with her father."

During a short recess, Douglas and Richardson compared notes while having a smoke. "This has been some pretty nebulous testimony," said Douglas. "None of it is really capable of independent corroboration by someone not a close friend of the defendant. Mary was the one who first claimed there existed a similarity in handwriting between the Greenwood and the Burroughs letters and she prompted the Devlin sisters to support her assertion.

"Mary and Louisa Devlin are the only ones who ever saw this disappearing postal clerk and heard him provide a description of Burroughs. Why didn't the defense send someone to the Post Office and find out who had worked at the gentleman's window? Certainly they would have had records of the name of the individual they paid to work that day. And Miss Devlin's pocket book where she marked down the date of the second letter seems to have conveniently disappeared too. It all makes me kind of skeptical."

Richardson commented, "The prosecution had a couple of opportunities to discredit this witness and let them slide by. She at first testified that the defendant had no gentlemen admirers then, a few seconds later, testified that she went out to the theater several times with men from Burlington. And, of course, the names of these men are forgotten so they can't be called as witnesses."

Douglas asked, "If she didn't know how to charge the gun, how did she manage to shoot Burroughs? She must have learned somewhere and I'm still doubtful that anyone without practice using a pistol could hit an intended target."

"Yes," said Richardson. "And the prosecution did not bother to take the opportunity to point out that, except for Jane getting hit with the brush, all of these examples of Mary's supposed insanity were interrupted before any great damage occurred, leaving the jury with the impression that she was frequently violent and out of control. They are the kind of 'almost disasters' that could happened to a lot of people."

"I think Wiley is tilting in favor of the defense in his ruling to admit the letters into evidence in the first place and then in keeping the prosecution from questioning the basis on which Louisa Devlin made her judgment about the similarity of the handwriting of the Greenwood letters to the known Burroughs letters. Maybe it calls for a conclusion of the witness but it seems to me she should be able to say what the features of the handwriting are that she considers to be alike."

"Probably not significant enough to get a new trial but it is something we should keep ourselves alert to as the trial goes on," said Richardson.

When the trial resumed, the defense called Dr. Calvin M. Fitch, the doctor who treated Mary in Chicago, to the stand. Mr. Bradley asked, "When were you called in to see Miss Harris?"

"I think I can remember that there were consecutive calls made about the 22nd, 23rd, 24th, and 25th of September, and I think they were for her. I saw her at intervals of three or four weeks, for some two or three months."

"During these visits, state whether or not the nervous system was much affected."

"Very seriously indeed."

"State to the court, as a physician, how she was affected, and the effect of that disease upon her mind."

"At the time to which I allude, I found her suffering under severe congestive dysmenorrhea, arising for the most part as a consequence of the irritability of the uterus. Such uterine irritation always affects the nervous system, in some subjects more so than in others. In some instances it develops into insanity and, indeed, a disturbance of the uterus – uterine irritability – is with females one of the most frequent causes of insanity."

"Can you describe to the jury any circumstances tending to show the influence of this nervous affection upon her mind, will, temper, or disposition?"

"My intercourse with the entire family was entirely professional. I do not remember ever having been there except when I was called professionally, and I knew nothing whatever of her social or private relations. I had not even heard Mr. Burroughs' name mentioned at the time to which I allude. All that I knew of her at that time was what I saw of her physical condition. I saw that her nervous system was very much excited and she was suffering at the same time a great deal of pain. Her eye was wild. On the occasion of the first severe attack to which I allude, I think they had sent for me the day before, but for some cause I did not get there until the following morning if I remember right. They told me she had been suffering a great deal. I think I was told she had not slept during the night."

"I now ask you, as an expert, what is the effect, looked at from the position of a physician, in such a case as you have described, of a moral cause of disappointed affection, connected with the subject?"

"We know that among the moral causes of insanity, disappointed affection is one of the most frequent; and we know that among physical causes, uterine irritation is one of the most frequent. The combination of these two causes we should naturally expect to produce a very much greater effect than either would induce alone."

"In a case in which there was not only disappointed affection, but where the party believed, whether truly or falsely, that the relations which had subsisted between them had been broken off by insult and injury, what effect would that have upon such a case?"

"Such an impression as that, whether correctly or falsely produced, would naturally affect almost any person, even if such person were not of a peculiarly nervous temperament. Such impression would of course affect a nervous person much more. It would affect with especial force a person laboring under the peculiar physical disability to which I have alluded. Combining the three causes together, you can see that the effect produced upon the nervous system would be much more intense than any one of them would produce singly."

The defense asked that the testimony of Policeman Walker and Secretary McCullough be read to the witness. That being accomplished, Bradley then asked, "Assuming that Miss Harris was contracted in marriage with the deceased, that she had an ardent affection for him, and she believed, whether correctly or falsely, that he had thus broken off the engagement and endeavored to inveigle her into a house of ill fame, her physical condition being such as you have described, what would be the effect of her meeting suddenly with the party against whom she thought she had causes of accusation?"

"The effect most necessarily and obviously would be the most intense nervous excitement. It might be that that excitement would be entirely uncontrollable. Circumstances less than those have in many instances produced entirely uncontrollable excitement – an irresponsible condition of the patient or subject. Whether or not in this case it did so, I am, of course, not able to say."

"Is there not a marked distinction between general insanity and paroxysmal insanity?"

"There is. There are many cases on record of paroxysmal insanity. In one case, a young woman in good health and temper, a cook, but suffering from dysmenorrhea, was, whenever she was laboring under these paroxysms of pain, very violent, making murderous attacks with a knife upon all who offended her. As the pain passed off, she would seem to recognize the nature of her acts, and become as quiet and kind in her disposition as ever."

"State whether or not, under such circumstances, the patient does not often know exactly what he is doing, and yet finds himself unable to control his actions?"

"Yes, sir. The case of Henrietta Cordier, who killed the child of a neighbor, Madame Boline, against neither of whom she had any malice, is in point. Instead of being influenced by malice, she had apparently courted the good will of the child for weeks, until finally succeeding one day in inducing Madame B. to let her take the child to her chamber, cut off its head as soon as she got it there.

She remained in the room with the dead body for about two hours, until the mother came and called for the child. Henrietta told her the child was dead and when the mother came into the room, she threw its head out into the street."

"You have heard the testimony of Policeman Walker, Mr. McCullough and Miss Devlin. Assuming them to be speaking truthfully, would it be your opinion that the party was insane and what would be the nature of that insanity?"

"I could not very well give a general answer to that. Assuming that all these moral influences, of which we have spoken, as true, that she had been very much attached to him, and that, under such circumstances, she had encountered him in the Treasury building and taken his life, I should at least be led to believe that there was a strong probability of her laboring under mental alienation. I should not be willing to swear positively that such was the case, because all these causes might operate upon some patients without inducing insanity – absolute insanity. Any person would naturally be much excited under such circumstances and I think that it nothing peculiar.

"But the contradictory statements she makes to Mr. McCullough and to the officer who had her in charge, are matters of a different character and would look a great deal more like a serious disturbance of the intellect. She would not likely, under such circumstances, willfully tell a falsehood. Mr. McCullough evidently thought she was telling the truth to him, and the officer seemed to think that she was telling the truth to him from her manner. But there is direct contradiction there and, if the witness is usually credible, such contradiction, under such circumstances, would argue very strongly for a serious mental disturbance – mental alienation. And we know that all the causes had previously existed, moral and physical, which might lead to such a mental alienation."

Mr. Wilson led the cross-examination by casting doubt on the qualifications of the witness. "Do you consider yourself an expert on the subject of insanity?"

"I have the same acquaintance with it that any educated physician is expected to have."

"What experience have you had in the treatment of insane persons?"

"I have had no special experience, for the simple reason that insane persons are generally carried up to the Insane Asylum, and placed under care there."

A twitter spread through the audience and Judge Wiley scowled his disapproval.

"You never have given the subject any special attention?"

"I have seen quite a number of cases of that description. Few physicians make it a subject of special study for the reason I have stated. But every physician, if he be an educated man, is expected to have a certain amount of knowledge on the subject. In minor cases, the physician may treat the physical cause of the mental disturbance and not send them to the asylum."

"Will you describe if you please, in what respect the symptoms described on your visit were different from ordinary cases of difficult menstruation."

"All cases of difficult menstruation are attended with more or less disturbance of the nervous system. The difference is simply in the intensity – the degree. This was a very severe case. There was a great deal of nervous excitement. The disturbance seemed to be out of proportion to the amount of pain the patient seemed to have endured. Hysteria may result from uterine irritation, and nearly always does."

"Were the symptoms in this case such that you considered it a case of hysteria?"

"We do not look for so much actual suffering in

hysteria. We may have, and often do have, cases of hysteria without any great amount of suffering on the part of the patient, or any great amount of previous irritation. In cases of hysteria, too, it is sometimes difficult to determine just how far the nervous symptoms are due to disease and how far to habit. The dividing line between actual insanity, caused by a disturbance of the uterus and hysteria, might be sometimes as difficult to draw as the line between mental disturbance, arising from any strong emotion, and insanity as a consequence of such emotion – as difficult as it is to tell when a chicken ceases to be a chicken and becomes a hen."

"Did you see anything to lead you to suppose that there was any injury to her capacity to control herself in regard to her acts?"

"I merely saw her for five minutes at a time, and, of course, I could have no opportunity whatever to form an opinion on that point."

"Did you have occasion to observe whether her power of discrimination between right and wrong had been affected at all?"

"I do not think any of my visits extended beyond fifteen minutes and no ethical question would be likely to come up in that time."

"After hearing the testimony read and the alleged indications of insanity exhibited, would you judge her to have been insane when she committed this act?"

"What I said in regard to that was this: that the nervous excitement that Miss Harris exhibited at that time might perhaps have been nothing more than would have been exhibited by any person who suddenly found herself under like circumstances. What looks to me most suspicious in this case, and most evidence of insanity, is the entirely contradictory statement made by her to Messrs. McCullough and Walker."

"A point of clarification, your honor," said Bradley.

Addressing the witness, he said, "But you added that, I understood, that if it were shown that at that time she was just recovering from one of these attacks to which reference has been made, that you should naturally expect, on any great cause of excitement being brought to bear upon her at that time, a very much greater impression would be produced upon her than at any other time?"

"Yes, sir. It would naturally and necessarily be so."

Judge Wiley addressed the court, "It being late in the day, the court will adjourn and continue tomorrow at 10 o'clock."

On the steps of the courthouse, Douglas and Richardson discussed the testimony of Dr. Fitch. "It sounded as though he was talking largely in a theoretical vein at the beginning. On the one hand, he said that he saw her about five minutes each time and knew nothing of her personal relations and had never heard of Burroughs. On the other hand, he spoke of hysteria being caused by dysmenorrhea and, when combined with disappointment in love, how it could cause insanity. Yet, he would not allow himself to be pinned down that that was what happened in this case. He allowed as to how the reaction of Miss Harris could be just a common reaction of a normal person who found herself in such circumstances."

"It was only when he accepted all of Bradley's assumptions about Miss Harris," said Richardson, "about her relationship to Burroughs, her suffering dysmenorrhea the day that she shot him, her being suddenly confronted with the cause of her suffering there in the hallway of the Treasury building – it was only when making all of these assumptions that he could talk of a combining of three influences that might cause Miss Harris to kill the deceased."

"But," said Douglas, "the defense did manage to get

him to imply that her confession to Officer Walker was an instance of mental alienation – a severe form of insanity - because it contradicted what she told Mr. McCullough. That was a sharp move by Bradley – now they don't have to spend time trying to explain why she said she warned Burroughs that she would have her revenge if he didn't follow through on his promise of marriage. It was just crazy talk!"

"The case of the woman who cut off the child's head added a nice touch too," added Richardson. "In that case the murder's logic is so bizarre that anyone trying to figure it out would just be going on a fool's errand. So too, in this case, one should not waste time looking for some method in her madness."

CHAPTER 8

Richardson and Douglas were chatting on the steps of the courthouse before the courtroom was opened on the seventh day of the trial. "I did some studying on handwriting analysis last night," said Richardson.

"Really," said Douglas, appearing impressed with the other reporter's diligence. "What did you learn?"

"It seems that people who regard themselves as experts in that art start with the assumption that, while people learn to write with a particular system, they develop idiosyncrasies in the way they form letters and words. These mannerisms are thought to remain constant, even when the writer is trying to disguise his writing.

"The experts focus on the shape of the letters and their proportion, the slant or angles of the lines forming the letters, the connections between letters, the nature of the curves and whether or not there is retracing. For example, one writer may form a round and fat capital 'A' while another may make it thin and angular. The slope of the cross on a 't' may be upward, straight across or downward.

"People also differ with respect to the pressure they exert on the pen or pencil, whether they make pauses as they write, the amount of space they leave between words and a bunch of other things. The belief that these differences in handwriting are related to differences in character has been around for hundreds of years."

"Wow! Sounds like one would have to be specially trained to take all those things into account," said Douglas, "not like the casual assessment you or I might make of whether or not one sample of handwriting is like another."

"The experts go about it in a systematic way, making tables of each form for the letters in one sample of handwriting and comparing it to a similar table constructed for another sample. If there are a lot of differences, then they judge the samples to have come from different parties."

"They don't rely on similarities, then?" asked Douglas.

"No" replied Richardson. "But the thing is that the experts disagree just about as often as the man on the street. The methods have not really been tested and it is doubtful if they are very reliable. Even the basic assumption that each person's handwriting is unique has not been demonstrated. The whole thing is very subjective."

"Hmm. Then any conclusion drawn about who really wrote the Greenwood letters is on pretty shaky ground."

"That's what I would think. But the lawyers in this case seem to think that anyone sufficiently well acquainted with the person who wrote the documents in question should be able to discern a true instance from a false instance. You would think that the prosecution would at least raise the question about the accuracy of determining the source of a sample of handwriting."

"Yes, you would think so," said Douglas.

The crowd began to move into the courtroom, which was again packed with observers and a number of ladies occupying seats inside the railing. Mary came in with her usual entourage just before 10:00 o'clock.

Judge Wiley signaled the defense to begin and Bradley recalled Louisa Devlin for one question: whether or not she had observed any change in the flesh of Miss Harris after she received the Greenwood letters. Miss Devlin responded that Mary's flesh had "fallen away" after receiving the letters. Bradley then called her sister, Jane Devlin, to the stand. After some preliminary questions, he asked "Did you ever see Mr. Burroughs, the deceased, in 1863?"

"I have seen Mr. Burroughs at the boarding house two or three times," the witness answered. "The first time I saw him was on the Monday after she came there. She came on Saturday and I saw him on the Monday following. I met him at the door. He asked me if Miss Harris was in. I told him she was not, and he wrote his name on a card and gave it to me to give to her, which I did."

"When did you see him again?"

"I saw him a few evenings afterwards. He was then at the door speaking to her, as I came into the passage. She had a cold, and he proceeded to muffle around her a shawl which she had on, and told her to take good care of herself – keep in her bedroom until she got rid of the cold."

"After that, when did you see him next?"

"Not until sometime during the summer, at our store. I saw him a second time at the store during that summer."

"Did Miss Harris' good health, cheerful disposition and good temper, which you previously testified to, continue during that summer?"

"It continued until the fall."

"How long was the interval between the last time you saw him in the store before these Greenwood letters were received?"

"It was about five weeks, I think, after this, that I saw the two letters referred to. I am not positive."

"Have you seen any letters in her possession purporting to be written by Burroughs before the two letters signed J. B. Greenwood?"

"Yes, sir. I have seen several letters."

"You heard the letters read on the day before yesterday. Did you recognize any of those as the ones you saw?"

"Yes, sir."

"Have you seen a sufficient number of those letters to enable you to form and express any opinion as to his handwriting?"

"Yes, sir. I thought they were in the same handwriting."

"When these letters signed 'J. B. Greenwood' were produced, state whether they were or were not, in your judgment, in the handwriting of the deceased?"

"I thought them to be of the same handwriting as the letter she had shown me, and which I had read – the letter of 7th August, 1863."

"Look at this letter of September 8 and tell the court where and when you saw it."

"I cannot remember the day but it was in our store and my sister took the letter from Mary, read it, and said she would answer it in her name. None of us could guess who the author of the letter was and we had no suspicion regarding it."

Douglas wrote on his note pad, "So the handwriting of the first letter was not so obviously that of Burroughs?" and showed it to Richardson. Richardson nodded that he understood the implication.

"Do you remember where and when you saw this

second letter dated September 12?"

"It was at our store on Monday. I do not know the day of the month. My sister asked Miss Harris to go with her to the post office to ascertain from the clerk who came for the answer to the former letter."

"What happened when they returned?"

"I do not remember what passed on their return, more than Miss Harris told me a few days afterwards that she had found out it was Mr. Burroughs who wrote those letters, by the description the post office clerk had given them, and that he wore a ring, which she had given him, on his finger."

Richardson wrote on his note pad, "It wasn't significant enough to mention on the day that it happened?" and showed his note to Douglas, who acknowledged it by a nod.

Bradley asked, "Did you go with Miss Harris to make inquires as to who was the author of that letter?"

"I went to the house where Miss Harris was asked to go in those two letters – No. 94 Quincy Street. We rung the bell and asked for the lady of the house. She came and one of us asked if the gentleman had called on the Friday before to meet a lady there. She said, 'Yes, he had called at noon and remained several hours, but that the lady did not come.' She said the gentleman told her the lady lived on Clark Street and that her name was Miss Harris. He told her he would take his seat by the window, that she did not need wait on the door, that he would go to the door himself when he saw the lady coming. I asked her to describe the person and she said he was a man of medium size, rather round shouldered, and had black hair and beard, with bright eyes."

"Did anything further pass?"

"I asked if he belonged to Chicago and she said he used to belong to Chicago but was now engaged in Government employ at Washington."

"Anything else?"

"I asked her, if it was not too much trouble, if she would call at our store and we would show her a picture to see if she could recognize it as the person who called at her house. She did call on Saturday afternoon about four o'clock, some two or three evenings after our visit. Miss Harris showed her the picture of Burroughs."

"Is this the picture?" (Handing a *carte-de-viste* to the witness).

"It is. She took the picture, looked at it for perhaps a minute or two – and then said that was certainly the person that called at her house."

"What effect did this produce upon Miss Harris when at the door of that house and after she had received this information from that woman?"

"When we first went to the house, she was perfectly cool, and asked the woman some questions, but soon got very much excited, and stopped asking any questions, but stood silent and trembled. She made two or three exclamations, saying 'Oh that was Burroughs!' She said he had wronged her, cruelly wronged her, and taken her from her home."

"Can you state whether or not Mr. Burroughs was in Chicago at the time of the receipt of that second letter, or about that time?"

"It was some day about that time – I cannot say what day precisely – I saw Mr. Burroughs get in a car going out to Cottage Grove. He got in on the corner of State and Monroe Streets. He appeared to be coming from the post office."

"Was this before receipt of the letter on the 12th of September?"

"I think it was before. I told no person that I had seen him. Sometime afterwards, when Mary was positive it was Burroughs who wrote the letters, I told her I had seen him."

"What was the effect these letters had upon Miss Harris' health?"

"They rendered her very thin and pale and yellow-looking."

"State whether, within a short period, you observed any fact showing a great degree of excitement about her and, if so, what that fact was?"

"The first time I remember seeing her excited was about the latter part of September, 1863 before Dr. Fitch visited her. She came out into the yard with a window-brush, and struck me several times with it. I asked her why she did it, but she gave me no reply."

"Do you recall any other incidents?"

"I remember her getting really excited several times and tearing up books, clothing and such things, but I do not remember the dates."

"How did she sleep?"

"I know she slept very little at night, often crying all the night and keeping me awake. Many times at night, when I would say I would not put up with her crying, which kept me awake, she would get up and go to the next room and lie on the floor until morning, without any clothing but her night clothes. It was January and the weather was intensely cold and there was no fire in the room."

"Did she make any other attack upon you?"

"The second Sunday in January, 1864, she ran at me with a carving knife, without any provocation whatsoever."

"What immediately preceded this attack upon you?"

"She had a letter or letters in her hand and she asked, 'Did I wish to read a fine letter?' I looked at it and seeing it was from Mr. Burroughs, I told her I did not want to hear any thing more about such a mean, contemptible fellow like him, and not to mention his name in my presence. She then made at me with the carving knife, and I ran out the door."

"How long were you absent from the room and what happened when you got back?"

"About half an hour. Mary wanted to go out the window into the street. My sister prevented her from doing so but she insisted on going into the street. My sister finally opened the door rather than have her go out the window. She went out and my sister told me to follow her and see where she went. She went round two or three blocks, then stopped a car on Madison Street and started to get in but did not. Then she went down Clark Street and into the Tremont House, the best hotel in Chicago. My sister and I went to get Mr. Harris, a friend of hers from Burlington and all three of us went to the Tremont, but she refused to come home. Then, about dark, she came home of her own accord."

"After you went to Janesville, were there any incidents of the same character?"

"I have seen her several times very much excited. When in those spells, she very seldom said anything and always sat looking on one object for nearly an hour."

"Was her eye fixed on a particular object or simply on vacancy?"

"I do not know. Her eye was apparently fixed on something."

"Was there any incident that occurred shortly before she came to Washington?"

"About a week before she left for Washington we had a sister who came to visit us. She was exhibiting a very handsome piece-quilt of silk which she had made. Miss Harris got it from her and commenced to tear it to pieces. It was with great difficulty that it was taken from her."

"Does the prosecution wish to cross-examine?" asked Judge Wiley.

"Yes, your honor," replied Mr. Wilson. "How old was Miss Harris when you first saw her?"

"I do not know. I have heard that she is now twenty-one."

"What day of the month and time of day was it when you saw Burroughs getting into the car on the corner of State and Monroe streets?"

"It was in the afternoon about the time of the receipt of the letters of the 8th and 12th of September. It could have been either before or after. He passed me on the street."

"Did you speak to him or he to you?"

"No, sir. I never had an introduction to Burroughs and never spoke to him but on the one occasion when he gave me a card for Miss Harris."

"When did you tell Miss Harris about having seen Burroughs?"

"It was sometime, a day or two, after I heard of his marriage. That occurred on the 15th of September."

"Did you express any opinion to Miss Harris as to the authorship of these letters?"

"Not until after we had been to this house on Quincy Street."

"Was your sister present when the subject of the authorship of the letters was discussed – when you were talking together?"

"Yes, sir. I don't remember who mentioned it first. I remember myself saying that the writing looked much like his. I don't think anyone else had mentioned his name up to that point."

"You, then, were the first one that suggested his name in connection with the letters?"

"I might not have been. The letters were looked over before."

"When did you go to the house on Quincy Street?"

"It was the afternoon of the 16th or 17th of September."

"Had you any suspicion as to the character of the

house when you went there?"

"Yes, sir. I had heard its character mentioned by a detective officer who came to our store and by several others of whom I made inquiry. My sister was the first to make an inquiry."

"Who first spoke to Miss Harris of the character of the house?"

"We all knew it could not be a very good house, being on the street it was."

"How long had you lived in Chicago up to that time?"

"About seven or eight months."

"How far was Quincy Street from where you lived?"

"One block."

"Did any gentleman friend accompany you to the house?"

"No, sir."

"Did you see any person there other than the keeper of the house?"

"I saw several girls there in the back department."

"Did you see any gentlemen there?"

"No, sir."

"Who first made the inquires of this woman as to the person who had engaged a room there?"

"Miss Harris, but then she stopped and seemed to get excited and then I made all the other inquires."

"What opinion did you express at the time."

"I expressed no opinion at the house but after we came home I said it was certainly Burroughs, that I had everything to convince me it was him."

"Will you state whether or not you, at any time, had any misunderstandings or quarrels with Miss Harris?"

"No quarrels whatever – only when she would be in these tempers of which I have spoken. We have been good friends otherwise, without interruption. I always said to my sister she was crazy, and that I could forgive her for anything she did."

"What prevented her from injuring you with that carving knife?"

"I got out of the door before she overtook me. She attempted to get out of the door but I locked it."

"What expressions did you hear her make use of in regard to Mr. Burroughs?"

"I have never heard her talk very much about Mr. Burroughs. She did tell me that he had deceived her, and he told me all about their engagements and so on. I often heard her say she would sue him for a breach of promise of marriage."

"What reply did you make to that?"

"I often told her I would not let on I ever heard he was living, and would drop him."

"While in Chicago do you know of her receiving attentions from a young gentleman of your own name?"

"I have known her to receive attentions from no gentleman other than Burroughs, either of mine, or any other name."

"Do you know of her receiving letters from any other person?"

"No, sir."

"When she left for Washington, did you have any apprehensions at permitting her to go away from you? Did you say anything to her on the subject?"

"I do not know as I said anything. I had no control over the girl. She was at liberty to go where she pleased. She said she would return very soon and resume her duties at the store."

"Did you ever hear anyone in your presence advise her in regard to this suit for a breach of promise?"

"My sister advised her to drop the matter altogether, and to have nothing to do with him."

"Were any steps taken to put her under medical treatment of any kind, except consultation with Dr. Fitch?"

"None that I know of."

"Did you ever make complaint of her conduct to any person except Mr. and Mrs. Harris?"

"Not that I know of."

"She was entirely capable of attending to all business you required of her?"

"Yes, sir."

On re-examination Mr. Bradley asked the witness, "Being in the millinery and fancy business near by Quincy Street gave you the opportunity of knowing the character of the streets in the neighborhood, did it not?"

"Yes, sir."

"State if you had any male friends in Chicago at that time upon whom you could properly have called to go with you?"

"No, sir; I had not."

"Had you ever seen this woman at the house on Quincy before you visited or after she called at your store about the picture?"

"No, sir."

"State whether Miss Harris was not, except at these intervals, fully capable of managing her own or anybody else's affairs?"

"Yes, sir, she was, except at these intervals."

Judge Hughes, for the defense, rose and asked that Joseph H. Bradley be sworn. He then proceeded to question the defense counsel on his relationship to the accused and what he observed while interacting with her before the trial began. Mr. Bradley did so, emphasizing her nervousness and relating several instances of peculiar behavior, during which Miss Harris would evidence "paroxysms" of extreme excitement, a heated head with imperviousness to cold draughts, a rigid appearance of her face and strange look of her right eye, and at times seemed not to appreciate the fact that she was confined to jail and charged with murder.

Bradley considered all of these symptoms and other episodes that he described as evidence of Mary's mental impairment. To cloak his testimony with the shroud of science, he read notes from a journal as if they were empirical observations and punctuated his account with measurements of the defendant's heart rate and assessments of the temperature of her head and hands.

He painted a picture of a naive young farm girl who had suffered all her life, felt unloved and as if she had no friends, was beaten and persecuted. At the same time she had given no one cause to hate her and dearly loved those who showed any kindness toward her and would do anything in the world for them.

He obtained and related the history of her relationship to Burroughs, emphasizing the influence he exerted over her development, the molding of her character and the control of her behavior. She was portrayed as initially being a young light-hearted girl who had fun playing pranks on Burroughs but was drawn to him out of sympathy for a good man fallen by misfortune, a sentiment that by degrees gradually turned to an absorbing love. From a very early age, Bradley argued, Burroughs had lead Mary to expect that they would be wed.

The attorney dispensed with the embarrassing facts of Mary's interview with the reporter from the *Washington Chronicle* by describing her intense emotional reaction when the matter was broached and interjecting that he did not believe the account himself. He embedded the event in his own testimony as to her quickness of apprehension, keen perceptions and distinct memory. And, suddenly, her entire newspaper confessional was lost in a flood of verbal legerdemain as his testimony moved on to more compelling matters.

Judge Hughes continued, "Will you now state whether, from your acquaintance with Miss Harris, and the facts you have just recounted to the jury, she is in your opinion of sound mind, either generally or partially?"

"Applying the facts which have come under my own observation to the experience I have heretofore had in similar cases, and to what I have read on the subject, I have no hesitation in saying that Miss Harris is not only of sound mind, but has an uncommonly good mind. I have no hesitation in saying - indeed I am perfectly confident - that in certain ways her mind is affected, not by nervous irritation alone, but by moral causes. When a fact or substance is suddenly presented to her mind, connected with these moral causes, or during this state of excitement of her mind, she is incapable of thinking and acting in regard to that subject with reason or discretion.

"She is subject to certain impulses which control her will in reference to the same matter; and that is what I understand to be paroxysmal insanity from moral causes. As far back as 20 years ago, I began to study this subject. Her case is not a case of hysteria; but the affection, whatever it may be, proceeds from physical and mental cause combined."

"If there was any special subject that seemed to disturb her intellect more than another, I wish you would state it?"

"Her relations to Burroughs in his lifetime, and whenever any reference was made to his widow or family. When the nature of the defense was made known to her, it completely overwhelmed her. Her modesty and sensibility were shocked, and she said she would rather have died then set up such a defense. She said to me, 'Do you think I am insane, Mr. Bradley?' I said, 'No, except under certain circumstances.'"

"What would be the effect of her unexpectedly meeting with Mr. Burroughs?"

"He was the subject of this moral affection of Miss Harris. I know from her what her impressions and what her beliefs were in regard to him. Whether delusion or actual fact, the effect upon her mind would be the same. I think that no human being, unless it may be what is sometimes called a 'mad doctor,' who has great experience in such things, can form any conjecture as to the effect which would be produced upon her mind if she were laboring under the trouble of a deranged system. But, whatever the effect might be, in my judgment it would be utterly uncontrollable by herself, and arise from an impulse, and not a mode of action governed by sound reason."

Douglas poked Richardson and pointed to what he had written on his note pad: "Unexpectedly meeting with Burroughs? Didn't she seek him out in the Treasury building? How is that unexpected?"

Richardson looked at Douglas and smiled.

"Mr. Carrington, do you wish to cross-examine the witness?" asked Judge Wiley.

As the District Attorney moved toward the witness, he asked, "You have had a great deal of experience in these matters in the course of your professional life, and you have often had occasion to put in this defense of insanity, have you not?"

"Yes, sir. Four times, I think, in criminal cases," replied Bradley.

"You speak of her distress at the announcement of the character of the offense and the nature of the defense. At any other time when the name of Burroughs was mentioned, or the letters read, did you observe any such indications of suffering?"

"No more than we would associate with a distressing subject. I have never noticed any degree of excitement except at periods I have mentioned; more remarkable still, I have never once heard her speak with harshness and severity of Burroughs."

"How long would these spells continue?"

"Sometimes five minutes. On one occasion they continued for as long as two hours. I never knew them to be exhibited more than one day at a time, except for the 22nd and 23rd of May and the noon of the 26th of May. I do not mean to say that she was not under great excitement before I saw her, but that it was not developed to me."

"She was at other times entirely capable of directing her conduct?"

"Yes, sir. Not only that, but she showed a remarkably clear comprehension in the preparation of her case, independent of this matter of insanity, which was never broached to her until the time I have mentioned. Also, among the peculiar marks of her character was the amiability of her disposition and her open cheerfulness."

His testimony concluded, Bradley arose from the witness chair and again assumed the role of defense attorney. "The defense calls Mr. Robert Beale," he said.

The warden at the jail took the stand. Bradley asked him, "On the morning Miss Harris was first imprisoned, did she know you were there?"

"She did not. The door of her room was open, and when I got there I heard a voice. She was walking with her back to me, and, therefore, did not observe I was by. She had her hands clasped, and was walking up and down exclaiming. 'I would not have killed him for the world. I loved him better than I do my life.' Then she stopped for a moment, and then added, 'Oh! I would have died for him, but he would have ruined me.'"

"At any time did you observe any marked peculiarity about the appearance of her eye?"

"Yes, sir. It was on the 20th of June – I made a note of it at the time – when going into her room, and taking a seat opposite her, she looked at me very intensely for awhile, her eye seeming to be entirely suffused. The pupil of her eye was so completely covered up that you could not see it at all. In fact, it did not look like an eye at all.

After sitting by her for a few moments, looking directly at me, she said, 'Well, I am very glad you have come.' I then asked her how she felt."

On cross-examination, Mr. Wilson asked, "What facilities for going about the jail were allowed Miss Harris?"

"She was confined pretty closely until her physician wrote a letter, which I brought to the Court, stating that it was necessary, from the condition of her health, to have her taken out of the room. I then gave her the privilege of the passage, and let her come down when I was there."

"No further questions."

Bradley called to the stand Miss Anna McWilliams, a clerk in the Treasury Department who had occupied the same room as Miss Harris in a Baltimore boarding house just before the latter came to Washington.

"Was Miss Harris sick whilst there and just before she came to Washington?"

"Yes, sir. She complained of a sore throat and seemed to have a cold."

"Had you at that time had any conversations with her in regard to her purpose in coming to Baltimore?"

"Yes, sir. I often heard her mention her affairs during her stay in Baltimore. On the Saturday night before she left she said she anticipated visiting Washington, but could get through her business in the course of an hour or two, and would return on the same day."

"What did you do on Saturday night?"

"We remained in the parlor together until ten o'clock. I retired first. She came up to the room about an hour later. I went to sleep and left her awake until a very late hour, probably between one and two o'clock, sorting some letters."

"Did she state what she was going to do with those letters?"

"She said she merely wanted to arrange them for the

purpose of taking them to Washington the next morning if she felt well enough to go. She said she intended instituting a suit in Washington against Mr. Burroughs for a breach of promise, and was going to put the letters into a lawyer's hands.

"I told her to give herself ample time in getting to the depot for her return, as I had been disappointed quite often in getting to the depot too late for the train. She said she would give herself at least three-quarters of an hour to get to the depot. We were going that evening to the colored people's school. Henry Ward Beecher was to review the colored scholars."

"Did you see her when she was starting in the morning?"

"I saw her a short time before she started. She left in the 40 minutes past nine train."

"Do you know if she brought those letters with her or not?"

"I did not know at the time, but I understood _____ "

Mr. Carrington arose and angrily said, "Never mind what you understood!"

Bradley frowned at the prosecutor and continued, "Do you know whether Miss Harris did or did not leave any letters on her pillow?"

"Yes, sir. She left two."

Mr. Wilson led the cross-examination by implying that the defense had presented only the parts of what transpired that would support their position. "Please state the *whole* of the conversation of which you have given us a part?"

The witness retold much of what she had already testified but also related that Miss Harris told her she had no intention to recover damages from Burroughs but was determined to let the public know that she was not the creature they supposed her to be. She said she would never have left her home to go to Chicago except on

Burroughs's account and that he had deceived her by marrying another woman. Her object in visiting Washington, she said, was to determine if he was currently in the city and then placing the letters in the hands of a lawyer during the coming week. She had read five or six of the letters to the witness.

The defense called Mr. William H. Brown, a Treasury Department employee who was about five feet in front of Burroughs when the shots were fired. On cross-examination by Mr. Wilson, he told the Court, "After the first shot was fired I turned suddenly around, looked to see where the shot came from, and saw a lady standing in the center of the hall, in the act of cocking the pistol a second time. I looked to see if it was any one I knew, for I did not comprehend the case at all. I had an impression that, perhaps, it was some sport but seeing her raise her hand to fire again, and no one in front of me but Burroughs, who had seen her and gone past me, I started towards the stairs. I did not know but what she was insane, as she had a sort of wild look, and was firing at random. Therefore I thought, if that was the case, she was as likely to hit me as any one else, or, if shooting at Burroughs, still as liable to hit me as him, so I accordingly started on after Burroughs. When I reached the stairs, glancing around and seeing that he was going to take the left-hand stairs, I went down on the right hand."

"Slowly or rapidly?" inquired Mr. Wilson.

"I don't think I went very slowly." A twitter of laughter went through the crowd, followed by a scowl from Judge Wiley and a rap of his gavel.

Daniel Voorhees took over for the defense, calling Dr. Charles H. Nichols, Superintendent of the Government Hospital for the Insane. "How long have you occupied that position?" asked Mr. Voorhees.

"Nearly thirteen years. I have practiced medicine for twenty-two years and I have specialized in the study of the mind for eighteen years now."

"I will simply recall your attention to the facts that have been testified to in your hearing; and then from these facts, if true, and from your own personal examination of the defendant, ask you to give us your opinion as to her mental condition."

"At the request of two gentlemen interested in Miss Harris, neither of whom has been present during this trial, nor in any way connected with it, so far as I know, I visited Miss Harris in jail first near the latter part of February or the 1st of March, not long before the adjournment of Congress. I saw her about five times, the last on the evening of the day of the President's funeral."

"Now, Doctor," Voorhees said, "be kind enough to give us the result of your investigations and your opinion as to her physical and mental condition."

"I have prepared a skeleton of my views, thinking it would save the time of the Court, and I will read them if there be no objection."

Glancing at the attorneys representing the prosecution and seeing no objection raised, Mr. Voorhees said to the witness, "Proceed, sir."

"I believe I have heard all the evidence bearing upon her mental and bodily health which has been given before this court since Saturday morning. From my personal observations of Miss Harris, made as stated, and assuming the testimony under oath, relating to the state of her mind, to which I have listened, to be true, I am led to the following conclusions:

"Miss Mary Harris's brain and nervous system are large and active. The nervous temperament largely predominates over the other temperaments of physiologists. It appears that she has been affected with painful dysmenorrhea from the autumn of 1863 to near the present time. Her mental faculties are stronger and more active than the average of women. Her temper is highly sensitive and spirited, but kind and placable.

"She has not enjoyed the advantages of much moral or mental training. Her character was that of an uncommonly sprightly and engaging girl, who had attracted the notice and regard of highly respectable gentlemen and ladies in Burlington, Iowa, who esteemed her for her intelligence, honorable ambition, and virtue. Both her physical constitution and health, and her mental and moral constitution are such as to render her unusually susceptible to either a physical or moral cause of insanity.

"She has been exposed at the same time to the physical and moral agencies which frequently cause mental derangement, and those to whose effects she was peculiarly susceptible. First, painful dysmenorrhea. Secondly, disappointment in love – the sudden and unexpected breaking off of a long continued engagement of marriage, in a manner most calculated to deeply wound the sensibilities of a nervous, proud, and virtuous young woman, and to disturb her reason.

"From the moment of this disappointment in love – this great shock to her delicate moral sensibilities – there was a material change in her spirits and health, and she at times exhibited acts of insane violence. She was unquestionably insane at times during the period between the disappointment and the homicide. The circumstances attending the homicide by her, are better explained by the assumption that it was an act of insanity, than that it was an act of malice or revenge. The state of her body and mind since the homicide is calculated to corroborate the theory that there is a continuous morbid susceptibility to mental disturbance, and that the homicide was an act of insane violence."

"Doctor, in your interviews with Miss Harris as a physician, were you apprised of the condition of her health. In other words, from your consultation with her after seeing her in jail, can you fix what her mental conditions was most probably on the 30th of January?"

"To give the weight which my knowledge upon that point has upon my own mind, I will mention that at the first interview I had with her, as well as at subsequent interviews, she impressed me with the conviction that she was a person not only of virtue and cheerfulness, but of uncommon candor. I may say that during the first and second interviews, I was inclined to doubt her insanity. It does not occur to me how I came possessed with the idea that her mental disturbance was connected with her menstrual periods. At any rate, I did get that idea in some way, and at one of my interviews, I think it was the third, I asked her whether she was unwell at the time of the commission of the homicide. She replied that she was.

"I may mention that I was so much impressed with her womanly delicacy and sensibility that I put the question by writing it upon a card, to make it as inoffensive to her as possible, and she returned her reply in writing. She stated to me in this reply that she had been unwell for three days before she came to Washington, and that was the cause in part of her deferring the visit to Washington."

Richardson quickly paged back in his notes and found that Mary's Baltimore roommate had testified that she seemed to have a cold. He wondered to himself if the doctor had presented his question to her in so delicate a way that it was ambiguous and she could honestly answer that she was ill, meaning having a cold, and was not acknowledging that she was having painful dysmenorrhea, as the doctor concluded. Or, perhaps, the question was deliberately presented so that it was ambiguous and the affirmative response could be interpreted so as to favor the defense.

The doctor's claim that he didn't know how he connected her mental disturbance with her menstrual periods also seemed disingenuous since the association was common knowledge in the medical profession. "Maybe I'm just being too suspicious," Richardson thought to himself.

Voorhees asked, "Doctor, in your experience and knowledge of this subject, assuming that fact to be true, how is it regarded by men in your profession as a cause of mental disturbance?"

"It is a frequent cause of mental disturbance. I have frequently seen cases that only occasionally exhibit mental derangement. Gentlemen of my profession are in the habit of calling it paroxysmal insanity."

"Is a knowledge of right and wrong any longer considered as a test of insanity?"

"I do not consider a knowledge of right and wrong, in the abstract, as a test of insanity; or even a knowledge of right and wrong in respect to any criminal act that may be committed by an insane person. I, perhaps, in justice to my profession, should say that that view has never been taken by it, though the views of your profession have never been as clearly defined upon that point as have those of mine. I am aware that a knowledge of right and wrong has been, by certain jurists, particularly in England, held to be evidence of responsibility in criminal cases."

"Describe to the jury what is understood in your profession by the term 'insane impulse'."

"By 'insane impulse' I understand that an individual is impelled, in consequence of disease of the brain, suddenly to commit an act that he is unable to restrain himself from committing. In some instances there is, probably, a consciousness of the nature of the act; but in most instances I think there is not."

Bradley interjected the next question: "Do you mean physical disease, or one created by the causes to which you have referred, when you speak of a diseased brain?"

"Perhaps it will be a sufficiently categorical answer for

me to say, that I believe that the brain is always diseased, either in substance or functions, in every case of insanity."

"Now, Doctor," Voorhees inquired, "what is the recognized effect by men of science upon the human mind of continuous and protracted thought upon any one subject, and especially if accompanied by violent emotions of disappointment, or even of exciting joy?"

"Such mental habits are frequently the exciting cause of insanity. Disappointment in love is a more frequent cause of insanity among women than men."

"Does protracted thought upon the subject of disappointment give rise to bereavement and what you call 'insane impulse'?"

"I should think it does, though every species of insanity may be produced by a single cause, and, *vice versa*, every known cause of insanity may give rise to one form of that disease."

Judge Wiley, citing the time of day, called for an adjournment with proceedings to continue the following day, Thursday, July 13, 1865.

CHAPTER 9

As arranged on the previous day, Dr. Nichols met with Mr. Bradley at a small restaurant on Pennsylvania Avenue for breakfast prior to the beginning of the day's session in court. When Nichols arrived he found that Bradley had already staked out a table at the back of the room. "Good morning Joseph," said Nichols as he shook his old friend's hand.

"Morning Charles," replied Bradley. The waiter took their orders and the two gentlemen enjoyed coffee while awaiting their corn pone and codfish balls.

"How is Lucy?"

"Not too well," said Bradley. "She's been ailing for quite a spell now. Losing two young children was hard on her but I think there is something else making her feel so tired all the time."

"I'm sorry to hear that, Joseph. Tell her that my wife and I will remember her in our prayers."

"Thank you Charles. No offense to the medical profession, but the ordinary doctors haven't been any help. My homeopathic physician, Dr. Verdi, is trying some things with her which seem to give her some comfort."

"I have no difficulty with that, Joseph. You can't object to anything that works just because it is from a different specialty. Is it true that Joseph Junior is working in your law firm now?"

"Yes. Both Thomas and Joseph Jr. are working in the firm now. A. T. has a good organizational mind and spends a lot of time managing the office. Junior has a good understanding of business law and a flare for the courtroom, like his old man."

"Well, Joseph, what do you think I can expect when the prosecution cross-examines me today?"

"It shouldn't be too bad. Lawyers are hesitant to be too hard on a prominent person such as you. But I asked you to meet me here today so the prosecution doesn't blindside you and I want to give you some time to think about your answers before you are put on the spot," said Bradley.

"I appreciate that," said Nichols, "although I have been questioned in cases like this before."

"Yes, I know. Some of them were cases we worked on together. But we want to reduce the surprise element - it doesn't hurt to be prepared."

"Right," said Nichols. "A cleaver lawyer can get you to admit a little bit here, a little bit there, or get you to concede some degree of merit in what they say, and then twist it around to come to some conclusion that is counter to your views."

"We want to anticipate and be ready for whatever moves they make," said Bradley. "In this case, I think they'll ask you how you arrived at your conclusions, to provide your reasoning for the statements you made, and they will be looking for any opening to discredit your testimony. So your logic has to be sound, even if you just claim that it is based on your vast experience in similar cases. Remember that none of them know as much about insanity and how the mind works as you do."

"I can rationalize most anything," said Nichols with a smile.

"I know you can," said Bradley. "Carrington will try to get you to cede the point that Miss Harris was rational and could tell right from wrong at least part of the time and that she wasn't always controlled by violent insane impulses. Then he will try to put you in the defensive position of disproving that one of those times was when she committed the crime. In other words, you'd have to muster an argument that she was crazy at the time or was controlled by an insane impulse. And if you do that he will come back with a quantitative rejoinder: 'Certainly, Dr. Nichols, she wasn't *so* insane that she couldn't tell that murder was wrong! Doesn't she bear *any* responsibility for her actions?'"

"I don't know if I can prove that. I'll have to give it some thought. Some ideas are beginning to form in my mind."

"They'll try to present evidence to the effect that Mary showed premeditation and planning in carrying out the crime," said Bradley, "and they will assert that such demonstrations of reason are inconsistent with the concept of insanity. Similarly, they'll argue that she acted out of revenge and that the presence of *any* kind of motive is contrary to the notion of insane impulse."

"The idea that it was an insane act proceeding from a deranged mind trumps all of those considerations. There is also the fact of her painful dysmenorrhea that is a physical cause of her insanity."

"Yes, by all means don't forget the disturbed uterus. While you doctors usually associate that condition with a diagnosis of hysteria, I think we can make the point that it can cause other kinds of mental disorders as well."

"That's true. Many causes can produce a single mental disease and a single cause can have many mental manifestations. And who but a doctor is qualified to make observations about a woman's private parts?"

"That's the idea. Just don't back down on any of your previous testimony. Repeat what you have said before or respond so as to minimize the significance of any point they make."

When they finished their breakfasts, Bradley left first so that when they arrived at the courthouse separately, it would not appear that they were conniving on testimony. Dr. Nichols lingered behind, drinking another cup of coffee and rehearsing possible responses to questions he might be asked.

***

The large number of people in the courtroom reflected the increased interest and press coverage of the trial. There were a great number of ladies in attendance, occupying seats inside the railing as well as outside. Shortly after ten o'clock, the prisoner and her entourage were escorted in, Miss Harris occupying her usual seat.

Mr. Carrington began the cross-examination of Dr. Nichols. "Will you be kind enough to state to the jury the facts upon which you base your opinion?"

"I base my opinion," Dr. Nichols replied, "upon the facts and occurrences testified to by the Misses Devlin and Dr. Fitch and on my belief that she was insane between the disappointment and the homicide is corroborated by what I observed myself of her condition, and by the facts and circumstances to which Mr. Bradley testified. In fact, by my entire knowledge of the case, obtained in the manner stated yesterday."

"State in detail, if you please, any remarkable incidents that occurred within your own personal observation which induces this opinion?"

"No very remarkable incident, bearing upon the state of her mind, occurred within my personal observation; no incident that, in itself, would convince me that she was insane. During the first interview I had with her, and at the close of the second, I think, I was under the impression that she was not insane – at least entertained strong doubts of her insanity. I was much impressed with her apparent candor and the probable truthfulness of her statements in regard to herself. She declined to see me twice because she was suffering from fever and restlessness, according to the guard.

"At my second interview, she told me she was very much indisposed at the time I called, and upon further inquiry, she said it was at her monthly period. At the last interview I had with her she was suffering from the erysipelas, described by Mr. Bradley, and she then exhibited more nervous agitation than I had observed at the previous interviews. It was the evening of the day of the funeral of the late President and she expressed great apprehension lest further violence might be committed by his assassins, and particularly to herself."

"Will you repeat those expressions as near as you can recollect them?"

"I cannot be positive in respect to her words, but I think she said she was afraid they might get in here (referring to her own room) and do violence to her. I think she said murder her, but it is the general character of her expression rather than the words that I remember distinctly. I am sure that is the nature of the apprehension she expressed.

"I would like to make an explanation just here. I was unable to recollect on yesterday how I obtained the idea that she suffered from dysmenorrhea. Upon reflection, I remember well that I learned from the prisoner herself that Dr. Fitch, who testified in her case on Tuesday, had visited her in Chicago, and I wrote to him. In reply, he informed me that he attended her for congestive dysmenorrhea."

"Doctor, will you be kind enough to state the technical name of the insanity with which she was affected?"

"I should denominate it a case of periodical or paroxysmal mania."

"Will you state its nature and character, and its effect upon the person?"

"The term, mania, is applied to that kind of insanity in which the excitement is great and general. The term paroxysmal, or periodical mania, is applied to that form of mania, the active symptoms of which recur sometimes pretty regularly, and at other times at irregular periods; and between them there is a greater or less remission in the activity of the disease. The mind is excited and the understanding more or less deranged. The will is either impaired or misdirected. Sometimes the energy of the will is greatly increased, beyond what is natural to the individual."

"To what extent was she affected by this insanity and how far did it affect her mind and her will while under the influence of it?"

"While under the influence of these paroxysms of mania that I presume still exist, I presume her mind was so affected as to cause her to have violent impulses and to be unable to restrain them and also to entertain either unfounded views and feelings or entertain ones that had a foundation, with a morbid energy so as to make them appear to her much more important than they would in health."

"While under the influence of this mania, was she incapable of giving a rational answer as to the moral quality of her acts, or to estimate the moral qualities or criminal nature of her acts?"

"My impression is that Miss Harris, if her attention had been arrested so as to give a direct or categorical answer to any question of that kind, would probably have given a correct one."

"Do I understand you to say that, under the influence of periodical mania, her will was so far impaired as to render her unable of self-control and render her acts involuntary?"

"I think so."

"Doctor, I will put a hypothetical case, so as to test the principle to which you have averted. Assuming it to be true that a woman armed herself with a pistol, saying that she would have revenge at the risk of her life; that she went to the Treasury or some other building in this city, inquired for a particular party and, after seeing him in his room, then concealed herself, and as he was passing by shot him, and then fired a second time at him; would you say, from your personal observation of the prisoner, and from the evidence of insanity that you have heard, that her mind was so far affected, or she was so insane, as not to know she was doing wrong, and violating the law?"

"Objection!"

"Overruled," said Judge Wiley. "The witness will answer the question."

"I will say, in reply to that question, that no amount of premeditation and preparation to commit a homicide, in my judgment, precludes the idea that that homicide was an insane act. I, however, deem it equally due to the truth of science to say, that if there is evidence of premeditation and preparation, a much closer scrutiny should be made in respect to the existence or non-existence of insanity, if insanity is supposed to exist. In other words, such premeditation and preparation are calculated to throw more or less suspicion or doubt upon the existence of insanity, or that the act was an insane act. If the facts cited in the first part of your question were proved to my satisfaction, it would not alter my convictions in this case, that the act of homicide was an insane act."

"My object is to get at the degree of insanity. I want to know whether a party so affected as you describe would be capable, under such circumstances, of understanding the moral character and quality of the act?"

"I can answer that directly or categorically by saying 'Yes' but by saying that in my judgment it was an insane act and that covers the question of responsibility."

"Assuming the same facts to be true, would you express the opinion that the will of the party was so affected that the acts were involuntary and beyond the control of the party?"

"I would."

"Do persons laboring under this peculiar species of mania generally act with any well defined motive?"

"They frequently act with a motive that in their own minds is a well defined one."

"How is it with regard to the spirit with which they are prompted – is it more the spirit of revenge and hatred against the person injured?"

"I should say that the spirit in which insane persons commit homicides is as various as the cases. As a general rule, it arises from some delusion, or the morbid exaggeration of some real fact."

"In determining whether a person is insane or not, how would your judgment be affected if it appeared that the person was prompted by a spirit of revenge or hatred against a particular person?"

"My answer would be no different from my reply to the question of premeditation and preparation, just substituting the words revenge and hatred."

"Are not the presence of revenge and hatred inconsistent with the idea of that insanity to which you have testified?"

"I can hardly say that. If those motives do not appear to exist I should the more readily conclude that it was a case of homicide by an insane person – an insane act."

"What, in your judgment, is the present condition of the prisoner's mind?"

"I will repeat what I said the other day. The state of

her body and mind since the homicide is calculated to corroborate the truth of the theory that there is a continuous morbid susceptibility to mental disturbance and that it (the homicide for which she is on trial) was an act of insane violence."

Mr. Wilson at this point interjected, "But you have already said, Doctor, that from the facts alone that came under your observation while you were in attendance on the accused, you could express no opinion as to the sanity or insanity of the party."

"No, sir. I believe I have not said that. I will now say that I do not think I could express a *positive* opinion, from my own observation alone, in respect to her sanity or insanity at the time of the homicide."

"Your opinion, then, is formed as well from your observation as from the testimony of the witnesses who have testified as to her condition prior to this homicide and also her demeanor after the homicide?"

"It is."

"Now, Doctor, be good enough to state what facts in the testimony of other witnesses enable you to form your opinion."

"Objection, your honor," cried out Mr. Bradley.

"Overruled," said Judge Wiley.

"The Misses Devlin testify to a material change in her physical and mental condition immediately following a disappointment. That change, in itself, is a morbid one – is disease. The *character* of the change was such, immediately upon its occurrence, as to indicate either mental disease or a susceptibility to it. She then exhibited, from time to time, what appeared to be symptoms of actual mental disease. The symptoms to which I refer were the nervousness and excitability, the loss of sleep, the loss of appetite, the loss of flesh, and the change in her spirits – her mental depression. Those, I believe, are all the principal features of the change first noticed.

"Dr. Fitch testifies to her suffering under a painful and severe form of dysmenorrhea, shortly subsequent to the disappointment. It seems to me impossible to do justice to science and speak of the symptoms simply without connecting them with the cause and showing how they harmonize.

"In the first stage of the case," Dr. Nichols continued, "I perceive a constitutional susceptibility to mental disturbance from certain causes. I then find that her moral and womanly sensibilities were deeply wounded; that she suffered from a painful dysmenorrhea. These were exciting causes of insanity and occurred independently of the constitutional tendency to mental disease.

"Then it seems to me that the manifestations of a particular form of insanity, the continued emaciation, irregular and insufficient sleep, the depression of spirits, and an occasional outbreak of insane violence, of a character which harmonizes with the form of the disease that I suppose to have existed. Those instances are the attack upon Miss Jane Devlin, upon a customer in the store, the cutting up of the quilt (which was, so to speak, a very *natural* insane act), her effort to leave the house at such an unseasonable hour at that season of the year and in her state of life, connected with the remark which indicates – I do not think it proves – some indefinite purpose in regard to her own life. The remark itself, in connection with her depression of spirits and state of mind generally, gave rise to the suspicion in my mind that I have indicated."

"Now, Doctor, you have heard all the circumstances of the homicide, will you be good enough to indicate what symptoms of insanity you are able to mention that have been adduced here in evidence on that subject?"

"It is due to science to say that, so far as I understand the circumstances connected with the homicide, as testified to in my hearing, that they do not of themselves prove the existence of insanity, though I think they are consistent with what usually occurs when an insane person commits a homicide. There appears to have been no effort to commit the act secretly. The best opportunity of committing the act was not embraced, as I think a sane person would have done. There were no efforts to escape, no attempt to palliate the crime by alleging provocation. On the contrary, she expressed her sorrow that she had done it and her great distress in consequence. I base my statement upon the testimony of Policeman Walker, Secretary McCullough, and Mrs. Woodbridge."

"Will you please state all the facts adduced in the testimony, outside of your own observation, that you predicate your opinion of insanity?"

"Aside from what I saw of Miss Harris myself, I based my views upon the testimony of Mr. Bradley. He testifies to so many incidents that I find myself unable to mention them all. But I recollect his mention of the frequency of her pulse, the manifestation of great nervous and mental disturbance in the expression of unfounded apprehensions, if not positive delusions; loss of sleep and insensibility to cold."

"Then you regard the prisoner as actually diseased in mind from the date of her disappointment to the day of the homicide?"

"Yes, sir. Miss Harris may have committed, and probably did commit, a great many acts for which she should be held to legal and moral responsibility but she was liable, at times during that period, to commit acts arising from mental disease for which she should not be held legally and morally responsible. In my view, in order for an insane person to be responsible for an act, the act must grow out of insanity. Comparatively few persons are so insane as not to do many acts for which they are responsible and for which they should be held responsible."

"Doctor, there is testimony that upon one occasion a carving knife was used in an attack on Miss Devlin. Of course there was a generally diseased mind that produced the attack but what I want to know is what the immediate cause of that manifestation was?"

"I do not know. If, for example, a quarrel existed at the moment of using this carving knife, my inference would be that she used the carving knife in consequence of her state of mind, when she would not have done so if she had been in a sound state of mind. But as no reference was made to such a quarrel in the testimony, of course I do not suppose that such a quarrel took place."

"Then, Doctor, I will ask you if these paroxysms of insanity, in your theory of the case, were liable to occur at any time, irrespective of the appearance or non-appearance of any one individual?"

"My strong impression is that paroxysms were more likely to appear at the monthly periods. But I think she was liable to have them at other times, that they were likely to occur independently wholly of any immediate exciting causes, and that they might appear at any time. A little indisposition arising from a cold, a bilious condition, fatigue, or anything of that kind might produce a paroxysm of excitement."

Possibly to distract the prosecution from following up on the question of the paroxysm being in response to a particular individual, Mr. Hughes interjected, "I understood you to say in your cross-examination, that in cases of this kind the act proceeded from insanity?"

"Yes, sir."

"I desire you to give your opinion from what you know of this case, whether the act here proceeded from an insane impulse?"

"I am of the opinion that it did."

Returning to his original inquiry, Mr. Carrington asked,

"Upon what occasions, from all the circumstances of the case, those manifestations were most likely to be exhibited – upon seeing what person or things?"

"I think those manifestations of insanity were most likely to occur upon seeing the person that had disappointed her, or that she thought, at least, had disappointed and greatly wronged her."

Judge Wiley announced a recess for lunch. Douglas and Richardson headed outside to the cart of one of the street vendors plying his trade outside the courthouse. Selecting coffee and German sausage on a bun, they took their lunches to a bench under a large shade tree. "Well, I don't think the prosecution did much to shake the testimony of Dr. Nichols," said Douglas.

"No, he stuck to his guns, alright," commented Richardson. "According to the good doctor, rationality, premeditation, planning, knowing right from wrong and having motives like anger or revenge don't count in determining insanity. Seems the DA was expecting that, by showing such characteristics in the defendant's behavior, he could prove that she is a sane person. Is there any way that she could be shown to not be insane?"

"About the only thing I heard was that if she had picked a better time and place to kill him, that would have shown her sanity! He said that she also didn't try to get away, but that was not true – she did try to escape but got lost trying to get out of the building and got caught."

Richardson laughed. "Amazing, isn't it? This disease that she is said to have can show up in a regular or irregular fashion, it can affect the mind in a greater or lesser degree and it can impair or misdirect the will so that the person so afflicted may or may not be able to control their violent impulses."

"It can occur at any time but is more likely to appear if the woman is having her monthly periods," said Douglas. "What do you think about this idea about a irritable uterus causing painful dysmenorrhea and driving a woman crazy? I've talked with a few women who say they have painful periods too but they have not killed anyone yet."

"I don't know," said Richardson. "That seems to be the current theory of mental disturbance in women or at least of hysteria. I don't know how you could prove it. In fact, I don't know how you can prove anything in psychiatry. Their concepts are so fuzzy and flexible that they can explain most any occurrence."

"One thing the prosecution could have done was to make more of the fact that much of Nichol's deductions were based on the testimony of Bradley and the Devlins, not on his own observations," said Douglas. "He even said that, if he were to rely only on what he observed himself, he would not be able to conclude that she was insane. Carrington or Wilson could have pointed out that neither Bradley nor the Devlins have the qualifications to be considered expert witnesses and they are far from being impartial observers in this case."

"Yes, they could have done that and it makes you wonder if there was some reason for them avoiding it or if they are not paying attention or are just plain incompetent."

"By the way, one of my friends in New York found out from someone he knows in Burlington, that Miss Harris was born in 1841. That makes her 24 years old. She's only one year younger than Amelia Boggs. Seems the defense has run the clock back by about three or four years!"

"Interesting," said Richardson. "I think I'll send a wire to Camp Douglas and see what I can find out about Burroughs's military service."

CHAPTER 10

After the break, Bradley called James A. Conner, a Treasury employee who was on the third floor of the Treasury building at the time Burroughs was shot. He testified that he dropped to the floor when the first shot was fired and from there saw Miss Harris fire the second shot, walk by him and descend the west front steps. He said that she "seemed to be under great excitement," was "very pale," and "Her eyes looked wild to me, as far as I could see."

At the conclusion of Mr. Conner's testimony, Mr. Bradley announced that the defense rested its case, whereupon the prosecution began to offer rebutting evidence. Mr. Wilson recalled William W. Danenhower, who was Burroughs's initial supervisor when he began to work in the Treasury Department.

"You have already stated that you knew Mr. Burroughs. Please state what opportunities you have had to become acquainted with his handwriting?"

"In July, 1863, Mr. Burroughs came into the Fourth Auditor's office and worked at a desk alongside me until the middle of December, 1863, when he left, and went into the office of the Comptroller of the Currency. During that space of time he copied and wrote letters under my direction, which I examined critically, and therefore became familiar with his handwriting."

"Will you examine these two letters, dated Chicago, September 8 and Chicago, September 12, and envelopes (handing same to the witness) and state if you have seen them before, and if so, where?"

"I saw those letters last Saturday morning and examined them. There was also another letter with them in this envelope, dated August 7, signed A. J. Burroughs."

"You testified as to the handwriting of a number of letters that were shown you the other day. Will you be good enough to state whether you believe these two letters to be in the handwriting of Mr. Burroughs?"

"I do not."

"State the degree of confidence that you can express in your own experience."

"I have examined them very critically. Mr. Burroughs had a very peculiar way of making a capital 'I' and if you examine the letters that I saw on last Saturday you will find those capital 'I's are very similar, and nearly exactly alike in every instance, whether made large or small. He generally wrote a large, bold hand but when he would write upon a small sheet of paper, he would not write so large."

"State whether this pile of letters was shown you, and if so, whether you at that time separated these two from the others, and expressed any opinion as to the handwriting?"

"They were all in one package, and handed to me by Mr. Bradley. After examining the package, I remarked to him, 'These two are not in his handwriting.' He then took these out and tied up the package of letters. Three he took out. There is no letter – no capital letter particularly, in these letters – that resembles in the slightest degree

Burroughs's writing. His 'W's' and 'H's' are different."

"Will you state your recollection as to the time when Mr. Burroughs left the city of Washington in September, 1863?"

"The records in the Fourth Auditor's office show that his leave of absence was from the 7th of September for the space of twenty days. I recollect distinctly that for some two or three weeks prior to his leaving he was in search of a house. I believe that he left here on the morning of the 10th of September."

Jumping in before the formal time for him to do so, Bradley asked, "Do you *know* when he left?"

"I am positive that was the time as I am of almost anything in regard to dates. I know it was two or three days after he got his leave and I know for what reasons he was detained here, the circumstances of which I can state, if allowed."

Judge Wiley allowed the cross-examination to proceed as Bradley asked, "Had Mr. Burroughs left the city before that?"

"A month or so before, and was gone, I think, something like ten days. I do not know the time he left nor the date of his return, but it was sometime in August. My recollection is that he was only back some two or three weeks from that trip before he obtained the leave of which I have spoken. He made a short trip to Chicago and back – at least that is where he intended to go, and I suppose he did."

Continuing to try to assail the witness' testimony, Bradley asked, "Look at this letter, dated August 7, (handing it to the witness). Is that in Mr. Burroughs's handwriting?"

"Yes, sir."

"I will ask you to look at the signature to this letter dated August 7 and these dated the 8th and 12th of September and state whether or not you perceive a resemblance in the letter 'I' or 'J' in those two, though very roughly done, to the 'I' and 'J' in the other letters?"

"There is a similarity between them but it is not sufficient for me to say they are alike. This 'J' in the Greenwood letter doesn't come down below the line, as Mr. Burroughs always made his 'J'. The only similarity that I see is in the dates. The figure '3' is something similar. I do not see any resemblance about the '6' or August 7. One of these '6's' might have been made by the pen going up, and stopping abruptly, and the other might have been made by coming up around."

"Look at 'Chicago' in these three letters?"

"Well, sir, these two letters are very much alike. They look to me as if they were written in a natural hand. There is a difference here of four days in the date, and unless he kept a *fac simile* he could not have copied the 'Chicago' so as to form such a close resemblance."

"I understand you to say that this letter of February 11, 1861 was a genuine one (showing it to the witness)."

"Yes, sir."

Having failed to dislodge the witness's statement, Bradley then went directly to the jury, acting as if they were to disregard the witness's testimony and asked them, "Here look at this and form your own opinion!"

"Here, here," said Mr. Wilson. "This is not the proper course to pursue! You can't just disregard a witness's testimony because you don't like it!"

Somewhat sheepishly, Bradley responded, "I simply called the jury's attention to the fact that they might, by comparison, form their own opinion with regard to the letters. We do not doubt that the letters were written in a disguised and fictitious hand, but we want the jury to make up their own minds."

Wilson then called John N. Goode who indicated that he lived in Chicago and was introduced to Miss Harris in the fall of 1863. "I saw her nearly every week in Chicago in the fall of 1863. I do not see much difference in her manner. She is not as cheerful, has not so much hair on her head, looks paler and is not so fleshy, but I see no material change."

"What was the occasion when you saw her?"

"I was then at a friend's house where she was. There was some little card playing and one thing and another. She seemed very cheerful that evening – seemed to enjoy herself very much. I played cards with her there for a little while. Her manner when I last saw her in Chicago, about an hour or two before she started for Baltimore, was about the same as it was that night. She was living at the time I first saw her at Mrs. Lacey's, on Monroe Street."

Mr. Carrington inquired, "Did you notice any indications of ill-health on the part of Miss Harris?"

"I did not at that time observe any indications of ill-health, either mentally or bodily. I saw nothing at all remarkable in her conduct. During the whole time I was acquainted with her I observed no remarkable incident that attracted my particular attention. She told me she was going to Baltimore, and stated she expected to be back in the course of ten days, or two weeks at the farthest. She did not say in whose company she was going nor did she ever in any conversation allude to Mr. Burroughs."

"Do you wish to cross-examine the witness, Mr. Bradley?" asked Judge Wiley.

"Cross-examination waived, your honor," replied Bradley.

The prosecution called the deceased's brother, Reverend Doctor John C. Burroughs to the stand. Mr. Wilson began the questioning, "State your profession and how you are presently engaged."

"I am a clergyman and at present acting as President of the University of Chicago."

"How long have you been President of that

University?"

"Since 1858."

"How long had your brother resided in Chicago before coming to Washington?"

"My impression is he came to Chicago in the early spring of 1860."

"Have you ever seen the accused before?

"I suppose I have seen the accused before. I have not seen the face of the party here since I have been in court, and therefore cannot identify her."

"Will the defendant please raise her veil?" asked Judge Wiley. Mary only partially complied with his request, raising her veil just above her nose and dropping it quickly.

"Do you know the prisoner?"

"I caught a glimpse of her features."

Bradley interjected, contentiously, "If the witness states that a lady called to see him in September, 1863, under the name of Miss Harris, we admit that the prisoner is the person."

Wilson continued, "State whether or not, in September 1863, a person called to see you in Chicago relative to two anonymous letters. State what occurred at that interview and whether or not these letters, dated September 8th and 12th, were the subject of conversation."

"I do not think I would be able to identify the person from that glimpse of her features. I will state, however, that in September, 1863 two ladies called on me in Chicago, one of whom introduced herself to me as Miss Harris. Miss Harris then introduced me to the other lady."

"Do you recognize any person present as the one to whom you were introduced?"

"I do not remember the name by which she introduced her, nor do I recognize any person here, or have I since seen any person whom I recognize as that lady for the reason that I have no distinct recollection of the features of the other lady. I did not regard her sufficiently at the time to fix her features in my mind at all."

"What time in September was this?"

"It was either the 16th of September or within one or two days of that. After the introduction, Miss Harris put to me the question whether my brother were in town or not. My reply was that he was not, that he had been in town but had left for Washington. She then produced one or two letters – I am unable to say which – stating to me that she had reason to believe that they or it was written by my brother. I asked her if I might see the letter or letters. She handed it to me and I read it or them."

"Just refer to the letters you have there, and state whether they are the ones which were shown to you?"

After carefully reading the Greenwood letters, Dr. Burroughs said, "They are. After reading the letters, I said to Miss Harris, 'Those letters were not written by my brother. The handwriting is not only not his, but he could not counterfeit such handwriting as that.' I then continued, 'Miss Harris, you have known my brother a good while, and you are acquainted with his handwriting.'

"I said further, that at the date of the first letter, September 8, my brother was in Washington, while this was a drop letter – dropped in the Chicago post office at that time, as shown by the stamp on it. I said, 'I know that this is so, and can swear to it.' I gave the reasons why I knew it: that I had correspondence from him, and knew when he left Washington and arrived in Chicago.

"I then turned to her and said: 'Miss Harris, I wish to know whether, in the long time that my brother has been acquainted with you, he has ever said anything to you or made any dishonorable proposition – that was the language I used – that justifies you in entertaining such a suspicion of him?' To which she replied he had not, and continued – with considerable feeling, as I observed – to say that he had always been her truest friend and had never said a word or done an act which was not in the highest honor; that she regretted that she had entertained the suspicion, and that it never would have entered her mind, but that it had been suggested by others, and that she could not think who else could have written them.

"Then she added, that neither the handwriting nor the circumstances justified her suspicion. That is the substance, but not the language she used. However, it is the exact substance. She then reiterated her regret that she had called on this errand, and requested me never to mention the circumstances to my brother. I told her I would not, with the understanding that the subject were dropped.

"I have omitted a circumstance which occurs to me at this moment. After asking her, as I have stated, whether he had ever done anything that justified her in the suspicion, I asked her further, whether he had violated any engagement to her? She disclaimed any such violation of engagement but added that there was a long correspondence, and that she had letters, or a letter, of his with her then. I asked her if I might see any she had and she thereupon produced one and handed it to me. I read it and then said to her, 'That is Judson's letter.' After expressing to her my regret that she should have had any pain or trouble on this account, she retired. I have not seen her from that day to this, to my knowledge."

"What opportunities did you have to become acquainted with the handwriting of your brother?"

"I taught him writing and have seen him write a great deal. I have written with him on trial to see which could form the best letters and to indicate to each other our modes of forming them. I criticized his handwriting a great deal shortly before his death, pointing out to him faults and errors in his mode of forming letters. I particularly found fault with him because he did not write plainly. He had kept books for me, made out bills, copied papers of various kinds and descriptions for me, and, of course, has corresponded with me very largely, from all of which I have obtained a knowledge of his handwriting and his mode of forming letters."

"Look at these two letters, dated the 8th and 12th of September and state, in your opinion, they are or are not in the handwriting of your brother."

"As I said at that time I say now, that they are not in the handwriting of my brother."

"Will you state at what time in September, 1863, your brother arrived in the city of Chicago."

"To the best of my knowledge, on Friday morning, September 11th."

"Lest there be any misunderstanding will you be good enough to state how long it takes a person leaving here on the morning of one day to arrive in Chicago by the ordinary course of travel?"

"It takes thirty-six hours, I think, to go from Washington to Chicago."

"State when he left Chicago, how long he remained during that visit, and where he stopped at?"

"He stopped at different places: at Mr. Bobb's, at my own boarding place, at the Lake-View House, some four or five miles out of town."

"When did he leave Chicago?"

"On the evening of the 15th of September, at, I think, six o'clock, p. m."

"On the 14th of September was any inquiry made of you as to your brother by a lady?"

"None, to my recollection."

Mr. Wilson asked the Court to direct Mr. Bradley to allow him to view the package of 92 letters. He had asked Mr. Bradley for them and had been refused. He wanted to know if he could not examine them under the eye of the

Court or of the clerk. Bradley did not think the prosecution should be allowed to see all letters in the bundle since only those which had been read were in evidence. The Court decided that the prosecution could only make use of such letters as had been read in the hearing of the Court.

Dr. Burroughs corrected his testimony, saying that an introduction to Miss Harris was unnecessary since he had met her a couple of times before. He also corrected the time his brother arrived in Chicago from 1860 to 1861. It being late in the day, the Court was adjourned.

Richardson remarked to Douglas as they descended the stairs to head for the streetcars, "Danenhower took an analytic approach to the handwriting, much more like the experts and much more credible than the claims of the Devlins. The Reverend Doctor Burroughs, who certainly would be well acquainted with his brother's handwriting, further substantiated his conclusion that the Greenwood letters were not written by Burroughs. I think the prosecution gained some ground there."

"Danenhower also was able to nail down the date that Burroughs left Washington, which was after the first Greenwood letter was mailed in Chicago," said Douglas. "That makes it unlikely that Burroughs could have written and mailed it, unless he had an accomplice."

Richardson added, "Then there is the question of Mr. Goode, who said he saw Mary every week in the fall of 1863. That makes him sound very much like a suitor and puts the lie to the claims of the defense that Mary entertained the attentions of no other men. But that wasn't clearly spelled out by the prosecution."

"I thought Burroughs' brother sounded rather hostile and contentious, don't you?"

"Yes," said Richardson, "he didn't sound very appealing in a personal sense, but that shouldn't detract from what he could attest to. It seemed to pass by the lawyers for the prosecution, but I found it interesting that he quoted Mary as saying that the claim that Burroughs wrote the Greenwood letters was first made by someone else. Louisa Devlin testified that Mary was the one who had first noted the similarity in handwriting. He also denied the assertion made by Louisa Devlin that she had gone to see the Reverend on the 14th of September. Of course, he could be lying about that but I fail to see how that would benefit him."

"The fact that Bradley wouldn't allow Carrington to see all the Burroughs letters, except for those already read in court," said Douglas, "makes me suspicious that something is being hidden by the defense, or at least that they think it would create an impression they don't want bandied about or that it might contradict an impression they have deliberately created."

"Yes, and isn't it strange that Judge Wiley would rule so strongly in favor of the defense. How could more information about the relationship between Harris and Burroughs, other than the picture that Bradley presented, possibly bias the trial? I'm beginning to think that the judge has fallen prey to the charms of the defendant and the beguiling words of the defense."

Gerald D. Otis

CHAPTER 11

Miss Harris was brought into the Court with her usual entourage shortly after 10 o'clock on the eighth day of the trial. There were more observers than on any of the previous days and an even greater number of women seated within the railings, along with reporters such as Douglas and Richardson.

Judge Wiley denied Bradley's request to postpone cross-examination of Dr. Burroughs because it would be an unusual proceeding, so Bradley initiated the questioning.

"You said yesterday that you could not identify the prisoner from the slight glimpse you had of her face. I will now ask Miss Harris to raise her veil." She exposed her facial features. "Look at her now and see if you recognize her?"

"I think I do."

"What raises any hesitation in your mind as to recognition?"

"I never saw Miss Harris more than two or three times, I should think."

"Did she not spend an evening at your house with

your brother, previous to that time?"

"Not at my house."

"When I said at your house I mean at the University, the place where you resided, and which was under your control, as I understand?"

"It was not under my control."

"You lived there?"

"Yes, sir."

"Was there any company there by your invitation?"

"No, sir."

"No persons there upon your invitation?"

"It would be impossible for me to say – whether on that occasion – I cannot remember distinctly whether Miss Harris was there or not, it being a public occasion, of which public notices were issued. I may or may not have invited some persons."

"Did she not spend the evening at that place on a private occasion?"

"Not to my knowledge."

"Who came with her at the time to which you have referred, and who was with her?"

"I do not know who came with her."

"Who did you see in company with her there?"

"I have only an impression, sir, that she was introduced – probably to myself, more certainly to members of my family, by my brother."

"Did you or not see her repeatedly after that time, and before September, 1863."

"The instances were repeated after that, one, two, or three times. I could not say definitely how many."

"Were they or not sufficiently frequent for you to know her when you saw her – to recognize her at once?"

"Not at once, sir. The occasion I alluded to on the 16th, or one, two, or three following days in September, I did not recognize her at first view, but before the introduction of herself was through I did recognize her."

"After you saw her at the University, and when, as your impression is, she was introduced to your family, or to yourself, and probably by your brother, and after seeing her several times after September, 1863, did you not recognize her as you met her in the street?"

"I never recollect to have met her in the street."

"Where did you meet her?"

"Only on the occasions to which I have referred, as far as I can remember."

"Can you fix the date you saw her at the University?"

"To the best of my knowledge it was in the month of June, 1861. I cannot be perfectly positive as to the month."

"Can you fix, with any degree of certainty, the subsequent periods when she called at the University, and you saw her?"

"I do not think I could even tell the years."

"Do you know where she was living at the time she spent that evening at the University?"

"I do not, but I think I heard."

"Was she or not living at Sheldon & Company's booksellers there?"

"Not to my knowledge."

"You never saw her there?"

"Not to my knowledge. It is a place where I did not go very frequently – not once in three or four years before."

"Had you any conversation with Mr. S. Sheldon in relation to Miss Harris?"

"Yes, sir, one that was introduced by himself."

"Were you aware at the time you saw her at that social meeting that a long correspondence had been going on between her and your brother?"

"I had not the slightest idea of any correspondence between them."

"When did you first learn of it?"

"In this court."

"Then what did you mean when you said to Miss Harris, 'Miss Harris you have known my brother a good while, and you are acquainted with his handwriting.' How did you know she had known your brother for a long time, and was acquainted with his handwriting?"

"My answer to that is that I did not know. I do not remember the particular expressions used as I stated yesterday, but I had understood from my brother in general terms that from the time he introduced her there, in 1861, she was an acquaintance of his and had been for some considerable time past, and presumed that letters had passed between them. I also knew it from the fact that she alluded to it at the time; the letter, perhaps, being more particularly the basis of any knowledge I had in regard to correspondence."

Bradley read from the previous day's testimony and said, "By the testimony I have read it appears it was after this remark of yours that she spoke of the correspondence between your brother and herself, and not until afterwards, so it could not have been from what she said."

"She at the outset, or nearly at the outset, of the conversation, it will be remembered, presented me with two letters, saying that she had reason to believe they were from my brother, implying that she knew my brother's handwriting and had had correspondence with him."

"Please state whether anything was said in that interview of your brother having been married that day or the day before?"

"I think there was not."

"In point of fact, was he married on the 15th of September?"

"He was."

"Prior to his marriage had anybody called upon you to inquire whether he was in town?"

"Oftentimes."

"The day before his marriage?"

"Not to my recollection."

"Do you recollect of a lady calling to see you and inquiring whether he was in town, and after traversing the room, walking its full length, you replied saying he was not in town?"

"When?"

"On the 14th of September."

"I have no recollection of any lady calling on that day. I recollect of repeatedly standing and walking about the floor when persons, among others, ladies, have called, and remember that was my manner when Miss Harris and the other ladies called on the 16th or the two or three following days of September. I walked the floor because I was called from to attend to their inquires; was annoyed at being interrupted, which interruption was contrary to my instructions to servants; and I wished to indicate by this manner of mine to those who called that I did not sit down for an interview."

"Is your memory perfectly distinct that this interview with Miss Harris was not as early as the 15th of September? Where were you on the afternoon of the 15th of September?"

"I cannot recollect my movements. It must have been in the afternoon – after twelve o'clock – when I left the University to go to the center of the city – some three or four miles distant."

"At what time did the marriage take place?"

"The time between leaving the University and the occurrence of the marriage was spent by myself in making some purchases – clothing for myself which I wore to the wedding – a pair of shoes, and some gifts for the parties. I arrived at the house where I performed the marriage ceremony, I remember, at precisely four o'clock, though they claimed it was six minutes past that hour."

"Did your brother not start from that house for the

railroad?"

"He did."

"Did you not leave the house about the same time and go back to your residence?"

"I left the house with the wedding party, went with them to the depot, saw the party start on the cars at about six o'clock, and then proceeded to my residence."

"Nothing was said the next day when you saw Miss Harris about your brother having been married the day before?"

"Understand me. I do not say it was the day afterwards. When the interview occurred nothing was said about it, I think."

"Can you describe about the age and the appearance of the lady who came with Miss Harris?"

"I have only a faint image of her in my mind. I remember the part of the room where she sat, and have a faint, but only a faint recollection of her features. I should judge her, from the image I have in my mind, to have been a woman of from thirty to thirty-five years."

"Was she small or large?"

"It is my impression that she was rather slender, and pretty tall. I wish distinctly to state that those are very floating, faint impressions."

"Did you know either of the Misses Devlin by sight at that time?"

"I am not aware that I did. I was not aware that I knew the Misses Devlin until I saw them in this court."

"I understood you to say yesterday that you had never read either of these letters of September 8 and 12 until they were handed to you on the stand and never heard them read."

"I stated I had not read them, though I have repeatedly had them in my hand here. I had read clauses in them, but only one or two short clauses."

"When those letters were read by me, when standing

by the witness, were you not sitting where the gentleman with the white coat is, and making a memorandum in a little book?"

"I could not say. I have made memoranda here in court. As to hearing Mr. Bradley, I will say, that I have found it difficult, sitting there, by the desk of the District Attorney, to hear a good deal that transpired here."

"You have no recollection of having heard them read?"

"I have a faint impression that I was aware that they were being read."

"Is that impression any thing like as strong as the facts you have stated about that conversation and interview happening in September, 1863 – only two years ago?"

"No, sir. It is not."

"I will ask you, sir, if you were not entirely aware, in the spring of 1863, of a correspondence going on between your brother and Miss Harris?"

"I am unable to recollect any thing further than what I have already stated on that subject."

"You said yesterday that, in that interview, Miss Harris disclaimed the fact of any engagement existing between your brother and herself. I will ask you whether you have not said on more than one occasion that you were aware there was an engagement between them – and that her want of education was the impediment to marriage."

"I have not."

"Do you know Miss Ann Riordan of Chicago?"

"I have met a Miss Riordan since my brother's death and have spoken with her twice since that time in the store where she attends."

"Did you or not go to see her in order to get evidence in relation to this case?"

"I went to see Miss Riordan in order to learn what facts she knew bearing on this case."

"In the course of the conversation with her did you or not tell her that you were aware of an existing engagement between these parties, but that the defective education of Miss Harris was a sufficient reason for not carrying it out?"

"I did not."

"Nor any thing to that effect?"

"Nor to that effect. I may have said something in some slight degree approximating that, which I could detail to you if the jury wish. As near as I can recall what I said to Miss Riordan in any way bearing on that point was that I was aware the parties – my brother and Miss Harris – had been acquainted. I cannot remember any expressions but my general idea was that they had been acquainted with each other – perhaps interested in each other, and think it very likely that I may have said that I presumed my brother might have entertained the thoughts of marrying her, but when circumstances changed, and he was unable to afford Miss Harris the means of education, he abandoned the idea. I presume I have said that to Miss Riordan. I have said it repeatedly since the occurrence, as a presumption, and not based on knowledge."

"Did you or not write a letter to the Reverend Mr. Johnson of Burlington, Iowa, with a view to engage his assistance in procuring evidence for this case?"

"I wrote to the Rev. Mr. Johnson, I recollect, making inquires in regard to this case. Whether asking his assistance or not I do not know. I may have done so."

"Did he decline?"

"He did not."

"Have you the letter here?"

"I have one letter of his here, but not that one."

"After receiving that letter from Mr. Johnson, did you visit Burlington?"

"I did."

"Did you go to Burlington for the purpose of getting up evidence to affect Miss Harris on this trial?"

"I went to Burlington for the purpose of ascertaining what facts might bear upon the explanation and final trial of this case."

"Do you know a gentleman in Burlington – perhaps residing a little outside of town – by the name of Judge Newman?"

"I know a Judge Newman."

"Did you visit him with that purpose?"

"Yes, sir."

"Did you or not, in that interview, state to Judge Newman that your brother was engaged to Miss Harris at one time, but in consequence of her defective education and his want of means, failing in business, that the marriage had not been consummated?"

"I did not."

"Or words to that effect?"

"Nor words to that effect."

"What did you say to him?"

"I stated to him my theory of their relations. Just what I have previously stated, and received his reply."

"You did not tell him that you knew they had corresponded for a long time, that you believed or knew they were engaged to be married, and that the marriage had not been effected by reason of her want of education and your brother's want of means, or words to that effect?"

"As to the effect of all of the words that you have used?"

"Yes, sir, as to the whole or any part."

"As to any part of them: you inquire as to whether I told him I knew they had corresponded. Without remembering positively, I presume that I used the expression, 'I was aware they had known each other, and corresponded,' as I have often expressed myself on other occasions; otherwise not to that effect."

"Did you, during the past spring or summer, visit Janesville, Wisconsin where the Misses Devlin reside, for the purpose of procuring testimony for this case?"

"I visited Janesville, Wisconsin for the same reason I visited Washington."

"Did you, at Janesville, have a conversation with a Mr. Dame, who, I think, is an auctioneer?"

"Not to my knowledge. I know nothing about a man by that name, nor about any auctioneer in Janesville."

"You never then did say to Mr. Dame that if he would come here and testify his expenses would be paid, and it would be worth $200 to him?"

"I never spoke to any such man that I know of."

"Did you, while in Janesville, procure the attendance of any witnesses to come here?"

"I did not."

"At whose insistence, then, were the two witnesses, Mr. Strong and Mr. Mosely, summoned here?"

"The history of that matter is that, at the time I was in Janesville I called upon the District Attorney there and asked his advice as to what was proper in this case, that having been the home of the party who had shot my brother. He referred me to the United States Marshall, Mr. Burbee, as a party who would know more, or be able to ascertain facts better, than any one else. I do not remember in what precise form he put it. I saw Mr. Burbee, and requested him to look up the facts in this case – everything bearing upon it. He has done so from time to time, and on being advised that this trial had opened, in Chicago, I wrote – or telegraphed, I think – to Mr. Burbee, to send any witnesses that he knew of, or such witnesses as he had previously indicated. I cannot tell in what form I put the expression."

"Did you or not see those witnesses in Janesville yourself?"

"I saw Mr. Mosely, and I may have seen Mr. Strong, but not to my recollection."

"Did you make inquires of anybody in Chicago besides Miss Riordan concerning the bringing of witnesses here on the part of the prosecution?"

"Yes, sir."

"Did you see Mr. Goode there?"

"I did."

"Did you have an interview with him on this subject?"

"I did."

"Did you learn from him what he would testify to?"

"I did, in general."

"Did you see Mr. Hartwell?"

"I did."

"Learn from him what he would testify to?"

"In general."

"When Mr. Hartwell was about to come here, did you furnish him with the money to come?"

"I did not."

"Did you give him an order to get money for it?"

"I wrote a note at the depot as I was starting for Chicago. Mr. Goode replied to me that Mr. Hartwell had not the means at hand of paying his railroad fare. I wrote a note to a gentleman asking him if he would see that Mr. Hartwell had the means of paying his railroad fare, or something to that effect."

"Did you not give Mr. Hartwell an order on a gentleman in Chicago, whose name you will recall if it is so, for the money to pay his expenses in coming on here?"

"I have answered just what occurred on that subject."

"To whom did you give that memorandum?"

"To Mr. Goode."

"To whom was it addressed?"

"To Mr. L. C. B. Freer, of Chicago."

"Commonly called Judge Freer?"

"Yes, sir."

"You wrote a note to him to furnish how much?"

"I do not think I specified a sum. I may have done so."

"Had you seen or conferred with them before as to the testimony they could give?"

"I had, both of them."

"Any other person in Chicago?"

"Yes, sir."

"Did you employ an agent in Chicago to obtain some information in regard to it?"

"I did not, with the exception of asking my counsel there to make an inquiry for me. I do not know whether I was employing him or not, for I am unable to say whether he did or did not charge for his service."

"Had you been to see persons whom you requested him to see before?"

"There occurs to me one person whom I had seen whom I afterwards requested him to see, and it is possible I might think of others by taking time. The one that occurs to me is Mr. Lambert."

"Who else?"

"None others occur to me."

"Miss Riordan?"

"I never asked Judge Freer to see her. I think / have been to see her."

"Do you not know that after you had visited these parties some one dressed as a gentleman, at your instance, went around and represented himself to be Mr. Bradley, her counsel from Washington, come on her account to obtain information?"

"I know that no one ever did it at my instance and I know of no one ever having done it at all. The first I heard of it was the other day from you in open court. No, I think Dr. Fitch had mentioned the same thing to me the night before, or shortly before, that that impression existed."

"As a friendly service have you asked any one to go to

the same persons whom you had previously visited and see them in regard to this case, or employed any one to do so?"

"I cannot at this moment remember any other persons than Miss Riordan, whom I had visited with a view of making her a witness, and the witness Lambert. As I said before, I believe I asked Mr. Freer to see him. I think I asked Mr. Goode and Mr. Lambert, one or both, as they were acquaintances, friends, as I understand it, to Miss Riordan, to see her in regard to it, whether she was willing to come here or not. With that exception I am unable to remember any instance of the kind. It is possible some may occur to me."

"During your inquires in Chicago did you become acquainted with a woman named Ellen Mills – see her?"

"I did not. I heard of her."

"Ascertain where she lived?"

"I heard where she lived."

"You say you started for this place last week, on the 5th of July, and you say prior to that you did not request or employ any one, or send any one to see her?"

"I had spoken to a person, a policeman, and told him it might become necessary to see her."

"Who was that policeman?"

"Mr. Douglas."

"When did you learn from Douglas that she lived at 94 Quincy Street?"

"Well, about a month ago, without being at all positive."

"Did you promise Douglas any compensation for his services?"

"He had rendered no service. I did not retain him for service."

"Was anything said between you as to compensation?"

"Not by me."

"Well, by him?"

"He made allusion to the subject at the time, it occurs to me – a sort of supposition in regard to the matter. As near as I remember his expression was that the witness was a loose and worthless woman; that he did not believe she would ever come here, and that by spending a little money – the matter of $100 or $200 – he could get on the same train with her and take her to any place he had a mind to."

"What did you say in regard to that?"

"I made no reply that I remember. It was a mere allusion of his."

"Let me interrupt and call a short recess here," said judge Wylie.

CHAPTER 12

The defense continued with the questioning of Dr. Burroughs.

"You say that your brother arrived in Chicago on the morning of the 11th of September, 1863. Where did he go on Friday night?"

"I did not positively fix the 11th as the day of his arrival."

"Where did he go the first day he came there?"

"I do not personally know of his movements. I only have it from tradition."

"Cannot you say whether or not on the day of his arrival in Chicago he came to your house?"

"I could not say that because I have already said that it was only to the best of my knowledge that he arrived there that day."

"Cannot you state that he came to that house the day on which he did arrive?"

"On the day on which he did arrive, according to the best of my knowledge, I think he passed the night at my house, but of this I am not certain."

"Where was he on the next day – Saturday?"

"In the after part of Saturday he visited me at my boarding place, in company with his intended wife and another friend or two."

"Where did he stay the night?"

"I am not positive. My impression is that after accompanying the ladies home, he returned and passed the night at my house."

"Where was he on Sunday?"

"I am not positive about his stopping at my house on either Friday or Saturday, but if he did he left our house on Sunday morning."

"When did he return?"

"It is very uncertain in my mind. I think he returned and passed Sunday night at our house and went into town with me on Monday morning."

"Where did he stay Monday night – the night of the day before his marriage?"

"I have no recollection of that subject."

"Where did he dress for his marriage on the afternoon of Tuesday?"

"I do not know."

"Were you actively interested in the fact of that marriage – taking a great deal of interest in it?"

"Yes, sir."

"Will you state how you can recollect with so much distinctness all that passed at the time Miss Harris called to see you, and yet your memory be so indistinct in regard to this matter of your brother, about which you were so much interested?"

"Yes, sir. I will state how it is. The reasons why I remember so distinctly what occurred at the interview with Miss Harris are that on inquiring for my brother, and on her producing those anonymous or fictitious letters, saying that she had reason to believe that he wrote them, I was considerably startled; and the thought flashed across my mind that my brother having been acquainted with this girl, as I knew the notice of his marriage in the paper had attracted her attention; and that she likely felt that she had some claims upon him, and had come on that account.

"The impression of these circumstances, as is natural, I think, very vividly fixed in my mind the connection between the appearance of the marriage notice in the papers, and their call. I therefore could not fail to remember it; while the other matters being of no particular consequence, and being very much occupied always, I gave myself no concern about them."

"I will ask you in connection with this matter, if you did not introduce your brother to the lady who afterwards became his wife?"

"I do not know that I introduced him."

"And not present when he was introduced?"

"I do not know where, and on what occasion he was introduced. She was in the immediate neighborhood of my residence when my brother lived with me. When he was first introduced to her I do not know."

Judge Wiley called a short recess, apparently to attend to an urgent need, during which Douglas and Richardson remained in their seats.

"What on earth is going on here?" asked Douglas. "He can't identify Miss Harris? He quibbles about the place where he lives? He can't remember events and can't hear what was said in court? He has only vague impressions or faint images? He splits hairs in his responses to questions and then ends up answering them anyway. He seems to be so obstructionist in dealing with the defense that it almost sounds like he is hiding something or is guilty about something."

"He certainly is not making a good impression on the jury," said Richardson. "He appears to be trying to avoid answering questions about his involvement in finding witnesses in Janesville and Burlington. I wonder if the

Reverend Burroughs and Carrington didn't talk about this before he went to those places. In fact, I have a hunch that the DA may have been trying to get around congressional restrictions by having the preacher do the leg work and pay for the witness's travel if they needed it."

"Now that wouldn't surprise me," said Douglas. "The defense did score some points by implying that the reverend had hired someone to pass himself off as Bradley to get information about the case. And they did jump on the insinuation that Ellen Mills was paid to disappear for a while, although I think the reverend may have offered the quotation from the police officer as an illustration of how she was a loose woman and would be an unreliable witness. He seemed surprised when they twisted the quote to imply that he had paid for her silence."

"It will be interesting to see how all these young men will testify – Mosely, Strong, Goode, Hartwell. Were they all Mary's suitors? Even if they just met and knew her, it casts doubt on the notion that Mary was interested only in Burroughs."

Judge Wiley returned to the courtroom and took his seat on the bench. "The defense may resume its cross-examination of the witness."

Bradley asked Reverend Burroughs, "Since you have been here do you recollect any conversation that you have had with any of the witnesses from Chicago or Janesville, on the subject of the testimony they would give?"

"Mr. Strong, Mr. Mosely, Mr. Goode and myself came on together – that is, I met Mr. Mosely and Mr. Strong in the cars. Mr. Goode and myself stopped at the same hotel, and we have met incidentally since, but not by any arrangement. The matter of the testimony has been alluded to."

"You have mentioned three – are there not four?"

"Yes, sir. Mr. Goode, Mr. Lambert – no Mr. Hartwell – I am reminded by that that I have confounded the names of Mr. Lambert and Mr. Hartwell in my testimony once before – Mr. Mosely and Mr. Strong."

"Do you mean to say you did not have an interview with Lambert, the policeman?"

"I had an interview with both Lambert and Hartwell but I remember that I have interchanged their names in the testimony before, as I did just now."

"State whether you have had any conversation with any of the witnesses summoned from Chicago or Janesville, since you have been here, about the testimony they would give in this case?"

"In a general way."

"Explain what you mean by 'in a general way'?"

"I have not sat down for a cross-examination of all the points that would be embraced in their testimony, but have understood from them in a general way what would be its bearing, and I think very likely that I have communicated what would be the bearing of mine."

"Have you or not said to some one or more of them, 'However this case may look now, wait till you are examined' or words to that effect?"

"Something like that it occurs to me was said when, the other day after the adjournment of court, the remark was made that the testimony was pretty strong, and I said that the other side was yet to come, or perhaps I said that the rebutting witnesses are yet to give their testimony."

"Do you recollect of having asked any one of them what the effect was out of doors, and your reply to him, 'Wait till you are examined'?"

"I remember a conversation with one or more of the witnesses, whom I met on the street, regarding the general impression of this case in the community, and remarked, when he gave his impression of the general feeling outside of this community, that the rebutting testimony was yet to come. I do not recollect of saying to any one 'Wait until you are examined' or anything of the kind."

Judge Hughes took over from Mr. Bradley. "Did you understand, at the time the policeman talked to you about this Mrs. Mills, that her testimony was material to this case – that she was sought for as a witness of the defense?"

"I understood that she was sought for as a witness for the defense."

"Then you fully understood that when these remarks were made, spending of a couple of hundred dollars to take her out of the way, that it was carrying off a witness whose testimony was desired?"

"I did."

"You made no reply?"

"None that I remember."

"There was no expression of disapprobation on your part?"

"None whatever."

"How long was it after the marriage until your brother's wife returned to make her first visit to her friends?"

"He was married on the 15th of September. She returned to make her first visit the following summer, arriving, I think, in July."

"Did he come with her."

"He did not."

"Do you know whether he went part of the way from Washington?"

"I know nothing only what I have heard him and her say."

"How long after that until he came to Chicago?"

"He arrived in Chicago in the month of September, I think."

"His wife was then in Chicago, was she not?"

"Yes, sir. He stayed fully three weeks, part of the time at his father-in-laws and he spent a week with me a little distance outside of Chicago."

"Did he inform you, about the time of his contemplated marriage with his wife, of any embarrassment that he felt in consequence of his relations with Miss Harris?"

"He did not."

"Was your brother's relation to Miss Harris ever the subject of conversation between you previous to his marriage?"

"I do not think it was."

"Was it afterwards?"

"Yes, sir. It was casually alluded to."

"Was your brother very expert with the pen?"

"I considered him so."

"Was he capable of varying it?"

"I do not think he was very much."

"Do you know who wrote the letter of September 8?"

"I do not, nor that of September 12."

"Did you see when Miss Harris visited you a likeness of your brother?"

"Yes. Miss Harris showed it to me."

"Did you endeavor to get it from her?"

"I have an indistinct recollection that I said to her casually that I would like to have that."

"Your witness," said Hughes, glancing at the District Attorney.

Carrington began by asking, "You have been asked, sir, in reference to your visit to different places. I suppose you felt it was your duty to have this case thoroughly investigated as far as you could?"

"My motives, as far as I understand them, were principally these: that in the presentation of this matter at the time of its occurrence, and as I understood it was to be presented by the defense, my brother's reputation and character were more or less involved; and at the request of his widow, for the sake of his child, I could not feel otherwise than interested so far as it affected his reputation in having those things cleared up."

"Was he the only brother you had?"

"Yes, sir."

"I would ask if you offered at any time to pay witnesses to come here, made any proposition of the kind, or encouraged others to do so?"

"No, sir."

Bradley interjected, "State whether you have or not said that this whole thing was founded in a conspiracy which you intended to explore, or words to that effect?"

"Objection, your honor," Carrington yelled out.

"Sustained," ruled Judge Wiley.

"I wish to reserve an exception to that ruling," Bradley stated.

"So noted," said Wiley.

Bradley tried again, "State whether you have not industriously sought evidence to taint the character of the accused."

"Objection, your honor! Dr. Burroughs is not on trial here!"

"Sustained," said the judge.

"I again wish to reserve an exception," said Bradley.

"Duly noted," said Wiley.

"The prosecution calls Mrs. E. A. Flemming," said Mr. Wilson. The witness came forward. "Please tell the court how you know the accused, Miss Harris."

"I reside at No. 142 Lexington Street, Baltimore. My acquaintance with Miss Harris was on the 6th of January last. She came to my house to board. She said her business was to go to Washington, that she was not well, and she was stopping in Baltimore for she did not know how long. Her object in going to Washington, she said, was to collect money for the Misses Devlin – the ladies by whom she was employed. That was what she told me the first evening she came there. Miss Devlin used to do business in Baltimore before going to Chicago. The prisoner remained at our house until the 30th day of January, the day she came to Washington."

"State what her habits were while visiting you, whether or not she visited places of amusement and with whom?"

"She did not visit any places particularly. Well, she used to go out occasionally to evening entertainments."

"In whose society?"

"That of Mr. Devlin, brother of the lady with whom she was engaged. He was the only gentleman she ever went out with."

"What did she say regarding her visit to Washington subsequent to the day you have mentioned?"

"She said she intended to come down and sue an old lover for a breach of promise. That she had been engaged to him for seven years, and that he had married another young lady, but had corresponded with her up to within a month of his marriage. She thought what induced him to marry this lady in Chicago was the fact of her having money. Her object in instituting a suit she said was merely to clear herself and let the world see that she was a virtuous girl."

"Did she assign any other reason for bringing this suit?"

"Well, she said something about two anonymous letters that she had received, signed Greenwood."

"Did she say anything further about the lady he had married?"

"She merely said that the father of this young lady was very wealthy, and she had understood and believed that Mr. Burroughs loved her, but married the other one because she was rich. She always held him, Mr.

Burroughs, in very high estimation – always speaking very
well of him."

"State what she said in regard to the delicacy, the
modesty, or propriety of Mr. Burroughs's treatment of
her?"

"Objection, your honor," said Bradley.

"Overruled, the witness will answer the question,"
replied Wiley.

"She said that she had always received the treatment
of a father from him, and looked up to him as such,
putting the utmost confidence in him. He had never
wronged her she said."

"State what she said in regard to still being in the
employment of the Misses Devlin and as to the payment
of her expense by them?"

"Objection!"

"Sustained."

"Will you state whether you observed on the day the
prisoner left Baltimore anything remarkable in her
deportment?"

"I do not know. I did the evening previous to her
coming to Washington. The Rev. Mr. Dudley was at the
house and while he was playing a hymn on the piano in
the parlor, she got up, picked up one of the ornaments in
the parlor, and went around to take up a collection. I
thought that very strange conduct."

"Did you observe that she was at that time unwell, or
complained of any disease, and if so, state what?"

"Yes, sir. She complained very much of her throat and
complained of being very weak. She had very little
appetite."

"Did you observe any thing else that was remarkable
in her conduct?"

"Yes, sir. Sometimes she would be sitting alone
apparently engaged in deep thought, and then she would
get up and all at once commence to sing a love song –

'First she loved him as a brother,

And he doubted her when her love was stronger.'

Then she would come to where I was, and appear to be in a very good humor."

The prosecution called Dr. John Frederick May, past Chair of Surgery, Columbia College and a physician that had been in practice in Washington for many years. Mr. Carrington posed a hypothetical case for the doctor's opinion.

"In the case of a young woman of highly nervous organization and vivacious temperament, and who has suffered from a disappointment in love, there is observed at intervals of greater or less regularity, at monthly periods, the following symptoms: irregular and insufficient sleep, depression of the spirits, and melancholy, outbreaks of violence of the following character – attacking a friend with whom there had been no previous quarrel with a broom, and on another occasion with a carving knife, throwing a pin cushion at a customer in the store in which she was employed, the cutting or attempted destruction of a piece of fine needle work belonging to a friend, awakening at an early hour in the morning and saying to a room mate that she must leave her, and going to walk upon the lake shore, insensibility to cold and shedding tears.

"State how frequently you have noticed in your practice such symptoms in cases of hysteria, or dysmenorrhea, and whether upon such symptoms you would infer the insanity of the patient?"

"It is impossible for me to say how frequently I have seen some of the symptoms enumerated. I have in cases of hysteria seen some symptoms like these, and others have been absent in such cases. Dysmenorrhea often occurs without any symptom that has been enumerated. But as far as answering such an abstract question as that I should say that if those symptoms occurred at the periods mentioned here, that they were symptoms of nervous excitement, dependent upon uterine irritability. I could not call that a case of insanity in the general acceptation of the term 'insanity'."

Carrington posed several interconnected questions concerning the insanity of a hypothetical patient but Voorhees objected to the witness answering. "Before he can be considered a competent witness, it should be ascertained whether or not he has made that branch of medicine a specialty. This is not to impugn the ability of the witness but because certain rules require that a professional man make a study of the subject upon which he professes to give an opinion." He argued that 'physician' as used in cases of insanity, applied only to those who made the study of the mind a specialty.

Carrington replied that the opinion of Dr. Nichols was all based upon the assumption of certain hypothetical causes, one of which was moral and the other physical and the prosecution desired to interrogate the witness relative to effects that might result from the *physical* condition of a party suffering under such causes as were stated in the question.

He further reasoned that the opinion of Dr. May and other educated physicians was worth more than the opinion of those who attended only to diseases of the mind because the former look at all physical causes for certain effects while the latter pursued but one branch.

"The defense assumes one state of facts to be fully proven and the prosecution assumes another, and they should certainly be allowed to put the question as they understand the facts. The jury is entitled to all the light they can get and the prosecution would be derelict in duty if they did not throw all possible light upon a homicide which, for its atrocity, is as the prosecution understands it, almost unparalleled in the annals of crime."

Carrington argued that Dr. Nichols gave his opinion on

a hypothetical case, the defense relying upon that hypothesis to prove the insanity of the accused. "The prosecution tries to meet that testimony and opinion, not by showing merely a hypothetical case but by adopting all the facts upon which the opinion of Dr. Nichols is based."

Mr. Hughes said this argument seemed to be but a commentary on the testimony of Dr. Nichols drawn up by the prosecution to which they desired Dr. May to swear.

Judge Wiley examined the witness, who said he was a practicing physician since 1834 and had opportunities to judge the effect of physical disease upon the mind but he stated he was not an expert on the subject of mental disease and it was not his specialty. Whenever he had a persistent and strongly developed case of insanity, he referred them to a specialist.

Judge Wiley said he was not the judge of the evidence. All he knew was that a hypothetical statement was submitted to the witness as an expert and the witness was asked whether a party thus affected was insane. The Court decided to admit the evidence but the prosecution adduced it at their own risk – it might subsequently be cast aside and the jury warned not to consider it.

Dr. May responded, "I will state that it would be with a great deal of reluctance that I would give an opinion in a case where life was involved, in regard to the mental condition of a patient, without knowing all the facts, antecedent and subsequent, connected with the case. But if the question is merely put to me as a hypothetical and abstract question, I am bound to answer it.

"I will state that, in my opinion, the antecedent condition of the patient, as mentioned in the first question, and the circumstances that are stated in the second and third questions as occurring at the time, would not, in my opinion, satisfy me of the insanity of the patient, in the general acceptation of the term, without there were facts before and afterwards to confirm that, of which I have no knowledge. The simple abstract question, as stated here, would not satisfy me that the patient was insane at the time of committing that act."

Court adjourned until the following day, Saturday, July 17, 1865. Richardson remarked to Douglas as they were leaving the building, "Well, Carrington got his own doctor to counter the testimony of Dr. Nichols."

"Yeah," said Douglas. "He did a pretty good job but the question asked of him was complicated to follow and I wonder how much of it the jury understood. Still, it ended on a positive note for the prosecution."

"But the defense continued to chip away at the Reverend Burroughs and made him look like he was colluding with the witnesses. He continued to give what seemed like evasive answers, which makes it hard to believe his testimony."

"That's true. On the other side of the fence, Mrs. Flemming testified that Mary went out with the Devlin brother while she was in Baltimore, one more strike against the claims by the Devlins and Bradley that Mary was interested only in Adoniram Judson Burroughs."

"It will be interesting to see what tomorrow brings," said Richardson.

"Yes. But right now I have to beat it back to my hotel room and finish writing my dispatch for today and get it sent off to New York on the telegraph."

CHAPTER 13

On previous days of the trial, crowds had assembled inside the railings of the bar, tending to cause a bit of confusion. Today, Judge Wiley ordered that no one be allowed to enter within the railing except members of the bar, reporters and jurors until court was opened. After that, ladies were allowed to occupy seats inside the railing. About 10:30, the prisoner accompanied by her several counsel and her lady friends was brought into the court.

Dr. May was cross-examined by Mr. Bradley. "What is insanity, Doctor?"

"While writers may make other distinctions, I think all the different forms of insanity can be classified or considered under four different types: mania, monomania, dementia, and idiocy."

"Do you acknowledge what is now called moral insanity?"

"I do."

"Is moral insanity also embraced within the four descriptions you have mentioned, except idiocy?"

"Certainly."

"Among the exciting causes of mental disturbance, is or is not disappointment in love set down as one of the prominent causes?"

"Unquestionably. I should say a very powerful cause."

"Among the physical causes producing any of these conditions of the mind, is not, in the case of females, the disease called to your notice yesterday by the District Attorney one of the marked cases?"

"I cannot in my experience recollect a case in which I could distinctly trace insanity as a result of that disease, positively. I will state this, however, that I have no doubt that where there was a tendency to insanity in a female that that disease would be more likely to develop it."

"How would it be affected by a moral cause, such as I have spoken of?"

"I should think it would aid in developing it."

"Is not paroxysmal insanity, as it is sometimes called, now a recognized subject of medical treatment?"

"Yes, sir."

"If, then, a disturbance of the mind should occur at certain periods, and when the female patient was suffering as described yesterday, the moral cause operating at the same time, when there was no shrieking or shedding of tears, but violent excitement of the mind, uncontrollable excitement, what would you say in such a case – would you call it hysteria, or dementia in any shape?"

"I consider hysteria to be a disease *sui generis*. I know there is a difference of opinion on that subject and that there are some physicians who consider hysteria as primarily existing in the brain. But I consider hysteria as a disease emanating from the uterus. I consider it affecting the brain secondarily and producing at times more or less disorder of the brain. Whether a person was suffering from hysteria or dementia would depend on circumstances. If there were antecedents that satisfied me that the patient's mind had been subject to paroxysmal insanity, I should consider that the condition you speak of was likely to develop insanity in a paroxysmal form. Hysteria is characterized by certain symptoms which cannot be mistaken."

"Have you seen cases of excitement produced by uterine disease in which the will of the patient was controlled by the disease, so that the patient was incapable of acting rationally?"

"I have, acting very irrationally."

"If, in examining into the past history of the patient, you should find instances of disturbance in the mind and the conduct of the patient at certain periodical intervals, and inquiring into the personal history of the patient, should find moral causes existing at the same time with those physical causes, would or would not that to a great extent influence your judgment, as applied to the case under examination by yourself?"

"Undoubtedly, it would."

"A hypothetical case was put to you yesterday, Doctor. Now I put one to you. It is as follows:

"A little girl not more than ten or eleven years of age – still in the dress of children of that age – attracts the attention of a man almost old enough to be her father. She had very few advantages of mental or moral culture. He is an educated man, experienced in the business and affairs of life. They are thrown into daily association, he being engaged in mercantile business, and she, the little girl, in a millinery and fancy store convenient to his place of business.

"He plays with her as a child, she sits on his knee and receives and returns his caresses which this intimacy continues between them, he being the trusted friend of the lady by whom she is employed, and is daily at her store. He fails in business, and then comes to keep and post the books of the little girl's employer. He has a difficulty in the church of which he was a member, and is expelled, and goes to this child, just budding into womanhood, for relief and sympathy. She believes him to be good – good to her, at least – but persecuted and reviled by the world. He is a Baptist; she a Roman Catholic.

"She now forms new associations. Prepared by his culture and instruction, she is admitted into the best and most refined and cultivated society of the city in which she lived. He leaves that city to seek employment elsewhere, and opens a correspondence with her, which he cautions her to conceal from her employer. She is eminently open and truthful, yet at his bidding does conceal the correspondence.

"Her parents discover that this correspondence is going on. Her father is enraged. Her friend's visits then are prohibited. She counsels with one of the most intelligent and cultivated ladies, of ripe years, and having daughters of the age of the patient, and that lady consents to permit them to meet at her house. He is now the declared lover of the patient.

"Step by step, intimacy between her and this lover had ripened into esteem, regard, and on her part the full confiding love of a woman who trusted everything to the man she loved. And she is formed, molded, trained by his plastic hand in her habits of thought, morals, and manners. She is absorbed into, and in all things controlled by him. She yields him her homage and they are engaged to be married. He keeps her constantly advised of his plans and schemes.

"Fortune frowns on his efforts and he is too poor to marry. He prevails on her to leave her father's house and come to him in a distant city and seek employment there, in order that she may be near him, and she yields. Shortly after she returns to her home. Again he prevails upon her to leave the parental roof and come to him, and she does so.

"Her nervous organization is fine and delicate, her mental faculties largely and well developed, her sense of female pride acute and strong. She is pure and virtuous, and continues so to this day. Her bodily health is remarkably good. She has more than ordinary flesh; a fine, pure complexion, and good vision. Her temperament is full of life and spirit, and her life happy, joyous, and gleeful.

"She has few associates, and those principally married ladies, or those older than herself. Her chiefest pleasure is her correspondence with him. Thus nearly five years are passed. In the meanwhile three different times had been assigned for their marriage and as often it had been deferred by reason of his want of means or employment.

"He is about to leave the city where he is residing to come to Washington in search of employment. Their correspondence had begun November 1, 1858, and continued down to the spring of 1863. When he is thus about to leave her, the last seen of them together at the time she was sitting on his knee, and he playing with her curls.

"Six months elapse. In the meanwhile he has succeeded in obtaining employment in one of the public offices here. She lives on in happy hope, and the summer passes without a ripple on her summer's sea.

"He left his home in March. On the 7th of August, 1863, she received a letter from him asking where he could see her. He had an interview with her, during the greater part of which he held her hand. What passed between them is not known, for no one heard what was said; but they seemed to part as ever – friends. On the 8th of September following she received another letter, which she believed was written by him; on the 14th a second, both begging her to meet him at a house of ill-fame. She inquired and received clear proof that these letters, though written in a disguised hand, were written by him. On being convinced of this fact, she was greatly distressed, and became wild in her excitement.

"A few days after this she discovered that four days after the receipt of the first of these letters, and one day after the receipt of the second, he was married to another lady in the town where the patient resided. Within less than a week after this discovery, on the first return of the period mentioned in the hypothetical case put by the prosecuting attorney, she was so sick as to require the attendance of a physician. A skillful physician was called, and he treated her for the physical disease, but knew nothing of her personal history, nor did he witness any mental disturbance. The sickness lasted but a few days, but her spirits were gone, her health was broken.

"She became silent, moody, melancholy; her flesh and strength wasted; her nights were spent in sleeplessness and tears. She went about her daily duties as usual, but with a broken spirit. Thus passed on two or more periods. At last her physician directed that she should lie in bed till after she had her breakfast. She then slept as she had from the first of May, 1863, in the same bed with the lady in whose employment she lived as clerk, and in the same chamber with that lady's sister. There was a vacant chamber adjoining, in which there was no fire, and against their remonstrance, she would get up from that warm bed and chamber, in the inclement climate of Chicago, in mid-winter, and go into that adjoining chamber in her nightclothes only, and sleep on the bare floor.

"During one of these periodical sicknesses, while the patient is still under medical treatment and required by her physician to keep her bed till after breakfast, in the winter time, in the high northern latitude of Chicago, and while she is occupying the same bed with the elder of the ladies with whom she lived, she stealthily got up from the bed – leaving the other, as she supposed, asleep - softly dressed herself, and approached the bedside of her friend, and believing she was still asleep, said in a low tone, 'I must leave you.' The friend threw her arms around her neck and said 'Why, where are you going?' She answered, 'I wanted to take a walk on the lake shore.' It was then but the gray of the morning, not quite day. The friend restrained her forcibly, and prevailed upon her to undress and go to bed."

Bradley went on to describe, in great detail, Mary's attack with a carving knife on Jane Devlin when the latter indicated she didn't want to read or hear any more letters from Burroughs; the apparently unprovoked attack on Jane Devlin with a window brush; Mary's throwing of a pincushion with a brick in it at a customer; her purchase of a Sharpe's four-barrel revolver, presumably to defend herself from Burroughs and his brother whom she believed were out to carry her off to a place of no return.

He told of her attempt to sue Burroughs in Chicago, that attempt frustrated by the process server's inability to find the accused party. When her attorney urged compromise, she refused saying she sought not financial gain but vindication of her character and clearing of her reputation. The attorney, Bradley reported, perceived Mary to become so excited with hate when the matter of her former lover trying to get her into a house of assignation was mentioned, that he felt it dangerous for her to meet him.

She then traveled to Washington to file a suit there but found that Judson was not at the Treasury Building, having gone to Chicago with his wife. Taking the first return train, she found that Judson's wife had arrived but he had not. The Devlin sisters moved to Janesville,

Wisconsin and Mary followed them about a month later.

"But change of scene," Bradley continued, "while it relieved and diminished the periodical exhibitions of a disturbed mind, did not cure it. Her life was the same – a brooding melancholy pervaded it. She performed all her duties as clerk and saleswoman, but she shunned society, and her spirits were gone. Periodically, sometimes not every month, but in two months at furthest, these exhibitions were revived, but with less violence until the latter part of December, 1864, when, while sitting with the two sisters she seized an expensive patch-work silk quilt from a third sister and began to cut and tear and destroy it. The attack required forcefully taking her to her room and locking her in. Prior to that, Louisa Devlin agreed to give her money to come to Washington to institute a suit for breach of promise, thinking that it might bring her relief."

Bradley spelled out the path Mary took from Janesville to Baltimore, where friends of the Devlins lived, beginning on January 1, 1865. Having a bad cold, she was detained for three weeks in a boarding house and then had her periodical illness. She shared her tale of being deceived and deserted by Burroughs with her roommate at the boarding house and confided her intention to file suit and defend her reputation. She showed her some of the letters Burroughs had written her and spoke of him with affection. They made plans to attend a lecture by Henry Ward Beecher when she returned from Washington.

Then Bradley portrayed as an innocent mistake the fact that Mary was armed when she went to Washington and left the letters, that she had said she had planned to show to an attorney, back at the boarding house.

"In the morning the small Sharpe's pistol and the bundle of letters were lying on the bureau. She had shown the pistol to the lady who occupied the room with her, and made no concealment about it. While making her preparations, she was called suddenly by the keeper of the boarding house and told she was late. She threw the bundle of letters into the trunk, and instead of them, put the pistol into her pocket and hurried down stairs to the cars, and thence came to Washington alone."

Allowing the jury and prosecution no time to linger on the question of Mary's motives as she departed from Baltimore, Bradley quickly moved into a gripping description of the murder itself. When she was arrested and placed in the room in the Treasury building, Bradley emphasized her degree of disturbance, saying, "... she paced the room in violent agitation; tore her hair; knelt on the floor and sprang up ; knelt to the justice, and was raised by him more than once; her face was convulsed but she shed no tear. Mr. McCullough, the present Secretary of the Treasury, came in and spoke to her. She asked if Burroughs was dead. He said he had often on the stage seen representations of mental agony, but he never witnessed the reality till then."

Bradley claimed the prosecution's territory by relating the policeman's testimony when she was arrested. "... on her way to the jail she told him that Burroughs had caused her to be driven from home and friends; that he had taken her to a bad house and had seduced her; that she had procured that pistol and came here to avenge the injury, and that she had done so. The policeman understood that she said she had got the pistol just before she left home, and came directly here for that purpose. He cautioned her against making any statements, yet she persisted in doing so. During the whole time she was greatly excited, and when they reached the jail she was so exhausted that she had to be supported by him and others into the jail."

Although he made no attempt to dispute the validity of the policeman's testimony (or the same statements made by Mary in her newspaper interview), he incorporated it as part of his own presentation and by doing so implied that it was just another example of her extreme excitement, not something to be considered important. Of course, it was also well embedded within a deluge of verbiage.

Bradley moved rapidly into more evidence that Mary was mentally disturbed. Two old friends from Burlington who visited her in jail testified that she was so changed in appearance, mind and manner during her periodical illness that they would not have known her had they not conversed with her.

She showed an insensitivity to cold, had a pulse of 120, cold hands and part of her head was hot. The pupil of her eye was so dilated as to cover the iris, she frequently visually focused on vacancy, did not believe Burroughs was dead, had seen him in jail, and talked incoherently at times. Later she displayed great violence of manner, claiming that bars could not restrain her. She believed she heard dreadful shrieks and cries coming from the hallways in jail.

This extensive monologue was directed to the jury and the audience as well as to Dr. May, who was still on the stand. Bradley posed the question, "I will now ask you whether you think she has been, at any time up to this period, the subject of mental or moral insanity?"

"I have no hesitation in saying that, having reference simply to the hypothetical case so minutely detailed by the counsel, Mr. Bradley, that the person labored under a deranged intellect, paroxysmally deranged, produced by moral causes, and assisted or increased by a physical cause, derangement of the uterus."

Douglas nudged Richardson and whispered under shield of his notepad, "He got him to reverse his testimony from yesterday!"

"How about that," replied Richardson.

District Attorney Carrington asked, "Will you state

whether, upon the hypothetical case presented to you, you could form, as a scientific gentleman, any opinion as to whether the homicide was the result of insanity or not?"

"I certainly could. I should say that a patient who had evinced the symptoms as detailed – the antecedent symptoms as detailed and the physical symptoms detailed – who had committed that act as detailed, labored at the time under paroxysmal insanity."

"Could you positively, as a physician, from the circumstances which Mr. Bradley has detailed, express the opinion that the homicide proceeded from an insane impulse; and that the party at the time of commission of the homicide was not sane, and was not impelled thereto by passion and revenge?"

Being careful not to make a judgment on the current actual case, Dr. May said, "I should say, with all due deference to you, that if you have reference to the case of the homicide now before this Court, that would be more properly a case for the consideration of the jury. But I will state, that taking all the facts as detailed by Mr. Bradley, I should consider, in the hypothetical case, the homicide to be the act of a person at times laboring under mental derangement."

"To which of the circumstances detailed by Mr. Bradley do you attach the most importance in forming your opinion?"

"It is the union of all the circumstances upon which I form my opinion, not upon any particular one. Upon a partial statement of those facts, I might give a different opinion, as I did yesterday."

Mr. Carrington called Dr. Noble Young, the physician at the jail and also the Chair of Theory and Practice of Medicine and President of the Faculty, Georgetown Medical College , to the stand.

"Did you see Miss Harris frequently while you were

there?"

"I saw her generally every day but sometimes there would be an intermission of a week or more."

"Did you ever observe any indication of insanity while you were there?"

"No, sir. My attention was not called to the subject at all. I generally saw her for the purpose of examining as to any physical disease, without any reference whatever to mental."

"Did you observe any particular physical disease – dysmenorrhea for instance?"

"No, sir."

On cross-examination Bradley asked, "When was her last periodical return?"

"I think from the 16th to the 19th of June. There is always a variation of several days, more or less."

"Do you recollect at all what the normal condition of her pulse is?"

"I do not think that I ever referred to it at all, except during the time that she was laboring under erysipelas, and I do not know that I examined it at that time."

Recognizing that he was not going to get anything to benefit his case from this witness, Bradley said, "No further questions, your honor."

Mr. Carrington called Dr. William P. Johnson, Professor of Obstetrics and Diseases of Woman and Children, Columbia College, to the stand. "You have been a practitioner in this city for a great many years?"

"Yes, sir."

"I wish you would state to the jury some of the more prominent symptoms which are exhibited in the cases of hysteria and dysmenorrhea?"

"Hysteria presents such an infinite variety of symptoms that it would be almost impossible for me to give a proper idea of the disease further than to say, perhaps, that it affects especially the muscular and nervous system, producing convulsions, and not infrequently gives rise to mental derangement. The repeated recurrence of this disease renders the individual still more liable to attacks, so that they become exceedingly impressionable – very slight causes inducing immediate and marked effect.

"Dysmenorrhea is severe menstruation, attended with pain, which is the most prominent symptom. But in connection with that, there are also other symptoms. For example, they frequently have just what I have described, paroxysms of hysteria, convulsions and delirium, which usually continue during the paroxysms – sometimes only a few hours, sometimes for a day or two, and sometimes for four or five days, going off and leaving the patient in full or ordinary health."

Carrington said, "I wish to state to you a hypothetical case and get your judgment on it. It is as follows:

"In the case of a young woman of a highly nervous organization and vivacious temperament, and who has suffered from a disappointment in love, there is observed at intervals of greater or less regularity, at monthly periods, the following symptoms: irregular and insufficient sleep, depression of the spirits, and melancholy, outbreaks of violence of the following character – attacking a friend with whom there had been no previous quarrel with a broom, and on another occasion with a carving knife; throwing a pin cushion at a customer in the store in which she was employed; the cutting or attempted destruction of a piece of fine needle work belonging to a friend; awakening at an early hour in the morning and saying to a roommate that she must leave her, and was going to walk upon the lake shore; insensitivity to cold, and shedding tears. State how frequently you have noticed in your practice such symptoms in cases of hysteria, or dysmenorrhea, and whether upon such symptoms you would infer the insanity of the patient?"

"I have no hesitation in saying it would be impossible to answer the question in the way it is put. In order to answer that question correctly, I should have a complete history of all the antecedent and subsequent facts connected with the case. I have not learned whether this patient at the time she proceeded to the building was suffering from dysmenorrhea."

Bradley interjected, "They assume, doctor, that she was in that condition."

"Then if that is assumed, and if, as we know she was liable to attacks of mental derangement at that time, while I could not say what was her motive, I could say that, seeing in her presence an individual whom she believed had wronged her, and being sensitive and impressionable, liable to have outbursts of passion from what might seem to us, perhaps, insufficient causes, I can understand that she might give way for a time, where a woman not liable to such paroxysms, having a strong nervous system, and not hysterical, might not have yielded."

"From your observation and experience," Carrington continued, "would you have expected the act of homicide to be the first symptom or indication of the presence of one of those spells?"

"I could hardly have expected that to have been the first, but then that would depend a great deal on circumstances – females are differently affected, as we have shown. If an individual has been brooding over a fancied wrong for a long time – an individual of that peculiar temperament we have described – I can understand that having seen that individual for the first time, perhaps after a long interval, that an impulse to commit homicide might have seized upon her, which it would not have done in a woman not so liable to such attacks."

"Would you have expected to find attending that impulse circumstances of apparent deliberation?"

"A hysterical patient of that kind might very well adopt an idea – and there is after all, between hysterical derangement and insanity, no line of demarcation – and brooding over it, in this condition of mind, premeditate an act of this kind, which would be perfectly compatible with the idea, that in the interval between her paroxysms she was of sound mind."

"In a case such as we have supposed, would you say that the patient had or had not sufficient power of control over mind and will as to avoid such an exciting influence?"

"Well, I suppose she might have kept away."

Judge Wiley asked, "Do you wish to cross-examine the witness, Mr. Bradley?"

CHAPTER 14

"But of course I do, your honor," Bradley responded. Turning to the witness, he asked, "Are there not numerous instances where, given all these conditions, the patient could not control herself and where they have gone to persons and asked them to hold their hands, or tie their thumbs with pack-threads because of this influence coming upon them which they could not resist?"

"Certainly," said Dr. Johnson.

"And are there not instances where, under just such conditions as you have described, moral and physical, a patient has been conscious of what he is doing and yet unable to resist it?"

"Yes, sir. I should think that might be considered as one of the phases of hysteria."

"Are there not well-authenticated cases in medical books where mothers have killed their own children, without any power to control themselves, laboring under precisely such description of things as you have presented to us?"

"That might occur, and instances have occurred."

"If the moral temperament undergoes as great a

change as the physical condition, is that, or not, a stronger illustration, morally and mentally, of the existence of mental disturbance as well as bodily?"

"Yes, sir."

"If accompanying a change in the condition of the body there is also a change in the condition of the mind, embracing in the mind all the facts, moral and intellectual, is not that evidence of mental disease also?"

"Certainly."

"Again, is not the departure from the natural and healthy character, temper, and habits, a very strong symptom, from which you would infer a disease of the mind?"

"It certainly shows some derangement of the mind of some sort."

"I now submit to you the same hypothetical case put to Dr. May, which you will please read carefully, and then give your opinion as to the condition of the patient therein described?"

After reading the description of the case, Dr. Johnson said, "It appears, from this history, that the patient has suffered, as I have stated previously, from dysmenorrhea, attended with marked symptoms of hysteria. Without being able to say whether she was or was not, at the time of the homicide, in an insane condition, she was certainly in that condition which had previously been characterized by evidence of insanity, and the cause, the most marked that could have occurred, was there to cause some condition certainly analogous to that which had existed from a much slighter cause – that is, from certain acts of alienation and of violence that she had committed before."

"Doctor, will you state what is the inference, treated medically, from these facts, upon the question of the condition of the mind?"

"I should have said that this patient was laboring

under this hysterical condition, and I want here to explain what I mean by hysterical. The ordinary acceptation of that term is not that which is meant by it medically. It is ordinarily understood as something more or less voluntary, as proceeding from a weak mind, and that the person, therefore is nervous, in the ordinary acceptation of that term.

"By the term, as used medically, we consider an individual suffering from hysteria as irresponsible for any act which she might commit. It is just as impossible for them to prevent violence as it would be for them to prevent being drowned, if thrown into water deep enough, and there allowed to remain."

Mr. Bradley called Dr. Thomas Miller, Professor of Anatomy, Columbia College and President of the Washington, D.C. Board of Health . "Were you in court this morning when I put a hypothetical case to Dr. May?"

"I was."

"What is your opinion as to the condition of the mind of the patient described in that hypothetical case?"

"I will state in one word that I concur entirely with the views and opinions expressed by Dr. May."

"State whether, especially at one period of your life, you did not pay particular attention to the diseases of the mind?"

"I did, many years ago, and was somewhat instrumental in having the present lunatic asylum established in Washington. I had special charge of the insane of the District for some years. They were at that time placed in the jail here prior to being removed to Baltimore."

"Your witness," said Bradley, glancing at Carrington.

"No questions," replied the District Attorney.

"The prosecution calls Dr. Flordoardo Howard to the stand," said Mr. Wilson.

Dr. Howard took his place in the witness box and Mr.

Wilson asked him to state his current position.

"I am Professor of Obstetrics and Diseases of Woman and Children, Georgetown Medical College."

"Will you please state some of the symptoms frequently observable in cases of dysmenorrhea and hysteria?"

"The symptoms of hysteria are very variable. It may assimilate almost any disease. Women subject to hysteria are generally very susceptible; sometimes subject to gloomy despondency and sometimes to joy. They go quickly from one extreme to another in their moral feelings. The attack of hysteria may be accompanied with agitation of the muscle, and there may be perversion of the intellectual faculty or not during the paroxysms."

Can the disease of dysmenorrhea be immediately detected upon a short visit to a patient?"

"A physician who made the proper investigation ought, I think, at his first visit, to decide whether his patient had dysmenorrhea or not."

Bradley, in cross-examination asked, "I believe you have read over the hypothetical case put by me. What is your opinion as to the condition of the patient thus described during the period of time covered by that statement?"

"I would suppose the patient thus described to be subject to mental alienation, and that she was subject to insane impulses – possibly suicidal or homicidal mania."

Mr. Wilson called Peter Hartwell to the stand. "Where do you reside?"

"In Chicago."

"Are you acquainted with the accused, Mary Harris?"

"I am. I have known her since 1863 – I think the spring of 1863."

"Will you state how often you have seen her, and when you lost sight of her before seeing her here?"

"During the summer of 1863, I think, I saw her nearly

every day. For the last twelve months I have seen her but very seldom."

"When did you last see her?"

"I saw her at the railroad depot."

"Did you see her the day before that and, if so, state where and under what circumstances you saw her?"

"I think two days before that I saw her at the passenger station of the Pittsburgh, Fort Wayne, and Chicago railroads about the first of January. I think the interview lasted about an hour."

"What changes did you notice in her appearance at that time as compared with her appearance when you had seen her before?"

"I did not notice anything particularly."

"Was her manner as to liveliness, vivacity, etc., at the time you last saw her the same as before?"

"I thought she appeared to be the same as usual."

"You have seen her since she has been here, have you not?"

"Yes, sir."

"What change have you noticed in her appearance as compared with either of the times of which you have spoken?"

"I have not seen her enough here to notice any change."

"Have you seen her face?"

"Yes, sir."

"At the time you saw her at the depot in January, did she state where she was going?"

"Yes, sir. She said she was going to Baltimore."

On cross-examination, Mr. Bradley asked, "How did you come here as a witness?"

"I was subpoenaed by the United States Marshal."

"Who saw you before then about this business?"

"Well, I had some conversation with Dr. Burroughs about it."

"Did anyone furnish you with the money to pay your expenses in coming on?"

"Yes, sir."

"Who furnished it?"

"Dr. Burroughs gave an order on Judge L. C. P. Freer to Mr. Goode, to give to me. I presented the order, and Freer accepted it and gave me the money."

"Dr. Burroughs has seen and conversed with you before that as to the testimony you would give here?"

"Yes, sir."

"Did you board at the same house with Miss Harris in 1863?"

"Yes, sir. For seven or eight months."

"During that time, how often were you in her company?"

"Very frequently. I would occasionally drop in the store to say something to the ladies and I would see her then."

"Do you mean to say that at that time she was more fleshy than she is now?"

"I think she was more fleshy than she is now."

"Do you mean to tell the jury that she had any more color than she has now?"

"I did not have an opportunity of seeing her face. I suppose, though, she had more color."

"You conversed with her here. Was she not more cheerful at home than when you saw her here?"

"Yes, sir."

Mr. Wilson called George F. Mosely to the stand. Where do you reside?"

"In Janesville, Wisconsin."

What is your occupation?"

"I am a book seller."

"What was your acquaintance with Miss Harris, the prisoner?"

"I became acquainted with Miss Harris about a year

ago and saw her from that time till the time of her leaving Janesville, which I think was in the latter part of December."

"How often did you see her and under what circumstances?"

"I saw her sometimes every day, at other times not so often, as she would come to my store on different kinds of business."

"What was her general demeanor?"

"She seemed usually to be cheerful and in fair spirits, quiet in manner, and quite self-possessed under all circumstances."

"Did you ever observe any extraordinary instances of conduct, or anything that appeared to you to be an evidence of insanity or mental derangement?"

"I did not."

"State whether or not, at any of these interviews, she said anything to you about her lover and, if so, what was said, as thus enabling you to arrive at her state of mind on that subject?"

"I do not think she did."

Bradley took up the cross-examination. "Did Dr. Burroughs talk to you about this case when in Janesville?"

"He has had some conversations with me in regard to it."

"When Miss Harris came into your store, did she come to buy papers, get change, or anything of that kind?"

"Usually."

"She did not sit down to have a chat with you?"

"No, sir. I think not."

"And this mere store acquaintance is all the acquaintance you have with her?"

"It is."

"By whom were you summoned?"

"By the marshal."

"Were your expenses paid?"

"No, sir."

E. H. Strong was sworn in and Mr. Wilson asked, "Where do you reside?"

"In Janesville, Wisconsin."

"Do you know the prisoner?"

"She boarded with me for about 10 days last year – in 1864."

"Did you ever see her subsequently?"

"I sometimes met her in the street subsequently."

"During the period she boarded with you, what was her spirit? Was she cheerful or melancholy? Did you observe anything remarkable about her?"

"I considered her laboring under mental depression."

"Did you observe anything else?"

"Nothing in particular."

"Do you know whether at that time she was unwell?"

"I do not think she was. I thought she was in delicate health."

"Did you observe anything singular in her conduct?"

"I did not."

"Do you know the witness, Miss Louisa Devlin?"

"Yes, sir. She was also at my house at the same time."

"How long did she board there?"

"Well, she came before Miss Harris, I should think about a month."

"How long did she carry on her business in Janesville?"

"I think she commenced business in May or June. She may have carried it on for a year."

"Do you know the general reputation of Miss Louisa Devlin among her neighbors, and if so, state what that reputation is for truth?"

"I do not. What knowledge I possess of the Misses Devlin is of a very limited character, and derived from very few persons."

"Did you have conversations with anybody, previous to your being summoned as a witness here, in this case?"

"Yes, sir. I had with the deputy marshal, when I was summoned, on the 4th of July last."

"What arrangements were made for the payment of your expenses?"

"None."

"Was nothing said to you about your expenses being paid?"

"Yes, sir, there was. The marshal read a letter to me, in which..."

The District Attorney arose and said, "I object to the witness stating the contents of any letter."

Judge Wiley ruled "The witness will not state the contents of the letter."

Bradley asked, "Who was the letter from?"

"The letter must speak for itself," bellowed out the District Attorney.

Bradley did not let go and asked, "Did that letter say anything to you about the payment of expenses?"

"I object," said Mr. Carrington.

Mr. Strong responded before Judge Wiley could get his "sustained" ruling out of his mouth, "The marshal said my expenses would be paid and $3 a day."

"Did he say from whom the letter was?"

"Yes, sir, Dr. Burroughs, and that if it was necessary he (Dr. B) would advance any funds which might be required."

Mr. Carrington said that he had no other witnesses in attendance to call and asked that court be adjourned until Monday, since the time for adjournment was near anyway. The defense counsel objected.

A juror got up and stated that some of the members were sick. Judge Wiley said the jury had now been on the case for eight days and if it went on much longer there might be no jury left to decide. He declared the evidence closed on both sides for the day and adjourned until ten o'clock on Monday.

Douglas and Richardson sat on a bench outside the courthouse to discuss the day's events before going their respective ways. "Today was the battle of the experts." said Richardson. "The big surprise was when Bradley got Dr. May to reverse his testimony after being presented with that elaborate detailed hypothetical case. That presentation was a *tour de force* for the defense. He referred to Mary as a poor innocent child about half a dozen times in as many sentences and implied she was completely enthralled with Burroughs."

"True," said Douglas. "The exquisite detail and dramatic presentation of *Mary's Story* by Mr. Bradley was brilliant. A hypothetical case, by definition, asks you to accept the assumed facts without question. The weak point, however, is the connection of the hypothetical case with the actual case before the jury. I thought the prosecution could have lessened the impact of Dr. May's testimony by pointing out where assumptions made in the hypothetical case have not been proven in the actual case. For example, the assumption that Burroughs wrote the Greenwood letters, the assumption that Mary's behavior prior to the murder was an indication of insanity, the assumption that Burroughs controlled and molded her views of the world more than did her sophisticated lady friends."

"If Mary's older lady friends were so intelligent and cultivated, why didn't they counsel her to not see Burroughs? And to add to your list of assumptions: the assumption that there was no calculation to her actions, the assumption that it was a simple oversight that she took her pistol with her to Washington and forgot her letters, the assumption that Burroughs didn't tell her of his upcoming marriage, perhaps on that meeting just after August 7th, or even the assumption that Mary was pure and virtuous."

"Oh, my God," Douglas said in mock astonishment, "you mean that all girls are not made of sugar and spice and everything nice?"

"Perhaps not," said Richardson. "However, all the other doctors, except for the jail doctor, Dr. Young, accepted Bradley's portrayal in the hypothetical case as being consistent with insanity. Bradley did his homework on mental cases well and knew how to ask questions of the doctors to get the response he desired."

"I heard a rumor that he had Dr. Nichols help him write up the hypothetical case he presented to Dr. May. Is that ethical?"

"I don't know. The hypothetical was long, confusing and in some places contradictory. Some judges have reprimanded lawyers for their omission of some facts or their selective inclusion of facts that should be decided upon by the jury in a hypothetical. It seems to be an ongoing problem that the courts are hesitant to address."

"What did you think of the other witnesses? The only purpose the prosecution seemed to have in calling them was to have them testify that Miss Harris didn't appear to be crazy to them - hardly expert testimony."

"I agree," said Richardson. "The ones from Janesville seemed to be only casual acquaintances, even if they did see her fairly often. Hartwell, from Chicago, said he saw Mary nearly every day in the summer of 1863 and that could have been used to argue against the assumption that she was socially retiring after Burroughs jilted her and maybe even that there was a relationship there. But the prosecution just let it slide. Makes you wonder just how prepared they were to try this case. Bradley just ignored the substance of their testimony, for the most part, and focused on making it look like the Reverend Dr. Burroughs bought their testimony, turning the witnesses to his advantage. That man is *very* clever."

"That's for sure," said Douglas. "See you on Monday."

CHAPTER 15

The courtroom had a greater attendance than on any of the previous days and women were especially well represented. Miss Harris appeared to be more cheerful than previously, looked around more frequently and took a greater interest in what was going on.

The arguments to be presented in court on this tenth day pertained to points of law. The jury was not required to remain in the courtroom and was allowed to leave. Miss Harris, with her lady friends, retired to the room adjoining the courtroom all afternoon. When it became evident that the entire day would involve discussion of legal questions, a large portion of the audience quietly left the courtroom. The reporters, Douglas and Richardson, remained in the courtroom to hear what principles the two sides wanted to establish as ground rules for the jury's deliberations.

Both defense and prosecution were allowed to offer "prayers" to the court - propositions about the legal-logical requirements in the case before it. Judge Wiley would then rule on which of these prayers he would accept and include in his instructions to the jury.

Mr. Wilson asserted that the only reasons for acquittal

were if the jury was convinced beyond a reasonable doubt that the accused at the time of the homicide did not have sufficient reason to know the nature, quality and character of the act and could not distinguish right from wrong in regard to the particular act of murder. It was not sufficient to show that the accused was merely susceptible to a diseased state of mind or that it was possible or even probable that the accused suffered from a diseased mind and was subject to fits of insane fury or paroxysmal insanity.

He maintained that she was not entitled to acquittal on the ground of insane impulse if they found that she had feelings of hatred toward the deceased, was conscious that she at certain periods was subject to paroxysms of insanity, previously armed herself with a pistol and sought out and killed the deceased as laid out in the indictment. What the defense had to show, according to Mr. Wilson, was that the act of homicide proceeded from a paroxysm of insanity occasioned by disease and not from criminal intent. He added that the jury, if they decided to acquit, should render their verdict as 'Not guilty by reason of insanity' and cite Statute 158, sec.5, 1857.

Mr. Wilson quoted several authorities favoring the idea that the burden of proof was on the defense to prove the insanity of the accused and that facts beyond a reasonable doubt would be required to convince the jury that they should render a verdict of not guilty. He said the test should be whether the accused, at the time of the commission of the homicide, understood right from wrong.

Mr. Hughes tried to combat Wilson's ideas by reading from some of the very authorities cited by Mr. Wilson to show that they had been overruled and that Wilson had unsuccessfully tried to manipulate the books. He used some of Wilson's authorities and others to make his case that the issue of knowledge of right and wrong is not critical to the existence of insanity and cited Brittain (*Man and His Relations*) to show how scientific and learned men showed a diverse opinion on the subject of the human mind.

Bradley's prayers were that the accused was entitled to a verdict of not guilty if:

she committed the acts in the indictment when she was unable to control her will and actions with reason and judgment, either because her mental faculties were being affected by physical disease or some involuntary moral cause, or both;

at the time she committed the acts she was moved by an irresistible insane impulse that controlled her will and judgment and arose from involuntary physical or moral causes or both combined;

the jury entertains a reasonable doubt as to the soundness of the mind of the prisoner at the time of commission of the acts since one of the elements of the crime charged is that she be of "sound memory and discretion."

Quoting from Wharton and Stille's *Medical Jurisprudence,* Bradley said that the government's view was "from the dark ages" and that modern authorities agree with the defense that if the accused acted without willful control, she should be found not guilty. T. Hartley Crawford, Judge Wiley's predecessor in this very court, had ruled affirmatively on similar questions raised in the trial of Daniel Sickles, the man who had killed the son of Francis Scott Key after learning the latter was having an affair with his wife. Indeed, Judge Crawford had gone so far as to state that the prisoner was entitled to the benefit of the doubt in the minds of the jury, as to his mental condition.

Quoting from Mr. Best in his treatise upon *Presumptive Proof,* Bradley said, "The onus of proving every thing essential to establishing of the charge against the accused, lies in the prosecutor." Judge Crawford too had decided the burden of proof never was shifted onto the defendant. Bradley maintained that the burden rests with the prosecution to prove every fact material and necessary to the commission of the crime beyond a reasonable doubt, including that the prisoner is sane and capable of murder, or else the jury is bound to acquit.

A second point that Bradley made was that the presumption of sanity is really a presumption of fact which, historically, had relieved the government from providing positive proof of that fact for the mere convenience of administering justice. That presumption is to be met by positive evidence, disproving or raising a doubt or question about that fact. So, if there is any evidence to show the party was of unsound mind, the burden of proof remained upon the government to establish the fact of sanity – a fact essential to the perfection of the offense. The burden of proof was not upon the accused to show that she was insane at the time of the crime and to show this beyond all reasonable doubt. Just as in the case of an alibi, it is a negative defense: the person cannot be guilty since she was absent (mentally) from the place where the crime was committed.

Bradley argued that the crime must have been committed by a person of sound memory and discretion against a reasonable creature, with malice aforethought. Sound memory and discretion, by which a party could understand his relations to his God, to his country, to his fellow-man, and himself, in the act which he was committing, were therefore essential to be proven by the Government. The government had themselves introduced evidence to raise a doubt of the sanity of the party at the time of the crime.

Finally, Bradley maintained that insanity, once shown,

is assumed to continue unless it can be proven otherwise. It is up to the government to establish the fact of a lucid interval at the time of the crime. The defense claim is, not guilty, because she was insane at various times antecedent to the commission of the act. The defense of insanity was not a "plea." It was a fact under the plea of "not guilty," to show that, although present in the body and acting, yet she was not there in the spirit, with understanding and reason, with "malice aforethought."

Before adjourning the Court so he could study the prayers offered by the two sides, Judge Wylie indicated his preference and respect for the opinions of his predecessor in presiding over the criminal part of the Supreme Court of the District of Columbia, Judge Crawford, thereby pointing to the direction of his sentiments.

Douglas and Richardson met outside the courthouse to compare notes on arguments of each side. Douglas said, "Looks to me like Wilson is implying that Miss Harris is feigning insanity because she has a clear motive, anger, and a clear intent, revenge. Of course there are other indicators of feigning that were not observed or not reported, such as intensification of symptoms when being observed, giving absurd answers to simple questions, feigning movements uncharacteristic of the disease, acting on suggestions given by the examiner."

Chuckling, Richardson added, "And some examiners use the whirling chair method, drug challenges, the faradic brush and stimulating with a pin with and without warning. Some even use emetics and then evaluate the torpor of the bowels. It would have been helpful to the prosecution if they had some other signs of feigning."

"Bradley managed to turn the burden of proof idea on its head, said Douglas. "Instead of accepting the common presumption that the person is sane unless proven otherwise, he claimed that the prosecution had to prove that the defendant had an interval of sanity at the time of the murder, since they themselves accepted that she showed periods where her sanity was in doubt.

"So if the defense is able to show that the defendant was insane at various times prior to the murder, in order to obtain a conviction, it is up to the prosecution to provide evidence that she was sane for that critical period of time. That is why the prosecution tried to demonstrate that Miss Harris showed premeditation and used cunning while in the Treasury building, and indeed tried to escape, even though she lost her way and was caught. All of that testimony was considered to be evidence for an unimpaired intellect. But it all seemed to get lost in the shuffle."

"I find it interesting, remarked Richardson, that psychiatrists are not allowed to testify as to what is normal behavior but can go on at length about what is abnormal. Normal behavior is considered to be in the realm of the jury even though psychiatrists are educated in normal behavior and development and probably can better distinguish it from the abnormal than can the jury. The result is an asymmetrical presentation of expert opinion which can distort the reality of the situation."

***

The Court reconvened on Tuesday at ten o'clock when Judge Wylie addressed the jury with regard to the prayers offered by counsel for the two sides. He said that insanity was the defense set up in this case, as no person but a person of sound mind is responsible in courts of law these days. The prisoner at the bar is either guilty of willful murder or else she is not guilty at all. Willful murder is where a person of sound mind and discretion unlawfully kills any human being in the peace of the government, with malice aforethought or implied.

He then ruled on the prayers asked by the two sides. He granted the first prayer of the defense but striking out the words "with reason and judgment." He granted the second prayer but refused the third, saying he was convinced the law is not as expressed in this prayer. The defense set up in this case must be made out affirmatively, beyond a reasonable doubt, by a preponderance of the evidence.

He rejected three of the prayers of the prosecution and qualified another. Wiley ruled that if at the time of the commission of the crime, the party labored under an insane impulse, produced by either physical or moral cause sufficient to dethrone her mind, or "if frenzy had mounted the throne of reason, so as for the time to dethrone reason," the party was insane. He said that if the prisoner was insane, she could not be made responsible for her actions by any conduct, declarations, or behavior on previous occasions, when her mind was under the government of her reason. He rejected the idea that the jury must cite an act of Congress and state the reasons by which they arrived at their verdict.

Wiley decided that the jury must be satisfied beyond a reasonable doubt that the prisoner was not merely liable to the insane attacks referred to, but that the act in question was committed by her while she was actually possessed and irresistibly controlled by the presence and power of one of them.

***

Wilson addressed the jury for his second-string closing remarks. "You are glad to see that the end of this long and painful trial is now not far distant. For nearly two weeks, with a thank-worthy and most patient attention, you have watched the complete unfolding of the dark texture of the prisoner's life, and the unraveling of the blood-stained threads, in warp and woof. Now you are to say whether the colors of that texture, its colors of crimson and of black, are but the shadows of unavoidable misfortune, or the badges of punishable guilt.

"The prisoner, although obscure and poor, has been able to summon to her assistance an array of counsel representing every phase of professional eminence and excellence. She is so fortunate as to be defended by one whose persuasive eloquence had made the borders of his own state too limited to contain his fame; by another, who has lately adorned a high position upon the Federal bench; by another, whose learning has been made conspicuous in many pursuits and offices; by another, the leader of our own bar; and by a fifth, whose talents and industry give promise of his high professional attainments. I say it is gratifying that the prisoner is thus defended, because we may rest assured that this eloquence, this learning, this experience, and this industry will not leave unvisited any corner of the domains of law, of science, of fact, of fancy, and will find out and exhibit all that there is or can be to palliate or disprove the blood-guiltiness of their client.

"The facts are these: the prisoner in the latter part of last December, armed with a pistol, sets out on a journey of one thousand miles in search of a man whom she hates, and who she believes, or alleges, has violated his promise to her. She stops in a neighboring city, leaves all her encumbering baggage there, and taking the weapon which has been her companion in her travel, she reaches her destination near noon. She goes to the Treasury Department and inquires for her victim by name, goes to his room and sees him at his desk. She conceals herself in the hall to await his coming. When he appears – when he is so near that her pistol's point can almost touch him – when it is certain that the ball must do its work – she fires. As he flies from her, wounded unto death, she cocks her pistol and fires a second time. She turns and walks slowly along the passage, descends the stairs, misses her way, corrects her mistake, passes through the outer door, and is about to descend into the street when she is arrested and brought back. She manifests rather less than more of the emotions that would naturally be elicited by such a deed.

"And we are to see whether, in the capital of this nation, in the very chambers of its civil life, men – aye, the very servants of the public – are to be done to death, are to be shot down, and no law found to punish the act, and no jury found to administer the law. We are to see if a young woman who fancies herself or, if you please, has been slighted, aggrieved, or injured, is with her own hand to execute the offender, and to receive the approval of those who are the sworn ministers of the law.

"Juries are the educators of public morals. What lesson do you propose to teach upon this subject? What precedent do you propose to establish? The counsel for the prisoner ask that you inflict no punishment and express no reproof. They interpose between the accused and the sword of justice a defense of insanity – a refuge always sought in cases where other refuge there is none.

"It is this defense you are to examine, not as a school of philosophers, not as a society of metaphysicians, not as a board of trustees considering an application for admission into an insane asylum, but as men of honesty and common sense, needing not the speculations and theories of the books, but having the instructions of the Court, and in them a guiding star, a chart, a compass and rudder, by which you may find and follow that rightful law whose aim it is in all the fluctuations of interest, in all the vicissitudes of fortune, to punish guilt, whether in high or low, whether in rich or poor, whether in man or woman.

"The defense has drawn from its arsenal of weapons not only the bullet that destroyed his life, but the poisoned arrows that are to pierce through his name and memory, and wound the heart of the widow and stain and discolor a child's reverence for a father who died ere its own life began.

"But their main defense is insanity. You must be satisfied beyond a reasonable doubt that the accused was at the time incapable, through disease, to resist the commission of the act. The defense does not propose to prove a general state of insanity but to show that just enough insanity existed to make this homicide no murder, and that the homicide having been committed, the prisoner has returned to a state of sanity. Their defense is paroxysmal insanity – a defense resorted to when defense there is no other.

"It has been their object to prove that in September, 1863, a change occurred in the bodily and mental health of the prisoner. They claim that this change was occasioned, first, by a disappointment in love; second, by a violation of a marriage engagement; and third, by a great moral shock; and to show whence these three conspirators against her reason came, they refer to the letters of September 8 and 12, 1863.

"In answer to all that, I refer you to the letter dated January 19, 1862 showing clearly that, whatever may have been the relations previously existing, they were broken at that time, and after that date Burroughs wrote to the accused but five letters, and had but four short interviews with her. He was the discarded suitor, she well satisfied with his absence and to have preserved her sanity. For in all the evidence of her acts during the eighteen months intervening between that time and September, 1863, we hear not a single note of 'sweet bells jangled out of tune, and harsh.'

"In the invention of the letters asking her to meet him at a house of assignation, she never could have been for a moment deceived, and had no belief that they came from Burroughs. The very witness first produced by the defense swears that it was physically impossible that he could have written them. They do not bear the least resemblance to his handwriting, Furthermore, she asserted only two or three days after, to Rev. Dr. Burroughs, of Chicago, that she had no reason to suppose they were written by Mr. Burroughs, and that she was sorry that she had entertained the suspicion, and would not have thought of it unless it had been suggested to her by others.

"A venomous and malicious attack has been made on Dr. Burroughs by the accused. But he is a truthful Christian gentleman, who has done his duty only, and is beyond the reach of the petty malice of his defamers. If confirmation is needed to add credibility to her story, we find it in the evidence where, more than a year afterward, she states that Burroughs had always treated her as a father. This bungling contrivance of the assignation letters gives to you no explanation of the homicide. To know its real motive, we have but to listen to the testimony of her friend, Miss Devlin.

"A change came over Miss Harris after the marriage of Burroughs. Up to that time she was cheerful and happy. To understand the significance of that we need no doctors learned in the symptoms of paroxysmal insanity and dysmenorrhea. We need only open the red leaves of the book of the human heart. She had loved him. She had, in coquettishness or for a worse reason, rejected him. He had married another. He was lost to her and she was jealous. Her love turned to hatred, her passion to revenge.

"It is not a new or strange story. This is not the first tragedy in which a woman has mingled with the wine of her life that 'poison more potent than a mad dog's tooth.' She tells her counselor that she hates Burroughs and does not know what she might do should she see him. A physician is called in soon after that to prescribe for bodily ailments, not to minister to a mind diseased. In the act of the homicide there is evidence not of insanity but of premeditation and of deliberation. 'If she was mad, her

madness had the strangest frame of sense. Such
dependence of thing on thing as never I heard in
madness.'

"In her subsequent conduct, while in jail, he who was
acting nurse, counsel, physician, and mental philosopher,
saw many touching and sentimental incidents, but an old
physician, who saw her every day, saw no evidence of
insanity of any sort. The defense has attempted to put the
prosecution in a position of antagonism with the medical
witnesses. We have too much respect for them as men,
and too high an estimate of their professional excellence
to oppose them. We agree with them in all they have said.
The prosecution and the defense each put to them
hypothetical cases and they gave their opinion on each.
The case of the prosecution was consistent with the
evidence; that of the defense was not.

"In the defense's hypothetical case, the following
facts were presumed to be true which do not appear in
evidence: First, there was a sudden breaking off of a
marriage engagement. Second, there was a serious moral
shock. Third, there was disappointment. Fourth, that the
accused did not avail herself of the first opportunity to
commit the act. Fifth, that she made no effort to escape.
Sixth, that she did not attempt to palliate the offense.
Seventh, that she was at the time of commission of the
act suffering from physical disease. Eighth, that there was
a sudden and unexpected appearance of the deceased.

"The disappearance of these facts, together with the
opinions of the physician that all the other peculiarities of
her conduct can be accounted for by the existence of
hysteria, effectually explodes the whole theory of the
defense. It is true that she was susceptible to disease, but
in that particular she is not different from us all. It is true,
that like Macbeth, she heard voices and saw visions that
had no existence, but in that respect she does not differ
from all who are visited by the specters of remorse, and

stung by the pains of an accusing conscience.

"In conclusion, we all know that in our own nature, in all human natures, there is a background of fire, and a world of fierce passions, of hatred, anger, revenge, and malice, that surge and storm against the barriers that confine them, and threaten at each moment to bring ruin upon ourselves and danger and disaster to the public peace. They are not to be kept in subjection by the refinements of metaphysics, or by the witchery of oratory, or by the pleasings of mercy.

"It is punishment and the fear of punishment alone that can keep our hearthstones unstained by blood, and the paths of our life secure. The pulpit may preach and the press may publish, and we may all approve those great solemn enactments of the law, and it is in vain, unless the juries of the land enforce those laws. If the prisoner at the bar was a responsible being within the instructions of his Honor, it is the law that condemns her, and though there may be tears for her womanhood, and pity for her youth, there should be punishment for her crime."

After Mr. Wilson's remarks, the court recessed until a quarter past one.

CHAPTER 16

Judge Hughes addressed the jury for the defense.

"May it please the Court, and you, gentlemen of the jury, it is essential to the discharge of your duty that you should well understand the issue which you have to try. The indictment charges the defendant with murder and in this charge is included the lower degree of felonious homicide – manslaughter. If the evidence satisfactorily shows the guilt of the accused beyond a reasonable doubt, you ought to find Miss Harris guilty of murder.

"If the proof falls short of establishing legal malice – that is, if the killing, instead of being deliberate and premeditated, was done upon sudden heat – you might convict her of manslaughter. Miss Harris has pleaded 'not guilty' and this requires the prosecution to prove every material allegation necessary to sustain the charge so that you may say that her guilt is established beyond a reasonable doubt. Otherwise, you must acquit her.

"Gentlemen, this killing was either a deliberate and

premeditated murder or it was no crime at all. It was either excusable homicide, committed in a state of mind which rendered the accused irresponsible for her act, or it was a homicide, although with great provocation, yet with sufficient degree of deliberation and premeditation to constitute the offense of malice.

"The accused, as you see, is a woman. It is the pleasure of the prosecuting attorney, in introducing this case, to comment on this subject. He warned you against sympathy. He warned you even against mercy and advised you that the laws of the land lodged the prerogative of clemency elsewhere. While he himself professed great sympathy for woman, he also professed that this particular female was an offender so black with crime, that she had excluded herself from the pale of sympathy on that ground. He said that she had manifested a savage disregard of human life, and later when the witness testimony ought to have dissipated any such impression from his mind, he, with great emphasis, in the presence of the Court and yourselves, pronounced this the most atrocious murder on record!

"It is not because the defendant is a woman that we expect an acquittal at your hands. She is young, and I was about to say that she is friendless, but she is not. I will say this in her praise, that whatever friends she has, she owes to her own unassuming merits. She has neither wealth, station, nor kinfolk, nothing to make her friends except her misfortunes and her good conduct.

"It is not because she is a woman. It is not because her parents and relatives, who should be here with her today, to sustain her in this trying ordeal, have been separated from her, and have become to her as aliens and strangers, through the acts of the unfortunate man whose life she has taken. It is not for that that we shall ask you to acquit her, but because she is innocent, because she has a right to a verdict of not guilty from you under the laws of the land.

"Whenever, in the very opening of a case like this, counsel of the learning, experience and ability of the prosecution serve notice upon the Court and jury, and upon all mankind, that they are seeking for a conviction upon mere technical grounds, and when throughout the progress of the cause the same disposition is manifested by repeated objections to testimony, and when, in order to induce the Court to give such instructions to the jury as were not law, for the purpose of conviction, old and exploded doctrines are exhumed, resuscitated, and appealed to, and when we see immediately behind the prosecution the party representing private vengeance in this cause, the prosecution so introduced seldom if ever, fails to be unsupported by law and by evidence.

"Gentlemen, the defendant comes here helpless, in the hands of a powerful government, and that government is the other party in this cause. True, the duty of the government is to enforce the law, to punish offenders, to protect human life but in no spirit of persecution and with no vindictiveness. The prosecution is presumed to be disinterested, presumed to be impartial, and absolutely to desire as the law desires that no innocent person should suffer, and to desire to prosecute his cause in the spirit of the law, which says that it is better that ninety-nine guilty persons should escape than that one innocent person should suffer.

"The prosecution has manifested an anxious desire to secure a conviction, urged on not by personal feelings of the district attorney but by some heart full of feelings of private vengeance and malice towards the accused and this became evident with the presentment of the principal prosecuting witness. And there is the mainspring in this case.

"The gentleman who just addressed you presented his theory that the murder was from jealousy, arising from disappointed love, and from disappointment at the marriage of a man who, according to his argument, this lady had rejected as a suitor. He denied, in the face of the evidence, that there was a continuous engagement of marriage.

"In spite of the natural goodness of his heart and the clearness of his intellect, he has had his judgment so warped by the private prosecutor in this cause that he can stand up here in the face of all the evidence we have adduced, and say that although he is willing to admit there were very intimate relations between these parties, and those relations at one time looked towards marriage, yet they were broken off and never again resumed.

"The fact is that there is a letter showing these parties had a lover's quarrel but afterwards had an interview, became reconciled and their affairs floated on in as smooth a current as before. If this not be so, why are these old letters here? Why is this picture here? Surely the man must be blind to not understand this, or he was never in love and had any of those lover's quarrels which are said to be so sweet and whose reconciliation appear as the green spots of memory. His theory is that she rejected him and afterwards when the disconsolate swain married another woman, she became jealous and killed him for it. The mere statement of the theory is a sufficient refutation of it and shows to what straits the prosecution has been driven.

"Then he speaks of punishment, the same cry for blood that has characterized this prosecution from the beginning. Punishment indeed! Who is to punish the betrayer of female honor? Who is to punish the serpent that with his slimy track pursues from early girlhood into budding womanhood the unfortunate girl, separates her from her family and friends, and leaves her alone and isolated, without father or brother to defend or protect her, and then throws her heartlessly upon the world? Who is to punish him?

"Ah! This unfortunate man no doubt thought that he could do this thing with impunity, because this girl was friendless. There is a just God, however, who administers justice in such cases, and he chose as the instrument of his justice, in this particular case, the poor unfortunate girl whose life had been forever blighted.

"That little girl (pointing to the prisoner) with that little hand poised the pistol which might, upon ordinary occasions, have been discharged a hundred times, or rather snapped (for they will not discharge one time in fifty) without any serious consequences, but with that toy of a pistol she was the instrument of punishment in the hands of God, and He took away her reason, and she stands here today secure from human justice. The overruling Providence, without whose consent not even a sparrow falls, brought punishment to the door of the deceased – brought it by the hand of her that he had ruined, and placed her in a position where she shall answer to Him alone for what she has done, and not to human laws.

"Gentlemen of the jury, one of the most painful duties that ever falls upon counsel, in the defense of an accused person, is to throw censure upon those who are dead – to bring up their faults, their crimes, and perhaps their wickedness – but when it is necessary for the defense, how can it be avoided.

"A man who leads a pure life, who deals fairly and honestly with his fellows, may be persecuted, may be hunted down, calumniated, but his character will only shine brighter for all that, if it can stand the test, and we know that so well that we would feel assured that an unwarranted attack upon this man would only recoil upon us, and do our cause an injury.

"But attacks are fatal where the conduct of the party himself has furnished the weapons with which to make them. We submit to you, gentlemen, that the unfortunate deceased has furnished everything necessary, not withstanding the boast of the prosecution that he died without a stain.

"Attacked! Yes, he has been attacked, but not by counsel. The sworn evidence in the cause attacks him. His own letters attack him. His inhuman cruelty, in seeking to destroy the reputation of this poor girl, when he had resolved to desert her, attacks him. His anonymous letters attack him. His assumption of the relation of husband for a most worthy and estimable lady, under the solemn sacraments of religion, occupying the position that he did to the accused in this case, attacks him. And one who has sought to sustain him in his wrongs, and one who has been the partner of his cruelty, and I might almost say the partner of his guilt, toward this young woman – even his own brother – attacks him.

"Gentlemen, you have more evidence before you to show that the Rev. John C. Burroughs is the responsible cause of his brother's death than you have to show that this unfortunate girl was. What! A doctor of divinity, who has come here and contradicted the statement of every witness in regard to the material points in this case, who has testified that his brother was not in Chicago upon a certain day, and therefore it was impossible for him to be at a certain place, who knowing that this prostitute, Ellen Mills, knew the fact, and could either sustain or overthrow him, for he himself tells you that when a detective or policeman told him that, with one or two hundred dollars, he could get her out of the way, he made use of no expression of disapprobation – not to be attacked?

"Yes, we will attack him. And the justice of God, that took away his brother's life will, in my humble opinion, bring to him his share of the punishment, for to him, a clergyman, reputation and credit are everything. If this trial does not condemn him with his congregation, and with all good Christian people in this land, then commend me to the standard of public sentiment in Chicago."

Hughes said that he earlier had supplied Dr. Nichols with the facts bearing upon the question of insanity in this case and asked him to use those facts to draw up a hypothetical case history. He then read the document so produced, which was basically the same as the hypothetical case presented earlier during testimony (but with a few added rhetorical embellishments) to the jury as a means of summarizing the position of the defense on this matter.

When he finished, he asked the jury, "If it fails to produce general insanity, which we do not claim that it did, is it not sufficient, upon the appearance in her presence of the man who had wronged her, to cause (using the language of your Honor) 'frenzy to mount up by the side of reason and hold its hands so that she would be an irresponsible being?'

"If this young lady could go through all this, could bear all this, and yet endure the sight of him and control of her reason, of her conduct, she has a heart and soul most obdurate. Dr. Nichols, an eminent physician in charge of an insane asylum with great experience in this branch of science has repeatedly sworn that the killing of Mr. Burroughs was the result of an insane impulse.

"Are you so hungry for conviction in this case – do you participate so much in the feelings that have actuated the prosecution – that with the sworn testimony of this physician, supported by that of every other doctor testifying in the cause, you can say that you require any further proof to satisfy you beyond a reasonable doubt, since such is the requirement of the law, that this girl was insane, in the sense we claim? We do not claim that she was generally insane all the time or even that she was partially insane all the time. We have repeatedly said she was subject to sudden attacks, overwhelming *paroxysms* of insane impulses.

"The District Attorney has declared that 'mad doctors' are not to be depended upon and that he would rather take one common-sense doctor than a host of them. He calls Dr. May and supposes a case that happened somewhere on the moon, I suppose, or in some distant country, for it is not the case before this jury. Dr. May answered that it was not a case of insanity but when Mr. Bradley proposed a hypothetical case taken faithfully from the evidence in this case, the common-sense Dr. May did not hesitate to respond that this homicide was the result of an insane impulse. The same for Dr. Johnson. When you find a verdict that this defendant is not guilty, you simply find the fact that you believe those witnesses. They are medical men, they are scientific men, and they know more about this matter than you or I, but whether that is so or not, they are the appointed witnesses that the law calls for to establish the defense.

"Burroughs excellent and worthy brother says he was going about Chicago for two or three weeks, all of which time the officer had a writ to serve on him and could not find him. Why was this? Why this dodging away from his wife on the trip back from Washington? Why the guilty manner in which he was married, and his hasty departure; his reluctance to go back, and his evident concealment when he got back?

"It was because there was ever present to that man the consciousness of the mountain of wrong he had heaped upon this poor woman, friendless, unprotected as she was, without her father, without a brother, without a champion. Conscience, which it is said makes cowards of us all, made such a coward of this man that he did not like to go to the great city of Chicago because this injured woman was there. He feared to be there and this is one of those pregnant and speaking facts in the history of his life that make the armor of his character, so much harped upon by the learned prosecutor, vulnerable at every point.

"After Miss Harris had her conversation with Mr. Davis, her attorney in Chicago, she looked across the street and suddenly was full of uncontrollable excitement and exclaimed, 'There is Mr. Burroughs!' It was fancy and delusion. She, unhappy girl, had become so excited, so crazed, if I may use that expression, upon the subject of this man, that although she had loved him for years, and knew his every feature, his walk, and every peculiarity by which to identify him, she took a perfect stranger for this man, and was about to go into paroxysms then. That was put on, I suppose? That was accidental?

"Had not the bullet been guided by the finger of an all-wise Providence, it would have passed him by harmless as the idle wind. She bought the pistol and remarked that Dr. Burroughs and his deceased brother had a plot to carry her off. Well, surely, that was no greater atrocity toward her than they had already perpetrated. They had carried off her happiness; they had broken her heart; they had blighted all her hopes of enjoyment. And she, with her unsettled mind and her deranged physical health, was haunted by the delusion that they might come to carry her away. I see no evidence, gentlemen, in these things, against insanity, no evidence of deliberate purpose, while I see much evidence to the contrary.

"If a killing is committed by an insane person, even temporarily insane, then there must be an acquittal. I have endeavored to show you, by a somewhat cursory examination of the testimony, that there is ample proof before you that this lady was insane when she killed this man.

"There are things, gentlemen, in this world that are more precious than life, and especially is female honor and female character. Yet, according to the law as it is found in the books, if Mr. Burroughs had imperiled the life of Miss Harris, she would have been perfectly justifiable, while she was perfectly sane, in taking his life. But having destroyed her honor, her happiness, and made her life a desert waste, without hope, had she taken his life in her sane moments, she would have rendered herself liable to punishment. This is a defect in our law, yet is it so written and so it must be administered.

"The District Attorney knew this and told you in his opening speech that you must not decide this question upon the law as you thought it ought to be, but upon the law as it is. But the fact is that Burroughs had so wronged her, that it became so consistent with human nature, so reasonable, so natural for her to have come here, with the premeditated purpose of taking his life, it would have been so appropriate to the passions, and the just passions of human nature, under the circumstances, that the counsel for the prosecution find a motive and an argument for a motive in these wrongs.

"The law is changed by courts, it is changed by juries, to suit the manners of the people, the spirit of their institutions, and the wants of society. These changes came long before the record of them is made in the books and for many a long year after the law has been radically changed, we find the judges constrained from the bench, contrary to their sympathies, contrary to their wishes, but because bound to find the law in the books, laying down as the law that which they think ought not to be the law, and that which the jury always takes care shall not be the law in its practical application to human affairs.

"After a while it gets into the books. At the present time in this country, to shoot down an adulterer in the act is manslaughter. And the man who does so, though he does it in the defense of his honor, must suffer if the law as recorded in the books applies. But there are provisions that no person shall be tried for a criminal offense, or be convicted, without a jury and in this country I do not believe that a single jury has ever found a man guilty in such a case.

"How is this? They are sworn to observe the law, they always receive it from the courts, and the Court always tells them how it is in the books. Why is it this way? The Constitution has provided that every man shall be tried by a body of men taken from his fellow citizens who are imbued with the spirit and manners of his country, and they in the application of the law will relieve any harsh and oppressive features.

"Thus it is that while juries will not say that a man is justifiable in committing a certain act, for that reason they find some other reason of a technical character for acquittal in such cases. I venture to say that at this day the common law of the United States, as established by usage and found in the practical application of the criminal code to cases that arise, is that the killing of an adulterer taken in the act, is excusable homicide.

"It is wonderful, gentlemen, to observe how in the progress of society the provisions of statutes and of laws are molded and changed to suit the wants of the people and the existing state of affairs."

Judge Hughes here cited several examples in which law as written was changed or reinterpreted in its administration to fit the spirit of the age and the necessities of the times. The counselor continued, "I would not insult any one of you by supposing for a moment that you would override the law and acquit any prisoner, however much you might sympathize with him, if you thought the clear requirements of the law forbade it. But this difficulty does not, in many of these cases, exist.

"Mr. Carrington said that mercy was an executive act lodged elsewhere than in this court. *But there is a mercy in the law itself*. There is a mercy in the mode of its administration, in the machinery appointed for its application to particular cases, which it is as much your duty to be governed by, which is as much a part of the law as the part that affixes a punishment for crime.

"One of these features is that the party should be tried by a jury; another is the doctrine of doubts. In a civil suit, a preponderance of evidence is enough but in a criminal proceeding, the jury is directed that if they have a reasonable doubt of the guilt of the accused person, they must acquit him. They may strongly incline to believe he was guilty. They may feel his conduct has been very reprehensible. They may feel that public morals, public justice, require that some rebuke or some punishment ought to be administered. Yet, if the doubt that the party's guilt is made to appear in the precise manner and form of the indictment, by competent proof, they must say to the accused. 'Go free.' The law recognizes, the books recognize, and experience proves, that by application of this principle many guilty persons are acquitted. But the law says better that it should be so. This is one of the merciful attributes of the law.

"Then again the law authorizes the defendant to put in a general plea of not guilty and the jury to give a general verdict. There is no judge, no attorney, no power on earth that can come in and require you to state the why or wherefore of your verdict. It is a matter between you and your conscience. The practical operation of this is that, in this country, certain offenses against human rights, against society, are committed which the law books have not revised to say are excuses for homicide, but the experience of men have.

"Another thing I want to draw your attention to is that the prosecutor told you that Washington city was a center of licentiousness and crime. That this was a place where people came to commit offense, and he made a sort of local appeal to you to make an example of somebody, to vindicate the general character of Washington. He said he hoped a Washington jury would maintain their dignity.

"Do you think it would be maintained by convicting an insane woman, because there is too much licentiousness in town generally? What kind of an appeal to a jury is that? Way out in the far West, in the trial of little suits before a justice of the peace, I have heard appeals made to excite prejudices against a town of people but I admit I was not prepared to hear such an appeal at the capital of the nation. A city of licentiousness!

"Wait until some unprincipled official, who has taken advantage of the disjointed state of the times to trample upon human liberty, upon human rights, and to disregard statutes, constitutions, and every sanction of liberty – wait until such men are dragged here, and they vindicate the law in Washington. In the meantime, let this poor, blighted, afflicted, ruined, and persecuted girl go. The law has no claim upon her. Let your verdict follow the partner of the deceased in this plot and let Washington justice travel to Chicago, and unmask there, before a confiding and trusting congregation and people, a man who wears the livery of Heaven to serve the devil under.

"Gentlemen, I am now through with this cause and knowing, as I do, that I shall be followed by a gentleman who will far more than supply anything I may have omitted, so far as I am concerned, I commit the case to your hands, with the most perfect and implicit confidence, that it will not take you long when you get this cause finally into your hands to record a verdict of Not Guilty."

After Wiley adjourned the court for the day, Richardson and Douglas retired to the Willard for a glass of Daniel Webster Punch while they compared notes in preparation for creating their reports for the day. The luscious concoction was made the night before and was composed of one bottle each of pure old French brandy, sherry, old Medford rum, champagne, and two bottles of claret, the juice of one dozen lemons, one pint of strong tea, sugar, strawberries, and pineapple to suit the taste, and absolutely no water. It was kept in a large silver bowl behind the bar and served in a tall glass with plenty of ice. Douglas and Richardson had beat the after-work crowd to the cool dark bar so the container had not yet been much depleted of this highly desirable beverage. Each of the reporters ordered a glass at the bar and carried them to a table where they could talk without being overheard easily. Douglas swirled a sip of the amber liquid around his mouth and said, "Damn, that's a good drink. One may not be enough."

Richardson lit up his pipe and lay out his note pad. "Wilson presented the sequence of actions Mary took in carrying out the killing and said she acted with hate as a motive and revenge as an object. She acted with premeditation and deliberation and tried to effect an escape. So *Mary's Story,* according to him, is not the story of a mind run amuck but one of normal human passions unrestrained by the fear of punishment, that results in a tragedy."

"And he pooh-poohs the insanity defense,especially the paroxysmal insanity defense, as the last refuge for the defenseless," added Douglas. "He characterized the Greenwood letters as a 'bungling contrivance,' which I guess means he thinks they were invented by the accused."

"Or her lawyers," smirked Richardson. "Most importantly, he specified, point by point, where the evidence in the real case differs from the assumed facts in the hypothetical case. You would hope that wouldn't be lost on the jury, but I'm sure the defense will try to undermine it."

"Now, for Judge Hughes," said Douglas. "He started out by reminding the jury that, if they didn't think she was insane, they should consider a finding of manslaughter rather than murder. Then he countered the DA's warning of being influenced by feelings of sympathy or mercy by warning them to be wary of acting out of a 'cry for blood,' like the prosecution."

"But he made no similar pledge for the defense," said Richardson. "Instead, he asks who is to punish the Burroughs brothers for their sins and then asserts that Mary's act was some kind of divinely administered justice. It was only with the consent of God that the unreliable pistol worked properly and the bullet did not go astray. Wow!"

"I think he must have gotten caught up in his own rhetorical flourish, since no one called him on it. He said he hated to speak ill of the dead but then went ahead and did so. He accused John Curtis Burroughs of being just as much the cause of his brother's death as Mary Harris and implied that he paid Ellen Mills to disappear, even though there is no evidence or testimony to that effect."

Having by now drained their glasses, the men strode up to the bar for a refill, then returned to their table. "I think I could stay in this nice cool spot and drink Daniel Websters all day," said Douglas.

"Yeah," said Richardson, "too bad we have to get our stories in in time to be run in tomorrow's papers."

"Well, I have a note here that says 'If you don't go along with what Dr. Nichols said, you must be consumed with the desire for vengeance,' "said Douglas. "It certainly sounded like that was what he was saying to the jury. He also said the prosecution's hypothetical case had so little bearing on the case that it must have taken place on the moon! He mocks the idea that Miss Harris could have faked her emotional misidentification of a stranger as if he were Burroughs when in her lawyer's office. He takes the preacher's evasiveness on the stand as proof of his guilt and he equates the breaking of Mary's heart to kidnapping. All of these claims are appeals to the juror's emotions and not to their logic.

"His last arguments have some merit, although I'm not sure how relevant they are in this case. He says the law isn't perfect and gives as an example the defect that allows killing in self-defense when threatened physically but not when female honor, happiness and hope can be destroyed under circumstances that would make killing a natural reaction."

Richardson said, "It is true that the law is a living and evolving structure and that juries, being imbued with the spirit and mores of the country, play a part in changing the law to fit current sentiments and circumstances. But it seemed that he was inviting the jury to find some excuse or technicality for acquitting, as has been done in cases of adultery. And he reminded them that they did not have to account to anyone for their verdict, they didn't have to give reasons for finding the defendant not guilty."

"I thought his last appeal was cleaver: Don't make an example of this poor girl to the citizens of Washington; go to Chicago and unmask the devil Burroughs before his trusting congregation."

CHAPTER 17

Daniel Voorhees was an imposing figure and his appellation – The Tall Sycamore of the Wabash – seemed quite appropriate. He was very tall, had an erect, regal bearing with light hair, dark eyes, and a full beard with a long goatee. His voice was intense and commanding which combined with powerful gestures to make him extraordinarily gifted in rhetoric. The representative from Indiana was serious in manner, possessed a magnetic charm, and had a command of language that could only be described as eloquent.

"This is one of the most remarkable cases ever submitted to a jury for trial. In many of its aspects it wears features more startling and extraordinary than we have hitherto met in the annals of jurisprudence. There is no man in this court room, no one throughout this broad land, whatever his experience or profession may be, who has ever seen its like in all respects before.

"A few months ago, in open day, in one of the public buildings of this capital, and in the presence of numerous observers, a human being was shot down by the frail hand of the prisoner at the bar, and sent to his final, dread account. The homicide mentioned in the indictment was thus committed. If it was deliberate, rational murder, then the blood of innocence is crying unappeased from the ground.

"But what are the elements which constitute this baleful crime? From that hour presaging woe to the human race, when the first man born of woman became a murderer, down to the present time, we have on record the frightful characteristics of the murderer. He is a being in whose heart the fires of malice and hate glow in perpetual flames, in whose face the image of God is blotted out, in whose eyes the light of mercy and love is forever quenched, who lies in wait like the tiger for his prey, and who strikes his unsuspecting and unoffending victim from motives of revenge or the lust of gain.

"Around such a being there centers every conception of horror which the human mind can embrace. All nature, animate and inanimate, the very earth and sky, recoil from him who bears the primal curse, and there is no communion for his blackened spirit this side of the abodes of the lost.

"But turn from this faint picture of a real murderer to the delicate, gentle being before you. We are told that deliberate and atrocious murder has been committed and that the criminal is in court. We are told that a brutal assassination has been accomplished, and that the lurking and ferocious assassin is in our presence.

"Where, gentlemen, where? Am I to be told that this heartbroken young girl, with her innocent, appealing face, and look of supplicating dependence on you, is the fierce and malignant monster of guilt which is described in the indictment and in the inflammatory language of the prosecution? Am I to be told that her heart conceived and her hand executed that crime for which the Almighty marked the brow of Cain?

"Let us pause and reason together for a few moments

on a primary question in this case. The whole life of this defendant, every trait of her character, all the general incidents of her conduct, have been elucidated and detailed in your hearing. Of what vice has she ever been guilty? In what immorality has she ever indulged? Not one, at no time and under no circumstances.

"Her life has been amiable, kind, affectionate, blameless, and pure. Troops of friends, of the best and most irreproachable in the land, have gathered about her in her quiet sphere at every stage of her checkered existence. These files of depositions declaring all her ways for nearly ten years past attest these facts. Can a young and generous mind, wholly uncontaminated with vice, unsullied and unstained by contact with the evil practices of life, without previous training even in the contemplation of crime, at once, while in a healthy state, in the undisturbed enjoyment of all its faculties, incur that awful grade of guilt at which civilized human nature in all ages stands aghast?

"Where is the hardened criminal who ever ascended the gibbet in expiation of his offenses who has not marked his downfall from small beginnings, increasing gradually and swelling in volume until he was hurled onward to the commission of those gigantic crimes for which the law claimed his life as forfeit? And yet, you are called on to believe that this defendant, at one single bound, sprang from the paths of virtue, gentleness, and purity, without any intervening preparation, to the highest and most revolting grade of guilt and ferocity known to human society.

"Those who have predetermined her guilt and passed a verdict in advance of the evidence and the law may indulge in this absurd and repulsive philosophy. In doing so, they may as well let the school houses be torn down and the churches abandoned. The instruction and moral culture of youth are useless and in vain. The precepts of morality and the principles of religion afford no security to the minds of their possessors from the sudden, instantaneous development of the most appalling wickedness.

"In the name of reason and universal experience I utterly repudiate this shocking theory. In the name of undefiled and virtuous human nature I repel it. In the name of innocent childhood and unstained womanhood, in the name of your own dear ones at home, I pronounce it a slander upon those holy attributes of the human heart which tend upwards, and ally us with heaven.

"I deny that Mary Harris is a criminal. I deny that any murder has been committed. I deny that this young prisoner is responsible for the death of A. J. Burroughs. I assert that his death was not a crime. He was not slain in violation of the law, for offenses against the law can only come by those who possess a sound mind and an unimpaired intelligence.

"And now, invoking your attention, I shall proceed to show you from the story of her life, which must constitute her defense, that it is not your duty to lay your hands in further punishment on the suffering head of Miss Harris, but that it will rather be your pleasing task to open her prison doors and bid her go free, attended by the charitable blessings of all Christian people.

"Who is this unfortunate defendant, and whence came she, when her weary feet bore her still more weary heart to this crowded capital? We see at a single glance a gliding, panoramic view of the life of an earnest, devoted girl. Our eyes first rest upon a point nearly ten years ago when Mary Harris was a beautiful and happy child, some ten years of age in the town of Burlington, Iowa.

"In that hour of tender childhood the evidence shows that Burroughs first met her and would to God that in that hour she had died! Gentle memories would have clustered around her peaceful grave, and this bitter cup whose very dregs she is now drinking would have been spared her. There is a mercy at times in death, for which the stricken soul longs and gasps as the parched and feverish earth does for the cooling rain. But He who notes the sparrow fall, and has a design in all the ways of men, ordered it otherwise, and she is here today, weary and heavily laden, but humbly submitting to the Providence by which her own will has been overruled and her actions guided.

"Burroughs at this time, gentlemen, was more than twice her senior, almost old enough to be her father. She sat upon his knee in the purity of unconscious childhood. He proposed to mold and fashion her mind by the superior force of his own age, experience, and will, in order that she might at a future period make him a suitable wife. There is no room to doubt upon this point. Let those ninety-two letters here produced in court make their appeal. They show us robust, developed manhood seeking the ascendancy over a confiding child. They show us maturity and strength striving for the mastery over inexperience and weakness.

"Under these circumstances, need I dwell upon the imperious nature of the influence which he obtained over her? The child became absorbed in the man. What else could happen? They walked the pathway of life hand in hand for many long years of hope and fond anticipation. He taught her to regard him as her future destiny. He was all the world to her. Her heart opened and expanded under the influence of his smile as the bud becomes a flower beneath the rays of the sun. She grew up to womanhood in unquestioning obedience to his will. The ties by which she was bound to him were the growth of years, and embraced all the strength of her whole being.

"And did all this have no effect on the subsequent condition of her mind when disaster came? He had carried her to the highest pinnacle of happiness and hope. She stood upon the summit of joyous expectations, and all around her was sunshine and gladness. Well might she exclaim to my learned and eminent brother, as she paced her prison floor, 'Oh! Mr. Bradley, you should have seen me then. I was so happy!'

"Yes, though poor and humble, yet she loved and was beloved and it was enough, she was content. For in that hour when a virtuous woman feels for the first time that she possesses the object of her devotion, there comes to her a season of bliss which brightens all the earth before her. The mother watching her sleeping babe has an exclusive joy beyond the comprehension of all hearts but her own. The wife who is graced by her husband's love is more beautifully arrayed than the lilies, and envies not the diadems of queens.

"But to the young virgin heart, more than all, when the kindling inspiration of its first and sacred love is accompanied by a knowledge that for it in return there burns a holy flame, there comes an ecstasy of the soul, a rapturous exaltation, more divine than will ever again be tasted this side of the bright waters and perennial fountains of paradise. The stars grow brighter, the earth more beautiful, and the world for her is filled with a delicious melody. This, peculiarly, is woman's sphere of happiness. There she concentrates all the wealth, the unsearchable riches of her heart, and stakes them all upon the single hazard. If she loses, all is lost and night and thick darkness settle down upon her pathway.

"It is not so with man. His theater is broader. No single passion can so powerfully absorb him. If disappointment overtakes him, a wide and open horizon invites him to new enterprises, which will relieve him of that still, deep, brooding intensity which is the pregnant parent of woe, insanity, and death to woman.

"Gentlemen, the language which faithful woman holds to the object of her love when the hour of separation is threatened is very old and very beautiful 'Entreat me not to leave thee, or to return from following after thee, for whither thou goest I will go, where thou lodgest I will lodge. Thy people shall be my people, thy God my God. Where thou diest there I will be buried. May the Lord do so to me and more also if aught but death part thee and me.'

"It was in this spirit that Mary Harris came to Chicago and resided with Misses Jane and Louisa Devlin. It was Burroughs still shaping her destiny. It was the man still pointing the course for the child to follow. And shall this be imputed to her as a fault? Will this prosecution, fed as I believe it to be from the springs of private malice, assail her because she trusted Burroughs and confided in his honor?

"Because he was false and broke her heart, you are called on to believe that this act abased her virtuous brow into the dust of shame. Not only do I pronounce this a slander upon Mary Harris, but it is equally a slander upon the truth, fidelity, and virtue of womanhood. She did no more than what the proudest, the purist, and the best have done in all countries at all times. She endowed him with the principles of justice and honor. She crowned his brow with a constellation of all the virtues and then trusted him. She turned her back on home, kindred, and friends and with him faced the world alone.

"Is Mary Harris to be condemned, to be carried to the horrid gibbet, that appalling machinery of death, terror, and lasting ignominy, in order that the conduct of A. J. Burroughs shall stand triumphantly vindicated? According to this new theology, falsehood has become respectable, treachery noble, and the base, cowardly betrayal of young, inexperienced female confidence, a qualification for a seat with the just made perfect.

"I can join in no such wretched blasphemy! I cling to the old and homely virtues according to whose teachings such conduct has been loaded with infamy from the earliest dawn of civilized human society. I take my stand on this universal verdict of all ages, this irreversible judgment of enlightened mankind. I say that such conduct is more injurious to morality than murder, that it is worthy of the punishment of death, and that he who is guilty of it ought to die.

"I do not place the defense in this case on that ground, but when the prosecution sees fit to tender an issue upon the character of the deceased in the face of the black and revolting record of his guilt, it is proper that it should be met. When an effort is openly made to debauch the public mind into the belief that vice is virtue, that turpitude is morality, and that crime against unsuspecting innocence is one of the adornments of the Christian religion, then I conceive that the voice of truth should be heard.

"Mary was looking forward to a future filled with honor and delight. In such a serene and happy moment as this, with no note of warning, the blow descended upon her naked head, shivering every hope with which her heart was tenanted, and dashing the temple of reason itself into ruins.

"Is this statement the work of fancy on my part? Is it not the sad, literal truth? Counsel has seen fit to attribute powers of eloquence to me, which I neither possess nor affect. I can only repeat to you a plain and simple story of wrong, misery, and madness, which you already know and which is far more eloquent in itself than any words I can employ.

"Seven years of love were spurned in an instant. Seven years of patient hope were turned into a moment of despair. He had lifted her up almost to celestial heights, only that her fall might be sufficiently great to dash her to pieces. In order to understand the effect of disappointment and misfortune, we must fully consider the condition of the mind when the shock came. In the present instance, we shudder at the bare contemplation of the mental agony of the defendant when she realized that she was abandoned by him for whom she had abandoned all but her honor.

"I am aware that the sufferings of helpless woman, under such circumstances, are too often discussed with a sneer. There are those, who pass for men, who aspire to be thought wise in the ways of the world, by talking and writing in flippant and witty strains in regard to woman, her sorrows and misfortunes. To such sage and philosophic minds there is no such thing as mental derangement, growing out of disappointed love or broken marriage vows. The defense of insanity in such cases is merely a cunning device of counsel. Well, gentlemen, I am consoled with the belief that there is nowhere in this court, either on the bench or in the jury box, one of these ready-made critics of human motives and human conduct, who are always deaf to law, to evidence, and to reason.

"I appeal to human experience. It is said that we are manufacturing a defense for this girl. This charge means that we are assuming facts in her behalf, which do not exist, that her condition at the time of the homicide was not such as we represent it.

"Is it not, therefore, a most essential ingredient of this defense to show that Mary Harris had been visited by those causes which have been recognized in all ages as the most prolific sources of insanity to her sex? Must we be told that we are standing on doubtful ground? Do men of sense gape and stare, because we show that the conduct of Burroughs made Mary Harris insane? Did such a thing never happen before? Is all this something so new that we are to be styled visionary explorers and reckless adventurers?

"Why, gentlemen, we are simply following a broad, sorrowful, and well-beaten track. It is thickly strewn with the wrecks of human happiness – with broken hearts and ruined intellects. Go to the asylums for the insane – those awful tombs of living death! See that once-beautiful, but now pallid and shrunken face, pressed against the bars of her cell. See the scorching frenzy of her restless and anxious eye. Her parched lips move, and she calls upon a name, which is strange to our ears. She prays sadly, perhaps to be allowed to go to him. She murmurs the broken lines of some song, which they sang together in the days of old.

"And then all of a sudden, as if a serpent's tooth had struck her bleeding heart, she shrieks out maledictions, and calls down the curses of God on his head. At last, she cowers down shuddering in her corner, where, chained to the barren rock of the past, her one perpetual memory, with beak and talons sharper and more ruthless than the vulture's, preys with ceaseless rage upon her vitals.

"The name she has called upon is borne by one who is the favorite of fortune, who wears the honors of the world on his brow, who has wife and children blooming under his roof, who has a high seat in the sanctuary – is a 'Christian without a stain,' – who has forgotten his victim and is happy. His name may not be Burroughs, but his conduct was not more false, and the ruin which he wrought was not more fatal to peace and life."

Here and there throughout the audience were heard the muffled sighs and sniffles of women. More than the usual number of men cleared their throats during this delivery.

"I have heard it urged that because, through all the long and intimate years which she passed with Burroughs, she kept the vestal fires of chastity alive in her heart, that therefore her sufferings could not have been so great, when he abandoned her, and attempted to stain her name with pollution, as if she had fallen. This is not my theory of female character. The just, the pure, the good, those who have never consented unto iniquity, are those who, as a general rule, are unable to relieve themselves from those burning memories of cruelty and injustice which so often bring distraction.

"Burroughs not merely left this girl alone in the world, robbing her of all the priceless treasures of hope which she had laid up in the future, but he endeavored, in the very wantonness of wickedness, to trample her in the mire under his feet, to make her an object of scorn, to taint her name with moral leprosy, and to consign her to odium and shame. I am aware that it is to be urged that Burroughs was not the author of the infamous Greenwood letters. I am ready for that issue. Tell me first, is there anybody else in the world likely to have approached Mary Harris in that way? Does a stranger thus approach a woman whose name is unsullied? Does a mere casual acquaintance seek thus to gain an intimacy with one whose virtue was never called in question? And who but Burroughs was intimate with the prisoner? If there was another, it would have been shown.

"The brother, Dr. Burroughs, has not slept on the track of the accused. He has spared neither labor nor money to bring before you every item of her brief and now miserable life which might bear hard upon her in this trying hour. He wrote to a brother divine at Burlington to engage his assistance. He went to Janesville to bring every hidden thing to light. He hunted up all those who had ever known her. He associated with policemen, and took them into his confidence. He labored day and night to rake together every grain of evidence which would weigh against her life in the scales of justice which you now hold.

" And if any one had ever sustained such a relation toward her except Burroughs, as would have rendered it even remotely reasonable that he wrote these letters, would he not have been discovered and held up in this investigation? If she had ever borne herself toward any one else in such a manner as to warrant a reasonable being in such an advance, that fact would have been proven.

"And, again, who would have used the language to Ellen Mills, at 94 Quincy Street, but Burroughs? The evening upon which he waited and watched for the meeting which his letter had requested, he said to the keeper of this abode of sin and shame that he would sit near the window, where he could observe the approach of his victim, and that he would himself go to the door and let her in.

"Why did he assume this task? Because, as he said, she knew him so well that she would trust him and come in. Who else but Burroughs did Mary Harris know so well? Who else could she so implicitly trust? And above all, who else could so confidently assert his power over her? Who but him, who had fostered the growth of her confidence from childhood up to womanhood? Who but him, on whose arm she had leaned so long and so fondly?

"'She knows me so well that she will trust me and come in.' This alone fixes the paternity of the Greenwood letters. This alone discloses who was that night waiting for this girl as plainly as if a beam of light had at that moment fallen on him, and made his guilty face visible to every eye in Chicago.

"More on this point. It was known to all here concerned as counsel for the government, and it was known to Dr. Burroughs within a few weeks after his brother's death, that Ellen Mills had minutely and accurately described the deceased to Miss Devlin and the accused, and had also recognized his photograph. It was equally well known that a clerk in the post office had done the same. For when these letters were received, the defendant, outraged by their character, took prompt measures to ascertain their depraved origin.

"We labored for months to obtain the testimony of

Mills and the post office clerk – they were important to us – but our efforts were in vain. (Turning to Dr. Burroughs) What efforts did you make? If the post office clerk did not say that it was your brother who called for these Greenwood letters and did not describe him, why did you not bring him here? If Ellen Mills never made similar statements, why is she not on the witness stand or her depositions on file? You have brought witnesses here from Chicago and Janesville whose testimony is so immaterial that it trifles with the time of the court. Yet instead of bringing these two witnesses here who could prove this vital point, we find by your own extorted admission, listening to the unscrupulous suggestions of a policeman, that one of them at least shall be carried out of sight by the corrupt use of money and the other one escapes us.

"There is but one conclusion to be drawn. These two witnesses would have sustained Louisa Devlin, and Dr. Burroughs and the prosecution knew it! The suppression of evidence is a grave and almost conclusive presumption against the party that resorts to it. This is especially true when the prosecution is sustained by the treasury of the government in enforcing the attendance of witnesses.

"Each of us, in taking our oaths, have invoked the name and help of God in the discharge of our duties. We are on holy ground. Life, life, that mysterious gift of the Creator, is the issue at stake. Its awful import should inspire every breast with a religious desire to aid this court and jury in arriving at the exact truth.

"What is to be said of one who admits that he has not done so? I learn that it is said that no attack can injure Dr. Burroughs, that his position is so exalted that no shaft can reach him. I have no desire to indulge in personal assaults, but no position in life, no assumption of superior piety and virtue, will ever shield the character of a witness who, in a trial involving life itself, conceals material evidence, and then attempts to supply its place by his own unsupported oath. Nor need counsel in such an instance waste their time in denunciation, for no language which our tongues could utter could paint his conduct in colors so dark, in a moral deformity so hideous, as he himself has painted it by his own testimony. Such a witness becomes at once powerless for evil before an intelligent jury. He is dead by his own act.

"And I submit here now, in all candor, in the face of this court, in the presence of my learned brethren of the bar, and to you the final arbiters of this sad and trying hour, that Dr. Burroughs stands in contempt of this court, for his collusion with the policeman, Douglas, to hide away a witness from its process; he stands in contempt of society, which requires all its members to aid in vindicating justice; he stands in contempt of you, in refusing to bring before you all the evidence in his power to establish a point on which he asks you to find in his favor; and he stands in contempt of the teachings of the merciful Master on the Mount, by coming here with deceit and treachery in his heart to strike this helpless, feeble, sick and lovely being, to whom his very name is an unendurable misery.

"But it is of no consequence whether Burroughs guided the pen or dictated to a confederate. The testimony of Mr. Danenhower is deemed material on this point. He says that the leave of absence on which the deceased went home to get married commenced September 8, and hence he could not have been there in time to write them. My answer is, first, that nothing is more common than for clerks to leave a few days in advance of the date of their permission.

"Secondly, in addition to the identification of Ellen Mills and the clerk at the post office, it is in proof that Louisa Devlin and Mary Harris both saw him at times corresponding very nearly, if not exactly, with the dates of these letters. This is conclusive. There are but two witnesses in the world who could have contradicted these facts. Dr. Burroughs knew they would not contradict them, and he therefore kept them away, with the aid of 'a hundred dollars or two,' as suggested by the policeman, and came here himself to contradict them.

"Why did Burroughs do this deed without a name for cruelty and perfidy? His motive was not the gratification of passion. Lust was not one of the elements in his calculations. Base and wretched as are such motives of action, yet, if it be possible, those that actuated him were still lower and more depraved.

"Look calmly at his situation. From Mary Harris he was about turning away without a word. He knew that such an act would be to her as appalling as the voice of doom. His conscience made him a coward. He could not face her with the story of his stupendous crime. He could not look into her confiding eye and tell her that his whole life towards her had been one mighty falsehood.

"Human nature, however depraved, was not equal to such a task. The past was filled with voices of reproach and terror to his guilty heart. The future frowned on him full of menace and warning. The present was haunted by a sense of conscious wrong from which he tried in vain to escape.

"He knew too that he was in her power. These letters which are here in court, and many others not here, arose in his memory. He recalled the one in which he says, 'And Mollie, if from any reason whatever I may change my views or feelings towards you, and I should feel like entering into a matrimonial alliance with any one else than yourself, I will promptly advise you of it.' He was about taking that fatal step but he had not the manly honor to fulfill his promise.

"He, however, like one who plans the commission of a crime, took measures for his escape. He was to be married in a few days to the unhappy lady who now mourns in her widowed home, and whose melancholy fate I deeply commiserate. He knew that when that fact reached the ears of Mary Harris, her cries, her sobs, her voice of wailing would ascend like perpetual lamentations in the air.

"She might, in her deep distress, utter his name to the world in such a way as to stain his character as a Christian. She might come near him some day and remind him that he once took a child from her parent's roof, and broke her heart. Aye, it was in her power to denounce him as false and infamous at all times and places, to pursue him, if she desired, as an avenging shadow, to rob him of peace, and to turn his days and nights into fear and alarm.

"But if her foot once crossed the threshold of shame she was in the fowler's snare and at his mercy. If this defendant had ever entered 94 Quincy Street, Burroughs would have breathed easy, and gone to his approaching nuptials a free and happy man, secure from molestation at her hands. Her mouth would have been closed forever. It was not her soul he expected to pollute, but her name.

"He intended to be able to prove that she was seen entering this wretched house and to hold that fact in terror over her. If she entered that house she would come out covered with an everlasting mildew. Her heart might be as pure as before, for she was unconscious of its character, but her name would be spotted with an incurable leprosy.

"If he could desert her without cause, is he not capable of committing the other crime? The one absorbing purpose of his heart at that time was to sever the tie that bound them together, and when we find him unwilling to do so by an interview, we are prepared to believe that he attempted to do so by consigning her name to ignominy and pollution.

"For the purposes of our defense, it is only necessary

to show that Mary Harris actually believed Burroughs wrote the Greenwood letters, and that they thus became one of the exciting causes of her mental agony and derangement. But I have also tried to show that she had overwhelming reasons for her belief – reasons from which there was no escape. No woman who truly loves ever willingly consents to blacken and deface her own idol. She rather clings to him in blind adoration long after the proofs of his treachery have become visible to all eyes but her own.

"And who will say that this defendant jumped to conclusions on this point against the deceased? On the contrary, when her fears and suspicions were alarmed, she proceeded with conscientious care. Step by step the painful truth was pressed upon her. The woman of Quincy Street described him. The clerk did the same But she did not stop there. This young girl, then but eighteen or nineteen years of age, gathered up the letters of the deceased, took his miniature, took all that related to her seven years of love and hope, and knowing the standing of the Rev. John C. Burroughs, knowing his religious character, went to him like a child to a father, and poured out her grief and her fears. How like the pure and noble girl that she was!

"But here we are involved in a contradiction as to the day on which this call was made. Dr. Burroughs says that she came on the 16th of September. I do not believe him. His brother was married on the 15th, and I do not believe him because, in order to free himself from reproach, it is necessary for him to fix his interview with the defendant subsequent to his brother's marriage. I do not believe him because Louisa Devlin and Jane Devlin swear it was on the 15th. You have looked upon those two honest, truthful faces and observed their patient candor under the most protracted examinations. They have been good angels of human nature in this cause. They were the friends of Mary

Harris in sunshine, and they have abided through darkness. Others may have shrunk from her side, but they have stuck closer because of her calamities.

"Are such pure and unselfish beings as these to be degraded by counsel in order to support the testimony of one who appears in this case more like a criminal than an honest man? Who failed to note that damning hesitancy of manner, which caused every eye in this court room to rest upon him with suspicion? Who could fail to perceive that he was weighing the effect – not the truthfulness – of his answers before giving them? Who ever heard an equal number of qualifying adjectives expressive of cautious doubt and uncertainty used in the same space of time as when he was under cross-examination? No, his oath will not weigh an instant in your minds as against theirs. You will believe, from the evidence, that the defendant and Dr. Burroughs met on the 15th and not on the 16th of September.

"There is another reason why it was on the 15th, the day of the fatal marriage. The law gives the prisoner the right to stand where I am standing, if she had the power to do so, and speak for herself. I am but speaking for her, and in that capacity, I have the right to say that it was the 15th, because she says so, because that awful day has left an indelible scar on her brain that fixes her recollection. And every word that has fallen from her pallid lips on this subject, has carried truth to my mind. Dr. Nichols has sworn to her exalted sense of truth and female virtue, and a mountain of oaths by Dr. Burroughs would not shake my faith in her integrity. I do not believe that at this dreadful moment she would purchase her life by the utterance of a falsehood, no, not even to escape that death from which we shrink back in speechless horror."

Judge Wiley called for a short recess and the reporters, Douglas and Richardson, took the opportunity to go outside on the steps and light up their pipes.

"No new information so far but Voorhees is masterful in weaving a tale and creating a spell," said Richardson.

"I thought his contrasting of the girl who sits accused with the stereotype of a murderer was a good opening," said Douglas, "the delicate, innocent, heartbroken young thing vs. the ferocious Godless monster, a merciless, cursed blackened spirit. She doesn't look the part. And how could she jump to being such a creature in a single bound with no intermediary steps in evidence? It's largely irrelevant to the case against her, but he implies that it strains the bounds of credulity. She obviously isn't that kind of murderer."

"He reiterates the idea that there has been no murder committed since that requires a perpetrator with a sound mind and unimpaired intelligence, taking for granted that the defense has proven Miss Harris to have been insane at the time of the homicide. And then he tries to evoke sympathy for his client by asserting that it would have been more merciful for her if she had died when she first met Burroughs. Thus," continued Richardson, "it must be part of some divine plan that overruled Mary's will and guided her actions. Like Hughes argued, it is God's will."

"They are still claiming that there are 92 letters that attest to the nature of their relationship," said Douglas, " even though there were only about a third that number that were actually entered into evidence and a request to read the others by the prosecution was denied."

"That's a minor bit of misinformation that registers in the minds of the jury but will not be contested for fear of being regarded as too picky," said Richardson. "But Voorhees really waxes poetic when he describes the presumed mind of the young girl in love.

"When the young virgin heart believes her love is reciprocated, she is ecstatic, rapturous and it colors everything she sees. She gambles everything on a single passion, unlike men who have many interests and are not so easily unbalanced. Burroughs raised Mary's expectations to celestial heights and then abandoned her and this calamity made her mad.

"It is a common story and he claims that insane asylums are filled with people with broken hearts & ruined intellects. All of Voorhees' biblical quotes about the beauty of woman's faithfulness further idolizes this state of mind, which presumably characterized Mary Harris before she was jilted by Burroughs. So he offers this as an explanation for why Mary went crazy and killed her lover. If the response of the observers is any indication, the narrative seems to have had the desired effect."

"He condemns the one doing the abandoning as having committed a crime worthy of the death sentence," said Douglas. "According to Voorhees, Burroughs robbed Mary of hope and then topped it off by trying to get her to step foot in a whore house and thereby taint her name with shame. And he did that because he feared she might denounce him publicly and injure his reputation as a Christian or pursue him like an avenging angel, making his life a nightmare. Do you think the jury is likely to buy that?"

"Voorhees deflected attacks by cynics by making fun of any detractors as being not 'real men' and asserting that they lacked an appreciation of law, evidence & reason. Then he launched into another attack on the Reverend John Burroughs, accusing him of colluding with the policeman to hide witness from court – the madam at 94 Quincy and the post office clerk. They could have testified as to the identity of the person who showed up at the house of ill-repute and the post office and Voorhees believes the preacher should have brought them there. Of course, he didn't mention that the defense had the same opportunity and didn't avail themselves of it either."

"Voorhees also didn't let pass the poor showing that the Reverend Burroughs made in court. He said he flatly didn't believe him and emphasized the doctor's evasiveness, hesitant manner and unnecessary qualifications and voiced the opinion that everyone in court was suspicious of him, thereby placing himself on the side of the audience."

CHAPTER 18

A bailiff appeared and indicated that court was about to resume. Douglas tapped the bowl of his pipe on the heel of his boot, letting the smoldering ashes fall to the ground. Richardson did likewise and they returned to their seats inside the rail. Representative Voorhees continued with his summation.

"Dr. Burroughs admits that Miss Harris came to see him in regard to his brother, and that she apprised him of her long and intimate relations with him. The Greenwood letters were submitted to him, as also her reasons for believing that the deceased wrote them. She was in grief and trouble on that account. She inquired whether he was in Chicago. He was forced to admit that he did not inform her of his brother's marriage.

"Why did he not tell her the truth? He says that he asked her if his brother had broken any engagement with her, and that she said he had not. The force of this answer will be fully appreciated when it is remembered that at this time the defendant was not aware that the deceased was married, and that this reverend witness was purposely concealing that fact from her.

"But he says that Mary Harris told him that no marriage engagement had ever existed between her and his brother. Now, gentlemen, if she had made such a statement to Dr. Burroughs on that occasion, it would constitute a marvel and a wonder in the history of human nature. Here was a young girl for the first time in her life in an agony of apprehension for fear she was about to be betrayed by the man whom she loved. The fact that she was engaged to marry him does not admit of a doubt. She carried with her the evidence of their engagement to show Dr. Burroughs as well as complaining of the feared breach of faith.

"The prosecution asks you to believe that, under these circumstances, she told an absolute falsehood that would deprive her of all claims upon the accused or of any right to inquire of his movements or conduct! Are we to believe that she bore false witness voluntarily against herself upon a subject of the most supreme and sacred moment, that while discussing her rights, she admitted she had no rights? That while hunting for him with nearly a hundred letters in her pocket promising marriage, she deliberately settled the whole case against herself by informing his brother that there was nothing whatever between them except the ordinary relations of friendship? What an interview, according to Dr. Burroughs! He must have foreseen this trial. At least he must have been qualifying himself to swear in an action for a breach of marriage contract.

"He asks her if his brother had ever made any dishonorable proposals to her, and she answers no, although at that time she was painfully aware that he had attempted to lure her into a house of ill-fame. Presumably he asks her if the deceased ever had broken any engagement with her and once more she answers in the negative. And then Dr. Burroughs ends the interview, forgetting to tell her that the object of her solicitude was married on the day before. Is there a man in the world of common intelligence who would believe this testimony? The defendant went to Dr. Burroughs for information and came away almost as ignorant as she went. Dr. Burroughs, on the contrary, made that the occasion to cram himself as a witness to every phase, which any judicial inquiry might ever assume between them. He says that he is here simply to protect his brother's reputation, and he certainly betrayed an early knowledge that it would need protection.

"Dr. Burroughs's testimony and all the witnesses he has brought here have but one purpose and that is the life of the prisoner. It is a bold demand for blood. Oh, spirit of eternal justice, what more is this poor shivering victim of man's cruel perfidy to suffer! It is not enough that one drove her mad, and caused her to cry out 'I am bound upon a wheel of fire, that mine own tears do scald like molten lead!'

"And must the brother come now and struggle to drag this wan, emaciated, and stricken being to an awful and ignominious death? Is he not satisfied with the ruin already wrought? Are you not ready to exclaim, 'Spare her, Dr. Burroughs, oh, spare her! Spare her for the sake of the name you bear. Enough she has suffered in that name. For the love of God and for the sake of His mercies spare her broken life. Do not press and trample on the fallen and undone. She may meet you no more in this world. You may forget her mortal agonies in the honeyed commendations of your followers.

"But there comes a day when the one who murdered her peace, and the one who now seeks to murder her life, will both meet their victim in the presence of the Great Judge, and in a court above the sun, where misfortune is not a crime, and where earthly distinctions fade away; where the poor are rich, and the merciful blessed, where the feeble are strong and the oppressor's rod is broken.

"In that awful presence they will be called to answer why, at their hands, Mary Harris was beaten and scourged to madness and death. Spare her, oh, spare her! Lest if you succeed in your purpose to slay her here, she will confront you in the eternal world as a bright angel, with her fair hair dabbled in her own innocent blood, shed by your hand, and there shriek into your shrinking ear, 'False, fleeting, and perjured!'

"Gentlemen, I sometimes tire of life when I see wrong and injustice spreading their prosperous branches as the green and flourishing palm. When those by whom offenses come in this world, who prey upon virtue and turn it into vice, who sport with innocence in order to poison it, who make a mockery of love and a plaything of truth, go not only unscathed of the law, but even applauded by the hired panderers to a depraved and debauched public sentiment.

"Gentlemen, I have now, to the best of my ability, proven that in the case of the prisoner there existed overwhelming causes of insanity. To establish this great fact, I have thus far dwelt upon her relation to the deceased, the hopes he inspired in her breast, the power he obtained over her will and destiny, their final separation, and the aggravating circumstances by which that separation was surrounded.

"Although these moral causes alone more than account for her subsequent condition, yet at this point I wish to barely call your attention to the testimony of Dr. Fitch. He is a gentleman of standing in his profession in Chicago, and attended the prisoner in her illness soon after Burroughs abandoned her. He states that he found her laboring under a painful disease peculiar to her sex. Every medical man in the world and every book ever written on that subject, declare that this disease is a constant physical cause of periodical, or, as it is more properly termed, paroxysmal insanity.

"I shall not dwell upon this fact but only remind you that she was suffering from one of those attacks when she entered the Treasury building on the fatal 30th day of January. In this most important feature of the case there is no conflict of testimony and no room for doubt or conjecture. Where then, in the whole range of judicial history, was there ever shown a more powerful combination of causes, in the same person, of mental derangement? The well-known moral causes existed in malevolent force and in fearful alliance with them was a physical disease which is recognized as one of the principal causes of mischief and malady to the female mind. Shall we, then, any longer wonder that, with her delicate nervous temperament, she fell before such a terrible combination?

"We behold, for once at least in our lives, a human being totally transformed. The change is complete in every respect. Physically she is no longer the same. Her former buoyant health withers away. The bloom in her face dies out, as it were, in a single night. Her already slight frame becomes still slighter. Sleep, the gentle nurse in whose arms the peaceful invalid woos the returning spirit of health, fled from her eyes. Burroughs had murdered sleep and her mind was fixed with an appalling intensity on the memory of the past, which was to her brain as a consuming fire. From this horrible spell there was no escape.

"We see her mind developing its changes in equal pace with her body. It is the seat of the canker which blighted her whole system and which no medicinal balm can reach. According to the evidence, she was up to that period the merriest and most joyous of her circle. But now the laugh was gone, no merriment kindled in her eye. The future was to her dead and she lived in the past and it was the charnel house of all her hopes and over it hung the mourning cypress.

"She grew weary of life. Who does not when all that gives life its value has perished? That is, in itself, one of the incipient stages of insanity. It is the offspring of that 'Black Melancholy' which all authors designate as one of the parent springs of madness.

"Had she succeeded in taking her walk by the lake after murmuring her farewell to her friend, there might have been an inquest and the usual verdict – one more unfortunate gone to her death. Perhaps there would have been an item in the papers the next morning. Men would read it listlessly over their coffee and forget it during breakfast. And yet in that item would have been contained the account of a wreck of more infinite and incalculable value than all the richly laden ships that ever sunk beneath the surface of the deep. It would have told of a ruin which calls upon Heaven, Earth, and Hell as its interested witnesses. It would have recorded a crime, which rises in mountain blackness against the soul of the betrayer of innocence.

"And what about those outbreaks of violence towards those who were the beneficent guardians of her daily life? We have found the development of suicidal mania and, alas, we now discover the unmistakable symptoms of homicidal insanity. Lost was her natural disposition to be amiable, gentle and affectionate. Do the moral affections and the mind all undergo a sudden and radical revolution, characterized by irrational actions, while all the functions are in a healthful condition?

"Can the dove change itself at pleasure to the kite or the lamb to the ravening wolf? If Mary Harris was not insane when she aimed a large and deadly knife at the breast of her dearest friend, the human character can assume the hues of the chameleon at will, and there are no rules by which human motives can be fathomed. She attacks Louisa Devlin and a customer. She is so violent that her friends imprison her by force and she destroys articles of domestic use.

"We show you a person sick in mind and body and assert that such functional disease of the brain ensued as to impel to this strange and irrational course of conduct. We are involved in no mysteries and have no need to resort to the malicious contrivance of a depraved heart or to the Devil for an explanation. We have the causes and the effects have followed. A mind over strained in the perpetual contemplation of a harrowing theme, and a body broken by painful disease, gave rise to a paroxysmal insanity which assumed the destructive form.

"We have heard from the prosecution, with an air of triumph, that there is at least one act on her part which clearly proves her a rational being – she bought a pistol. The real reason that she bought it was one of those frightful ideas which pursue the startled and suspicious minds of the insane. She believed there was a scheme between her false lover and his brother to pick her up in the streets some day and carry her away, where she would never be heard of again. She was haunted and pursued by this irrational fear and meant to be ready to defend herself. It was a wild delusion that is absolutely conclusive of a disordered intellect.

"Mary Harris comes calmly into court and does not rave in your presence. At certain times, when we catch a glimpse of her, she has exercised the attributes of reason. A number of witnesses have been brought here from great distance who say that she was not mad in their unobservant presence. We not only admit all this but we assert that there are intervals during which she is perfectly sane on all subjects. As Dr. Reid says, 'There are few cases of mania where the light of reason does not now and then shine out between the clouds. But the mere interruption of a disorder is not to be mistaken for its cure or its ultimate conclusion.'

"And Esquirol says, 'The insane group and arrange their ideas, carry on a reasonable conversation, defend their opinions with subtlety and even with a rigid severity of logic, give very rational explanations, and justify their actions by highly plausible motives.' Winslow refers to, 'the subtlety, extreme cunning, and extraordinary shrewdness of the insane, as well as the wonderful mastery they have occasionally been seen to exercise over their acknowledged delusions, whilst under the searching analysis of the ablest and most accomplished advocates of the day.'

"We forget that the mind is a many-stringed instrument, and that, while it requires every cord in a healthful state to create a perfect harmony, yet one may be strained and broken, and still the others when touched give forth their own unimpaired tones. It is a matter of history that Tasso composed his most eloquent and impassioned verses during paroxysms of insanity. Lucretius wrote his immortal poem, *De Rerum Natura*, when suffering from an attack of mental aberration. Alexander Cruden compiled his *Concordance* whilst insane. But in these most painful instances there was somewhere a hidden wound which would not heal, which bled at the touch. When it gaped afresh the whole instrument wailed forth in melancholy madness, and the stricken beings were irresponsible for their acts in the sight of God and man.

"In Baltimore we see the defendant fitful, nervous, gloomy, silent. She gazes steadily on space and sometimes breaks into a ghostly glee or sings in plaintive strains the broken fragments of some melancholy song telling of disappointed love. She spends a sleepless night poring over these fond letters of the deceased. The midnight is not more gloomy than her soul. She is communing with the lost – the lost hopes of other and brighter days – the lost hours of a radiant joy – the lost hours of love, of happiness and promise. She is amidst the tombs, and the demon, memory, absorbs and binds her captive. She takes no note of time. Thus, this lovely being came here and in this mood of mind she went to the Treasury building.

"Where is the evidence that she premeditated murder? The pistol itself is scarcely calculated to take life, and it has been shown that she obtained it under the influence of an insane delusion. She inquired for Burroughs. Was this a desire to kill? In the instant that he fell by her hand she implored God on her knees to spare him. Does the murderer beseech Divinity to spare his victim? She offered her life for his if he could be saved. Is this the conduct of one who lies in wait and assassinates in cold blood?

"As his life was ebbing away, she shrieked, 'Oh, God, I loved him better than my own soul.' Is this the language of one who, in the exercise of reason, has smitten to death an object of hate and revenge? The rigid features, the white and ghastly face, the blazing and tearless eye, the rapid and at times incoherent speech, imprinted on the mind of the Honorable Secretary of the Treasury for the first time in his life, the dreadful reality of absolute despair. He rendered a verdict of innocence when, with the instincts of the kind gentleman, he took Mrs. McCullough the next morning to visit her in prison.

"I now plant myself on sworn facts which you cannot disregard, except in violation of your oath as jurors. We placed on the stand a gentleman of eminent distinction as a physician of the diseased mind. Dr. Nichols has pursued this branch of science as a specialty for over twenty-five years and has been Superintendent of the Asylum for the Insane in this District for the past eighteen years. His reputation is known extensively throughout the country, and I may be permitted to say that he has deeply impressed me as a gentleman of profound intellect, a vigorous and correct thinker, and a most conscientious laborer in the vineyards of truth. Life, honor and justice are all safe in his hands.

"He comes before you and relieves this case of every difficulty. He lifts a weighty responsibility from your shoulders, and makes your duties light and easy to be discharged. He has heard all the testimony and visited the prisoner in jail several times in order to form a correct opinion. No man ever stood up in a court of justice more amply qualified to give an opinion.

"In view of all the facts which this girl's unhappy case presents to his analytical, discriminating, and scientific mind, he declares to you, as the result of his careful deliberations, that she has suffered from paroxysms of insanity, and that the act of homicide on the 30th of January arose from an insane impulse, and not from motives of hate or revenge – in his own language, 'that this theory is more in harmony with the truth than the other.'"

Jumping to his feet, the District Attorney yelled, "He did not say that!"

"He did say it," responded Voorhees, "and said it even in stronger language, I believe, than I have used, as the official record will show."

Judge Wiley said, "The Court Recorder will please read the relevant parts of Dr. Nichols testimony."

The record was read aloud to the Court and was found to be substantially as stated by the counsel for the defense.

"I knew that I was correct," said Voorhees. "Here then is the whole defense established by the highest evidence known to the law. The opinion of an expert is *a fact in the case*. No other witnesses can give an opinion at all. Dr. Nichols, therefore, proves as *a fact* that, from moral and physical causes combined, the defendant has labored under paroxysmal insanity, and that the act for which she is now on trial was committed during a paroxysm, and under an insane impulse. You have no legal right to find a verdict contrary to the testimony of Dr. Nichols, unless he is unworthy of belief, or has been successfully contradicted by other competent witnesses, whose opinions are entitled to greater weight than you attach to his.

"Another point made by the prosecution is, I dare say, without a parallel in the courts of any country which has been blessed with the light of civilization. The gentlemen who represent the government boldly and without a blush declare that the opinions of men, who like Dr. Nichols, have given their lives to the study of the mind in all its various and mysterious phases, are less reliable in the discovery of insanity than the opinions of those who have bestowed on them no particular attention on this great and difficult subject. The cry of 'mad doctors' has been raised, and we heard an appeal against them in favor of what were styled 'common sense doctors.'

"Gentlemen, I feel humiliated that I have listened to such language from such a source. Is there such an unappeasable rage to take the poor life of this prisoner that in order to do it these distinguished gentlemen are willing to resort to the lowest and most pernicious arts of the profession? Do they propose to deride the disciples of learning, the devotees of science? Will they stand up here in the noonday of human progress and enter the lists as the avowed champions of ignorance?

"Who are the 'mad doctors' whom this persistent sneer is leveled? They are those who have made the subject of insanity a specialty, who have given their days and nights to incessant and laborious thought, who have struggled with painful toil to alleviate the direst woes of their fellow men, to cure those wounds which the lash of misfortune inflicts, and to pluck from the diseased mind its rooted sorrows. And is it found necessary to stamp such characters with odium in order to convict Mary Harris? Shall we pluck from the scientific heavens their brightest and boldest luminaries, and accept darkness, gloom and mist again?

"The District Attorney is nearly two centuries in the rear of the still advancing column of human improvement. There was a period in the world's history when this assault on men of science would have relaxed the dull features of stupidity into a smile and caused blind superstition to nod its ugly head with approval. During such times the District Attorney, if he could have found an enlightened man of science, doubtless could have had him hung as a sorcerer or magician, along with the party whom he declared to be insane.

"Even now, today, there may be a cavern in which the owls and bats of ignorance, superstition, and gangrened prejudice yet inhabit, where the rays of liberal enlightenment have not yet penetrated, and where no beautiful thing has ever grown as a sign of progress. In order to ask for a conviction at your hands, he is compelled to repudiate the products of civilization, recede into the darkness of the past, and from the gloomy fortress of barbarism shower his missiles on the head of this most unfortunate being.

"In the name of bright-eyed truth, in the name of immortal science, in the name of the high, advanced banners of civilization, in the name of the stalwart, conquering spirit of gigantic progress, in the name of the greatest benefactors of suffering and diseased humanity, in the name of the liberal, humane, and learned professions of which I am an humble member, and in the name of an American court of justice, I protest against this attempt to break down and trample under foot the wisdom, the experience, and the labor of ages, and to destroy by an unworthy appeal to the basest prejudices of mankind, those safeguards which the proudest intellects of the earth have erected around such victims of misfortune as this young prisoner.

"And what have the 'common sense doctors' testified in this case? Upon a presentation of the case, detailing the evidence with wonderful fidelity and accuracy, every physician, without a single exception, who was placed upon the stand by the Government, concurred instantly and unreservedly with Dr. Nichols. Will it be said that Mr. Bradley did not submit a fair statement of facts to these medical gentlemen? You shall be the judge of that. Would he fabricate a case on which to obtain their opinions? The District Attorney and Mr. Wilson certainly do not mean such an imputation. Can a man at his time in life, at the head of his profession, eminent in it before some of us were born, beloved and respected by all – can he afford to attempt to practice a fraud upon you in your presence, when you have all the means of detecting it?

"No. He submitted the whole case, including his own accurate and most intelligent observations of her wretched condition in prison – a recital so vivid and eloquent in its faithful simplicity that thoughts of it swell the heart with emotion, and banish from our minds all idea of guilt in the conduct of the prisoner.

"Why, without one solitary witness to support their theory of the case, do the prosecutors so hunger and thirst for the conviction of this most desolate and bereaved of sorrowing mortals? Why do they clamor so fiercely against the barriers of the law and of the evidence, which encompass her about, in order to drag that sick and fragile body to a miserable death?

"Is it punishment they seek? She has suffered more already than the king of terrors in his most frightful form can inflict. If she had been broken on the wheel, her limbs disjointed and her flesh torn piecemeal by the most fiendish skill of the executioner, her torture would have been merciful compared to the racking which sunders into fragments the immortal mind.

"There is no arrow in death's full quiver that can give this young breast a new sensation of agony. She has sounded all the depths and shoals of misery and pain. She has lived in 'a whirling gulf of fantasy and flame.' Restore her by your verdict to the soothing influence of friends, of home. Let her go and lay her aching head on the maternal bosom of that Church which for eighteen centuries has tenderly ministered to her children in distress. Let her go and seek, in the love and mercy of the Father of us all, consolation for the cruelty and inhumanity of man.

"But it is claimed that a conviction must be had for the sake of example. You were told that the defendant came here from a distance – that the States were pouring their criminals in upon you, and therefore she must suffer as a warning to others. Such a statement is unjust to your people. You want justice, and justice alone, administered upon all.

"Who believes that this girl's life is required as an offering upon the altar of public justice? I repel this imputation upon the intelligence and humanity of this kind and hospitable District. When you are discharged from your protracted confinement and return to your homes, as you will in a few hours, ask those whom you meet there whether they desired you to cut the feeble thread of this girl's life by your verdict. I will abide by their answer. To no one has she appeared as the criminal, save to those who conduct and inspire the prosecution. To all others in your midst she has presented the sad spectacle of calamity and misery.

"Her purity, her gentleness, her guileless truth, shining out in every word and act, have won to her side in this dark hour your oldest, your best, and most honored citizens. Her prison abode has been brightened by the presence of the noblest and purest of her own sex, and delicate flowers from the loftiest station in the world have mingled their odors with the breath of her captivity. Men venerable in years, and strong in their convictions of the principles of immutable right, have been drawn to her assistance by an instinctive obedience to the voice of God, commanding them to succor the weak, lift up the fallen, and alleviate the distress of innocence.

"Add one more obligation for Mary Harris to remember until the grave opens to hide her from the world. It is in your hand to grant. The law in its grave majesty approves the act. The evidence with an unbroken chain demands it. Your own hearts press forward to the discharge of a most gracious duty. The hour is almost at hand for its performance. Unlock the door of her prison, and bid her bathe her throbbing brow once more in the healing air of liberty. Let your verdict be the champion of law, of morality, of science. Let it vindicate civilization and humanity, justice and mercy. I now, with unwavering confidence in the triumph of innocence, surrender all into your hands."

A long silence followed the end of Voorhees' speech, interrupted only by a deep single audible respiration by a female member of the audience. Jurors squirmed in their seats and cleared their throats. Judge Wiley lifted his gavel, hesitated, then pronounced the session at a close for the day.

Richardson and Douglas retired to Ebbitt's Grill on F Street for a drink while they discussed the trial and tried to formulate their newspaper stories to be published the following day.

"Voorhees mounted quite an attack on the Reverend Doctor Burroughs," said Douglas. "He indicted him for cowardice and purposeful deception in not telling Mary that his brother was married. He said his claim that she said there never was a marriage engagement was ridiculous and that he was just positioning himself for future litigation on that account. He asserted that the

Reverend was out for vengeance and made a derisive plea for him to act like a Christian with mercy and spare the poor girl. Then he added emphasis by confessing how he tires of life when he sees injustice flourishing and when people treat the virtues of innocence, truth and love as trivial amusements."

"Do you think he really believes that," said Richardson, "or is it just part of the defense strategy to create a living villain to distract the prosecution and the jury?"

"He certainly sounded like he meant it. If he didn't, I'd have to give him the highest marks for his skill in rhetoric. He also reminded the court that Mary was suffering from dysmenorrea, an identified cause of paroxysmal insanity, when she walked into the Treasury building and implied that Dr. Fitch's testimony supported that. But I don't think that it has been established as a fact that she had her period that day; it has just been asserted to be so by the defense attorneys and the prosecution hasn't contested that assertion."

"He paints a tragic tale of Mary being consumed by memories of the past and exhausted by a black melancholy, losing weight, sleep and her perkiness, said Richardson. "When combined with her broken body, a homicidal insanity results where she attacks her friends and eventually Burroughs. It all sounds very logical and terribly sad. Of course that is the effect that Voorhees wanted to produce."

"Yeah, said Douglas. And then there is the 'toy' pistol again, which she only bought because she was haunted by an irrational fear that the Burroughs brothers were going to kidnap her. But then there is no denying that the gun was deadly enough to take a life and you have to ask yourself: Why did she go to see this fearful brother and expect to get an honest answer from him? Wouldn't she be afraid that he might do something to harm her?"

"Voorhees used a great metaphor to explain the fact that Miss Harris doesn't look or act crazy and is able to exercise reason," said Richardson. "In a healthful state, the mind is a many-stringed instrument that requires every cord to create a perfect harmony. While one string may be strained and broken, the others when touched still give forth their own unimpaired tones. But the broken string constitutes a hidden wound which does not heal, which bleeds at the touch and causes 'the whole instrument to wail forth in melancholy madness.' Beautiful! He includes many examples of the talent shown by insane people and concludes that the individuals so stricken are not responsible for their acts in the sight of God and man."

"Yes, I was impressed with his use of that metaphor and how he used it as the backdrop for implying that she was in some kind of trance when she was in Baltimore." He read off his notes, "She gazes steadily on space and sometimes breaks into a ghostly glee or sings in plaintive strains the broken fragments of some melancholy song telling of disappointed love."

"Voorhees as much as said to the jurors, 'Don't wrestle with your decision. Rely on Dr. Nichols. He is an expert on the mind and what he says is a fact.' The representative derides the prosecution for being critical of the discipline of psychiatry and accuses the DA of being two centuries behind the times, repudiating the products of civilization, and allowing superstition to rule."

"Right," said Douglas. And besides, all the so-called ordinary doctors sided with Nichols anyway. He impugns the motives of the DA and insinuates he is out for blood and punishment. He makes an impassioned plea to let Mary go and not inflict more suffering on someone who has already been broken."

"And then he disputes the DA's characterization of the wants of the citizens of the District of Columbia, added

Richardson. "They don't need an 'offering on the alter of public justice.' They don't want to make an example of 'the humblest, the feeblest, and the most helpless.' Mary Harris is 'a sad spectacle of calamity and misery.' Finally, he pulls out all the stops by subtly reminding the court that she received flowers from Mrs. Lincoln and that men of great moral principle have been drawn to her assistance."

"I guess I would have to say that Voorhees summation ranks up there with the most masterful I have ever heard."

"Indeed," said Richardson. "He managed to weave together the facts that support his position with appeals to the sympathies of the jurors, while glossing over contradictions, in a most effective manner. No wonder he keeps getting re-elected!"

CHAPTER 19

In spite of the sweltering heat, the argument of Mr. Voorhees was listened to with rapt attention. The marshal tried to restrain the buzz of many voices, as the prosecution got ready to present their closing statements. Miss Harris, who had become exhausted, was not present in the courtroom when Mr. Carrington summed up the government's case.

Carrington approached the jury box. "May it please the Court and you gentlemen of the jury, I congratulate you that we are now rapidly approaching the termination of this long, tedious and painful investigation. Permit me, as the legal representative of the Government and of this community, to express my high appreciation of the kind, patient, courteous, and respectful attention which you have given to the evidence, the instructions of the Court, and the argument of counsel. I am sure that not only from respect to my official position but in consequence of the personal friendship and esteem, which I flatter myself you all have for me, that you will listen attentively to every word I utter and every sentiment I express. It is quite obvious that you have determined to discharge your high and solemn, duty conscientiously. I shall not again remind you of the oath, which you have taken to decide this case as every other – according to the law and the evidence.

"Gentlemen of the jury, you see before you on trial a woman. It is a case somewhat unprecedented in the history of this tribunal. I plead the cause of woman. Go to yonder churchyard and see that mother weeping over the honored grave of her only boy. He has fallen in his country's cause. Who is she? Nobody, in comparison with Mary Harris, the heroine of the day. See that wife diffusing life, light joy, and hope around the family circle – the idol of a husband's heart and the guardian angel of her children. Her little curly-headed girl is kneeling by her side, and repeating her evening or morning prayer.

"Rise from your knees, my pretty child, you are wrong. When your little heart is wrung, don't go, as your hymnbook says, and tell Jesus. Arm yourself with a deadly weapon and avenge your own wrongs with the red hand of violence and of crime. Mary Harris, the model of female excellence, held up before the public for the admiration and imitation of our mothers, wives and daughters, has said that the ladies of Chicago carry deadly weapons and avenge private wrongs, whether real or imaginary, by private means and we intend to introduce this fashion into the city of Washington.

"Permit me here to say, that if the voice of woman could be heard – gentle, lovely, virtuous woman – she would denounce this slander of Mary Harris and the Devlins as an insult to every honest and virtuous lady in the land. I have known the inexpressible tenderness of a wife's, a sister's, and a mother's love. You all have. We each have seen the noblest exhibition of true female character during the unhappy strife, which has existed in our country for the last four years. Did you ever go to yonder hospital? See the young man. He is pale, attenuated, and emaciated. He has received some terrible wound while fighting in his country's cause. He is far away from family and friends. The agents of the Government are doing all that humanity and duty can suggest for his comfort and relief, but he is not satisfied. No kind mother stands by his bedside to cool the fevered brow.

"But hark! He hears woman's gentle voice, perhaps one that he has never heard before, but it is woman's voice. It falls upon his ear like the name of home in some distant land, or raindrops in a thirsty desert. She administers to his wants, and whispers words of comfort and of consolation. He revives. He shoulders his musket and strikes another blow for his Government and his flag. Perhaps his last hour has come. Ever faithful, gentle woman points him to a Savior's dying love. As the world recedes from his view, like a true and valiant soldier of the cross, he triumphs over death and the grave.

"When the noble daughters of America were kneeling by the bedside of the dying soldier, where was Mary Harris? That was a time when an appeal was made to every woman who had a heart to love her country and her race. Where then was Mary Harris, the model of female excellence? Arming herself with this instrument of death, practicing the use of deadly weapons, going in company with one of the Devlins to Quincy Street to a house of assignation without a protector, and at last imbruing her hands in the blood of one who had drawn his sword in his country's cause.

"And you are called upon to approve, justify, and applaud this cruel and bloody deed. Are we Christians? Do we live in a Christian age, a Christian community, and do we worship the Prince of Peace as the only true and living God? Gentlemen of the jury, have you considered the awful responsibility that rests upon you? I have, and I pray that God may give me grace to discharge my duty.

"Behold, here, ladies, gentlemen, and little boys and girls. You are educating public sentiment. The judge upon the bench, the district attorney, and the jurors, should not only be men of common sense and of sterling integrity, but of the purest morality. Will you by your verdict say to these little boys and girls that a woman who arms herself with a deadly weapon and imbrues her hands in her brother's blood, and commits murder in vindication of female virtue which has never been injured, is a model for their imitation?

"*O tempora! O mores!* I appeal to an honest jury of my country to beware how they record a verdict so hostile to the cause of justice and religion, and which will be borne by the telegraphic wires to all sections of the country, and which will be read by the present and succeeding generations. Oh, gentlemen of the jury, let us rebuke this spirit and vindicate the sacred cause of religion and of law.

"Appeals have been made to your sympathies and that is all, as I will show. Sympathy! Sympathy! Sympathy! And nothing else, and with unusual zeal and eloquence. Good Heaven! Behold what an array of counsel. In Joseph H. Bradley you behold the Ajax Telemon of the defense. In my friend William Y. Fendall you behold the young, the ardent, the amorous Tydides, not casting his javelin at the goddess of love as she flies through the air on her way to heaven, but, with his armor off, kneeling at her feet."

The audience erupts in laughter.

"In Judge Mason you behold the sweetly speaking Nestor of the Grecian camp."

More laughter sweeps throughout the room.

"In the Honorable Daniel W. Voorhees you behold the fierce, implacable, irresistible Achilles, and even old Agamemnon (pointing to the judge on the bench) his self, can never look at the gentle sufferer without a sigh expressive of his sympathy."

Even the jury is unable to control their laughter.

"And there sits the lovely Helen, bathed in tears, surrounded by her female attendants, urging on these sturdy warriors to deeds of superhuman valor. Here I stand, aided only by my efficient and accomplished assistant.

"Gentlemen of the jury, am I not an object of commiseration? I saw some of you crying, but I think you cried in the wrong place. Were you concerned for me? No! No, gentlemen, don't be alarmed. Courage gentlemen! I stand clothed in celestial armor, behind the broad aegis of the law, and their javelins fall harmless at my feet. I hold up the law, and thus I roll back the tide of sympathy that has been pouring into the jury box. I remind you of your solemn oaths, and then you dry your tears, and nerve yourselves to the discharge of your stern and solemn duty.

"As my friend, Mr. Wilson said, what do we care for Mary Harris? So far as she is concerned, you may put her in a bandbox and send her home – not to the Devlins, however – God forbid – but to her father."

The laughter is now reduced to mainly chuckles.

"And I will tell you, before taking my seat, how it can be done without doing violence to any man's conscience.

"It is the principle, the great principle for which I contend, that the majesty of the law must and shall be vindicated. I said in my opening address and I now repeat, that we must be cruel only to be kind. We must punish the guilty to protect the innocent. Obedience to the law is the safeguard of us all. Loyalty to law and government is obedience to God. Crime must be punished because God commands it. You are the ministers of his justice upon earth.

"If you wish to shield yourself behind the opinions of the doctors I have no objection. But I have no idea that a doctor shall swear to one state of facts, and see an honest and intelligent jury of my country make themselves ridiculous before the whole world by swearing to a different state of facts, or rendering a verdict inconsistent with the opinion expressed by these scientific gentlemen, who have perhaps said enough to mislead the jury, if what they have stated be not properly explained by the law officer of the Government.

"They were themselves exceedingly cautious not to commit the blunder which they invite you to perpetuate upon the records of this court. What doctor has sworn that this woman was so insane at the time the homicide was committed as to render her irresponsible in law for her conduct? None. None of them would dare to do it. He could not do it, in my judgment, without committing the crime of perjury, and I will prove it.

"If this jury acquits this woman upon the ground of insanity, you swear to a fact, and you perpetuate upon the records of this court a fact, which will not only make you ridiculous, but which is utterly inconsistent not only with the evidence, but with the opinion of every physician who has been examined within your hearing. But permit me, gentlemen of the jury, to proceed more logically to consider the case at bar.

"There are four questions, as I stated to you in my opening address. First, was the homicide charged in the indictment committed within the jurisdiction of this court? Second, was it committed by the prisoner at the bar? Third, if it was, is it a case of excusable homicide, upon the ground of insanity, or for any other reason? Fourth, if it was not excusable homicide, is it murder or is it manslaughter?

"I will consider the first two propositions together and in so doing, I have only to briefly recapitulate the evidence.

"Gentlemen of the jury, the curtain rises. The scene is laid at a boarding house in the city of Chicago. The heroine of the bloody tragedy makes her appearance – a good, sprightly, black-haired girl. She was without either father or mother at that time. It is then she forms the acquaintance of Louisa Devlin, another beautiful, charming, and accomplished lady. Louisa Devlin invites her to go to her millinery establishment. Prompted by an 'insane impulse' she accepts the invitation."

There is a renewed outbreak of laughter in the audience.

"What sort of a millinery establishment was it? I wanted to find out, and in the most courteous and respectful manner, for no one is more courteous to a lady than myself, I asked her how many young ladies she had in her employment. She threw herself back on her dignity and said, 'That is my business, and none of yours.' There is Miss Harris in a millinery establishment, the character of which the proprietress is ashamed to describe."

Judge Hughes rose and said, "May it please your Honor, I dislike to interrupt counsel, but where, in a closing argument, the evidence is clearly misstated, an interruption is not only tolerable, but it is the duty of counsel, whose client is affected thereby, to so interrupt. There is no evidence here whatever as to the character of Miss Devlin's house. It is true the District Attorney did ask her how many persons she employed in her house and she replied, 'That is my business.' An appeal was made to the Court, and the Court directed her to answer the question, but a discussion springing up at the time, the question was lost sight of and no answer was given."

"May it please your Honor," Mr. Carrington countered, "I did not interrupt counsel in their argument and I hope they will not in mine. If I misstate the evidence, which your Honor knows I will not do intentionally, I have no doubt you, sir, will correct me."

Judge Wiley ruled, "A counsel in the closing argument, knowing that there is no one to come after him, ought to studiously keep himself within the prescribed limits, unless he wants to be interrupted at every stage. He ought not to pervert or misstate the evidence – I do not mean to say that you have done so in this case – but I do think that there is nothing in the refusal of Miss Devlin to answer that question to justify the suspicions which have been inferred by the counsel."

"Is that a question of law, your Honor?" asked the District Attorney.

"It is a question of law, sir," said Judge Wiley in a stern manner.

"Gentlemen, after the attack which has been made upon Dr. Burroughs," began Mr. Carrington, before a perturbed Judge Wiley interrupted him.

"You shall not retaliate upon Miss Devlin for an attack upon Dr. Burroughs. You must confine yourself to the legitimate application of your remarks to the evidence of the Misses Devlin. It is an abuse of your position to make such an attack as that upon such grounds."

"What had I said, may it please your Honor."

"You know, sir!"

"You had not heard, sir, for I had not completed the sentence. What I intended to say was this: that after the attack which had been made upon Dr. Burroughs by the learned counsel, had I not a right (they justifying that attack upon the testimony of the Misses Devlin) to attack her testimony."

"You shall not retaliate upon the Misses Devlin. You have a perfect right to attack the Miss Devlin's testimony as to its inconsistency, either with itself or with the other evidence, but to launch out in such a latitude of inference as that you were going upon, in regard to the character of the house of the Misses Devlin, whose reputation has not been attacked, either for truth or in any other respect, I cannot permit it in a closing argument."

The District Attorney attempted to proceed. "You will bear in mind, gentlemen of the jury, that I did not interrupt the learned counsel. You heard the attack upon Dr. Burroughs, of which I shall have something to say hereafter. You know I must not dare to lay my fingers on the Misses Devlin."

Again, an exasperated Judge Wiley comes down on Mr. Carrington. "The Court did not say so. I will not permit you to misrepresent the Court or the witnesses. The Court has given you express permission to comment upon all the evidence given by the Misses Devlin, and compare it with itself and the other evidence in the case, and sift it to your heart's content. But upon the mere refusal of one of those ladies to tell you how many clerks she had in her place of business, the Court will not permit you to launch out in the great latitude of inference you were going upon."

The District Attorney began again. "With the permission of the Court, and you, gentlemen of the jury, I will say that I do not think any witness contradicted Dr. Burroughs. They justify their attack upon him from inferences drawn from what he said. I thought I had the same privilege, but I bow with due deference to the decision of the Court. In this case, as in every other, I intend to discharge my duty in the fear of God, and without the fear of man. No man can say with truth that I was ever seen to cower or to falter in the discharge of my official duty."

Clearly angered by Carrington's sarcasm and effrontery, Judge Wiley said, "Well, you shall not go on in that way. The Court will not permit a controversy between you and it to be decided by this jury. You shall not utter another syllable on that subject. I will put you in the hands of the Marshall if you do."

Mr. Wilson said, "Ed, why don't you sit down and collect your thoughts. I can take over until you are ready."

"No, I will complete my argument. Again I say, and I will endeavor to argue under the instructions of the

Court."

"Well, proceed," said Judge Wiley tersely.

"I *will* proceed."

"In order," added Judge Wiley.

"I was about to argue as to the inference to be drawn from the testimony of the woman Devlin, her manner, and her answer to the question which I put, which I thought was competent, but I understand his Honor to say I was wrong in that opinion."

Judge Hughes stood, raising his hand, and said, "I hope a suggestion from me may assist the District Attorney in the discharge of his duty here. I have no disposition to embarrass him in his argument, and I am sure that he must be able to perceive the awkwardness that results from keeping up a controversy of this sort, and I trust he will confine himself to the evidence, and relieve me of the necessity of any further interruption. As to attacks upon Dr. Burroughs, they were legitimate in the case, and I expect him to make such a reply to our argument on that point as may seem proper."

Judge Wiley said, "It was a very unpleasant thing for me, and I was reluctant to interrupt counsel in the course of argument, and would not have done so in this case, although I observed the impropriety of it, had it not been called to the attention of the Court by the counsel on the other side.

"This is a case of the greatest importance, and I am resolved that it shall be conducted orderly and properly, and especially am determined to see that the counsel for the United States, who so ably represents the interests of the Government here, endowed with natural gifts of eloquence and power with the jury, shall not in a closing speech travel beyond the limits assigned to counsel on these occasions."

Mr. Carrington straightened his posture, paused, and began, "Gentlemen of the jury, before proceeding to discuss the question of insanity, I shall be pardoned, I trust, for saying a few words in reference to the brother of the deceased. Permit me, gentlemen, to ask you one question: Suppose that one of our ministers – such a man as Dr. Gurley, Dr. Samson, Dr. Gillette, or Father Maguire, men to whom we have been in the habit of looking up to, not only as our spiritual fathers, but as our teachers and exemplars – should go to Chicago as a witness, and a woman, who admitted she had been to an assignation house without a protector (no matter for what purpose) should be put on the stand to assail the reputation of such minister for veracity – what would you think of it?

"You know, and we all know, what would be your opinion. Now, the Rev. John C. Burroughs stands in Chicago just as either of these eminent gentlemen to whom I referred stands in Washington."

Bradley interrupted, "Who testified to that?"

Addressing Judge Wiley, Carrington said, "Have I not a right, your Honor, in argument, when the gentlemen have departed from the evidence to –."

Wiley, cutting him short, said, "The legal presumption is that his character is good."

Bradley, contemptuously, "Go on. It won't hurt us."

"It *may* not hurt them, gentlemen of the jury. They seem to think there is a strong prejudice against the whole Burroughs family, judging from what Mr. Voorhees said of the popular clamor and the feeling in the community against Dr. Burroughs, and from what Judge Hughes said on the same subject. I think they are mistaken. If this jury has any prejudice, which I do not believe, but if you do, I will simply say that you have sworn to decide the case without prejudice. I intend to show you that you cannot discredit Dr. Burroughs without branding one of the best men in the community with the crime of perjury, and falsifying the record of the Treasury Department.

"Who is John C. Burroughs? He has told you he is
president of the University at Chicago. Well, I am one of
those men who do not believe that the office makes the
man, but that the man makes the office. I admit that
there are hypocrites, wolves in sheep's clothing. But it is
not so in this case. It may not be amiss here to say,
among other things, in order to show you the character
and position of Dr. J. C. Burroughs, that he was, during the
life of the distinguished orator and statesman, Stephen A.
Douglas, one of his most honored and trusted friends, and
the remains of that illustrious man now rest within the
enclosure of the university over which he presides."

Judge Hughes, interrupting, said, "Dr. Burroughs
made a speech against the remains being placed there."

Carrington went on, "He has, too, been the friend and
co-laborer of our fellow townsmen, Dr. Samson and Dr.
Gillette, and is therefore entitled to your respect and
confidence. If what I now say could be heard in Chicago,
the good people there would say, is it possible that Mr.
Carrington has deemed it necessary to pass an eulogium
upon Dr. Burroughs? It is a presumption. It is not
necessary to defend him against such attacks, even when
made by Judge Hughes and the Honorable Daniel W.
Voorhees.

"Now what has this estimable man, who holds a
commission from our Savior, which he has never
dishonored, done to induce these unjust assaults? Why,
gentlemen, his offending consists in his offering to
advance money to certain witnesses, that they might thus
be enabled to come here and vindicate by their sworn
testimony the character of his murdered brother, a soldier
and a public servant, who died at the post of duty by the
assassin's hand, without a stain upon his honor.

Is Dr. Burroughs to be condemned for this noble,
generous and manly act? Had he not consented to do it,
he could not have been regarded otherwise than as the

wretch he is represented to be. Had he offered to pay a witness to swear falsely, he would have been guilty of subornation of perjury. I, in that case, would have been as prompt and vehement in his denunciation as any one could be, and would instantly tell you his testimony was entitled to no weight at your hands. But every honest man, instead of censuring, must commend the noble zeal he has displayed in his efforts to remove the stigma which is sought to be cast upon his dead brother's character and name.

"Again, gentlemen of the jury, it was said that he offered witnesses three dollars a day. That is not so, in point of fact. I know that he said he had a letter from Dr. Burroughs but the evidence will show that the witness distinctly stated that the marshal said, on his own responsibility, that he would get three dollars a day – that being the fee allowed witnesses in some of the States. Nothing was said in the letter regarding it."

Bradley interrupted again, "The witness stated that the marshal said that Dr. Burroughs had written he would advance any money that was necessary."

Carrington replied, "He said the marshal might draw on him for expenses. Of course he did and he was right in so saying. He would have reflected discredit upon himself had he not done so.

"Again, gentlemen of the jury, they say that he is contradicted. In what respect? In regard to his brother being in Washington at the time these 'Greenwood' letters were written and mailed and that he has testified falsely in regard to these letters.

"All I have to say is that if he has, so also has Danenhower, one of the most intelligent and estimable gentlemen in this community. The records of the Treasury Department are false if the testimony of these gentlemen be false. Danenhower swears, and those records confirm his statement, that A. J. Burroughs was in the city of

Washington on the 10th of September, and these letters are dated on the 8th and 12th of September, and dropped in the post office at Chicago. From these facts it is conclusive that Dr. Burroughs has testified truthfully upon the point."

Yet again, Bradley interrupts. "I do not know whether it is proper to interrupt the counsel, but I would like to remark that Dr. Burroughs swore his brother was in Chicago on the 11th of September. He could not, then, have been here on the 10th."

Carrington replied, "Why not? Is that not impossible?"

"It takes thirty-six hours to get to Chicago," said Bradley.

Carrington continued, "How is it possible that he could have written the letter dated on the 8th of September? And it is obvious that the author of the one is the author of the other.

"Again, gentlemen of the jury, he is charged with endeavoring to keep away a witness – one Ellen Mills – desired by the defense. Is that so? What is the evidence on that point? We do not ask any favors, gentlemen of the jury, but we ask justice.

"The evidence is that Dr. Burroughs inquired of the officer whether this woman would be summoned, or could be relied upon. The officer replied that she was a woman of bad character, and would not appear as a witness unless she was paid, where upon Burroughs, like an honest man, declined to summon her. He, supposing her testimony to be important in the case, wanted to summon her for the United States but, hearing she was a corrupt woman, refused to have anything to say or do with her.

"It is said by the gentlemen that they wanted her here, and that her testimony was very material to the case. Why didn't they summon her? They had the right, and could have got her here. Or, if they did not want to bring her here, why did they not have her deposition taken – a privilege, strange as it may seem, granted to them by act of Congress, but not granted to us in criminal cases.

"They say they did not like his manner. Did you ever, gentlemen, observe a more solemn and impressive scene? There sat the murderess and near her were her friends and companions. There stood the witness, his heart wrung with anguish, for his brother had been murdered and he was the natural protector of his widow and his orphan child. Here, by the table, sat the ablest counsel in the country, eager to catch at every word he uttered, for the purpose of assailing his testimony."

Judge Hughes asked the Court permission to read from the official report the testimony of Dr. Burroughs related to his conversation with the policeman about Ellen Mills. After he did so, the District Attorney continued.

"Is not that exactly as I have stated it? Dr. Burroughs consults the officers as to whether he shall summon this woman or not. He discovers she is a corrupt woman and, like an honest man, he declines to have anything to do with her. But they say that this minister of the Gospel is to be censured because he did not read a lecture to the detective and this prostitute, Ellen Mills. What does the Bible tell us to do in such cases? 'Do not cast pearls before swine.' Dr. Burroughs observed the Divine injunction. That seems to be his only fault.

"I understand the object of the assault, gentlemen, and I think you must perceive it. These gentlemen know they cannot injure Dr. Burroughs in the estimation of the public, or in your estimation, but they desire to divert me from the prosecution of Mary Harris to the defense of Dr. Burroughs, to divert your attention from the murderess to the brother of the deceased whom they have portrayed as a villain. But I am too old a war horse to be caught in that way.

"There are three ways of contradicting a witness.

First, by assailing his reputation for veracity. Why didn't they attempt that? They dared not do so for the reason he stood too high. Not a witness, with the host of friends this beautiful murderess has, could be found to assail his reputation for veracity.

"Second, they can try to show that he has made different statements at different times in regard to the same transaction. Was not the statement of Dr. Burroughs clear, consistent, honest? He would say now what he said yesterday, or would say tomorrow.

"The third mode is by proving a different state of facts by another witness. What witness contradicted him?" Turning toward Louisa Devlin and pausing for a moment, he said, "Yes, Louisa Devlin! And how does she contradict him? Why, in regard to an immaterial fact and – you will, your Honor, pardon me for I do not wish to go against the instruction of the Court – is John C. Burroughs, the honest, Christian gentleman, to be denounced in court, and is my mouth to be sealed when they rely upon the testimony of this Louisa Devlin? Who is Louisa Devlin? When asked about her business, her color would come and go. By her own admission, she went to an assignation house on Quincy Street on a fool's errand."

Bradley again interrupted Mr. Carrington. "I must interrupt the counsel there. Louisa Devlin never went to that house."

Carrington continued, "Jane Devlin did." Turning to Louisa Devlin, he said, "I wonder if any man ever called her ducky, his darling, his rosebud, or his sugar plum."

Guffaws arise from the audience. Judge Wiley scowls and raps his gavel.

"Do you suppose it would have given her paroxysmal insanity?"

More laughter ripples through the audience and the judge makes three raps of the gavel.

"I have no doubt it would have excited her very much

for, judging from her looks, she ain't used to it."

Judge Wiley, in despair, doesn't even raise his gavel as more laughter spreads throughout the courtroom.

"And this is the woman upon whom they rely to contradict the honest, Christian gentleman? She is indeed the Iago in this bloody tragedy for Mr. Bradley told you, in his opening address, that this was the old story of Othello. It was hatred and jealousy that urged Mary Harris to the commission of this atrocious murder, for you remember that she told her lawyer that her love had turned to hatred.

"Gentlemen of the jury, it was the desire of money that prompted Louisa Devlin to fire the jealousy of this love-sick girl, preparatory to a suit for a breach of promise of marriage, expecting to share the damages, and I will prove it from the evidence before taking my seat.

"Notwithstanding the eulogium pronounced upon her, I say that she is a woman without delicacy, without refinement, and without sensibility for during this trial she has sat here giggling while her friend was on trial for her life, as though she were on a debauch in Quincy Street, Chicago, at the house of Ellen Mills."

Bradley stood and asserted, "May it please your Honor, I denounce such an accusation in the strongest terms that man can. There has not been one word of reproach cast upon Miss Devlin from the beginning to the end of this trial, and I do say that no gentleman would use such language towards a woman."

Carrington in a rejoinder, said, "I shall not be betrayed into any indiscretion if the object is to insult me. I have only discharged my duty as in my humble judgment seemed proper. I make the same remark in regard to the attack upon Dr. Burroughs."

Bradley said, "I do not wish to insult you but I do say the man who denounces this woman without the evidence in the case warranting it trespasses beyond the license of counsel, and abuses the character of gentleman."

Carrington remarked, "All I have to say is that I return the insult – your conduct has been ungentlemanly."

Taunting his adversary, Bradley said, "You can return the insult as much as you please. I despise you. Say what you please to the jury, I shall not interrupt you again. Here is a chip on my head. Come and knock it off."

There is laughter throughout the courtroom.

Judge Wiley tells a clerk to summon the marshal and addresses the District Attorney. "Mr. Carrington, the Court will not permit you to go on without expressing a strong condemnation of language of that kind, which it thinks entirely without foundation in the evidence."

"Thank you, sir," added Bradley.

Carrington asked, "Will your Honor be kind enough to make some remarks of that description in regard to the attack upon Dr. Burroughs?"

Wiley responded, "That occasion has passed. I understood the attack upon Dr. Burroughs to be confined to the character of his evidence, compared with itself, and compared with the evidence of other witnesses. I thought it was a pretty severe investigation, to be sure, but then it was not a mere calling of names and denunciation, without evidence to support it of some kind, whether sufficient or not.

"I do think that this denunciation upon the Misses Devlin's moral reputation, outside entirely of the evidence in the case, ought not to have been made and is deserving of the strongest and severest censure which the Court can declare. I had hoped, Mr. Carrington, that you would not go beyond what you knew, and especially in regard to a female witness, who is here, in all appearances, without a protector."

Bradley added, "And who challenges the closest investigation as to her character. I speak with the authority of gentlemen of the highest reputation in this country."

Wiley said, "I do not wish to prejudice the case at all by what I have said, either one way or the other, and I hope the jury will not so regard it."

"I thought I was entirely justified by the evidence. I may be wrong, but I think my attack is not half so severe as that made upon Dr. Burroughs."

"You must not retaliate upon the Misses Devlin," said Wiley.

"This witness is introduced under my protection," said Bradley. "I am responsible for introducing her as a lady of reputation and character, and I regard the attack upon her as an attack on me. I know her from the reputation of men of the highest character in the country – Mr. Armstrong of Baltimore and Mr. Shoemaker of Adams Express Company, and others."

"I refer to the whole city of Chicago in regard to the Rev. Dr. Burroughs," said Carrington. "When he is denounced, I thought it was my duty to expose properly the testimony of the Misses Devlin. The Judge thinks I have gone too far, and so does Mr. Bradley. I will say, gentlemen, that it is not material to this case whether you believe either the Misses Devlin or Dr. Burroughs, or discard both of them.

Judge Wiley called a recess, hoping the counsel would cool off after a little separation. Following their usual custom, Bill Douglas and Francis Richardson went outside for a smoke and a cold drink from one of the street vendors who worked the courthouse area. Spotting a vacant bench, they sat down and exchanged observations on the progress of the prosecution's closing statements.

"I think Mr. Carrington made a mistake by starting out with a sarcastic account of Mary Harris as the model of female excellence," said Douglas. "Belittling her by comparing her to a grieving mother who lost her only son in the war or to a dutiful wife and mother tends to strike people the wrong way. Sarcasm is a two edged sword that can cut the user as well as the object of scorn."

"I agree," said Richardson. "It may also have been a mistake to try to place the jurors in the role of educating public sentiment by their verdict and implying that they would have an adverse effect on the whole country if they find the accused to be innocent."

"His humorous depiction of the defense counsel as characters in a Greek tragedy was a stroke of genius, however, " said Douglas. "He correctly points out that the defense has made eloquent appeals to the jurors sympathies toward the accused as a young woman from an impoverished family but characterizes himself as an object worthy of commiseration too since it is only himself and his assistant to battle this array of legal luminaries. He asserts that the prosecution is up to the task because they are fighting to uphold the law which protects us all and is a Godly pursuit."

"Then he moves back onto shaky ground, saying that the jury will make itself appear ridiculous to the whole world if they find Mary Harris innocent because that verdict would fly in the face of the testimony of the doctors. He claims that none of them have sworn that she was crazy enough to make her irresponsible for her conduct. But they all were testifying to hypothetical cases, not to this particular case of Mary Harris."

"He again tries to get the jury to strip the case of all the sentimentality and consider the case only in terms of his four questions. Everything else is irrelevant, according to the DA. While this may be logical in terms of the legalities of the case, it doesn't do much to win the hearts of the jury members."

"He really got himself into hot water when he tried to copy the defense's strategy of creating an object to hate in John Curtis Burroughs," said Richardson. "He tried to paint the Devlin sisters as unsavory and evasive and managed to raise Judge Wiley's ire. No matter what Carrington said, he just seemed to dig himself in deeper and he wouldn't let it go. Of course Bradley and crew took advantage of the DA's chagrin and tried to keep him rattled by peppering his closing with interruptions."

"I'm afraid his good points were lost in the emotion displayed by the judge and the way he came down hard on the DA," said Douglas. "He did indicate that the Reverend Burroughs did not pay anyone to stay away from the Court and only paid expenses for witnesses who otherwise would not be able to appear. He also reminded the jury that Congress did not grant the prosecution the right to get depositions while the defense operated under no such constraint. And he said that Danenhower's testimony placed A. J. Burroughs in Washington at the time the Greenwood letters were dropped in the mail in Chicago."

"He made another mistake when he identified Louisa Devlin as the one who went to 94 Quincy when it was actually Jane Devlin. Not a big deal but it made him look like he was not really up on his facts."

"He lapsed into sarcasm again when he made fun of Louisa Devlin's looks and joked about her becoming paroxysmally insane if a man had called her rosebud or sugar plum," said Douglas. "Then he spun this unsupported theory about Louisa Devlin expecting to share in the damages from a law suit and thereby to fire up Mary's jealousy. Wiley again came down hard on the District Attorney for what he called his retaliatory attack on the Devlin sisters."

"It got pretty hot when Bradley, declaring himself the protector of Miss Devlin, taunted his adversary to knock a chip off his head and Wiley threatened Carrington by summoning the marshal to have him carted off to jail!"

"Carrington sounded kind of pathetic when he asked the judge to reprimand Bradley for the language he used about Dr. Burroughs and was rebuffed. The judge said the interrogation of the Reverend was not merely name calling without any evidence and was confined to the nature of his testimony."

"The comment he made about Judson Burroughs having raised his sword in the defense of his country reminded me of what I had found out from the folks at Camp Douglas," said Richardson.

"What was that," asked Douglas.

"Burroughs never took part in any military action. He was commissioned as a Captain after he recruited a company of soldiers, but he left the 127th Illinois Infantry Regiment just before it was to leave for the battlefield. He told his superiors he had received a higher commission as a major someplace. But that is about the time he started working in the Treasury Department."

"Whew! The guy really was a scoundrel," said Douglas.

"Seems to have been," said Richardson. "They also had no record of him ever having had a broken leg. It was just another lie he told Mary."

Douglas shook his head in amazement.

CHAPTER 20

The bailiff stuck his head out the door and notified the people standing around that the trial was about to resume. Richardson and Douglas extinguished their pipes and headed inside. The District Attorney was just beginning to continue his account of Mary Harris's actions that resulted in the homicide.

"In conversation with her lawyer, Miss Harris tells him that her love for Burroughs had turned to hate. 'Heaven has no rage like love to hatred turned, Hell hath no fury like a woman scorned.' Out of her own mouth do I condemn her. Prompted not by 'insane impulse,' but by hatred she comes to the city of Washington to institute a suit for breach of promise of marriage.

"She does not put her writ in the hands of the marshal, but she goes in person to the Treasury Department – let us admit with the writ in one hand and the pistol in the other. She inquires for Burroughs and is told there are two gentlemen there of that name. And this presumably insane woman asks to see Adoniram J. Burroughs, examines the register, finds his name, is shown to his room and looks in. She does not fire as old

Mrs. Woodbridge is in the direct line of fire.

"She retreats down to that clock and there takes her stand. There was time to hear the ticking of the clock, observe the movement of the minute hand. There was time for the clerks to be discharged and young Burroughs to make his arrangements for the next day. There was time for passion to pass away and reason to resume its sway. There was time for 'insane impulse' to pass and the power of volition to return.

"He passes by and she fires at him deliberately. He falls and she fires a second time, aiming directly for his head. Then she endeavors to escape and losing her way feels the heavy hand of justice upon her. She is arrested but is cool, calm, collected. She told the officer that this man injured her. She wanted revenge and would have it at the risk of her life. She showed no emotion until the bleeding mangled corpse of her murdered victim is brought into her presence.

"And this is the evidence of insanity? No, gentlemen of the jury, it is evidence of sanity. It is woman's nature speaking out. Proud, cruel, ambitious woman, like Lady Macbeth. So, Mary Harris, having accomplished her purpose, and when she sees before her the bleeding evidence of her guilt, suffers the pangs of remorse. This is sanity. Can you interpret it to be evidence of insanity?

"Science, as the learned counsel understands it, calls this 'insane impulse.' Science, as I understand it, and as I think you understand it, call it murder. The law, as they understand it, calls it 'insane impulse.' But the law as I understand it, and as the Judge interprets it, as I shall contend, calls it murder. Common sense calls it murder, cruel, revengeful murder, unrelieved by a single mitigating circumstance, and it is idle to shut our eyes to a stern and solemn truth.

"Now, gentlemen of the jury, if this be science, as they understand it, in my judgment it is time that the great portion of us, I include myself among the number, should be dressed in strait jackets and locked up in the Insane Asylum."

Smirking, Bradley commented, "I agree."

"If a man or a woman, prompted by revenge, can lie in wait and commit a deliberate, willful murder, and science calls it 'insane impulse,' of course Mr. Bradley will agree with me when I say, 'Dissolve society into its original elements, raze your churches, your courts of criminal jurisprudence, close your Bibles, and tell your daughters to learn to be marksmen, and to arm themselves with a pistol and the assassins dagger.

"When the husband goes out to work for his daily bread, his wife should stand by his side with a pistol in one hand and a Bowie knife in the other, to protect him against the 'insane impulse' of some wicked revengeful woman who wishes to gratify her revenge against him perhaps for some youthful indiscretion.

"It is throwing open the doors wide to violence and crime, and I ask, 'What man in the community is safe, if a jury so far mistakes the law as to acquit this woman upon the ground of insane impulse?' By such an absurd verdict you say to every wicked woman in the city of Washington, kill a man for revenge if you please, and then take care to tear your hair, cry, and cut up a few antics, and we will call it insane impulse, and thus we will not only approve, but applaud the act.

"Now, I think I understand every man on the jury. You are anxious to acquit this woman, and this may be creditable to your hearts. But I undertake to show that this is a case of murder, and that this woman is not *scientifically* insane. She is not *legally* insane. She is not *practically* insane. She is not *generally* insane. She is not *periodically* insane. She is not *spasmodically* insane. She is not even *hypothetically* insane."

Even the judge smiled at this turn of phrase.

"She is as sane now as she was before the murder. This idea of insane impulse is but a legal contrivance to hide behind. These Western gentlemen, members of Congress, come here to charge me with relapsing into a state of barbarism. Science, as they understand it, says insanity is that state of mind that leaves a person unaffected except just when he wants to commit a crime.

"They admit that the woman is sane today, admit that she was sane before the homicide, but claim that she was insane at the precise point of time she committed it.

"The learned counsel for the accused have with great art endeavored to place the counsel for the Government in antagonism to Dr. Nichols and the other physicians who have been examined here. But if you adopt the opinions of these physicians, you are bound to convict the prisoner at the bar. Has Dr. Nichols or any other physician dared to testify that this woman, at the time she committed the homicide charged in this indictment, was insane, and so insane as to be irresponsible for her conduct? He has not done it. He could not do it without committing the crime of perjury. Let him take his place in the jury box and, judging from the opinion, which he has expressed as a witness, as an honest man he would render a prompt and decided verdict of conviction. I should be glad to see him in that jury box, and relieve this merciful and kind-hearted jury."

Bradley, with a smirk, said, "I should be glad to put him there."

Carrington continued, "He has testified most cautiously. I charge you, gentlemen of the jury, as you value the cause of truth, of justice, and of public security, to understand the opinion before you endeavor to shirk your responsibility, by shielding yourselves behind it. I shall warn you, for if you render a verdict of acquittal on the ground of insanity, it will be inconsistent with the opinion expressed by each and all these scientific gentlemen. And you will render yourselves ridiculous and the intelligent portion of the community will say, either that you do not understand your duty or that the law officer of the Government did not explain it to you properly.

"Dr. Nichols expressed an opinion upon a purely hypothetical case, not upon the case at bar. He did not hear the whole evidence-in-chief offered by the prosecution, or any of the rebutting evidence offered by us, and he assumed, as proved from the evidence, that he did not hear, facts which are not proved."

Wiley said, "Dr. Nichols heard all the evidence. He did not speak from a hypothetical case."

"He did not hear the testimony of Mr. Everett, one of the most important witnesses examined on the part of the prosecution, and he did not hear any of the rebutting evidence. And in addition to this, he did not even upon the evidence he did hear, express the opinion that this woman, at the time the homicide was committed, was so insane as to be irresponsible for her conduct. Your Honor should have stopped him if he had, for it would have been allowing the physician to transfer himself from the witness stand to the jury box.

"No! The responsibility is upon you, gentlemen of the jury, and you cannot as honest men avoid it. I shall not shield myself behind the opinion of any one, and I charge you, as honest men, not to avoid your duty, by endeavoring to do so."

Wiley stated, "Dr. Nichols was present from Saturday morning, the second day of the evidence, and remained in court each day until the time of his giving his testimony."

Bradley commented, "He had read to him the testimony given on Friday, and he gave his opinion upon all the facts, assuming the evidence to be credible."

Wiley added, "Yes, Dr. Nichols assumed all the evidence to be credible and assuming that fact, he gave certain opinions upon that evidence. If the jury differ from him, if they believe that this evidence or a part of it was perjured evidence, or unworthy of belief, to that extent they can set aside the opinion of Dr. Nichols as an expert. But if they think that the evidence heard, considered, and weighed by Dr. Nichols is credible, they are bound by the opinions of Dr. Nichols as an expert."

"If your Honor please," said Carrington, "you will remember that upon cross-examination the witness assumed to be proved certain facts, and he went on to state them. Now, I wish to show to the jury that the doctor assumed as proved what was not proved in point of fact."

"Certainly, you have the right to do that," said Wiley.

"Then, gentlemen of the jury, I will proceed. The opinion of Dr. Nichols, as I have already stated, is expressed upon an assumed state of facts. First, he assumes as proved that there was a marriage contract, which was broken. Secondly, that the prisoner was melancholy in consequence of disappointed love. Thirdly, that she had received a dishonorable proposition from her lover, contained in these Greenwood letters, or believed she had. Fourthly, that she was suffering from dysmenorrhea at the time.

"If these are the facts upon which his opinion rests, and I show you that these facts do not appear from the evidence, the opinion is hypothetical and cannot be regarded by you in forming your verdict. He erects a superstructure upon these four stones and I intend to remove them one by one, and the entire fabric falls to the ground.

"First then, gentlemen, was there a marriage contract? A marriage contract, like every other contract, requires the consent of both parties. I defy you to discover a marriage contract from any of the 92 letters offered in evidence. Even if we admit, for sake of argument, that there was a marriage contract, I maintain that the lady herself violated it.

"Look at this letter. I cannot read it, gentlemen. Perhaps it should be read. I saw some of you crying. What are you crying about? I cannot cry. I will have to get my friend Mr. Bradley or Judge Mason to cry for me."

Bradley commented, "If you had half as much sensibility as we have you would cry also."

"Cry for what," said Carrington holding up the letter. "Perhaps I committed a mistake, gentlemen. I should have put some one of these ladies on the stand as an expert. This letter echoes the groans of a discarded and despairing lover. The lady discards her truehearted, honorable lover and he, like a man of honor, offers to return her letters and her portrait and try his fortune in another quarter. The lady, exercising a woman's right, in a spirit of coquettishness, discards the man she loves and then, fired by the demon of jealousy, murders him for marrying another, her superior in all respects.

"What then is the opinion of Dr. Nichols worth when he assumes she was suffering because her lover had violated his promise of marriage? Is it dishonorable to love a pretty girl and tell her so? And when discarded by one pretty girl, is it dishonorable to love a prettier and a better girl and to tell her so?

"Burroughs loved Mary Harris tenderly and devotedly, if these letters breathe the spirit of true love. He was discarded by her and, meeting another lady, her superior, loved her, offered her his hand and heart, and like a true hearted woman, she neither flirted nor coquetted with him, but promptly gave him all that a woman has – a woman's love.

"It is said that the prisoner suffered from melancholy, too, in consequence of disappointed love. Gentlemen of the jury, was she melancholy? We all know what suffering from insane melancholy means. In looking through the evidence we see this poor, melancholy, love-sick girl playing cards, attending parties, conversing with a young gentleman on the very morning she started for the city of Washington, bent upon her murderous purpose, and collecting money for the Misses Devlin in her usual good health and spirits. Did she suffer from disappointed love? True love, gentlemen, is a noble, pure and generous passion. It refines the manners, purifies the heart, elevates the thoughts, gives zest and delight to every energy and to every aspiration.

"Did Mary Harris love the man she so cruelly and inhumanly murdered? No, gentlemen of the jury. The kind, gentle, and loving wife, may, in a moment of passion, speak an unkind word to her devoted husband but when she sees him in danger or distress, she will rush to his assistance.

"Did the tender and sacred flame ever burn in the heart of this cruel and revengeful murderess? To say that she ever loved with a pure and holy love, A. J. Burroughs, is an insult to every honest and virtuous woman in the land. What then becomes of the opinion of Dr. Nichols when he assumes as a fact proved in the case, that the prisoner was a poor melancholy, love-sick girl who committed this horrid crime while in a state of insanity? If a woman is to be excused on this ground, you give a *carte blanche* to any lewd and wicked woman to commit violence and crime.

"Thirdly, Dr. Nichols assumes that the deceased was the author of the Greenwood letters, or that the prisoner supposed he was, and thus she received a great shock to her moral sensibilities. Adoniram J. Burroughs was not the author of those letters. I appeal to the testimony of the Rev. John C. Burroughs, corroborated and confirmed by the testimony of Danenhower, and the records of the Treasury Department.

"The prisoner knew he was not the author of those letters for at the suggestion of the Devlins she went to the house of the Rev. J. C. Burroughs and was satisfied from that interview that he was not the author of the letters, and she returned to her home entirely relieved of all suspicion. It is true the Devlins were not satisfied, and it was not their purpose to be satisfied, but Mary Harris was.

"What then becomes of the opinion of Dr. Nichols? Her sensibilities were not shocked but, on the other hand, the sensibilities of the deceased were shocked in consequence of the unexpected discardal by the woman he truly and honorably loved.

"Fourthly, Dr. Nichols assumes that she was suffering with dysmenorrhea at the time the homicide was committed. This is not so in point of fact, judging from the evidence. Mrs. Flemming testifies that she saw her the day previous to the homicide, and that she complained of a slight sore throat but otherwise was in good health.

"No girl could be suffering with that complaint without its being known by an old woman with whom she was boarding at the time. Every old woman in the country understands the complaint and knows how to cure it – simply by putting the patient to bed, applying a few warm bricks, and administering a little hot tea."

Laughter arose from the male part of the audience, followed by a rap of the gavel.

"Mrs. McWilliams saw her shortly before the homicide and her testimony is inconsistent with the idea of her suffering with dysmenorrhea at the time of the homicide. Dr. Young, the physician of the jail, testifies that she was *unwell* on the 16th of June. The homicide was committed on the 30th of January, and therefore, in the regular course of events, it is possible, but not probable, that she was suffering with dysmenorrhea at the time she murdered Burroughs.

"Gentlemen of the jury, if you acquit the prisoner by assuming that she was insane from facts like these, you perceive that you render a verdict utterly at variance with the evidence.

"In order to acquit this woman upon the ground of insane impulse, you must be satisfied with the evidence that she unexpectedly met with the man who had injured her, or whom she supposed had injured her, and suddenly drew her pistol, which she happened to have about her person for no particular purpose, without being able to restrain herself, or appreciate the character of the act she was committing.

"By way of illustration, just as a person suffering with typhoid fever would suddenly seize some deadly weapon laying near him, and strike either friend or foe. Is that this case? Shall I repeat the evidence? She armed herself with a pistol, tracked up her victim, concealed herself, laid in wait for him, fired at him, and then, deliberately stepping into the center of the hall through which he passed, cocked her pistol and fired a second time.

"Now, in regard to Dr. May, I have a word to say. This eminent physician, in reply to a hypothetical case put by me, said he did not think the supposed patient was insane. Judge Hughes says I brought this hypothetical case from the moon. If that is so, then Mr. Bradley's hypothetical case was borrowed from some distant planet, for I do not think that he has presented the facts of this case so accurately and so fairly as I have done.

"They are both hypothetical cases, and the Court should not allow the doctor to express an opinion upon any other, for it would contravene a familiar and well-settled rule of law. In answer to Mr. Bradley's hypothetical case, Dr. May says the patient was insane and upon cross-examination he gave his reasons for it.

"First, he assumes that the prisoner had been suffering from melancholy resulting from disappointed love; second, from a shock to her moral sensibilities; third, that she did not attempt to escape after committing the homicide; fourth, that she did not know the man was dead after she killed him. It needs no doctor, nor does it need any ghost from the grave, to tell us that such a person was insane.

"But is that *this* case? I have already argued that she was not suffering from melancholy, resulting from disappointed love; that she had received no shock to her moral sensibilities. Did she not attempt to escape? The evidence is that when Burroughs fell, having endeavored to escape from the building, she lost her way and was arrested in the basement.

"Did she not know what she had done? She told the officer that Burroughs had injured, had seduced, had ruined her, and she was determined to have revenge at the risk of her life. She shows no emotion, to be sure, until she sees his mangled and bleeding corpse and then she suffers, as I have already said, as any other sane woman would, however depraved, the pangs of remorse.

"It must have amused you, gentlemen of the jury, to have seen the senior counsel for the defense – the father of the bar, the venerable Joseph H. Bradley – appearing in the double capacity of counsel and witness – of lawyer and doctor! When the learned counsel took the witness stand, he reminded me of an old lawyer – to put a hypothetical case, – who came out to Western Virginia for the purpose of practicing law. He settled in the village, rented an office, swung out his shingle, and the next morning the following advertisement appeared in the village paper: 'The undersigned will practice law in this town. Fees moderate, except when evidence is furnished.'"

The audience again laughed. Judge Wiley made no attempt to restrain them, instead directing his attention to the counsel for the defense.

"Mr. Carrington, do you intend, sir, to impugn my motives?" thundered Bradley from across the room.

"Certainly not. But let us analyze his testimony. He

says he observed a peculiar dilation of the pupils. Have you never observed that before, gentlemen of the jury? Did you never see the gentleman's pupil dilate when he was replying to some attack that I had made upon his client in a desperate case?

"Again, it is said that she could not sleep and in the silent watches of the night, when honest people were sleeping quietly, she heard unusual and unearthly sounds. Is there anything remarkable in this, when we remember that she had stained her conscience with innocent blood, and that she was suffering the pangs of remorse?

"After the murder of Duncan, Lady Macbeth advised her husband to sleep, to think no more of his crime, or it would run him mad. He cried, 'Sleep no more; Glamis hath murdered sleep!'

"But, gentlemen of the jury, I shall not trouble you by reviewing the whole of Mr. Bradley's testimony. I see nothing in it inconsistent with the sanity of the prisoner, in view of the fact that these vagaries to which he testifies, occurred subsequent to the homicide – after the excitement was over and the prisoner was confined in jail.

"Mr. Voorhees asked if I intended to charge Joseph H. Bradley with fraud? Certainly not. He knows and my brethren of the bar know my regard and respect for him. If any man on the street should charge him with fraud in my presence, I would be prompted by an 'insane impulse' to knock him down."

"Thank you, sir," commented Bradley.

"But I will continue this discussion no longer. You know this woman is not insane. If you acquit her upon the ground of insanity, it will be a pretext only. If you wish to acquit her, do it because you want to do it but do not render yourselves ridiculous by listening to this nonsense of insane impulse. Just remember, you have taken an oath to decide this case according to the law as it is, and not as you think it ought to be.

"How often do you hear this defense of insanity? It is relied on in every desperate case of murder and honest and intelligent jurors generally treat it with contempt. If some poor, trembling criminal in rags and tatters should dare to make such a defense as this, it would be hooted out of court.

"Why should a different rule be adopted in the case of Mary Harris? Why was she not subjected to the inspection of the jury? For your custom is, when the defense of insanity is made, to examine the prisoner carefully for yourselves and form your opinion from a personal inspection and examination of the accused. But it was not so in the case of this veiled and mysterious murderess.

"Whenever I hear this defense of insanity, it reminds me of a remark that was made to me by my predecessor, Mr. Fendall, father of one of the defense counsel. He had just purchased a book on homicide and he met up with old Col. Benton on the street. 'Why,' said Col. Benton, 'your money has been misspent. There are only two defenses in cases of homicide in this country – self-defense and insanity.' "The old colonel was right. If a man injures another and the injured party kills him, he pleads self-defense. If a man kills one who has never injured him, it is said that there was no motive and therefore he was insane.

"The result is, that skillful counsel may persuade judges and jurors, who have not the firmness and intelligence to discharge their duty, to give unbridled license to the crime of murder. If you approve of this defense by your verdict, it shall be against my earnest and solemn protest. I now solemnly protest against this libel upon the laws and religion of my country, When the excitement of the day passes off, and murder, crime and blood run riot in your city, no man or woman shall say it was I who did it.

"You have heard a great deal said by the learned

counsel about the dark ages. But even in the dark ages, in the age of chivalry, when the bloody code of honor was the rule, the injured lady called upon her hero, and the dispute was settled by the wager of battle in an open field, under a clear sky, where man met man face to face and beard to beard. They never employed the assassin's dagger to redress even the blackest and foulest wrongs.

"If this injured lady had been governed by the bloody code of honor, she would have appealed to her father, to her brother, or some friend – perhaps to the young Tydides. In this country a thousand swords would leap from their scabbards to avenge a look that threatened with injury or with insult an honest and virtuous woman.

"Gentlemen of the jury, we do not sit here to administer law according to a bloody code of honor. We are Christians. We live in a Christian age and are a Christian community. We can neither recognize nor tolerate any redress of wrongs, whether real or imaginary, except by an appeal to courts of justice.

"Gentlemen of the jury, it is idle to close our eyes to the truth. It was not insanity, either paroxysmal, scientific, or by whatever name you may be pleased to call it, but it was jealousy! Jealousy! I have seen a personification and representation of the passions upon canvas – hatred, envy, malice, revenge, and jealousy. In this collection of imaginary demons the most horrible to behold is the green-eyed monster, but it is no excuse for crimes. It never has been and never can be where the law is properly administered. Mr. Bradley in his opening address admits that this is a case of jealousy. You remember his remark, 'It is the old story of Othello.'

"But Othello gave his doomed wife a chance to ask for forgiveness before he killed her. Not so with Mary Harris, who struck young Burroughs down and sent his soul into eternity without a word of warning or time to breathe a single prayer. Othello relents after the deed was done but not Mary Harris. She is now seen, like a horrid ghoul, burrowing in the grave, and feeding her revenge upon the remains of her murdered victim. Through her counsel, her organ and representatives who speak her sentiments and represent her views, she endeavors to destroy the reputation of his only brother, the natural guardian and protector of his widow and his orphan.

"There was another person behind the scenes, pulling the wires, when this dark and dreadful deed was committed and that was Louisa Devlin. I do not mean to say that she expected to profit from the murder of Captain Burroughs, but her object was to profit by a suit of breach of promise of marriage. While the prisoner may have been satisfied after her interview with Dr. Burroughs, the Devlins were not.

"They fired the jealousy of this love-sick girl by claiming that Burroughs was the author of the Greenwood letters, not withstanding what his brother said, and urged her on to institute this suit for a breach of promise of marriage. The prisoner, finding she could not maintain that action, no doubt contrary to their expectations, in a moment of jealousy, revenge, and disappointment, committed this terrible murder.

"Now I reach the last, and indeed the only real defense to this indictment. I approach it with fear and trembling, for I do not see how I can meet it successfully, in view of the extraordinary but powerful sympathy that has been elicited on behalf of the prisoner. It is this: she is a pretty, delicate, little woman. That is all.

"This is really the only defense and you know it. If you acquit this woman it will be because she is a woman and all this nonsense about insanity and moral justification are simply to afford you a pretext. It is said that she wanted to be the wife of the deceased. Wife, indeed! That name is sacred as heaven itself. It is associated in our minds with all that is good, amiable, and attractive.

"What sort of wife would this woman have made, who had the heart to conceive and the hand to execute this bloody deed? What if a man hears that his wife has been to an assignation house – no matter for what purpose – and has conversed with the proprietress of that infernal den – no matter what subject – inhaled its pestilent atmosphere, or that she has gone to a prostitute and inquired if her lover was faithful to her? His love would turn to disgust and he would dash her, like a loathsome weed away, if it wrung his very heart-strings.

"I admit that Burroughs once loved Mary Harris with an intensity and ardor which is creditable to his heart, if not to his head. He was affectionate, demonstrative, and violent in his attachments, but honorable and true. He calls her 'ducky,' 'darling,' 'rosebud,' and 'sugar plum.' This is the ordinary language of love but it is too tame."

Gentle laughter arises from the audience.

"No term of endearment is too strong to be applied by a man to the girl he loves and no demonstration of affection too expressive. Think back 20 years ago of the sweet words you have whispered into the ears of the girl you love, and the notes that you have written her in those halcyon and happy days. How would you like to have them exposed to the vulgar gaze of the public? If such demonstrations are evidence of insanity, you and I and every true-hearted man, should be dressed in straight jackets, and turned over to the tender mercies of Dr. Nichols, this propagator of the new and dangerous doctrine – this modern philosopher of the humbug of 'paroxysmal insanity.'

"The last problem is: what is the quality of the homicide? Is it murder or manslaughter? There was neither passion nor sufficient and recent provocation for it to be manslaughter. On the contrary, it was willful, deliberate, and premeditated, and committed under circumstances of great aggravation, showing a heart regardless of social duty, and fatally bent on mischief. It is a case of murder – cold-blooded, cruel, causeless murder.

"Notwithstanding the strictures of the learned counsel for the accused in regard to my reference to the place where this homicide was committed, I repeat that it is, in my judgment, a fearful aggravation of her guilt that she slew a public servant while at his post of duty, and who drew his sword in his county's cause in that hour of national danger and distress, when loyal, patriotic men constituted the great wealth and the chief hope of the republic.

"Let it not be said that eminent criminals, defended by prominent public men, may commit a crime with impunity in the federal metropolis. Why did not this prisoner, I repeat, take the life of the deceased in Chicago, if he injured or if she supposed he had just injured her? Did she suppose, as many do, that here she could gratify her revenge with impunity? The citizens of Washington are a law-loving, law-abiding and a religious people, but it is a rendezvous for thieves, murders, garrotters, and adventurers of both sexes and of every variety – a sewer for all the vices and immoralities of the age in which we live.

"Our only hope of safety is in the firmness and fidelity of the judiciary. I plead the cause of law, order, and religion and if you dishonor the records of this court by an approval of this bloody deed, it shall be against my earnest and solemn protest. Washington is a central and radiating point. We exert an influence in all sections of this great confederacy. Besides, strangers judge our people from the manners and customs of the federal metropolis.

"I charge you then, gentlemen of the jury, to remember the solemnity of your position, and take care how you outrage the public sentiment, and libel the community of which you are the representatives on this occasion. I can read your thoughts. You pity the prisoner at the bar. So do I. You wish to shield her from the consequences of her crime. I have no objection to this, provided the law is enforced. How is it to be done? It is the simplest thing in the world.

"The legislature, in its wisdom, has provided for such cases. Convict the prisoner, and then commend her to the mercy of the Executive. Do this and your object is accomplished without violence being done to any man's conscience. If the prisoner deserves clemency, she will receive it. But in my opinion, stern, inflexible justice is true mercy. I would have you temper justice with a spirit of mercy, but I would not have you sacrifice the cause of justice to mercy."

Judge Wiley addressed Mr. Carrington, "Does that conclude the prosecution's closing statements?"

"It does, your honor," said the District Attorney.

The judge then turned to the jury and told them the Court had laid down the law. He said he felt they understood the law and he would now submit the cause to them without further charge. He commented, "I hope you have made up your minds and will soon render your verdict."

At 4:00 o'clock he remanded them to a room where they could carry on their deliberations after taking care of any bodily needs. Richardson and Douglas remained in their seats as the jury walked out.

"Carrington made some valid points," said Richardson. "Mary told her own lawyer that her love had turned to hate. She did not put her writ in the hands of an attorney when she came to Washington but instead went to the Treasury building and killed Burroughs after premeditation and after enough time for any insane impulse to have passed. Afterwards, she tried to escape, was cool, calm and collected and told the police officer who took her to jail that she wanted revenge."

"He said if this was insanity, we should all be locked up and Bradley agreed that the District Attorney should be locked up," said Douglas with a laugh.

"Carrying the analogy to a ludicrous level," said Richardson, "he exclaimed that if this was insanity we should destroy our churches, courts and bibles and teach our daughters how to shoot and use daggers! And in an attempt to get the jurors to identify with Burroughs, he asks, 'What man is safe from a youthful indiscretion if the jury acquits a wicked woman? Think back 20 years to what transpired between you and the girl you loved. How would you like to have your words and love notes exposed to the vulgar gaze of the public?'"

Douglas remarked, "Carrington used a nice turn of phrase when he said that Miss Harris was not scientifically, legally, practically, generally, periodically, spasmodically or even hypothetically insane. He said the idea of an insane impulse and the paroxysmal insanity defense were merely legal contrivances. As they are used, they leave a person unaffected except just when he or she wants to commit a crime."

"But he slipped up again when he said that Dr. Nichols was not present to hear all the evidence," said Richardson. "Judge Wiley corrected him by saying he was present from the second day until after he gave his testimony. That reinforces the perception that he didn't have all his facts straight."

"Yet he did enumerate all the facts that Nichols assumed were true but were not actually proven, said Douglas. "It was never proven that a marriage contract existed and Mary did appear to reject A. J. Burroughs at least once. It was assumed that the prisoner was melancholy because she was disappointed in love but she attended parties, played cards, and conversed with young gentlemen. Carrington denied that it had been established that Mary truly loved Burroughs. It was assumed that she received a dishonorable proposition from her lover but it was never proven that Burroughs was the author of the Greenwood letters and Mary didn't believe it herself at first.

"It was never proven that she was suffering from dysmehorrhea at the time of the murder. No young woman could have hidden that fact from an old woman like Mrs. Flemming and she didn't notice it. Dr. Young testified Mary was 'unwell' on the 16th of June and the murder was committed on the 30th of January so, mathematically, it is improbable she was suffering from dysmenorrhea at that time. Since these facts do not appear from the evidence, Dr. Nichol's opinion has to be based on a hypothetical case."

"Carrington makes light of the disorder by saying the standard cure is tea, hot bricks for heat and bed rest," said Richardson.

"There were a lot of snide comments exchanged between Carrington and Bradley," said Douglas. "The DA made fun of Bradley acting as both lawyer and doctor and Bradley responded by acting as though his motives are being impugned – whether he actually believed it or not is another question. Carrington, in defense, questions the validity of Bradley's testimony about the symptoms of his client."

"When he again disparages the insanity defense as humbug, Carrington cleverly quotes defense attorney Fendell's father as saying there are only two defenses to homicide: self-defense and insanity. The implication is that the defense is disingenuous about their claims of insanity but that is all they have to work with. He claims their only real defense is that Mary Harris is a pretty, delicate, little woman - the insanity claim and proffered moral justifications for her actions are just a pretext for acquitting her on the basis of sympathy for a woman."

"He turns the defense assertion that he, Carrington, is

from the dark ages around on them by saying that we civilized Christians no longer operate by a bloody code of honor but rely on the courts for justice."

"Returning to his opening statement," said Richardson, "he finishes up with a plea to clean up the image of Washington from being 'a rendezvous for thieves, murders, garrotters, and adventurers of both sexes and of every variety – a sewer for all the vices and immoralities of the age in which we live.' He was asking the jurors to not simply assess the facts presented in court but to look at how their verdict would be perceived by potential critics of the justice system and of the District of Columbia. In addition, he asserted that safety for the citizens lies in a judiciary that is firm and adheres to its duty."

CHAPTER 21

The jury returned at 4:10 and the clerk, Mr. Middleton, asked "Gentlemen of the jury, have you agreed upon your verdict?"

The foreman, Mr. Thomas Schrivener, answered, "We have."

Mr. Middleton said, "Look upon the prisoner at the bar. Do you find her guilty as indicted, or not guilty?"

The foreman answered in a loud clear voice, "Not guilty."

A tremendous cheer arose and nearly everyone in the courtroom appeared to be gratified. Many people were trying to shake hands with Miss Harris and a few caught her hand. She was kissed by Mr. Bradley, but immediately fainted. Bradley swept her up in his arms and took her to an anteroom in the courthouse to avoid the crowd. After Mary recovered her composure, Miss Louisa Devlin and Mr. Voorhees accompanied her in a carriage from City Hall to an undisclosed location.

Richardson and Douglas looked at each other in amazed silence for a moment. "Wow! They pulled it off," said Douglas. "I didn't think they could do it, at least not Scot-free. I thought the jury might go for manslaughter."

"Clearly, it looks like everyone's sympathies were for the defendant," said Richardson, "except maybe that of the prosecution. Judge Wiley was certainly biased in favor of the defense and his strong criticism of Mr. Carrington no doubt hurt his case. So heart wins out over head! All of the logical arguments of the District Attorney's Office fell on deaf ears. Poor little Miss Mary was just the instrument of God's wrath toward that scoundrel, Adoniram Judson Burroughs, and his brother, who was portrayed as a vindictive accomplice in his brother's treachery. Even without genuine proof of most aspects of the defense thesis, they were able to convince the jury through insinuation, innuendo and oratory."

"If I ever kill someone, I am for sure going to get Bradley as my attorney," joked Douglas.

"Of course, the prosecution made a number of errors in pursuing their cause," said Richardson. "They were so convinced that it was an open-and-shut case that they didn't anticipate many of the moves by the defense and collect information and testimony to counter them. They tried to strip the case down to just four basic questions that were devoid of sentimentality, and that did nothing to win the hearts of the jury.

"It is true that our judicial system shows both reason and compassion and that these different functions are sometimes assigned to different parts of the system or stages of the process. But trying to get the jury to trust that some other judicial body would show the *right* sentiment was not a convincing argument for those harboring sympathetic feelings toward the defendant, especially after what happened with Mrs. Surratt."

"Carrington claimed, incorrectly, that Dr. Nichols was

not present for all the evidence and misidentified Louisa Devlin as the one who went to Quincy Street, which suggested he wasn't on top of the facts in the case," said Douglas. "He didn't find out what Mary did during the month she was alone in Chicago after the Devlins moved to Janesville. Did she see Burroughs then? Did she practice using her pistol?"

"And he didn't raise any doubts early on in the trial about Mary being melancholy as a result of her rejection," said Richardson, "or about her actually having painful dysmenorrhea on the day she killed Burroughs, or about Devlin's testimony that she had no gentlemen admirers. He could have leveled more pointed questions toward the men that Mary spent time with, especially Peter Hartwell, and he didn't question the Devlin brother at all after it was suggested that she said she was going to marry him."

"The prosecution let pass the whole issue of the selection of letters which were presented in court when they could have demanded full disclosure right from the get-go," said Douglas. If they had been on their toes, they could have made a big deal about the assumptions built into the testimony of Dr. Nichols in cross-examination rather than waiting until their final summing up. They could have clarified the differences between a hypothetical case and the actual case of Mary Harris."

"Trying to paint Louisa Devlin as a conniving strumpet and questioning the nature of her business without any supporting evidence got him into trouble with the judge and made Bradley a hero for stepping up and defending her, said Richardson. "And Carrington caused a backlash in the jury by his use of sarcasm and his belittling of Mary's patriotism and love for Burroughs. So too did his attempt to make an example of her. Such tactics made him look like he had lost his objectivity and wanted to convict her on irrelevant grounds."

"Besides taking every opportunity to play on their

heartstrings, the defense may have also helped the jurors to rationalize their decision by suggesting that they could rely on the conclusions of the experts – the doctors being so much more knowledgeable about insanity. They could even go beyond the rules of evidence - make history and establish a precedent by their verdict."

"We've got to get out of here and get our stories filed for tomorrow," said Richardson. "It has been a pleasure discussing the case with you. I think it has helped both of us to do good reporting."

"Same here," said Douglas. "I have to get back to New York as soon as I'm finished here. Maybe we can get together the next time I'm in town."

"Sounds good. How about we meet for a drink at the Willard?"

"That's the ticket! The Round Robin is my favorite place in Washington," said Douglas as he picked up his notes and made haste toward the door. "I'll send you a note when I'll be in town," he shouted back from the doorway.

***

Later that day Mary met with Bradley and thanked him profusely for having saved her life. She said that she would be forever grateful and, with tears in her eyes, that she loved him. Bradley, tearful himself, responded, "I love you too, little lady. What are you going to do now? Do you have any plans?"

"Yes, I am returning to Burlington tomorrow to see my parents and my friends. I'm not sure how it will go there, what with all the notoriety I have received. I may have to go someplace else if things don't work out."

"Don't you worry, Miss Mary," said Bradley. "If you need help for your mental problems, just call on me and I can prevail upon Dr. Nichols to have you admitted to St. Elizabeth's. And I still have some connections I can call upon to help you find work, if you need to support yourself."

Two days later, in a column of news highlights, it was reported in the *New York Times* that Mary Harris. "the heroine of the late remarkable trial," was leaving for Burlington, Iowa where her parents live while the Devlin sisters were returning to Baltimore to reopen their millinery business.

The July 20, 1865 headlines on the *New York Times* were presented in "decks" of varying size, as was the custom, and read:

Miss Harris Acquitted

Extraordinary Close of a Remarkable Trial

A Court of Justice Rivaling a Political Caucus

Browbeating and Bullying the Public Prosecutor

Sensitiveness of the Judge on Free Speech

The Jury Make a Show of Deference and Retire

They return in Five Minutes and Pronounce a Verdict of Not Guilty

Tumultuous Joy of the Multitude

Curious Antics of One of the Defendant's Counsel

He Rushes Upon Her and Wildly Kisses Her

Bears Her Tenderly to Her Carriage

The Boys Shout "Hi! Hi!" and the Trial is Over.

The newspaper account included extensive coverage of the closing statements by the defense and prosecution. Its editorial comments disparaged the proceedings, especially during the closing hours, as being disorderly and disgraceful. It criticized both sides for the use of insolent language and the judge for being ineffective in controlling the excesses of the attorneys and lacking the dignity necessary for being on the bench. It characterized the closing statements, "comprised of the stump speeches of Mr. Voorhees and the rambling arguments of Mr. Carrington," as being confusing and more like a political convention than a dignified trial in the sacred halls of justice.

The *Brooklyn Eagle,* on the same day, compared Mary Harris to the heroine "Lilly Dale" in an English novel of the time. Lilly Dale, like Mary Harris, was jilted by her lover, remembered only his best qualities and was sad that her pure love was not reciprocated. But she recalled that episode in her life with sorrow, not anger, and did not set out to kill her former lover. The article concluded that the verdict in the Harris trial would encourage others to look up to the bad example of Mary Harris who is "supported by her enthusiastic rable," and not the good example of Lilly Dale.

"Pointing out that Voorhees had abandoned the claim of insanity and replaced it with the claim that Burroughs was rightfully punished with a dog's death for his offenses, the article stated that the verdict proclaimed there was no crime committed. "A woman who may fancy herself injured by her lover, may take the law into her own hands, though as in this case, no injury may be alleged against her person, and for anything that was proved, no suspicion may have been thrown on her character. This is 'law' and has been sustained for perhaps the fiftieth time by an American jury!"

Another article in the *New York Times* on July 20th noted that the trial had been followed throughout the country with great interest, not because the incidents of the crime were extraordinary, not because the social positions of either the deceased or the accused was eminent, not because the counsel were distinguished, not because any new principle was expected to be settled by it, and not because the verdict was expected to be different than it was. Instead, the author contended, the popular interest in the case was because "the times are rather dull, and an episode of this kind furnishes a lively subject of gossip amid the grave public questions now before the country."

The verdict, he wrote, illustrated a settled principle in American law - "that any woman who considers herself aggrieved in any way by a member of the other sex, may kill him with impunity, and with an assured immunity from the prescribed penalties of law." Even if the man has not harmed the woman physically, assailed her honor or roiled her feelings, she may kill him without notice, and without any penalty whatever, if she feels he did not conduct himself according to what he told her.

The following day, July 21, 1865, there appeared in the *New York Times* an article entitled "Photography Viewed in the Light of Social Science." The author satirically presumed to have read a response by a woman to an advertisement in which it was stated that a woman could obtain a husband for 25 cents. "But, wrote the author, " in view of the late disgraceful farce at Washington, to what may not this correspondence lead?"

"What if the picture of the future husband the smart young man sends to the lovelorn woman happens to be a likeness of you, the reader? What if you learn from her big brother that his forty-eight year old sister is demanding an immediate marriage? Your protests that you never heard of her are not listened to.

"It won't do; she may come down from Peoria with a pistol, she may waylay you in a public hall, she may gently split your pericardium with a conical bullet, and you may die, as you ought to, under the circumstances. What then?"

"During her trial it is found that you must have promised to marry her since how else would she have your picture. She must be insane since how else would she fancy such an ordinary fellow as you? She most definitely was insane at the time she shot you since 'there is a method in madness,' and since only an insane woman would not have wanted to rid herself of a person like you. And, to amplify and make the most of such points against you, or rather against your memory, you will find wily judges and client-kissing counsel always at hand; or if they should fail here, a change of venue to Washington will secure them."

On July 24th Carrington wrote a letter to the editor of the *Washington Chronicle,* complaining that many newspapers had selectively published only certain portions of what transpired in court and asking for publication of a full report of what was said so that the public could decide for themselves whether he acted improperly or went beyond the limits of his professional license. He obtained the help of Mr. Celphane, the court reporter, in transcribing the relevant portions of his report, which he hoped would be more objective than what had so far appeared in the press. The article comprised nearly the whole of Mr. Carrington's speech, including his defense of Reverend Doctor John C. Burroughs.

Dr. Burroughs himself wrote a letter to the editor of the *Christian Times,* which was republished in the *New York Times* on August 14th. His intended audience was not the general public but his Christian friends who had shown him kindness and sympathy and whose judgment he trusted. He praised the press in general and the *Chicago Tribune* in particular for a fair presentation of the facts and the merits of the case in spite of the distortions imposed by the lawyers for the defense.

He said that he knew his brother was acquainted with Miss Harris since 1861, possibly had been introduced to her, had seen her in Judson's company a couple of times and had heard him refer to her in kind terms. Neither he nor any member of his family knew there was anything between them other than friendship. At the time of his murder, none of them, including those to whom Judson confided his relations to ladies, could remember her name or recollect her appearance when supplied her name.

Dr. Burroughs related that before their engagement, Judson's wife spoke freely of Mary Harris and her relationship with Judson and after the revelation of their correspondence in court, she indicated there was nothing there she didn't know about. A month before his wedding he spent a week in Chicago and mentioned to his wife in a letter that he had just seen "Mollie," told her of his intention to marry and she had informed him of her engagement to Mr. Devlin of Baltimore. Months later he told his wife he had received a Chicago paper containing a notice of the marriage of Harris and Devlin.

Reverend Burroughs related Judson's wife's claim that they had arranged a meeting with Mary in Baltimore on their way home to Washington but were prevented from doing so because of an accident. Neither he nor any of Judson's friends had heard anything about a suit for breach of promise of marriage before his death.

Dr. Burroughs believed that Bradley would not allow reading of the remainder of the letters because there existed in them evidence which would refute the presumption of a promise of marriage. He didn't believe there was a legal basis for even admitting the letters as evidence because they were so mutilated, containing erasures, cut-outs, unfinished sentences and lack of signatures.

He contended that only the Devlin sisters attested to the resemblance in handwriting of the Greenwood letters to the handwriting of his brother. And he found it preposterous that Judson would be so stupid as to make an appointment at an assignation house a mile and a half from where he was to be wed only an hour and a half later. He was content that the trial would pass into history as a "farce," "mockery," "outrage," and "shame," as many papers described it, but he lamented the loss of his family's youngest member and of a man to play the role of father and husband to those he left behind.

In January of 1866, some six months after the trial ended, an article appeared in the *American Journal of Insanity* entitled "The Trial of Mary Harris." The unnamed authors, presumably the editors, began by saying that murder justified by insanity and applauded by the people of Washington is not without precedent. Taking a poke at representatives of the government, they stated, "Individuals chosen to uphold the national dignity, and high in social position, have furnished repeated examples of this kind." After citing several examples, they commented, "No sane person can believe that a man who disappoints a woman by refusing to fulfill a promise of marriage, is worthy of death," even if he tried to despoil her good name. Yet this was what happened in the Harris trial. This case differed from these others in that the perpetrator was a woman and, they contended, this constituted an appeal to the strong sentiment of sympathy characteristic of the American people. Whether or not she was insane had nothing to do with it.

Richardson was one of the first to read the piece and immediately wrote a letter to his old friend, Bill Douglas, enclosing a copy of the article. Douglas persuaded his publisher that there might therein lie a follow-up story on the Harris trial and convinced them that he needed to go to Washington to check it out. When he arrived, he immediately went to Richardson's office on Newspaper Row to leave a message that he was in town and arrange for a meeting. The following day they met at the Round Robin in the Willard Hotel.

Taking their Daniel Websters' to a convenient table, they began to discuss the *Journal of Insanity* article. "The psychiatrists did not contest the authorship of the Greenwood letters and they did not question Louisa Devlin's account of going with Mary to the Quincy Street house, or the claim that Mary was melancholy and had painful periods," said Douglas.

"True, but they did believe that Mary's erratic behavior was a voluntary yielding of control to her wayward feelings, aimed at generating a kind of morbid sympathy from her lady friends," said Richardson. "They implied that neither Louisa Devlin nor her sister, Jane, took these acts as serious or dangerous because they did nothing to prevent a recurrence, thought she was able to discern right from wrong, and acknowledged that no one was ever seriously harmed by the defendant."

"They characterized Judson's letters as 'silly and extravagant' and said that the Court initially ruled that the case for insanity should be made on the basis of questions more immediately connected with the deceased," observed Douglas.

"Yes, but then the testimony was admitted anyway as proof of *a* cause of insanity in general, not of *the* cause of insanity in Mary Harris," said Richardson.

"They criticized the Court's ruling that the jury did not have to justify it's verdict as an invitation for them to 'gratify their own impulses in a verdict of acquittal.' They seemed to feel the ruling set aside psychiatry's hard won legal definition of insanity."

"There were a number of other concepts that they ridiculed as being of merely metaphorical as opposed to scientific or legal usage: 'diseased physical condition,' 'moral cause operating,' 'stinging to madness and for the time displacing reason from its seat.' Looking at his notes, Richardson quoted the article, 'But if a jury may find insane impulse where there is no insanity in either the common or legal sense, we do not see that anything more is needed.' Obviously the mad doctors didn't see any evidence of insanity!"

The elite members of the American Psychiatric Association who wrote the article made a gesture of deference to Dr. Nichols, crediting him with a special sense for detecting mental disease, and so hesitated to criticize him. But they had no such hesitation when it came to Joseph H. Bradley, who they saw as "either an eager and unscrupulous advocate in behalf of his client," or as "a kind and too susceptible old gentleman, won over by the seductive manners and the real distress of a hysterical girl." They thought that, while some of the medical witnesses were simply ignorant about mental disease, all in the courtroom were in sympathy with the accused, including Judge Wiley.

"Their most severe critique was reserved for the evidence used to support the claim of insanity," said Douglas. "Listen to this: 'In the first place, no delusion, in the medico-legal sense of the term, was exhibited by the prisoner at any time in her history. The temporary visual and aural hallucinations which she seems to have had in Chicago, and while in jail, are the natural result of excitement, and not worthy to be mentioned. Indeed, no prominence is given them by anyone.

"Any degree of mental enfeeblement is also disclaimed for her. There remains, then the plea of 'moral insanity,' which we maintain has not, and cannot have any place in the sciences of law or medicine. But whether with the design of concealing the weakness of their theory, or from want of knowledge, the phrases 'moral insanity,' 'homicidal impulse,' 'insane impulse,' 'uncontrollable excitement,' etc., are used indiscriminately, and seemingly as often as possible. Another phrase is that of 'periodical or paroxysmal insanity,' which is used to denote a single species of disease, instead of two, as it should be understood.' They just ripped apart the defense's whole argument for Mary's insanity!"

In order to find for insanity, the psychiatrists wrote, there must be no natural explanation for the act and there must be some other precursor of mental illness such as heredity, previous attacks, head injuries, brain fever, pregnancy, etc. Neither menstruation, either with or without pain, nor disappointed affection warrants causal status in determination of mental derangement.

"It was pointed out that neurotic girls, during puberty, are likely to develop an attraction toward someone of the opposite sex and, if this attraction is met with no encouragement, it may give rise to a case of disappointment in love which is said to overthrow their minds," said Richardson.

"Uh huh, but the psychiatrists do not consider Mary Harris to be an example of this dynamic," said Douglas, "because the evidence, as they see it, does not show any deep-rooted, serious attachment between the parties."

The authors of the article explained that hysteria is a disorder in which the individual may yield up control of the will when prompted by "selfish and depraved desires." The hysteric may show violence and threats only when it may be done without much consequence. The usual goal is to obtain sympathy or notoriety, but steadfastness on the part of the interlocutor can suppress some manifestations of the neurosis.

"So they believed," said Richardson, "that what they called 'the flattered vanity and excited ambition' of Mary Harris was quite naturally changed, by Burroughs's scandalous conduct, into 'deadly hatred and the desire for revenge.' These feelings were, in turn, expressed in an hysterical neurosis, especially during the menstrual crisis, and the facts testified to by Dr. Fitch and the Misses Devlin are simply those of hysteria, and hysteria alone."

"The writers concluded that 'moral insanity' is indistinguishable from moral depravity and for that reason it is not allotted a position in the list of mental diseases," said Douglas. "Clearly, this is a devastating indictment of the defense attorneys, the judge and of the whole trial. The obvious implication is that the verdict was a miscarriage of justice."

"I think I'll title my column about this article as 'Harris Got Away With Murder, Say Psychiatrists'" said Richardson.

"I was toying with the title, 'Psychiatrists Think Bradley Was Seduced by Hysterical Client,'" said Douglas.

Both men laughed. "Well, it was certainly a spirited and colorful debate," said Richardson. "Of course, we had suspicions all along, but this article shows that renowned psychiatrists rejected the arguments of the defense, the testimony of one of their own and that of other doctors, and the unwitting collusion of the judge. No one involved in the case escapes without some stain on his reputation."

***

Mary made the trip from Washington to Burlington in three days, allowing a day stopover in Chicago to visit old friends. When she arrived in Burlington, her father had a buggy at the station, ready to carry her home. On the ride out to the farm, Mary inquired as to the welfare of her siblings and how the crops were doing. "Was the corn knee-high by the 4th of July?" asked Mary.

"Yeah," grunted her father. "You know you have cast shame on our whole family?"

Mary could smell the alcohol on his breath and feared angering him to the point where he would give her the back of his hand, as he had done when she lived at home. "I was found not guilty, father. There were a lot of well-known people in Washington and even New York who did not blame me for what I did."

"Well, back here people say you got away with murder and use you as a bad example to their daughters. You should have obeyed me when I told you not to carry on with that feckless slacker. You broke your poor mother's heart."

"I'm sorry, papa," said Mary, already regretting her decision to return to Iowa. "Can I stay here a while until I have a plan for myself?"

"You can stay but there isn't any more money than when we sent you off to work for Mrs. Alexander in the millinery and fancy goods store. You'll have to be able to carry your own weight pretty soon."

When she got into the house, her mother hugged her but then broke into tears. Drying her eyes, she asked, "How are you getting along, then?"

"I'm still having a hard time believing all that has happened to me, mama. People in Washington were very good to me and helped me get through the ordeal of the trial, but I am exhausted and need some time to get my bearings."

For the next few days Mary cleaned around the house and helped make meals. She told her mother about the trial and the eloquent defense that Representative Voorhees mounted on her behalf, which made her feel like she had some value in this world. She related the strong support and near constant visitation she received from Mrs. Abbey of New York. She told of the tender treatment she received at the hands of her main attorney, Mr. Bradley, and of how he had enlisted the help of his wife and daughter to make her time in jail less onerous.

Suspicious that anyone would want to extend a hand to help a poor Irish farm girl from Iowa, her mother said, "And what did he expect to get from you for all this graciousness?"

"Nothing, mother. He is just a kind old man who likes to help those less fortunate than he," Mary said while at the same time wondering if her Washington benefactor had a more personal interest in her than he had let on. Then she dismissed the idea as too unlikely.

"Um," said her mother with a doubtful tone.

Mary went to see her old lady friends in town. Mrs. Alexander was hospitable but did not offer Mary a job or suggest where she might look for employment. Mrs. Phelps, who had been so kind when she was in jail in

Washington, now seemed more remote and indicated that she and her husband were both very busy, requiring her to cut short their visit.

Mrs. Winters was her usual direct self. "Look, Mary, this is a very traditional community, except for down by the river. People are afraid of associating with you, thinking their friends will consider them to have loose morals simply by talking to you. The priest and preachers in town have been calling you a Jezebel and using what has happened to you as a lesson for their young parishioners. I don't give a shit what any of them think of me, but I don't have any job to offer you either. I suppose you could go down to one of the gin mills on the bottom land and become a lady of the evening, but I don't see much of a future in that."

"I don't think I have much of a future in Burlington, Mrs. Winters. I probably won't be able to find a way to make a living here and my parents are ashamed of me. I'm sad and discouraged. I think I should return to the East where I have some real friends that might be able to help me."

The next day she boarded a train headed back through Chicago to Baltimore. She found lodging at the same boarding house where she had stayed in January, before she had shot Burroughs. She called on her old friends, the Devlin sisters, and they rehashed the course of the trial and laughed at the chagrin the defense had visited upon the prosecution.

Louisa Devlin offered Mary her old job back but Miss Harris indicated she wanted some time to think about her future, without the necessity of keeping a schedule and meeting an employer's expectations. When she got back to her room, she sent a letter to Mr. Bradley asking if she might have an appointment with him and awaited his reply.

Within a few days she received his answer: "Please,

dear lady, come meet me at my office on Monday next at about 3:00 pm."

When Mary arrived at Bradley's office she gave Dorris her name and said she had an appointment to see Mr. Bradley at 3:00 o'clock.

Perplexed by the lovely woman standing in front of her, Dorris said, "You're Mary Harris? Mr. Bradley has spoken of you often in glowing terms but I didn't realize you were such a pretty young thing. Please have a seat and I'll let Mr. Bradley know you are here."

Bradley appeared at his office door with a broad smile on his face and a twinkle in his eye. "How nice to see you again, Miss Harris. Please come into my office. Can I have Dorris get you anything to drink?"

"No thank you, Mr. Bradley." After he closed the door, he hugged her briefly and ushered her to a large overstuffed chair that made her feel like a little girl again. "Mr. Bradley, my stay in Burlington did not go well. My parents are disappointed in me and ashamed to be seen in my company. There are no jobs for me in Burlington and even old friends shun me. I am terribly sad and confused." As a tear rolled down her cheek, she said in a quavering voice, "I don't know what to do. Am I as evil as they seem to think? What is to become of me? I keep thinking that there is no place in the world for a sinner like me."

"Now, now, Mary. Let's think this through. You have just had a most harrowing number of months in jail. You lost the man you thought you loved and some people have turned against you. But still there are those who think highly of you and adore your nimble mind and your gentle ways. I count myself among your admirers. There has to be a future that we can fashion for you. All we have to do is figure it out."

"I hope that is true, Mr. Bradley. You have been so very kind to me, I don't know how I can ever repay you. I need some time to think. I need to sort out my feelings and find out who I really am. I am so upset and discouraged that I don't think I would even be able to work and take care of myself. I guess I should just go and jump into the Potomac!"

"There, there little Miss Mary. We can solve this problem. Maybe you could use some time at Saint Elizabeth's. I can contact Dr. Nichols and arrange for an admissions interview. After his testimony, I'm sure he will get you in and see that you get the treatment you need. I'll look in on you from time to time to make sure you are being treated properly."

CHAPTER 22

The following day, Mary met with Dr. Nichols and was admitted to Saint Elizabeth's Insane Asylum, just over the bridge past Uniontown in Maryland. Dr. Nichols arranged for her to see a psychiatrist once a week during her stay. She used her other time in arts and crafts activities and helped with the physical operation of the hospital. Because she had an almost photographic memory for things she read, she was allowed to work in the accounting office.

The handsome young psychiatrist, Dr. West, who treated Mary, was just out of his residency. She was immediately attracted to him, wanted him to like her and felt they were close friends after just a few sessions. As time went on, she told him of her heartbreak when Adoniram Burroughs jilted her and she dramatically related to him her trip to the Treasury building when she shot her former lover, portraying herself as her defense attorneys had during the trial. As she had done with Joseph Bradley, she related how lively and enthusiastic she had been in that relationship and she even hinted at their sexual activity.

"We had such fun those times we met in towns away from Burlington. Sometimes we would spend half the day in bed."

His virility aroused, the psychiatrist pressed for greater detail: "What did you do?"

"Why ever do you ask that, Dr. West?"

"Well, ah...I just thought it might help me understand your situation better. Sometimes a person's preferences can help in making a diagnosis."

"Oh, I see," said Mary, playing along with what she knew was a ruse. Pressing her dress down on her abdomen with both hands, she said with a throaty laugh, "Well, I guess I could say that we put our separate parts together in various interesting and pleasurable combinations."

Not wishing to appear more lascivious than was appropriate for a doctor, the psychiatrist did not pursue his earlier inquiry. Mary knew she had awakened in him a greater degree of interest than existed before. In following weeks she would continue to try to impress Dr. West by telling of her accomplishments and popularity in other areas of the hospital. And she continued to be discretely flirtatious, sometimes "accidentally" brushing against him with her breasts as she entered or left the interview room, or turning in such a way as to show her cleavage.

But Mary was easily frustrated and, if Dr. West did not comply with her requests for special privileges, she would pout or fail to show up for the next appointment. When she did return, she would force him to jump through hoops to regain her favor, giving him subtle cues as to the direction he should take in order to get that delightful and provocative patient back into the room. Her mastery of the relationship with Dr. West did much to repair the self confidence that had been damaged by her return to Burlington and the brief time she again lived with her parents. She lavished praise on the good doctor, telling him he had saved her life and given her new hope for the future.

Perhaps Mary's most significant encounters occurred with Barbara Blackwell, a very perceptive and understanding nurse with whom she met daily over the next year. Walt Whitman had influenced Barbara when she worked with him in the Armory Square Hospital, on Seventh Street across from the grounds of the Smithsonian Institute, treating soldiers injured during the war. Like "The Good Gray Poet," she saw the value in listening compassionately to patient's stories, giving them individual attention, valuing their emotional reactions and providing practical tokens of their value. She was different from the other staff at Saint Elizabeth's because she ignored diagnosis and focused on the narrative of Mary's life as she lived it, trying to fashion it into a more or less coherent and unique story, like Whitman did with his injured soldiers.

Mary was a bit leery of Barbara at first because the older woman did not seem to be impressed by her notoriety and often answered a question with a question, displaying no trace of where she stood on the particular issue. "My parents were ashamed of me after I got back home. I didn't expect that after all the kindness shown to me during the trial and all the good people who helped me while I was in jail. Do you think I am despicable for what I did, Miss Blackwell?"

"I am not a judge, Miss Harris," said Barbara. "Generally, I don't think it is a good idea to kill people, but sometimes a person can get so worked up that it seems like the right thing - maybe the only thing - to do."

"There were times that I felt that way about Judson. When I thought about decorating and living in a house in Washington, getting all dressed up to go out to some ball or function, raising a bunch of kids, having distinguished friends in the nation's capitol, and then when I pictured his horrid rejection of me, I became so angry I wanted to destroy everything around me. Then there was the humiliation of it all in front of my lady friends...I didn't want him to shatter my dreams and get away Scot-free."

"That was a big loss for you. We humans usually can get that angry only when we have staked everything on that one other person. Without him, we think we have no value at all," said Barbara.

"Yes, without Judson I thought I was nothing. I wanted him to feel the emptiness I was feeling or at least to feel ashamed of what he had done."

"Do you think he felt that when you shot him?"

"No. I think all he felt was fear."

"You are probably right about that. So, the effect that you intended didn't really work out with the method that you had employed?"

"No. I just lost all possibility of ever having him as a friend and I got myself into a lot of trouble."

"Do you suppose there is some other way that you could appraise your value – some way where it is not tied to what some other person does or thinks?"

"I don't know, Miss Blackwell. I've always thought a woman's value was dependent on being a good wife and mother, being able to keep up a household, being a helper to her husband. I know there are women who choose not to have husbands or family but I always thought they were a little odd."

"Maybe we should talk some more about how one goes about measuring one's worth," said Barbara.

In subtle and gentle ways, Barbara helped Mary to more fully appreciate and accept the feelings which had motivated her crime. She did not judge Mary for her actions but simply treated them as methods she used to achieve goals within the world as she had constructed it at the time. Barbara suggested other possible constructions Mary could have placed on events, proposed alternative actions she could have taken at each choice point, and explored with Mary why she did not avail herself of these options and instead chose the path she followed. She also discussed with Mary what different goals she could have set for herself and what conditions would have had to be present in order for her to subscribe to these other goals.

Mary found the exploration of her actual self and her possible selves captivating and, in the process, gained a great deal of confidence in her powers to understand herself and make more deliberate decisions. At times, though, it was difficult for Mary to face up to the facts and deal with the chagrin she experienced when looking at her former self. "How could I have been so stupid? I always had my doubts about Judson. Why didn't I listen to them? Why couldn't I have just said, 'To hell with him' and gotten on about my life? Why was it so important for me to show my lady friends that I was grown up just like them and could get a man to marry me?"

Implicitly connecting the answers to such questions to beliefs Mary acquired in her childhood, Barbara said, "Tell me about growing up in Burlington, Mary. What was it like on the farm and why did you go off to work in town at such a young age?"

Barbara did not allow Mary to simply get hysterical when difficult questions arose, but helped her remain rational and analytical when addressing them and encouraged her to persist until she found a "good enough" answer. Sometimes, after much discussion, they decided the question couldn't be answered unless they had God-like powers or that there were too many unknowns so that it was pointless to try to figure it out. Time was better spent in looking to the future.

***

Joseph Bradley visited Mary every week while she was

in the hospital. She shared with him what she was learning about herself with Barbara but was evasive when discussing Dr. West. She told him about her successes in the accounting office and proudly showed him the craft projects she had completed. He provided encouragement and support. He often found himself overwhelmed with sympathy and admiration for this poor little girl who had been through so much and still had the spunk to keep trying to make a life for herself.

Such sentiments were nothing new for Joseph. While he made a comfortable living, he had not become extremely wealthy like other members of his family since he often took cases *pro bono* because some humanitarian principle was involved or when the individuals in the case aroused his sympathies. Ordinarily, Joseph took the fatherly, protective role and did not introduce his needs into the matter, but his wife was ailing at this time and he shared his fears and frustrations with Mary. Mary was flattered that her protector should seek her counsel and she was able to articulate her ideas about what his wife must be feeling and even gave some suggestions for what he might do to comfort her. He appreciated the feminine perspective and felt some relief at being able to talk about it with someone outside the family.

Eventually, as her confidence increased, Mary began to think of life outside the institution. She wanted to get a job and support herself, but her courtroom fame in Washington made that difficult. Bradley had an idea and wrote a letter to one of his father's old friends at the Post Office in Philadelphia. The man responded immediately and said that he would be delighted to find a position for anyone recommended by the son of his old friend. Within the month, Mary was on a train to Philadelphia to begin a career of federal employment. A newspaper article noted her release from the hospital "showing no signs of any dangerous malady of body or mind."

Mary fared very well in the bureaucracy because of her amazing memory for the written word. William H. Walkup, who described himself as a close friend of Miss Harris, said that she could read two columns from any document that she had never seen before and immediately repeat the text literally correct from memory. Relatively quickly, she moved from an entry-level mail handler position to one with more responsibility and authority.

Mary developed a reputation for being lively and enthusiastic, qualities noted and prized by both Mr. Bradley and her psychiatrist. But, as relationships endured, her friends often found her effusive manner to be a cover for superficiality and a lack of genuine sympathy. She was inclined to idealize a person whose approval she desired but she was sensitive to criticism and, if she perceived some slight, her feelings were easily hurt and she would shift to a total devaluation of that person. Some of her co-workers disliked her need to be the center of attention and others resented her inclination to manipulate people in order to get something she wanted.

One time, a co-worker was in line for promotion to a position in the accounting department of the Post Office, a position that Mary thought should be hers because of her good memory and facility with numbers. Knowing that her immediate supervisor, Jeremy Hadley, frequently spoke with the person who was to make the final decision, Mary "accidentally" implied that the woman, Leona Green, was hiding something unsavory.

"I hear that my good friend Leona Green is up for a position in accounting," said Mary.

"Yes," said Mr. Hadley, "I think she would be a valuable addition to that department."

"Why, certainly. Leona is a very dependable worker and she definitely needs the extra income now, after what happened...."

"What was that? I hadn't heard of any difficulty," said Mr. Hadley.

"Oh, I shouldn't have said anything, Mr. Hadley. I'm sure she has settled the matter by now."

"Was it anything that could compromise her effectiveness on the new job?"

"Oh, no, Mr. Hadley. It was really nothing. I'm sure she must have told her supervisor about it. Just forget that I said anything about it."

Leona Green was mad as hell about not getting the job and spared no effort in trying to find out why. Eventually she found out that Jeremy Hadley raised doubts about her. She confronted him to determine the nature of the complaint and, after a withering tirade, he finally revealed his conversation with Mary Harris.

Leona screamed at Mary, "What did you tell him about me?"

"Why, nothing at all, Leona. I just said you could use some extra income now since you lost your apartment and had to find a new one. I don't know how he could have made anything derogatory out of that! I liked Mr. Hadley when I first came to work here, but now I'm beginning to think he maybe doesn't have the discretion and managerial skills to be in the position he is in."

Of course, when Jeremy Hadley heard from Leona Green that what Mary was referring to was only that Leona had lost her apartment and that she was now bad-mouthing him to boot, he began to view her with a jaundiced eye, paying closer attention to her statements and getting clarifications of her intended meaning, and double-checking what she claimed others said or did. He inquired of her co-workers the nature of their transactions with Mary and did not like what he was hearing. Determined to straighten the young girl out, he set an appointment with Mary for a performance review.

Mary became quite anxious that her game might have been found out and had a recurrence of her "spells" that required her to take time off work. Preempting a dismissal from her job, Mary sent a letter to Mr. Bradley stating that she was having a relapse and needed to be readmitted to St. Elizabeth's. Mr. Bradley, ever the fatherly protector, sent an immediate reply. "Come to Washington forthwith. I have talked with Dr. Nichols and he will admit you. I will meet you at the railroad station. Let me know when you will arrive." It was signed, "Love, Joseph."

***

Mary's second admission to Saint Elizabeth's was much like her first but she had a new psychiatrist to break in. She looked forward to the challenge, more confident in her seductive capabilities than she was on her first admission. Barbara Blackwell was still there but Mary was hesitant to resume their daily sessions. Barbara seemed to know too much, or intuit too much, about her. "She gives me the willies," Mary thought. "It's almost like she can look right into my soul and see the wickedness there. Not that I am wicked, but it feels like that is the object of her gaze."

Mary made up excuses for not meeting with Barbara but eventually the tall nurse said to her, "You seem to be avoiding me, Mary. Is there something you are afraid I will do to you?"

"No, Miss Blackwell, I have just been very occupied since I got back," Mary lied.

"I see. Well, I have talked with Dr. Nichols and he has arranged for a time in your busy schedule for you to see me. He agrees with me that you need a cathartic resolving action in order to put your demons to rest."

"Demons! Demons! Do you think I am possessed, Miss Blackwell?"

"Of course not, Mary. I was simply speaking in metaphor. What I meant was that you need to experience

383

genuine emotion as you talk about the things that bother you. You seem to often live in a world of 'Let's pretend' where you cover up your true feelings and beliefs with something that is more acceptable to you."

"There is nothing that bothers me. I don't hide my feelings!"

"Then why are you back here? Maybe we should seek an immediate discharge for you today."

"No, no. I didn't mean that," Mary backtracked. "I know I have problems. I know I do things I shouldn't do that get me into trouble. But I can't help myself." Mary paused. "I am frightened, Miss Blackwell."

"I know you are, Mary. It is frightening to step into a world that you do not know. But maybe you can discover that you *can* help yourself, you *can* think and act differently and have better results than you have had in the past."

Thus began Mary's second round of treatment at Saint Elizabeth's Insane Asylum. Joseph Bradley was still visiting Mary as often as his busy law practice would allow. They would go on walks around the grounds and sometimes he would get her a pass to go into town to shop or attend some event. They talked about her activities in the hospital, about his work, about their interests, hopes and desires. They began to understand each other's families, at least as perceived by one of its members. Joseph told Mary about his wife's long illness and declining health, which worried him a great deal. They became very fast friends and looked forward to their meetings.

***

In 1867 Bradley was persuaded to take on the case of John H. Surratt, one of the Lincoln conspirators who had managed to escape the fate of the other plotters (including his mother) who were tried by a military commission and hung while the trial of Mary Harris was taking place. Surratt made his way to Canada, where he was hidden by two priests, and then traveled via England to Italy, where he became one of the Papal Zouaves, an international military regiment formed to assist the pope in his struggle against Giuseppe Garibaldi's movement for Italian unification.

A friend with whom he had attended school betrayed Surratt, and the Pope, learning Surratt was accused of helping to murder the President of the United States, immediately had him arrested and held for deportation back to his home country. However, Surratt managed to escape by making a daring leap down a sheer precipice. He made his way to Malta and finally to Egypt, but was eventually found by American detectives and returned to Washington.

Forty-one year old Richard T. Merrick, a well-known Washington lawyer, was the primary attorney on the case, conducting most of the witness interrogations. The 65 year old Bradley took a secondary role for the defense. His son, Joseph H. Bradley, Jr., went to Canada to round up witnesses and made the opening argument for the defense. The prosecution was composed of Bradley's old nemesis, E. C. Carrington and his assistant, Nathaniel Wilson.

Fortifying the government counsel was 50 year old Edwards Pierrepont, a graduate of Yale and the New Haven Law School. Pierrepont had practiced law in Columbus, Ohio, before moving to New York where he served as judge of the New York Supreme Court from 1857 to 1860. During the war he was a member of the military commission handling the cases of state prisoners in federal custody. Originally a Democrat, he turned Republican, served as an advisor to Lincoln and organized the president's 1864 reelection campaign. The judge was George P. Fisher, another Democrat turned Republican who had been appointed to the Supreme Court by Lincoln.

On some days during the trial, Judge Wiley, the

magistrate in the Mary Harris case, assisted him.

The prosecution had a four count indictment. The first count accused Surratt of actually having shot and murdered Lincoln. The second count alleged that Booth did the actual shooting but Surratt was present "aiding, helping and abetting, comforting, assisting and maintaining" Booth in the murder. The third count included all the other conspirators in aiding and abetting Booth and Surratt in the murder. And the fourth count accused the conspirators, with other unknown persons, of agreeing together to kill Lincoln, with Booth being the one who carried out the assault in pursuit of their unlawful conspiracy.

The defense construed the crime as a simple murder, albeit of an important person, but no different in the eyes of the law than the murder of a vagabond. The prosecution construed it as a more serious crime involving treason, the murder of a head of state, conspiracy to murder all the members of the president's cabinet as well as the vice president, and an attempt to throw the government into chaos and anarchy. They believed that, for such a serious crime, all parties involved were equally guilty of murder - there were no "second degree" participants or "accessories," either before or after the fact.

The trial was long and arduous. The initial jury was quashed because it was not selected according to procedures required by law, so the first week was taken up by selecting a jury of talesmen. Some 172 witnesses were called, including Ulysses S. Grant and Thomas Lincoln, the assassinated president's son. The proceedings were to spread over three months before they were completed.

Given their view of the crime, the prosecution should, perhaps, have just focused on proving that Surratt was a part of the conspiracy and therefore guilty of murder in the first degree. Apparently they did not feel confident that their argument would persuade the jury. Instead they called witnesses to place Surratt in Washington on the day of the assassination and to associate him with the now deceased conspirators.

The defense contended that, while Surratt may have been part of the original conspiracy to kidnap Lincoln, that conspiracy was abandoned as unfeasible and he was not a part of a conspiracy to murder the president: that was all Booth's idea. They used the alibi strategy, attempting to prove that Surratt was at Elmira, New York at the time of the murder. They called witnesses or made logical arguments to discredit government witnesses who had identified Surratt as being in certain places at certain times and doing certain things to further the conspiracy. Of course, the prosecution then called their own witnesses to discredit the defense witnesses. And the government convinced the court to not allow into evidence the register from the hotel in Elmira where Surratt stayed on the night of the assassination.

This ruling by Judge Fisher, which blocked Bradley from proving Surratt's alibi, as well as several other rulings showing a bias in favor of the prosecution, convinced Bradley that there was a conspiracy by the government to hide it's rush to judgment in the military tribunal that resulted in the hanging of Mary Surratt and the other plotters. Bradley believed that the Supreme Court had decided, in principle based on a different case, that the tribunal by which Mrs. Surratt was condemned and executed was illegal, unconstitutional and without legitimate authority. Politicians and lawyers had denounced her execution as murder with insufficient evidence to prove her guilt. Bradley thought the actors in the military trial were just trying to protect themselves by making another sacrifice, John H. Surratt, to satisfy the public lust for vengeance.

That argument fell on deaf ears in the Fisher Court. The prosecution claimed they bound the defendant with chains of evidence linking him to the murder of the president. Bradley considered them forged or false links in a fabricated chain, "covered over with the gloss of eloquence polished by ingenuity." He felt their chain of evidence was so flimsy that "it breaks at the touch." And he was convinced that Fisher's rulings in the present case continued the cover up. Bradley stewed about it for several days.

On July 1st Merrick had made a comment suggesting that some of the witnesses were "fit for the penitentiary" and Bradley had chimed in with a quip of his own that the witness waiting room was itself a "penitentiary." One of the witnesses, Dr. McMillan, took offense at the implication he was a criminal and made some hostile remarks to Merrick when he was questioned by him. Judge Fisher, who had been making out passes for a friend at the time of the hubbub in court, wasn't paying particular attention to what happened and criticized Merrick, rather than the witness, for his offensive remarks.

The following day, Bradley complained to Judge Fisher about his censure of Merrick and asserted that there was no provocation given by the counsel. Judge Fisher had the transcript of that part of the previous day's proceedings read and then lectured both Bradley and Merrick about treating witnesses with respect while also admonishing Dr. McMillan to hold his tongue.

"I have never seen witnesses cross-examined with so much asperity as in the case now pending. It does not appear to me, therefore, as at all strange that witnesses should be worried into such remarks as this witness has uttered, especially when intimations are publicly thrown out as to their fitness for the penitentiary, and that, too, when some of the most respectable persons in the land, such as General Grant and Assistant Secretary Seward, are among the number. And not even was the effect of the remark allowed to stop with this intimation, but when attention was called to it by the district attorney, in the hope, I presume, that it would be recalled, it was repeated with the additional observation that the propriety of the remark could be shown.

"When such things occur, it is not at all surprising that witnesses should come here prepared to avenge themselves by making insulting replies to counsel. I deeply deplore it, and will endeavor, by most carefully observing all that transpires, to prevent a similar recurrence on the part of either counsel or witness.

"I would suggest to counsel on both sides that in the examination of witnesses, if they consult Quintilian and Allison in regard to their duty in this respect (and no doubt they have read the remarks of both these authors on the subject), they will find that those writers say nothing is to be gained by a bitterness of manner toward witnesses either on examination in chief or cross-examination, but that everything may possibly be gained by kindness and conciliatory manners; and I think it would be a decided improvement in this case if their suggestions were accepted."

The judge then called a recess. As he descended the bench, Bradley accosted the judge, saying, "Look here, Fisher, you have given me a series of insults ever since this trial began. What do you think you are doing? I'm not going to take that crap!"

Fisher responded, "I had no intention of insulting you, Mr. Bradley. I entertained only feelings of respect toward you."

Bradley, grabbed the judge by his throat. "Don't give me that bull shit! You don't give a plug nickel about me or about the law. All you're trying to do is cover up the atrocities committed by your political pals. I think I should just kick your ass all the way down Pennsylvania Avenue!"

The altercation was broken up, and the parties behaved more or less civilly toward each other in the courtroom, but Judge Fisher did not forgive and forget and Bradley knew he would pay for his impulsive display of anger in some way.

Bradley told Mary about that day in court, about how his blood rapidly came to a boil; he felt disgusted with Fisher and, uncharacteristically, lost his temper. "It just came over me like a black cloud. Bang! It was there full-blown. I felt like puking. I think I could have killed the bastard, if there weren't all those other people about. I'm never like that. I'm always in control, even when I am putting on some show for the effect it has on the jury."

"Yes, I think I know what that experience is like," said Mary. "Barbara tells me that it occurs when some hidden or buried thought-sentiment gets set off. Something happens, you may not know what, and this devil in you gets unleashed that wants to destroy everything in sight. Afterwards, when you come back to your senses, you wonder 'What got in to me? Why did I do that? That wasn't me.'"

"So you mean that you have some kind of vulnerability and something comes along and excites it and you go crazy?"

"Yes," said Mary. "I guess the reaction doesn't always have to be anger – it could be sadness or some enthusiasm...or even love."

"Hmm. Do you think you can ever figure it out? I mean, what the vulnerability is or what sets it off?"

"I don't know," said Mary. "Barbara seems to think you can but it may take a long time to do it."

"I've got to think about that some more. I've been kind of ornery lately. Lucy has been sick for a number of years and she has taken a turn for the worse in the last few months. The doctors don't seem to know what is going on, even Dr. Verdi. It is very frustrating and I want to kick their asses too!"

"I'm sorry to hear about your wife, Mr. Bradley. Give her my regards. She was very kind to me when I was in jail."

The trial dragged on for weeks. Many of the witnesses were surly, cantankerous or very particular and getting them to testify to what Bradley knew they knew was difficult. He was getting tired and was relieved to have Merrick and Joseph Junior there to help carry the load. And, in spite of the court frequently going against him (he registered 150 exceptions to Fisher's rulings), he was able to make some good arguments in his client's favor.

A few weeks later Bradley told Mary about Pierrepont's theory about Surratt's actions during the time he was in Canada and on the boat to Europe.

"He thinks that Surratt's readiness to see detectives pursuing him everywhere and his fear when anyone came near was proof of his guilt. He believes his heart was weighed down by a terrible sense of guilt and this caused him to unburden himself by blabbing about his horrid experiences to McMillan. Pierrepont claims that criminals always find relief by unburdening their heavy hearts in these kinds of confessions.

"He said he believes that criminals can not restrain themselves from returning to the scene of their crime and telling all they did because of the madness brought about by their awful guilty secret. I think there may be some criminals with a descent upbringing who do that but not all of them. In the case of my client Surratt, he may have been guilty about having participated in the conspiracy to abduct Lincoln but he wasn't guilty about the conspiracy to kill Lincoln since he wasn't a part of it."

"I see," said Mary as she thought about what Bradley had said about the burden of a guilty secret compelling someone to confess. She had a feeling it was true, but she was not yet ready to reveal her concealed knowledge to the one who had saved her. Deciding to shift the focus of the conversation to a less sensitive area, Mary picked up on the latter part of Bradley's comment.

"Yes, if he was feeling and acting guilty, it was not for the crime with which he was accused. But couldn't he also have just been afraid that he would be apprehended and wrongly convicted of the crime because everyone wanted vengeance?"

"That's what I think and that's what Surratt told me," said Bradley. "Pierrepont just likes to sound authoritative in front of the jury, like he knows everything about how the human mind works. I do that myself, sometimes, but I don't really believe it," Bradley laughed.

Mary laughed too, relieved that the topic had been exhausted, at least for the present, and they could move on to less stressful areas of discourse. But the idea of being betrayed by a guilty conscience that could evade the force of one's conscious will kept coming back to her from time to time.

After 62 days of testimony and argument, the case was finally given over to the jury. Fisher, in his charge to the jury, cast their duty in favor of the position taken by the prosecution. He started out with a quote from the Bible: "Whoso sheddeth man's blood by man will his blood be shed," and he cautioned them against a "morbid sentimentalism" that might close them off to the stern voice of justice and make them vulnerable to the "kind whisperings of mercy."

He reminded the jury of the heinousness of the crime, disavowed the idea that the earlier military tribunal was a murderous conspiracy and that the Supreme Court had declared it to have no authority, cautioned that the "benefit of the doubt" was not a speculative or capricious one, not a mere shadow of a doubt.

He asserted that the crime was on the same footing as treason or the killing of a king, that the idea of less than the first degree of involvement for anyone connected with the conspiracy made no sense to him and he held that the notion of an alibi should be looked at with suspicion.

He denied the defense's argument that the jury had the right to weigh both the facts and the law in the case and he belittled the defense's 150 exceptions to the court's ruling out of evidence as the mark of amateur lawyers. In short, with these and other instructions to the jury, Judge Fisher attempted to destroy the whole basis of the case for the defense.

The jury retired to deliberate just before noon on the 9th of August, 1867. By four o'clock many of the spectators had gotten tired and went home. Judge Fisher went home for two hours and returned. Rumors floated around the court room. About 9:30 bedding was brought in for the jury and Judge Fisher left for the night.

At 12:30 the next day the crowd which had been waiting rushed into the courtroom after the deputy marshal came in and stationed the officers. The attorneys entered the room and there were more rumors flying about the room. At one o'clock the prisoner was brought in and smiled when Mr. Merrick indicated there was a report that a rescue would be attempted. Five minutes later the judge ascended to his seat on the bench and the jury was brought in. The court clerk, Mr. Middleton, asked if the jury had agreed upon a verdict.

It must have come as quite a surprise to the prosecution and Judge Fisher when the jury foreman, Mr. Todd, handed Judge Fisher a note indicating the jury was hopelessly divided and was convinced they could never arrive at a verdict. They asked to be dismissed at once because of family duties and ill health of several members.

Judge Fisher asked if anything was to be said from either side and Mr. Bradley arose and said that any discharge of the jury would be against the protest of the prisoner, who did not want to sit through any more trials. Mr. Carrington said he would leave it to the court to decide and Judge Fisher subsequently discharged the jury, perhaps hoping to frustrate Bradley one more time.

It was interesting that, in spite of the judge's attempt to stack the deck, the jurors had voted eight to four for acquittal.

Judge Fisher immediately announced: "I have now a very unpleasant duty to discharge, but one which I cannot forgo." He then read the charge against Joseph H. Bradley for contempt of court for having accosted him in a rude and insulting manner.

CHAPTER 23

"No court can administer justice or live, if its justices are to be threatened with personnel violence on all occasions whenever the irascibility of counsel may be excited by an imaginary insult. The offense of Mr. Bradley is one that even his years will not palliate. It cannot be over-looked nor go unpunished as a contempt of court. It is therefore ordered that his name be stricken from the rolls of attorneys practicing at this court."

Mr. Bradley rose to his feet and asked, "Is the court adjourned, your honor?"

"It has not been, sir," replied Fisher.

"Then, sir, in the presence of the court and this assembly, I hereby pronounce the statement just made by the Judge as utterly false in every particular."

"Crier, adjourn the court," said Fisher.

"The court is now adjourned," said Mr. Malloy.

"Well, then, I will say now...," Bradley began.

"You can say what you please, sir, and make a speech to the crowd, if you like," said Fisher as he began to leave the bench.

Bradley yelled, "You have no authority to dismiss me

from the bar. That must be the act of three of the judges of the Supreme Court."

"Very well, Mr, Bradley, you can make the proper appeal."

As Fisher made his way to a car to go home, Bradley followed him closely. When Fisher got into the car, Bradley handed him a note dated August 6th, four days earlier. It read:

Sir:

You have insulted me and besmirched my honor. I demand the satisfaction due a gentleman and would hope that you would meet me at a mutually agreeable location outside the District of Columbia and away from the public eye where our difference can be satisfactorily settled in the way of gentlemen. You may bring whatever seconds you deem appropriate and I shall do the same. I await your reply.

Joseph H. Bradley, Esq.

Officer McHenry stood closely by the side of Bradley as he handed the note to Fisher. Armed friends of Surratt and armed friends of Fisher were nearby and a crowd of one thousand had blocked up the street. They began to move back in fear when someone shouted "He's going to shoot!" and additional policemen moved to disperse the crowd.

Bradley and a number of friends left for his office. After a short time inside, he came out with his brother Charles, of the National Bank of the Republic, and they headed down Louisiana avenue, followed by a crowd of friends and curious onlookers, who were excitedly discussing what had just happened.

Most members of the bar united in their bitter denunciation of Judge Fisher who they felt disgraced himself by using his official power to avenge a personal grudge. They called a meeting to be held on Monday morning to discuss what might be done on Bradley's behalf.

Depressed and angry that he could no longer practice law in the courts of the District of Columbia, Bradley filed a writ of mandamus to the Supreme Court of the District of Columbia, which was heard in 1868. Bradley argued that the Supreme Court of the District of Columbia, as reorganized by the Act of March 3, 1863, was a different court from the criminal court mentioned in that act, though a judge of the former held the latter court. Hence the Supreme Court had no power to disbar an attorney for contempt of the criminal court. The question was whether there was or was not a criminal court in the District as distinguished from its Supreme Court.

After considering that question in the context of the history of the court system in the District of Columbia, the court ruled that "the conduct of Mr. Bradley was not merely a contempt of the authority of the Supreme Court of this district, but was also gross misbehavior in his office of attorney, and that for this reason also, his offense was cognizable by the court in general term, irrespective of the doctrine of contempts." It therefore ordered that Bradley's name be stricken from the roll of attorneys allowed to practice in the court.

Bradley was crestfallen. Lamenting his situation to Mary, he said, "Forty years practicing before that court and I'm kicked out in disgrace. I don't care what the court said, he didn't have the authority to ban me. Dammit! And I was defending the poor bastard for free, even paid for the witnesses to come down from Canada out of my own pocket. I know I shouldn't have attacked Fisher but the guy is an asshole and a hypocrite and doesn't deserve to be on the bench."

"There, there, Mr. Bradley," said Mary, reversing the roles they had while she was in prison. "I still care about you and I know you have a lot of friends that believe the same way you do. You'll get back to practicing in the courts, you'll see."

Bradley continued to stew about the injustice he felt was done to him. Then his wife died in 1869, after a long illness, and he went into a black mood. Everyone around him felt like they were walking on eggshells, fearful that anything they said would bring on a flood of self accusations or a torrent of invective. Mary, for the most part, avoided his surliness, but there were times when he visited that she was reminded of her father's frustrated ambitions and consequent rage. Her approach to Joseph's despair and discontent was one that had worked for her in the past.

"I know, Mr. Bradley. Let's get all dressed up, go into the city, have dinner and go to the theater. We can pretend we are on a date and that all this sadness has long passed! Wouldn't you like to squire a pretty young girl around town, Mr. Bradley?"

Surprised and amused at the thought, Bradley smiled for the first time in months and straightened his posture. "Maybe that's what I need," said the distinguished barrister as he tried to identify that long dormant feeling stirring inside. "I've had enough grief. It's time for some fun! And, Mary, I think we have known each other long enough for you to call me by my given name – Joseph."

Indeed, both parties enjoyed the evening out and Bradley's spirits were bucked up by the same youthful joy on Mary's part that he had found so delightful, at times, when he was defending her. But the Judge Fisher story was to have another chapter. On May 18, 1870 Bradley was walking to his office near City Hall when he encountered Judge Fisher, who had stepped down from the court and was just beginning his new duties as District Attorney.

"Now, sir, it is time for a reckoning," said Bradley as he struck Fisher sharply with his walking stick. The judge stuck out his foot as Bradley moved closer, tripping him and causing the two of them to go down on the pavement in a bundle. A number of onlookers rushed to break up the two old men rolling around in the gutter and escort them to their respective offices as the police dispersed the crowd.

Fisher's son, Charles, when he learned of the assault on his father, marched to Bradley's office to extract some revenge but was prevented doing so by a large crowd that had formed. His father and friends eventually persuaded him to give up the endeavor. The next day's newspaper headlines read: "Renewal of hostilities by Bradley – Assault with a walking stick and a roll in the gutter: 'All quiet on the Potomac.'"

Until he died in 1874, Joseph Junior handled all of the courtroom sessions for the family law firm while Joseph Senior occupied himself with office work. At the opening of the September Term of the Supreme Court, Thomas J. Durant, representing a large number of members of the bar, made a motion that Joseph H. Bradley be restored to the bar and the court immediately granted it. Bradley was gratified by the support shown by his peers but did only minor courtroom work subsequently, preferring to stay in the background.

By this time, Mary Harris had become a regular companion of Mr. Bradley, somewhat to the consternation of his family. "There's no fool like an old fool," many of them were prone to remark when the matter of their age difference arose. But they enjoyed each other's company and the surviving son and daughter preferred to see their father happy in his old age even though they remained a bit skeptical about Mary's intentions.

Mary had gone through several psychiatrists during her years at Saint Elizabeth's. While a couple of them had seemed genuinely interested in her as a person, her fear of not being in control prevented her from developing a truly trusting relationship with them. To keep them from getting very close, she would play the clown and entertain them with her wit or else bombard them with accusations that they weren't really interested or paying attention to what she was saying.

But most of her psychiatrists were smug know-it-alls who's primary objective was to confirm their pet theories using the data from her life. Some fancied themselves as no-nonsense practical types that had to goad patients into conventional behavior. Instead of support and understanding, they offered instruction and jargon-filled interpretations. Some were cynical men who regarded mental patients as useless riffraff whose only function was to help the physicians learn about craziness and provide them with a source of financial support. Some wanted to purge patients of their demons by giving them some foul tasting concoction or by forcing them to recite all of their sins and their painful memories, reacting with exaggerated facial expressions of emotion just before announcing that the time for the session was up.

Mary had perfected the pseudo-sexual style that she had used with Dr. West and it provided her with a bit of amusement when things got dull in the hospital. She would provide a fetching image of naive sensuality yet stay just out of reach as the men made fools of themselves by lavishing her with over-blown compliments or offering her privileges in hopes of getting some "favor" in return.

Mary's serious conversations were reserved for Barbara Blackwell. The nurse was a middle-aged woman who was of an intuitive turn of mind yet could maintain focus on a subject, not being distracted by fleeting impressions or thoughts. She was so different from Mary's own scattered and non-selective style. Talking with her was more like the sort of conversations you would have with a good friend over coffee than the interrogatory she sometimes experienced with a reputable doctor, but

Barbara would often surprise her patient with some connection made between events or with some insight that would make Mary's story more coherent.

Although she did not avoid them, Barbara spent less time and energy on trying to unveil early life experiences and more on what was happening in the present. She was a strategic adviser who understood Mary's anger and sorrow but cheered her on in her daily life. She never took notes, preferring to devote her full attention to what Mary was saying, yet she could remember most of what was said in earlier conversations.

At first Mary wondered just how well Barbara understood the relations between men and women and how much experience she had that Mary could benefit from. She felt uneasy about staying on the surface, thinking she might leave herself vulnerable to an eruption of hidden feelings that would sooner or later come out of nowhere and do her in. Yet she worried about getting in too deep, about letting down her guard and trusting too much, about not being vigilant enough. At times she felt that Barbara was looking at her and making derogatory mental notes: flamboyant, manipulative, inauthentic, immature. At other times she feared that Barbara was about to tell her that her perceptions of being unlovable were not just distortions due to her mental illness but were, in fact, the truth.

Mary liked Barbara but she was not about to let her know it in their early sessions. She would often fight with her over silly things. She would tell her that she didn't like the way she did her hair or that she thought the decorations in her office were uninspired. Barbara didn't take the bait and reject her and she couldn't be thrown off the scent of some problem that needed to be exposed. Mary inquired if Barbara didn't like her because she was such a difficult and contentious patient and caused such uproar. Barbara responded, "Why Mary, didn't you know I love the challenge of a difficult patient?"

Mary knew that she was given to angry outbursts that alienated the very people she wanted around her and that, afterwards, she felt regretful for what had transpired and envious for that which might have been. She had succeeded in driving away Burroughs with just such impulsiveness and refusal to exercise control of her actions. She had a dream in which he had visited her in the hospital and asked her to come with him to a party. Before Mary could accept the invitation, in the dream, a parade of elephants came through the ward and separated them. Barbara commented, "Maybe you hope he hasn't forgotten about you? Sure would have been nice if the clamor of the parade hadn't kept you two apart."

Mary was pursued by a number of demons - her conscience for having shot Burroughs, her ambivalent feelings toward her distant mother, her fear of a father who might explode in violence at any moment, her resentment for having been "farmed out" of the family home at such a young age, her sense of loneliness and doubt that anyone could truly love her for herself. She wanted to be close to others but at the same time feared getting too attached and running the risk of being abandoned.

"So being either too independent or too close is hard for you," said Barbara. "I wonder what it would take for you to be able to strike the right balance, or to be comfortable both when you are close and when you are on your own?"

Eventually, Mary began to regard her sessions with Barbara as a time and place to say the things she could say nowhere else and express the feelings that would be disparaged in the outside world. She could give voice to what she had formerly kept silent with the hope that she might better understand herself and come to terms with desires and thoughts she could not accept and find a more effective way to be in the world. She developed a knack of looking at herself from a more objective viewpoint and became more detached from repetitive patterns of thought and behavior that had trapped her into the compulsions of her darker moments.

Finally, she was ready to strike out on her own, without there being someone readily available to listen to, and treat as important, every new wrinkle to her life story. While she felt fragile, like a person walking along one of those narrow footpaths in the side of a cliff, she knew that it was up to her alone to overcome her resistance to letting go of her support. Of course, she was not left to float on the breeze, devoid of any back up. Barbara would always be there if she needed her on an out- patient basis. And Bradley was there to keep her connected. He helped to find her a job in a bookstore and to find an apartment in Georgetown, near where he lived.

***

Mary and Joseph participated in the life of the ever expanding government city. Joseph, having grown up in the District and in a prominent family, could provide endless history lessons. The christening of new buildings occurred several times every year and the opening tours were attended by most of the politicians and dignitaries. The first run for president by a woman, Victoria Woodhull, occurred in 1872 and was the occasion for much public discussion. The stage debut of Buffalo Bill's Wild West Show took place in the same year. 1873 saw Ulysses S. Grant's second inauguration but many of the events were canceled due to frigid temperatures.

Mary enjoyed going to various Shakespearian plays such as the *Merchant of Venice* and *As You Like It*. Joseph liked tutoring her on the plots and contexts of the plays and seeing Mary become a more sophisticated woman. They also enjoyed laughs over more contemporary romantic and comedic plays such as *Kiss in the Dark* and

Did You Ever Send Your Wife to Georgetown? Mark Twain came through town reading excerpts from *The Gilded Age: A Tale of Today*, which satirized the greed and political corruption in post-Civil War America. And then there was the amazing piano performances of Blind Tom Wiggins, who could imitate a composition played by another player completely from memory while adding his own embellishments. New art work was being continually added to the Corcoran Gallery, requiring additional visits.

Balls and parties were popular and Joseph was always invited to those involving prominent people in the city. He enjoyed the envious stares of his male contemporaries as he introduced his young and beautiful companion and was amused by the critical glances from their dowdy wives. He knew they were wondering whether or not they were intimate and how they did it, but he had no intention of letting them know that the relationship was chaste.

Joseph had not experienced sexual intimacy for several years because of his wife's long debilitating illness. He had at one time had a brief affair but was bothered by not being true to his marriage vows and ended it. He had learned to turn off his desire by diverting his attention to work or some other activity. Now that his wife had died and he no longer had the constraints imposed by a guilty conscience, his age had reduced his ardor and he had difficulty unlearning his inhibitory habit.

One evening at Mary's apartment, after a wonderful day together, Mary hugged Joseph and asked, "Joseph, do you not like me in that way?"

"What way is that, Mary?"

"You know. *That* way," as she moved his right hand to her abdomen.

"I didn't know you had any romantic interest in an old fart like me, Mary. And I'm not so sure I can still get it up anyway."

"Maybe we should try it, just to make sure," said Mary

as she led him to her bedroom.

Joseph was hesitant about removing his clothes as Mary shed her dress and underwear. "You won't laugh at me and my wrinkly sagging skin?" asked Joseph.

"Don't be silly, dear," said Mary. "You know I love you for your real self. Let me help you with those clothes." Mary helped Joseph get out of his suspenders and pants and he removed his shirt. Then she slid his shorts down below his knees and steadied him as he got them off his feet. Leading him to the bed, Mary said, "Now you get in first and just lay on your back while I amuse myself for a little bit."

Mary moved in beside him and they kissed passionately as Mary gently massaged Joseph's relaxed parts. She put her left nipple in his mouth and watched his tongue flick around the erect membrane. She pushed his finger into her wet vagina and increased the pace of her manipulation. Then she leaned over to practice her buccal arts.

It was not long before Joseph exclaimed, "Well I'll be damned! It still works."

Mary climbed aboard and enveloped Joseph's turgid organ. Slowly, she began thrusting her pelvis in his direction, savoring all of the attendant sensations. Timing her movements and her own excitement to coincide with her partner's progress, the crescendo occurred for each of them at the same moment.

After a few minutes, Mary lifted herself from Joseph's chest and, looking him in the eye, said "Well, counselor, I guess you're not ready for the grave just yet!"

"I'll say. I had forgotten how great that feels," said Joseph. "I guess I'll have to see Dr. Verdi to see if he has some potion to help me along. Once just isn't enough!" He wondered if Mary had bestowed such pleasures on Adoniram Judson Burroughs, but he had the good graces to keep his thoughts to himself.

Dr. Verdi did, indeed, have an herb that assisted Joseph's amorous adventures and Mary and Joseph sang his praises on many a day. Joseph had a lightened step as he pranced around the nation's capitol and Mary felt more content and secure in their relationship.

So secure, in fact, that one day as they were laying in bed after having sated their desires, Mary confessed to Joseph that she and the Devlin sisters had concocted the Greenwood letters because they thought they had to make Judson out to be more vile than he actually was in order to win the law suit they had planned. "Louisa and Jane felt like Judson should pay for his betrayal and I agreed to give them a share of whatever proceeds might be obtained. I wanted him to suffer too but I knew that I had to portray myself as being simply out for vindication of my good name or a jury would think I was just a gold-digger."

"I kind of figured that but I didn't want you to tell me so that I could argue whole-heartedly for the story we presented," said Bradley.

"Louisa, Jane and I rehearsed the story about the post office clerk and the assignation house so often that we almost believed it ourselves. We knew there was no one who could be found to contradict it."

"Did Judson ever see you and tell you he was going to marry the Boggs girl?"

"Yes. He saw me in August of 1863 and told me he was going to marry Amelia. I was hurt but I didn't want to show him my humiliation so I told him I was engaged to Mr. Devlin."

"Then the account by Judson's wife as told by John Curtis Burroughs was correct?"

"Yes it was. I was stewing about how Judson had hurt me and thinking about harming him for a long time. I practiced with my pistol outside of Chicago, after the Devlins moved to Janesville, and got to be quite good with it. I had a fantasy that if I wounded Judson,he would feel pain like I was feeling pain. I thought he would see how much he meant to me and come rescue me. I don't know how I could have been so dumb, but that's the way it was."

"Well, it's all water over the bridge now," said Joseph. "It certainly would not serve any useful purpose for you to sit in jail for 20 or 30 years. Best to just let it be."

***

During the summers Joseph liked to live out at the old family farm in Chevy Chase, Maryland. His father, Abraham, had purchased the 218 acre parcel in 1814 and added an additional 15 acres four years later. He invited Mary to spend some time with him at the place where he grew up and she accepted.

"I love this place," said Bradley as they drove through the gate in the rough hewn three-rail fence. The main house was a two-story brick building to which an almost equally sized wooden structure had been added. It had a second story balcony running the whole width of the back of the house and below it were numerous chairs and tables suitable for outdoors living. Ivy climbed up the seven posts supporting the structure and roses made their way up the side of the house to the lath screening on one end of the overhang.

"The main brick part of the house was built in 1722 by Colonel Joseph Belt. My dad added on the rest. Over there," he pointed to a smaller L-shaped two story house with wooden siding, "is the tenant house."

Bradley stopped the buggy between the two houses and an older black woman with a full length apron covering the front of her dress came running out. "Welcome home, Mista Bradley. I've got everything prepared for your stay."

Bradley said, "Mary, this here is Sophie, the best cook in the whole world. Sophie, this is my friend Mary Harris who will be staying with us, I hope, for the rest of the summer."

"Pleased to make your acquaintance, Sophie," said Mary. "You certainly have a beautiful place to live. And everything looks so well maintained and fresh."

"Mista Bradley has been very kind to me and I got's ta return the favor as best as I can," said Sophie. "I hope y'all will enjoy your stay. If there's anything you need, please just let me know. I'm sure you will love this here country livin' as much as I do."

Joseph and Sophie carried the luggage into the house. "Mary will be staying in the bedroom next to mine on the second floor," said Joseph. "If you would, please turn down the bed and make sure there is water in the wash basin."

"Yes sah, Mista Bradley. What would you like for dinner?"

"Why don't you surprise us with one of your scrumptious meals, Sophie. Whatever you make is always delicious." Turning to Mary, he asked, "Would you like to freshen up after our ride from Washington?"

"Yes, and then I would like to see the grounds." Sophie showed Mary to her room and Mary unpacked her clothes and washed her face. She then got into a pair of riding pants and blouse and rejoined Joseph, who had shed his city clothes for the casual attire he usually wore on the farm. The two of them walked out the door and began a tour of the nearby grounds, strolling down a well-worn path.

"Back in 1814 when the British ransacked Washington, several members of the cabinet, along with their valuable records, came here to hide out. My father, Abraham, brought with him the records of the Post Office Department."

"You must have been proud of your father," said Mary.

"Oh, yes. He died in 1838 at the ripe old age of 93. They buried him at Verona, N.Y. where he grew up. Dad and his brother Phineas shepherded the growth of the post office from the time it moved to Washington from Philadelphia. Phineas was a straightforward man, not refined or fashionable in manners but he managed to accumulate a goodly estate. Dad was of a different temperament. He loved to read and study. He liked to think about the possibilities and often talked about philosophy and metaphysics. When he was 70 years old he wrote a treatise called *A New Theory of the Earth*. For leisure he wrote poetry. He liked farming and domestic pursuits, and was frugal and moderate in all his wants."

"Do you take after him?"

"I guess I do more than does my brother Charles. Dad used to come out here to get away from the hectic life in the District. He used to live a comfortable, easy life out here where there were fewer required social obligations. Phineas and his boys would come over and we would play all over the place. I used to know damn near every rock, shrub and tree on the place. Dad used to often enjoy the fellowship of his old pal, Henry Clay, and they would sit out on the back porch drinking mint juleps and talking about big ideas. We kids were always included in the conversations if we weren't off playing. They'd encourage us to think about important things and they never made fun of our naive comments."

"It sounds like you had a marvelous childhood, Joseph," said Mary. "Not much like mine."

"We did," said Joseph. Leading Mary over to a well pump, he said "Here. Have a drink of this. You'll never find any water more pure and sweet than this."

Taking a sip from the old coconut-shaped dipper, Mary said, "H'm. It is really good."

"Smell that air," said Joseph as he inhaled in a dramatic manner. Smell those flowers. Isn't that truly marvelous?"

Mary mimicked him and nodded her assent. "It reminds me of those carefree days when I was just a little girl on the farm in Iowa, before they sent me off to work for Mrs. Alexander."

"Lucy and I used to have the two boys and our daughter out here every summer when they were growing up. They were always so active and full of life. I tried to be the kind of father my dad was. I guess I succeeded because they all turned out to be great kids and outstanding adults."

"I'll bet you were a great, loving father," said Mary wistfully.

It was near dusk and Joseph pointed to the golden sunset in the west. "Now isn't that as exquisite as any painting you will see in the great halls of government?"

"It is truly marvelous," said Mary.

The couple retired to the main house where Sophie had prepared a supper of baked ham with a mustard and peach glaze, new peas from the garden, and freshly baked bread. Desert consisted of peaches from the tree in the side yard, poached in honey, sugar and peach brandy. Mary tried to restrain herself as much as possible, in the interests of maintaining her figure, but the intensity of flavors and the variations on a theme were beguiling.

"How grand," said Mary. I have never had such an enticing meal. I think I may have overdone it," she said, patting her stomach. "I bet I will have pleasant dreams tonight!"

The next morning Mary awakened at dawn to the smell of grass dampened with dew gently wafting through the open window of her bedroom. Poking her head out the door, she noted that she and Joseph were the only ones on the second floor and Sophie had not yet started to work downstairs.

Silently opening the door to Joseph's bedroom, she

slid into bed beside him. He was half asleep as she kissed him and rubbed him into tumescence. Mounting the recumbent lawyer, she unleashed a passionate embrace, which terminated with deep sighs of relief. Mary disengaged herself, smiled at the grinning old gentleman, and returned to her room to clean up and prepare for the day.

Descending the stairs, she was greeted with the smells of freshly brewed coffee, corn pone and codfish balls basted in eggs and milk and baked to a golden brown. "Good morning, little lady," said Joseph as he put down his second cup of coffee and rose to pull back a chair for Mary. "We are going to have a good breakfast to keep us going for the rest of the morning when we take a buggy ride around the farm and the nearby area. How did you sleep?"

"I slept very well, like a kitten. And I had a charming dream where I was in a most enchanting kingdom. Everyone treated me like a princess – it was fantastic!"

Sophie observed the crimson blush in Mary's cheeks, looked at the still grinning Bradley, and smiled. "I'm glad you two had a good rest. It always seems to lift the spirits."

Mary and Joseph chattered nearly without interruption as they rode around the forests and fields on the farm. They stopped at a roadhouse for lunch. Nearly everyone who came into the establishment seemed to know Joseph Bradley and came over to the table to greet him, wish him well and chat about the crops. Joseph introduced Mary as his "dear friend." Although most knew who she was from local gossip, out of deference to Mr. Bradley, no one made any reference to the trial.

When they were alone, Mary commented softly to Joseph, "One of these days you're going to have to make an honest woman of me."

EPILOGUE

Mary Harris and Joseph H. Bradley were wed in
Philadelphia on Wednesday, October 31, 1883
(Halloween). She was at that time 42 years of age and he
was 80 years old. They had a prenuptial agreement dated
the day before their marriage that was written by Bradley
on an ordinary sheet of legal cap paper and executed in
Philadelphia with William Downey as a witness. According
to the document, Mary, if she survived Joseph, was to get
1/5th part of Bradley's real and personal property. Mary,
in turn, released Joseph of all claims to dower (a provision
for a widow on her husband's death) to him or his heirs
and claim to any distinctive share she might have in any
personal estate. Mary was listed as "Mary Harris Harrison"
in the document which suggests that she had used an
assumed name after the notorious murder trial.

Bradley died at his residence, 1517 29th Street in
Georgetown, at 5:00 pm on April 4, 1887. He had just
turned 84 years old in March. According to the *National
Republican* of April 16, 1887, Bradley had executed a
lengthy will about two months before his death. In it he
asked that he be buried in the same grave as his wife

Lucy while Mary, if it was convenient at the time, was to be buried between him and his deceased daughter-in-law in Oak Hill Cemetery, West Washington. He made many individual bequests to family and friends. His residence was to be sold and the proceeds added to the income of his estate. From that income, Mary would receive $40 per month as would a woman by the name of Alice Sherman. The balance of the estate was divided into four equal shares. One fourth would be invested for the benefit of Mary and the principal would go to her children if she were to subsequently have any. Dr. W. W. Godding of St. Elizabeth's, was designated as Mary's trustee. Another quarter share went to Alice Sherman so long as she remained single. One fourth shares went to each of the children of his deceased son, Joseph H. Bradley, Jr.

Mary Harris Bradley continued to live in the District of Columbia. After Joseph's death, she again spent some time at St. Elizabeth's. In 1901 the *Times of Washington* published a story on the 36th anniversary of the murder called "Recalling A Tragedy." The article appeared on page three and occupied more than two columns. It started out stating, "There is not in local annals a more romantic story than that of the killing of Adoniram J. Burroughs, a Treasury Department clerk, in this city. Living in an obscure boarding house on Grant Place northwest, is Mrs. Joseph H. Bradley, formerly Mary Harris, whose acquittal on a charge of murder was a surprise to many; to her friends a fruitful source of congratulation." The author described the relationship between Mary and Burroughs, the events of the murder itself, and "one of the most remarkable [trials] to be heard in the District of Columbia." The report concluded, "Only the oldest residents know the story of her past life; for Mrs. Bradley, except to her few most intimate friends, never speaks of the 'forgotten' tragedy."

Mary died on October 27, 1926 at the age of 85 years.

Born in 1841 she was 10 years younger than Adoniram Judson Burroughs, 17 years old when she began to correspond with him, and 24 years old when she was tried for his murder. The deception about her age that was created in court was never discovered. Insofar as can be determined, she never remarried after the death of Bradley and never had any children. She appears to have outlived everyone else associated with this story.

John Curtis Burroughs resigned as president of the University of Chicago in 1874. Soon afterward he was appointed a member of the Chicago board of education, and in 1884 he was elected assistant superintendent of public schools in that city. In 1893 there was an elementary school in Chicago that was renamed to honor John C. Burroughs and it exists to this day. He received the degree of D.D. (Doctor of Divinity) in 1858 from the University of Rochester, and in 1869 that of LL. D. (Honorary Doctor of Law) from Madison University.

The University of Chicago went bankrupt in the late 1880's, owing its then president, Galusha Anderson, $3500 in back wages. Anderson cleaned out the movable property in the university building, including a number of oil portraits of early benefactors, friends and faculty of the university. These portraits included Dick Yates, Illinois Civil War governor; the "Little Giant," Stephen A. Douglas; Senator C. B. Farwell; two ex-mayors and several big donors; and that of the first president, John Curtis Burroughs. Anderson hung the portraits with "For Sale" signs in the shop of his barber, Lewis J. Frahm, on Cottage Grove Avenue near the vacant old university. Word got around the city and relatives descended on the place to buy up the likenesses of their famous kin. The last to be sold were those of the ex-mayors and Dr. Burroughs.

The other Burroughs who worked in the Treasury building at the same time as Adoniram was actually a cousin, John Burroughs. That John Burroughs became a famous naturalist and essayist, writing about conservation. His first popular book was *Wake-Robin* in 1871. He became friends with Walt Whitman, John Muir, Henry Ford, Harvey Firestone, Thomas Edison and Theodore Roosevelt. The last named would allow only Burroughs to accompany him alone when touring sites in the west later to become national parks.

Amelia Louise Boggs Burroughs gave birth to Judson's son, Charles Curtis Burroughs, on April 6, 1865. The boy died on his birthday in 1871 at six years of age. Amelia subsequently married Orris Glidden in 1870 and had a daughter by the name of Grace. In February of 1875, she married Norman T. Gassette, a 36 year old lawyer with two children. The latest report placed her in Paris, France living with her daughter.

As far as can be determined, the Devlin sisters continued in the millinery business in Baltimore.

Edward C. Carrington held the position of District Attorney for nearly ten years serving under Lincoln, Johnson and Grant. He later moved to Prince George County, Virginia and became a municipal attorney. He died on June 3, 1891 at the age of 66. He had a son of the same name, born in 1850, who also was a lawyer and he had a grandson of the same exact name who died in 1938 at the age of 66 years. Nathaniel Wilson, Carrington's Assistant District Attorney, died in the District of Columbia at the age of 79 years.

Daniel Voorhees served as a United States Representative from Indiana from March 4, 1861 to February 23, 1866 and again from March 4, 1869 to March 3, 1873. He was appointed to fill the Senate vacancy caused by the death of Oliver H. P. T. Morton and subsequently elected as a Democrat to the United States Senate, serving from November 6, 1877, to March 3, 1897. He was chairman of the committee to establish the Library of Congress and the Committee on Finance (Fifty-third Congress). Known for his passionate partisanship, stirring eloquence and devotion to personal liberty , he died in Washington, D.C., April 10, 1897 at the age of 69 years.

Judge James Hughes, after leaving Congress, was appointed judge of the United States Court of Claims and served from January 18, 1860, to December 1864, when he resigned. He was a member of the Indiana House of Representatives 1864-1866 and a cotton agent of the Treasury Department 1866-1868. He died in Wattsville, Maryland in 1873 and was buried in Rose Hill Cemetery, Bloomington, Indiana.

Andrew Wylie had been appointed by Lincoln to a new seat on the United States District Court for the District of Columbia (at that time called the Supreme Court of the District of Columbia) during a Senatorial recess in 1863. The Senate confirmed him in 1864 and he assumed his seat on the bench. He retired from the court on May 1, 1885, and went back into private practice in the District until his death at 91 years of age in 1905.

President Andrew Johnson appointed Cornelius Wendell as Superintendent of Public Printing. He served only from September 1, 1866, to February 28, 1867. He was done in by a political battle between the president and Congress, the latter deciding to elect John D. Defrees as the head of the Government Printing Office and make him an officer of the Senate. During his short term, Wendell had managed to avoid a major strike by government printers and began an 8-hour, 6-day week. In 1866 he had purchased for the GPO the first automatic reel-fed rotary press that printed on both sides of the paper. The press could put out 10,000 flat sheets, printed on both sides, in an hour. He continued to attend every National Convention of the Democratic Party until his death in 1870 at 59 years of age.

After he built the government hospital for the insane,

Dr. Charles H. Nichols more than doubled the grounds to 420 acres, increased the size of the buildings on three different occasions, and treated 4,000 patients. He was a member of many professional and benevolent societies and was for several years president of an organization of American medical superintendents of insane asylums. From 1873 to 1879 he was president of the American Psychiatric Association. He resigned from St. Elizabeth's in 1877 and became superintendent of Bloomingdale Asylum for the Insane in New York City. He died in 1889 at the age of 69 years.

Charles Mason is best remembered as the man who beat out Robert E. Lee for head of the class at West Point in 1829. A Copperhead who opposed slavery, he remained involved in Democratic politics until his death in Burlington, Iowa on February 27th, 1882 at age 77.

Charles H. Phelps became Judge of the Circuit Court in Burlington, Iowa. He and his wife, Eunice Alice (Webb) Phelps had three children. According to the 1880 census, Edward S., age 22 was a Deputy US Revenue Collector; Charles E., age 17, was a railroad clerk and Eunice A. was 6 years old. Phelps remained involved in local civic activities until his death at age 67 years in Burlington in 1891.

George P. Fisher was appointed by Lincoln, on March 11, 1863, to be a judge of the Supreme Court of the District of Columbia, which position he resigned in 1870 when he was appointed district attorney for the District of Columbia. He served as district attorney until 1875. On May 31, 1889 he was appointed by President Benjamin Harrison to be the First Auditor of the Treasury Department, a position he held until March 23, 1893. He died in Washington, D.C. in 1899 at age 82 years. Fisher was first buried in Oak Hill Cemetery in Washington but later reburied in the Whatcoat Cemetery at Dover, Delaware.

John H. Surratt was released on bail awaiting a new trial, which never happened because the government declined further prosecution and the statute of limitations ran out. He began to deliver lectures in which he admitted his part in the plot to kidnap Lincoln but denied any part in the assassination. His career on the lecture circuit was short lived because citizens were enraged that he should make any money from his crime. Surratt farmed tobacco, got a job as a teacher at St. Joseph Catholic School in Emmitsburg, Maryland and later was hired by the Old Bay Line steamship company on Chesapeake Bay. He ended up being treasurer of the company. He had four children with Mary Victorine Hunter, a relative of Francis Scott Key. Surratt died on April 2, 1916 of pneumonia at the age of 72, having outlived all other participants in the Lincoln conspiracy.

Richard T. Merrick continued to practice law in the District of Columbia. Georgetown University continues to offer The Merrick Debating Medal, founded by Richard T. Merrick, LL.D., 1873. The competitors for the medal must be members of the Philodemic Society,a 175 year old debating club. Merrick died in 1885 at age 58 and is buried in Oak Hill Cemetery in the District.

Edwards Pierrepont served as U.S. Attorney for the Southern District of New York from 1869 to 1870. President Ulysses S. Grant appointed him Attorney General of the United States on April 26, 1875. He was an active member of the "Committee of Seventy," a good government group in Philadelphia, best known for monitoring elections in the city and its suburbs. In 1876 he became Minister Plenipotentiary of the United States to Britain, serving until December 1, 1877. Pierrepont died in New York City two days after his 75th birthday in 1892 and is buried at St. Philip's Cemetery, in Garrison, New York.

One of the young men that Burroughs recruited for

the Union Army, Joseph Lee Heywood, survived battles at Chickasaw Bayou, Port Arkansas and Vicksburg. He became a bank cashier of the First National Bank in Northfield, Minnesota, the author's home town. In 1876 Frank James shot him to death when he refused to open the safe as the James – Younger Gang attempted to rob the bank. A few feet away outside the bank stood 41 year old Adelbert Ames, the man who commanded the unit that war correspondent and reporter Francis Richardson was assigned to at Antietam. Ames had received the Congressional Medal of Honor during the war and was, at the time of the bank robbery, coaching one of the local citizens on how best to shoot the desperadoes.

Richardson went on to become a well-known reporter in Washington and wrote an article about his experiences for the *Records of the Columbia Historical Society* in 1903. George Alfred Townsend did manage to get the Civil War Correspondent's Arch built at Gathland State Park in Maryland near the battlefield at Antietam.

The Old City Hall, where the trial took place, had a magnificent restoration in 2009 after having sat idle for 10 years. It now houses the District Court of Appeals. A Washington Post article reported that the building was "...successfully expanded with a sexy glass box atrium on the north side. Ugly street-level parking has been removed and placed underground. A new landscape has been introduced that not only flatters the building but also makes it accessible to people who have disabilities. The interior has been renovated as well, including a new underground courtroom large enough to handle the bar ceremonies over which the Court of Appeals presides."

The Willard Hotel has gone through several renovations over the years but remains at 1401 Pennsylvania Avenue and still has the Round Robin Bar. The present building, designed by Henry J. Hardenberg, opened in 1901 but had a major fire in 1922. The Willard family sold its equity in the hotel in 1946, and the hotel had to close in 1968. After a lengthy legal battle, the hotel reopened with the InterContinental Hotels Group as part owner and operator of the hotel. The hotel was restored to its turn-of-the-century elegance and re-opened on August 20, 1986. Additional restoration occurred in the late 1990s.

The court reporter, James Ogilvie Clephane, took notes in shorthand and from those produced copy for the printer, who set the type by hand, proofread the result and sent it to the press. Demand for fast turn-around was high but the process was slow and error prone. The Harris trial spurred Celphane to look for faster mechanical methods to produce the manuscripts. He began to invest in the inventions of Ottmar Mergenthaler, who finally produced the first Linotype machine in 1884.

The following characters are completely fictional: John P. Anderson, Judge Canby, Neil Bartlett, Clarice Cody, Doris, Bill Douglas , Dr. West , Barbara Blackwell and Leona Greene.

###

ABOUT THE AUTHOR

Gerald D. Otis was born in Northfield, Minnesota. He graduated from Northfield High School, attended St. Olaf College for two years then transferred to the University of Minnesota where he obtained his Bachelor's Degree. He earned his Ph.D. in Psychology from the University of Arizona in 1966. After completing a clinical internship at the Veterans Administration Hospital in Palo Alto, California he joined the University of New Mexico School of Medicine where he headed a research team in a longitudinal study of the career decision making process in medical students and physicians, taught classes and maintained a clinical practice. For 10 years after Dr. Otis left the University, he combined a private practice with the design and construction of sculptural furniture and computer programming. He has published numerous articles about the effects of psychological type on behavior, perception and attitudes and has received several awards for his efforts at fine woodworking. Following 16 years working for the Veterans Administration in Medford, Oregon, where he specialized in the treatment of post-traumatic stress disorder, Dr. Otis retired from clinical practice and now lives in Las Cruces, New Mexico with his wife Connie and two Bichon Frise dogs, Scuzzie and Brandi Alexandria. He previously published a biography of the heroic bank teller, Joseph Lee Heywood, who resisted Jesse James' band of outlaws and was killed in the process. He has also edited a book of poetry and is currently at work on a book about a life-long friend who was unjustly committed to a mental hospital.

www.ingramcontent.com/pod-product-compliance
Lightning Source LLC
Chambersburg PA
CBHW070350260626
47161CB00001B/85